An Untitled Lady

A Novel of Manchester

Nicky Penttila

This is a work of fiction. Similarities to real people, places, or events are entirely coincidental.

First edition published 2013 by Musa Publishing

ISBN 978-1-943192-00-7

A

An Untitled Lady

For John

PART ONE

ONE

Manchester 1819

N ash first saw her as an apparition, a gilt London trinket set down by mistake at a dusty crossroads three miles north of town. A straw bonnet atop a traveling suit of thick French silk perched on the largest of those seven mismatched trunks he'd later had to find space for in his life. But on that odd, chill May afternoon, he'd needed to make room for them only in his wagon.

"Lost your carriage, miss?"

The green of her too-wide eyes seemed to drink him in, but the corner of her too-full lips puckered down. Did his coat not meet her standards? It was good Manchester cotton, but cut for comfort, not frills. Or was it his ill-behaved hair, far too curly for this humidity? He broke her gaze to check the skies. Rain, but a half-hour away yet. Served her right to get sodden through, if she looked so askance at a worthy mode of transport.

1

"The letter said the stage should drop me here, and someone from the castle would fetch me." She looked up the track, the document clutched in her glove, hope drooping like her forlorn skirt.

That decided him. Fine-drawn females should not loiter in the fields alone, especially not in these times. "And here I am," he said, casting a leg over the side of the wagon to climb down from its seat.

She stood, an alert little rabbit, mouth twitching. Slimmer than he thought, and chin height at the most. "But you come from town," she said.

"Aye, and I'm not a fancy carriage, but I'm going the right direction. You've been waiting these five hours or more, if you took the daily coach. Shall I leave you, and trust someone else to divine your presence? Or do you dare take advantage of one of the few conveyances that can readily carry all this baggage?"

She rocked back on her heels and swung her arms up. He was sure she was going to slap them onto her hips, but the lady's training caught her, and she hesitated, dropping her hands into the pose of a prim schoolteacher instead. First point to her, then. He could fight fair.

"How far to the castle?"

"Straight, not three miles. In or out?"

She released her hands with the same tiny gesture of surrender he'd seen French sailors use after he'd boarded their ship. Even score.

She gave him wide berth, but wasn't above taking one handle of the largest box. Together, they hefted it into the wagon, pushing his cargo to either side. The paper wrap had torn on one of the bolts of cloth, showing a swath of dark blue. She reached for it, stroking, as if she couldn't help it.

"Is this silk?"

"Frenchie trade. Like what you're wearing."

She snatched her hand away. "You sound as if you disapprove."

"Bad bargain on my part." Nearly a fatal one, for his fledgling trading company. "Mancunians prefer local-made silks. And they'll look sidewise at the likes of you, too, half-mourning or no. Is that all that's in here?" He slapped a palm on the nearest trunk.

"Everyone in Bath buys their fabrics from France. We're not at war. And it's better quality."

"You're behind the times, miss. Manchester matches their best, and beats it."

"So says the man of sales." She followed him to the front of the wagon and held her hand out for him to help her up to the bench. Then she saw the anger on his face, and put her hand on her chest instead.

He forced his mouth into a grimace of a smile and willed his tone to be light. "I may be a lowly man of business, sure, but I also serve for a magistrate for this town. And I was born to Shaftsbury."

"Then it's welcome home for you, as well." She used the bench for a hand-hold, fortunately for him, as he was shocked to a standstill. He never called that bloody dungeon of a castle home. Why had he now? And what did she mean, "as well?" He didn't know her, and she would be hard to forget. Before he'd gained his seat, she'd already changed the topic.

"You are fortunate the Quinns will take your silks, then."

He tugged the reins a bit too hard, and his pair lurched into motion. Her shoulders swung back, her hands reaching past her hips to the wood of the seat to hold her steady. Served her right, her smelling like sunlight on grass, yet biting sharp as any asp.

A gently bred lady, with no companion, traveling to Shaftsbury. He knew of no poor relations, in Bath nor any place else. She didn't appear a lightskirt, not with those trunks. Nor a servant, with those cultured accents and pretty manners. Now she sat as if on a church pew, hands folded, yet her feet were braced wide, one on the side of the board, the other against his foot.

"You're the new housekeeper?"

She glanced at him, eyes narrowed, mouth cool. "Shaftsbury lacks one?" But she quickly looked down at her gloved hands, one still mauling that letter of hers. He felt a bumpkin, snapping at some lost girl merely because he could not snap at those who better deserved it.

"I'm sorry we haven't been introduced. I'm Nash Quinn."

She looked up at him, eyes wide. Cat's eyes, he decided, and the lips, turning up into the first smile he'd seen all day, a blooded rose.

"I am so relieved. I mean, your face, your hands, your hair. Just like your father." She stopped short, her smile falling away.

Nash concentrated with effort on the too-familiar track. He couldn't look at her. She'd thought him born on the wrong side of the blanket? Well, why wouldn't she? An earl's son in trade? It might have been better if he were a bastard.

"You knew the old earl?"

"I am sorry for your loss. He was a good man." Her mellow alto softened further, as if she believed it.

He might debate that, but for the moment he let it go. "How did you meet?"

"He was my godfather. My name is Madeline Wetherby."

"The little lost Wetherby?" He'd heard vague tales whispered of a blond child spirited away in dark of night.

"I could as easily call you the little lost Quinn. Your fa—" She stopped herself.

"My father did."

"I apologize for my rudeness."

"You'd as well apologize for your dropped R's and Southern speech. As well as your silks. You may have been born here, Miss Wetherby, but you don't belong here." Truly, on this cart, in this country, she looked as out of place as a dove at a cockfight.

Trying not to look at her and failing, he couldn't help but see the glint of moisture at the corner of her eye. He was a cad, just as his brother Deacon, the new earl, always said. "Don't. You know you'll need tannery skin to survive the castle."

"Your father was the one who wrote to tell me to come today. But he isn't here."

"It's him you're mourning? Deacon will make you welcome, no doubt. He has to. This blasted affair, begging your pardon, it's all for him. The grand summoning."

"How many are invited?" She pretended to flick a dust speck from her eye. He felt his chest ease.

"Eight or ten, I believe. But it's quality that counts. Well, nearly. The illustrious head of your house is expected, our Lord Wetherby."

He couldn't pretend not to hear her gasp, or see her shoulders hunch, as if warding off a blow. "Not a favorite, Miss Wetherby? Can't say I like him, either. But he's Deacon's best beau, so fair warning."

"Your own speech is an interesting combination of cant and King's English."

He snorted. "It's not me you're wanting to fight, little lost Wetherby."

She pursed her lips. "My shining knight in dull loom-spun."

All he could come up with was a repetition. "Save it for the castle."

Point and match to the lady.

MADELINE WETHERBY REFUSED to admit the idea that this might not be the happiest day of her life. Wasn't she here, in the storied Shaftsbury Castle, in the finest guest bedroom in the family wing? Hadn't the butler assured her that she was, indeed, expected? And didn't his master's letter promise her the world— or at least a decent family to belong to, at long last.

But thus far, nothing had gone to plan. The coach trip had taken more than the extra day she had allotted, her note confirming her arrival seemed to have gone astray, and Lady Shaftsbury was too busy preparing for supper to greet her. And here was Nash Quinn, safe and sound, not lost to the sea after all. Surely Lord Shaftsbury would have mentioned that piece of news.

Still, Maddie forced her face into a serene lady's mask even as the poor maid labored to smooth out the tangles in her hair. What could account for the queasiness in her middle? Could there be such a thing as too much happiness? The cold stone air of the castle sidled under the flush of her overtired skin, and she found she wanted everything over and done. The smiling, the shouts of pleasure, even the meal, though she hadn't eaten anything since morning.

And then tomorrow—tomorrow she would have a place, and a purpose, and the rest of her life secure. No more guessing what would please her betters. They would have to guess what would please her.

She shivered. The worry was worse than the thing itself, Headmistress Marsden always said. The north wind rattled the window's panes as it passed into the chamber. The butler had assured her the new silk curtains, Mr. Nash's delivery, would be up by nightfall.

What did that Nash Quinn mean—she had to be tanned leather to withstand the castle? Perhaps it was to guard against the chill; it couldn't mean to withstand the company. Though it might well hold true for him, the prodigal son. Not for her, though. Lord Shaftsbury had promised.

She stood and took a last look in the dressing-room glass. The gray of half-mourning suited her better than unrelieved black, her color was high, and the maid had managed to collect her hair into a properly missish shape. Maddie nodded her thanks, reached for her shawl, and took herself out into the hall. She stepped purposefully through a minor labyrinth of rough-hewn stairs to the door of what the butler called the receiving room.

Mr. Quinn paced outside the door, pulling at his cuffs. He looked almost guilty, as if she'd caught him doing something he oughtn't. His odd smile disarmed her.

"No nerves?"

He appeared the prosperous merchant, in charcoal trousers, a maroon silken coat over a simple buff shirt and classic cravat. Though they hadn't started so well, it set her heart at ease a bit to see a somewhat familiar face.

"Perhaps," she said.

"I know the feeling. But quickest started is soonest ended. What? Did I murder the line?"

"Not at all. I have a friend who is always saying that." She accepted his bow and his hand, so still against her own palm's buzzing blood.

She nodded, and at his signal the underservant opened the door for them. Maddie steeled her shoulders and stepped into her future.

The room, though, seemed to thrust her into the past. Gothic in its proportions and furnishings, its high post-and-panel ceiling dwarfed the two sets of people present. Dozens of wax candles fought the gloom to a draw. Even the tall windows gave no light. A storm was coming in.

"Mama first, or Deacon?" He smiled down at her as if he'd known her all his life.

Maddie released her death-grip on his hand, sheepish, but he did not release her entirely. "Lady Shaftsbury, if you please."

But before they had taken more than a few steps across the theater-sized chamber toward the corner where a proper lady was holding court, a tall bit of flash and finery sauntered up to intercept them.

Mr. Quinn stopped, making the man come to them. "The golden boy."

"The prodigal son." Deacon Quinn, eighth earl of Shaftsbury, shimmered in a closely tailored suit coat of gold shot with silver. Fine china, much too great for daily use.

"I see we're out of mourning."

"Oh, I couldn't wear that travail one more minute." He turned away from them, his arm sweeping the room. "Look, everyone. Even sober Nash has brought a gift."

"She's no gift. She's an invited guest. Same as all of us."

The new earl, or rather Lord Shaftsbury, turned his gold-flecked gaze back to her. "Have we been introduced?"

Maddie stilled the hornet's nest under her corset, and spoke as carefully and clearly as headmistress Marsden had taught her. "Small wonder my face is unfamiliar, My Lord. I last saw you when I was but four years old."

"Oooh, a mystery. Can you solve it, fair Ellspeth?" The flame of the earl's personality, or perhaps the lilt of his voice, had drawn a young miss to his side. Spectacled and tightly ringletted, she pursed her mouth in pretty confusion. The earl's gaze slid toward the rafters, as if he were trying to pull a memory from the shadows.

"Stubble it, Deacon." The cobalt blue of Mr. Quinn's eyes darkened as he bit out the words.

"Temper, temper. You've made me lose my train of thought. It's no good; we'll simply have to begin again. Do me the honor, dear brother?"

Mr. Quinn skipped the first part of the introduction. "Deacon, this is Miss Madeline Wetherby."

"Wetherby? Not the little lost Wetherby? A capital gift, indeed, on the occasion of my majority." He paid her a most courtly bow, leavened by an infectious grin as lopsided as his brother's.

She matched with a deep curtsey, and a tentative smile of her own. She wasn't sure how to take this overgrown puppy of an earl. "I regret that your father didn't live to see this day."

"Why? His departure is the very reason we can celebrate. I was a grave disappointment to him, you know, and everyone knew not to mention Nash's name."

The man beside her growled.

Lord Shaftsbury shrugged his slender shoulder. "Tell me you've changed your mind about the old sod now he's in the ground. Of course not. But enough about Nash; he's forever interrupting. Tell me, my angel, how you come to join us tonight?"

A stone seemed to lodge in her throat. He couldn't be serious. "You jest with me, my lord?"

The girl, Ellspeth, tittered, and Lord Shafsbury gave her a wink. "Just this once, no, m'dear. Clear up this mystery for us, tout de suite, if you please."

Did they really wish to play this scene as farce? The floor seemed to slide away under her. But she bent her knees and stood her ground. "Of course. I see. I was summoned—"

"A summons from a ghost. Familiar tale, indeed." He nodded at Ellspeth, who nodded double-time back, an eager mimic.

"Let her finish," interrupted Mr. Quinn.

"Pax, Nash. You were summoned?"

"To fulfill the contract."

Deacon's agile face stilled in expectation, eyebrows up. Even Mr. Quinn looked puzzled. Ellspeth had frozen mid-smirk. Everyone seemed to be waiting for a cue.

"Contract?" Mr. Quinn was the first to recover.

"Of marriage. To you." Finally saying the words, and hearing them aloud, Maddie felt the ground firm up beneath her.

But her announcement seemed to take all the wind from pretty Miss Ellspeth's sails.

She fainted dead away.

TWO

Deacon and Miss Wetherby prowled the old earl's estate office like caged tigers. Nash closed the door, caging them further but at least dampening the din from the hall and the opportunity for prying ears. The click of the latch set Deacon off.

"I should have you both tossed out," he said, sweeping his gaze wide to include both the lady by the bare bookshelves and Nash on the other side of the room. Then he clapped his hands together, face alight. "But by god, what a show! Have any more surprises planned?"

"I should hope not." The lady's skin shimmered, as if the muscles underneath were trying to rebel and being clamped down at the last moment. Nash moved toward her, unaccountably wanting to lay a hand on her shoulder, but held back. You didn't treat a lady as you would a spooked mare, even if she might benefit from a gentling. Especially then.

She shot away from him anyway, stopping near the night-dark windows. The rain had started in earnest, he saw in her wavering reflection.

Deacon paced to the desk, and then turned back to Nash. "Brilliant. I would never have thought of it. Do you think Ellspeth will cede the field now? Bad form not to, really."

The lady shuddered.

Nash fought the unexpected urge to comfort her. He was just as puzzled by her outburst as Deacon. Unlike his brother, though, he'd seen the flash of shock at Deacon's reception of her news.

She had expected to be welcomed.

Almost without realizing it, he was closer to her, within arm's reach. "You thought we would all know, didn't you?"

Deacon prattled on. "Come, come now, spill. You know you can't keep a secret, Nash."

"Bollocks. And I'm no part of this."

"What can you mean? Wait. Little lost Wetherby, are you in league with your uncle? This smells of his doing." Deacon's light tone darkened. "It's far too jocular for something my dear brother would do."

She snapped around to stare at him. "Absolutely not."

Deacon at last turned to look at her. His eyes widened, finally catching on. "You were serious?" He collapsed into the chair in front of the desk

"Pray, sit," Miss Wetherby said acidly.

Nash took his father's chair, realizing at the last moment that it swiveled. He braced his palms on the cleared expanse of the writing surface to steady himself. He rather liked this view of his brother, bewildered and in the beggar's seat. But Deacon was old news; the lady was the draw. With a raised eyebrow and a slight dip of his head, he directed her to the chair beside Deacon. She took the hint, stepping directly in front of it and sinking down slowly and so neatly she did not need the arms to support her. A lady, to the bone.

Deacon sat, hands twitching but mouth closed, his current of words at a brief ebb. Nash cleared his throat. They both looked up to him, Miss Wetherby in wariness, Deacon in supplication. He liked this power, too, and chose to use it on the lady first.

"Who sent you?"

"Your father." Her words cast a chill across the room.

"Merciful heavens." Deacon slouched in the seat, throwing an arm up, as if pleading with his god. "The man reaches out from his grave to direct our lives."

Nash waved his hand, distracting his brother and cutting the rant short. "Explain, please, Miss Wetherby."

She centered her round-eyed gaze on Deacon, who seemed to be staring at the ceiling. "We entered into a contract, sir, of marriage. I saw some papers, a draft. I was given to understand that you had promised, as well."

Lord Shaftsbury launched forward and slapped his hand onto his knee with a sound crack. She flinched as if it had been a physical blow. "I did no such thing. The man who promised you was already married."

"Not to him. He promised me to you. That is what I have been in training for all these years."

"I can't believe my father trained up another tyrant to replace him when he shuffled off. You, ma'am, are no lady."

Miss Wetherby closed her eyes, drawing in a breath as if containing her temper against the ranting of a child. "Who made the agreement is not my concern. I merely seek to honor it."

"You mean, you did not agree, either? That's rich. Two unhappy souls bound for eternity."

"Hold fast." Nash tried to regain the line of his thinking. "What do you mean, in training?"

She answered, again not taking her eyes from Deacon. "I'm to be your complement. I know the crops your tenants raise, and how they remedied the blight from aught nine. I can explain why the irrigation routes on your back twenty look askew but do, in fact, work. I've kept the books for Miss Marsden's Academy, including tenants, sharecroppers, and charity payments. I acted as chatelaine these past three years. And I've studied the history and maintenance records of Shaftsbury, as well as your places in London and the estate in Scotland."

Deacon sighed theatrically. "I suppose you've got my maiden speech in Lords written up, as well."

Though her jaw shut tight, her feline eyes started to moisten. She was as much the victim as they were. Perhaps more.

She must have believed his father, the old tyrant. Must have thought he had her interests at heart. She was wrong. They all were.

This time the breath she took in shook her shoulders, breaking training. "Do you wish to read the agreement? I have the letters in my trunk."

"She has it in writing." At Deacon's mocking tone, she narrowed her eyes.

"What do you know of contracts?"

"Nothing. He's the expert, ask him." Deacon looked to Nash for support.

Nash leaned back, careful not to swivel, and steepled his hands. "He knows as much about business as he does estate management." Irresponsible sot.

"That's not fair." Deacon's puppy eyes had long lost their powers over Nash.

Miss Wetherby appeared equally unaffected. "I have a contract with this family, with this estate. I have honored that agreement through my actions over these past six years. I have trained, worked, and waited. I have done my part. I expect you to do yours. As a gentleman." She shifted back, not crossing her arms but somehow giving the impression she had.

Deacon dropped the soulful look. "Don't know many gentlemen then, do you?"

"Stow it, Deacon. Miss Wetherby, we will need to look at your correspondence, yes. I assume you have no formal, notarized, contract?"

"But he promised." She worried at her bottom lip a moment, then a thought seemed to accost her "You believe I lie?"

"Do you blame us? You reappear, claiming to be a long-lost neighbor. The only person you claim to know is safely deceased."

"Your butler knew to expect me. And Mr. Perkins."

Deacon sighed, a shade less theatrically. "Perkins. Where is the man?"

"You dismissed him, remember? Said he smelled of the old earl."

"And so he did."

"But he apparently informed Emmett of Miss Wetherby's arrival on his way out the door."

She nodded. "He wrote to me for the details of my travel."

"Funny that he never spoke of it to me." Judging by the lady's moue of displeasure, she did not find it so.

"Deacon, think. Where would the old codger have kept such correspondence? You wrote him, as well, I expect."

"Dashed if I know."

This room was floor to ceiling bookshelves, like the library, but here the shelves were mainly bare. His father preferred to work in a Spartan office. To preserve his ideas of lineage and family pride, though, he had the family ledgers made up in beautiful bindings, neatly arrayed on the first two rows of shelves. He kept the family Bible here, too, with its record of births and deaths and families of origin. If only he had arranged his correspondence as neatly.

When Shaftsbury had died of sudden apoplexy, his desk had been a solid mound of correspondence. Only he and poor Perkins knew the method of it, and Perkins had taken that knowledge with him.

Nash pulled out the top drawer at the side of the desk. The quarterly books, half-completed, in their nude state before binding. Middle drawer appeared to be for dog toys. They had not had a hound in the house for years.

Deacon rose and drifted to the bookshelves. He ran his hand across the open page of the Bible, and turned to the flyleaf. "I'm still blessedly unattached on the family tree, thank heavens. And how on earth did my pater come to choose you?"

"You chose me, he said. You told him once that you loved me."

"When you were four."

"I believe you were eight at the time. I was not yet four."

Deacon tapped a finger on his cheekbone. "Eight years old. In the summer?"

In the bottom drawer, Nash found dozens of bundles of letters, each tied with string. He pulled them all out, making a paper dune on the surface of the desk.

"I remember now." Deacon clapped his hands, as if delightfully surprised by a cake made just for him. "The little heiress, all dimples and curls. An angel. But your hair was gossamer. Now it's mouse."

"The winds of time change us all, my lord."

"A fallen angel then. But you're still an heiress?"

"Deacon." Nash shot him a glare.

His brother raised both eyebrows. "What? Isn't that part of the contract?"

She shook her head. "I've nothing but the interest on two thousand pounds. Your father said I'd no need of anything but pin money as he'd provided me a husband." Deacon crossed his arms.

Most of the old earl's correspondents franked their letters. Nash quickly put those aside to his left, as a girl at boarding school was unlikely to have a peer to frank her correspondence for her. But one such package caught his eye, anyway, as it was in his mother's spidery copperplate. He set those to his right. Another set traveled under military seal.

"Who did the old man know from the Navy?"

"Just you." Deacon drew closer to the desk. "Good lord. Did he write everyone in the kingdom?"

Miss Wetherby rose, as well. "Perhaps I might assist."

"You would know your own hand, I trust." Deacon flinched

away as she neared. Nash pushed half the remaining stack toward her. She reached for the top set.

"It's no good. It will never do." Deacon shook his head. "If father orders it from beyond the grave, even if his ghost takes to haunting me in my sleep, I'll not marry you. That is the good part of being the earl."

"You cannot mean it." She dropped the pages and turned to look at him.

"I damned well mean it."

She drew her spine taut. "What will happen to me?" Deacon said nothing. "You would throw me into the streets?"

"Don't be hysterical."

"Why not?" Her voice cracked on the words.

"You'll return to the bosom of your family, none the worse for wear. We'll find you a chaperone somewhere. No one will be the wiser."

"The bosom of my family is a crypt." She sagged, leaning back on the table for support.

"Unfortunate. We'll send some blankets along."

"I wish your father were here."

"Be glad he's not, or we wouldn't be having even this civil a conversation."

"If your—if the previous earl had not passed away, would we even be having this discussion?"

He grimaced. "Likely not. But he's not, is he? Wait, hear me out. The earl—the old earl—ruled over us. Reigned, is better. An old-fashioned despotism. We could not question an edict, much less quarrel with one."

"Mr. Quinn did not quarrel?"

"Mr. Quinn," his voice dripped sarcasm, "ran away."

"So now you are free of your despot. Now you are king."

"Right. It's six months on, nearly, we're finally out of our black, most of us anyway, and we're dashed well enjoying our liberty."

"And the king is responsible for his kingdom."

"Responsible? I try not to think on it."

"And as earl, you maintain your properties and meet everyone's expectations of you, all your promises."

"Heavens, no."

"Because you are no longer merely responsible for yourself, but for your grieving mother, your workers, your staff."

"Mama takes care of all that."

"For the moment."

"You morbid little thing. Don't you threaten Mama. She won't have it."

Nash looked up. She had her back to him, fists on hips.

Deacon sat unmoving, staring at her as if she were Medusa in the flesh. "I've found them."

THREE

Even Maddie's plan to take a moment's solace in the bedroom while she retrieved her side of the correspondence was thwarted. Three underbutlers stood on chairs by the windows, under the direction of a fourth, hanging a familiar shade of silk. The old curtains, perfectly fine to her eyes, lay across the bed.

Her trunks also had been brought up, and two maids were unpacking, unfolding, and unraveling the lot of it. For a moment, she thought to tell them not to bother. She and her baggage might well be tossed out on the morrow.

But the longer it took the maids to pack it all up again, the longer she would need to stay here—and the more time she had to argue that she should stay forever.

Of all the scenes she had pictured in her dreams, all the conversations, all the visions of their first fateful meeting, she had never, ever considered that the new Lord Shaftsbury would have no idea of her at all. How could it be possible, when nearly all her thoughts revolved around him? It didn't seem fair, or right.

The trunk with her books and papers sat beside a dainty writing desk. She sank onto its matching chair and pushed the lid open. The bundle of letters, too big now to squeeze into her Psalter, lay under her books and before her music in a browned paper folder marked Accounts. She found it in seconds, but continued to lean down, pretending to rummage among her things. A tear fell on the missal, quickly wiped away. She would not cry. She could still make a success of this and it wouldn't do to fall apart in front of the help.

It took only a moment to gather herself back into order, if not ladylike serenity. She sat up, careful to avoid looking into the dresser mirror or at the window's reflection. She didn't quite trust her quickly found balance.

She had been holding this same folder the last time she'd seen the seventh earl of Shaftsbury, in Miss Marsden's parlor in Bath. That time it had held duplicates of the castle's accounts, carefully copied and with annotations. In previous years, it carried Latin exercises, history recitations, and, once, a poem to his honor.

Each year, usually the end of spring, she would present herself, surprised all over again at his attention. He had an old relation in Bath, he said, but he also wanted to see how she was getting on.

Each year, in her terror of not pleasing him, she would picture him an ogre, as stern and solemn as his letters. But when he appeared among the china and lacework in the parlor, he always looked more the squire than an earl, in dark clothes and sensible shoes. He was her first crush, and she dreaded that he would ever find out. Nash Quinn shared his square jaw and darkly handsome look; Deacon Quinn seemed fairy-born in comparison.

And, like his second-born son appeared to be, the seventh Lord Shaftsbury was nothing if not decisive.

"See here, Miss Madeline. You're old enough to be leaving school, but my little toad isn't ready for you yet. So my question for you is can you stand to stay here another three years, or shall we find a new occupation for you?"

Maddie had had to sit at that question. She was all of sixteen, and no one had ever asked her what she wanted to do before. "What choice do I have?"

"Stay here and Miss Marsden tells me she will let you continue to teach the young-formers. I'd have you pick up a bit more mathematics and the like, if you can find a suitable tutor. You'll receive your stipend directly, most of which will still go for room and board, but you'll be the mistress of the rest." He tilted his head, gazing steadily at her. What did he see? "That's one possibility. Another is you could travel, to Europe for example. Get yourself enrolled at university. Girls can do that there, did you know? Third, hire yourself out as a lady's companion. Trouble with that is you'll need to quit in a couple years to come back home."

"Back home? To Bath?"

"Shaftsbury. To marry the viscount."

"The viscount?" She couldn't hide the shock in her voice. Sure, she been training to run an estate, but as a housekeeper, or perhaps the steward's wife.

"Aye. It's a debt of honor, you know. Deacon saved your life."

She had no memory of it. "I thought you did that."

"On his instruction, so to speak."

Maddie was ashamed to remember how the thought someone would want to save her went beyond her understanding.

"No need to become maudlin, girl. You have grown up quite acceptably, by your own report as well as that of Miss Marsden's. You'll do."

"I don't understand."

"Deacon is no prize, see, but you'll have him well in hand in no time. And there are clothes presses full of benefits to being a countess. Problem is, you're ready now but he won't be for at least three years. We'll do the deal in '19. He'll be twenty-five that spring. You come up then. Perkins will send you the details. So what do you say?"

Maddie never was a quick study, and he'd just foretold for her an unexpected and wondrous future. Had she had leisure to decide, she might have chosen to travel. She had always wanted to search for Troy.

"I am betrothed?"

"Just so. You must act like you are, of course. No men on the side, if you know what I mean. And keep up your studies. The estate depends on you. You do wish to be part of the family?"

Through the long years since that meeting, there was nothing she wished more. Nothing she wouldn't do, and nothing she wouldn't learn, even including the common illnesses of sheep. She had lost her own family like a quick tear in a bag of apples, the sole survivor of a winter carriage accident. No provision had been made for her in her father's will—who thinks to change the will when a girl is three and her father a mere twenty-eight?

She owed the Quinns her new life and the promise of truly being part of their family—forever—stole her breath away whenever she thought on it too long.

Girls at school had complained, even whined, about their families and then happily went home for the holidays. She acted the good girl always, and never was allowed back home. But the earl's promise had changed everything.

She had dreamed of Shaftsbury castle. She'd memorized the floor plan, as well as the names of the surrounding villages and towns, even the waterways, hills, and mountains. She'd forced her mind to fathom accounting instead of the music that it loved. She'd learned about corn, and cows, and taxation.

And in the end, all she had done was for naught—because once again, a man had died and left poor instructions.

Suddenly, she realized she'd left herself open to ruin, as well. Here she was, alone and unchaperoned, in this towering wreck of a house. If she did not marry, she'd be seen as a lightskirt by anyone who mattered.

Perhaps a male might escape it, as Nash Quinn had. A grown female who left here alone was ruined, and one who stayed was ruined, as well. And a female who was rejected was ruined. Simply being a female seemed guaranteed to lead to ruin.

Who else would want a lady who knew everything about Shaftsbury, and nowhere else? Who couldn't sew a proper sampler? Who read Latin but couldn't make her hair bundle itself neatly? And who had few relations and precious little money to her name?

She must make this work. She must convince this flighty

new earl to keep his family's promise. Surely he would do his duty.

Maddie closed the trunk lid and pushed back the chair. She stood on jellied legs, willing her spine to firm. Grinding her jaw, she headed back into the lion's den.

❧

DISCOVERING a small bottle of rum in the bottom-most desk drawer, Nash took a swig. "This is all the earl's doing."

"I'm the earl, boy," Deacon growled in a fair, if higher-pitched, mimicking of their father. "And hand that bottle over." Draped against the back of the chair, legs outstretched, he took a longer draft, and then lurched up, sputtering.

"Is this Navy swill? It's undrinkable."

"Give it back then. I've had worse."

Instead, Deacon tried a smaller sip, to the same effect, and reluctantly gave up the bottle. "S'wounds! I see it now. The old toad did set this up. He used to say, 'You'll marry at twenty-five, boy, and give me a son by twenty-eight.' Think the lady has the same deadline?"

"Expect so."

"But why hasn't Wetherby said anything about it? He has plenty to say on most everything else. His own niece."

Cecil Lowe, the Viscount Wetherby, had stepped into the breach left by their father's death, but he was a piss-poor mentor to the new one. Nash wondered why. The old man had never cared for Wetherby. "We'll know soon enough. The sot must be coming tonight."

"He likes you. But he told me yesterday he had a score to

settle up north somewhere. Something about the quality of the help. Sometimes, I think he brings it on himself."

At least Deacon did not subscribe to all Wetherby's failings. Wetherby was a beautiful creature and nice in manner, but a menace to his tenants and a danger to the well-being of his estates. That's what comes when the second son inherits, his father would have said. Nash, also a second son, bristled, just as his father always intended. "You know they never can control their passions," the old man would say, another twist of the blade.

Deacon fell back against the chair. Nash would never have dreamed of sitting so slack in his father's presence. He wondered if he could do it even now. "This started out so well. I thought she was with you. You need a soft hand and tender heart to look after you."

That was the last thing Nash needed.

Deacon draped a hand over his brows. "Let's just hand her over to Wetherby. He'll have to take her, family obligation and all."

"Wetherby's no good. What would he do with a young miss?"

"You, then. She says she knows book-keeping. You might hire her, and give me my Perkins back."

"You made him cry."

"I'm sure you've toughened him up by now. Or living in that sooted-up town has." At the sound of the door opening, Deacon turned his head. "Just such a good citizen appears. Evening, Heywood."

"My daughter has the vapors, your mother is at her most shrill, and Cook is raging that our seating is delayed. Sounds like

I missed the party." William Heywood, the family barrister, took up the chair that Miss Wetherby had earlier graced.

"Another ghost from the past." Deacon raised his glass to the man. "Shall others appear? The weather is appropriate enough."

"A promise is a promise. Especially to your father, may he rest in peace."

"If only he would. Ellspeth is on the mend?" Deacon couldn't have sounded less interested.

"I expect so. But she's taken some sort of fright, and won't be down for supper."

"So we're odd-numbered at table. No wonder Mama is agog."

"Should be even enough. Wetherby rode in just ahead of me." Heywood shook his head, spreading rainwater from his sideburns across his lap. "The man's a menace. Filling the generals' ears with imaginary terrors." He looked at Nash. "And you are not much better."

"I am fomenting riot?" Then Nash remembered. A magistrate's meeting had been called for this afternoon. But a mislaid shipment of cotton had nearly stalled production at Malbanks mill, and he'd had to scramble to make good. He couldn't afford to lose a single customer in this economy. He had completely forgotten the meeting.

"Your voice was sorely missed. Is that brandy?" Heywood looked at the bottle hopefully.

Nash handed him the bottle and another glass from the drawer. "Piss water. So, they agreed to solicit for special constables?"

"A new army?" Deacon's delight did not spread to the others.

"As if a collection of rabid innkeepers and shop owners can keep the peace," Heywood said. "On horses, no less."

"Stupid enough," Nash agreed, "and dangerous. But I doubt it was such an even polling that my voice would have made a difference."

"You carry more influence than you think. Damn, this *is* pig swill." Heywood drained the glass but didn't pour another.

"Don't worry. Mama serves better at table."

"Thank you for that, my young lord. No, the bill you would have prevented, Nash my boy, is the ban on singing."

Deacon laughed. "Too many flat sopranos at church?"

"No, the cathedrals are safe, for the moment. But anyone out in the streets who engages in 'debauched' singing is fair game."

"Pray, how does one debauch a song?" Deacon said.

"Deliver it with an ironical tone. Or change the words to call for reform."

Nash snorted. "Now I'm doubly sorry I failed to remember. They've gone far enough. I won't miss any more meetings."

"I made sure of it. I named you to our new select committee. After Oldham, we need a tight group that can act fast and see sense. You're the new committee secretary, boy, so you'd damned well better be there."

"Our Nash, a politico?" Deacon fanned his face. "But won't they eat him? He's only been in the town for two years."

"Long enough," Nash growled. "And by the way, how are you managing with the estates?"

"And how is that fine French silk of yours selling? Mama says we might all be wearing mauve this season, thanks to you."

"Boys, boys," Heywood waved a hand. "Don't dirty your outfits before the party."

A servant announced that supper was served. Nash jumped up to help Heywood rise from the chair. "This new girl. Did she collapse as well, or will I see her at supper?"

Deacon waved his hand. "It's nothing. Just some scarecrow my pater fixed on to set me on the marrying path."

"Homely, then? Ellspeth shouldn't mind that."

"Rather lovely, in fact, in the Saxon way," Deacon said.

"And she's a complete stranger?"

"Not exactly." Nash held the door to let the older man pass. "She's a Wetherby."

Heywood stopped cold. "Not the Wetherby chit. I thought your father had forgotten her years ago. The idiocy of the peerage is only overshadowed by the idiocy of the people."

"You know her?"

"We'll see soon enough."

"IS THAT THE CORRESPONDENCE?"

Mr. Quinn's voice, echoing down the receiving room, did not sound ill. His face expressed irritation, perhaps, but not hostility. But Maddie reacted to his question with a lurch in her chest.

"May I have them?" He held out his hand.

She clutched the letters tighter. "Will they be safe?"

"To be sure." This time, his odd smile did not relieve her.

"These letters are everything to me."

"I do understand, Miss Wetherby. And we share an aim—we

would both see my brother wed and the estate under better management. But if it will put your mind at ease I give you my word: No harm will come to them."

She willed herself to meet his reach and loosened her fingertips, one by one, to give them over. She knew it wasn't true, but it felt as if she were giving away the former earl's friendship into the hands of others who might not treasure it as she did. But that was nonsense. Hadn't she nearly memorized their contents? And wasn't friendship in the heart, not on flimsy pages?

When he took them from her she felt a whisper of relief. At last, she wasn't carrying this weight alone. But when he handed them directly to the butler, she thought she might faint.

"Don't look so frightened. They'll be safer in the library. No crumbs."

She stared at him, startled. A joke? His smile lifted a bit higher on the right than the left. She tried to match it, but her lips were less biddable than her fingers.

He'd met her at the door as she re-entered the reception room. This time, she took in more of the furnishings, as well as the people. Fragile Louis XIV settees fought for purchase on the medieval slate floor, while drapery twice as long as her bed tried to tame the windows, if not the stormy dark beyond. Wax candles on nearly every surface succeeded at holding the night at bay, at least in the lower half of the room.

Two older men in addition to the golden-haired Lord Shaftsbury flanked a petite, ornamented dumpling of good breeding. None wore even the ghost of a smile. This was worse than the interview at the agricultural college.

Mr. Quinn must have sensed her anxiety, for he took her arm to draw her toward the fireplace. The simple gesture somehow calmed her, and her small smile of greeting was genuine.

The lady before her matched her affect. Lady Shaftsbury was blond like her eldest son, and blue-eyed, but the children must have come by their length of limb from their father's family, for she was as tiny as a second-form girl.

"Miss Wetherby, I am delighted to meet you." At Maddie's look of surprise, she continued. "We thought you were dead, didn't we?"

Maddie could only stare at her. Lord Shaftsbury trilled a laugh, breaking her stupor. She quickly made her curtsey, but her conversation lagged. "Dead?" she managed to croak out.

"George had stopped speaking of you, you know, and he didn't mention it on his deathbed."

"But he did speak to you of it." Did Mr. Quinn's warm baritone hold a trace of irritation?

"It was so long ago, dear. Deacon was away at school, so at least five years now."

"And what did he say, Mama?" Lord Shaftsbury sounded almost interested.

"Oh, 'the young Wetherby' this, 'the young Wetherby' that, that sort of thing."

"Nothing about this plan?" Mr. Quinn had voiced Maddie's question aloud.

"He would never share his plans with me. He had his dratted will for that." Her eyes darkened for a moment, and then she seemed to recover herself. "You're a lovely thing. Introductions? Here is William Heywood, the oldest friend of our bereaved family. Oldest living, that is. And of course you know your uncle. You must be so eager to reacquaint yourselves."

If Lord Shaftsbury was a golden child, all blond and blue eyed, Lord Wetherby, was his dark doppelganger, with his Byronic locks and nearly black eyes. And where the earl might be mistaken for a puppy, this man would never stoop to such playfulness. He was not as toweringly tall as she remembered, but the rest was the same. Maddie's hand went to her throat, touching the gold-bead necklace she always wore. A gift from her father, she had had to have it extended as she grew. Her pulse raced under her skin at the hollow of her neck.

The man nodded gracefully but slightly, his thin lips pursed in the perfect aristocratic bow. Maddie executed a fully proper curtsey. As she sank down, she imagined how a knight must feel kneeling before his liege lord, exposing his neck for praise or death. Her uncle appeared the ultimate gentleman, but her senses were on fire with fear. Why on earth was she being so fanciful?

"Little Maddie. How you've grown."

His mild words shot through her veins like poison.

Heat flooded Maddie's face, as if all her blood had fled to the top of her head. Just as fast, it was gone, leaving her eyes out of focus and her head too light. She fought for balance, swaying slightly. "Uncle."

She felt the disapproval of his gaze. Panic nearly overwhelmed her, weighting her legs down with lead. He couldn't hurt her now, here, could he?

Lady Shaftsbury clapped twice. "Let us go in, now we are all here." She held her arm to Mr. Heywood.

Lord Shaftsbury took her uncle's arm, leaving Mr. Quinn to escort her. "You make quite the impression on your little niece."

"She always was a timid little mouse," drawled the dark man.

𐫱

Nash had never seen such a deadly reaction to the fop that was Lord Wetherby. By the time they reached the hall, Miss Wetherby could barely stand.

Nash bid her sit in one of the seats for the older footman. "You're choking your air."

"What is that?" she choked out.

"Trouble breathing. Lean as forward as you can." Louder, he said, "Dashed corsets. I don't know why you women insist on strapping yourselves like sausages."

He told the nearest footman to fetch a glass of water. Crouching down beside the chair, he took her wrist as if to take her pulse. He knew already from the flush on her face and upper chest it was racing. Instead, he used his thumb to brush the pulse point at her wrist. She jerked back, her gaze flashing to his. But soon enough, the tension in the corners of her mouth eased, and she could sit without swaying. She pulled her hand away with a sniff, a sure sign she was returning to form.

She closed her eyes and took a slow breath. "I apologize, Mr. Quinn. I'm fine, truly. It's been a long trip, and I've thought about—dreamt about—this meeting for so long that when it happened I was overcome. That and the trouble with Lord Shaftsbury. And everything so muddled."

It sounded plausible, but it was not true. He felt it.

"Miss Wetherby, a mouse?"

She didn't open her eyes. "I was the one who had to chase the mouse out of the girls' room at school. But he's right. I've always been frightened of him."

"Fear doesn't need to be rational to be real." He heard his

mother's voice ordering people about in the dining room and frowned. "Perhaps it was the corset."

She rose carefully. "We mustn't dally."

"You don't need to impress him. Lord Wetherby may be Deacon's false lieutenant, but he's not ours."

"Let us see," she said, leaning a bit more on his arm than proper.

FOUR

Instead of the slightly warmer dining salon, Mama had set this meal in the echo chamber of the banqueting hall. Elaborate place settings for the six of them looked a forlorn hope against the long stretch of the scored oak trestle that their medieval forebears had supped on.

In this setting, the socially preferred even seating looked wrong. Deacon took the head, his back to the open-grated maw of a fireplace. To be proper, Mama should take the opposite end, but as it was six yards away, she wisely chose conversation over propriety. She sat at Deacon's right, along the length of the trestle, with Wetherby on her right. Heywood had Deacon's left, with two place settings beside him. Six candelabra illuminated the expanse of empty ebony wood after that.

Nash escorted Miss Wetherby to the seat next to Heywood, and sat himself on the rump seat. Not surprising that he would have to cede his place to the older man, but in a setting so obviously designed to recall the lineage and greatness of the Shaftsburys, even to using the heavy cutlery, it stung. That he would not need to avoid observing Ellspeth Heywood's moon-eyes at his brother all meal long was small consolation. He sent a silent plea to the gods of hospitality; let it be a short meal, not one of those four-hour monstrosities.

He did feel the blow to Miss Wetherby's aspirations, though. She should have been seated nearest Deacon; even Ellspeth could have claimed that position. What with the unhappy carriage ride, the shock of arrival, and now this, he nearly felt sorry for her. But she played the role of the martyred lady too coldly for his taste.

Still, her panic in the sitting room felt real enough. He expected that ladies like her did not often face back-to-back setdowns. So often in calm waters, perhaps they did not know how to roll with its swells.

Heywood cleared his throat, startling the servant setting his soup before him. "Now that you are an earl in truth and the King's law, Shaftsbury, do you show yourself at Lords this year?"

"I think not. You do not, do you, Wetherby?"

"Might be time. With all this hubbub about the country, it might do well to give a speech or two. Get your name in the dailies as a supporter of the crown."

Nash had never liked Wetherby, but he had to admit the man defined elegant, every bit the gentleman. He'd ridden from Wetherby in that Corinthian cravat and high-pointed green jacket, and took table better than even Mama. Perhaps he resented the man only because he was a second son, made whole by the death of his brother, Miss Wetherby's father.

On the other hand, Wetherby obviously had not been magnanimous in victory. He hadn't settled a fair dowry on the lady, as he should have done. Will and testament or no, she was family. Small wonder the lady, so round-eyed and attentive, shuttered her gaze when it passed over her uncle. As the Wetherbys sat directly across from each other, she spent most of the meal looking up the table. Nash most often had a view of the graceful curve of her neck, and a tawny curl that had escaped to dance along its length.

They weren't through the fish course before talk turned to deeper politics.

Surprisingly, Deacon made the opening salvo. "Mama, Nash has joined a select committee. He's charged with keeping the peace."

"Is that safe?" She touched the corner of her mouth in a pantomime of agitation.

Miss Wetherby's head snapped to face him. Reappraising the merchant? For a moment he warmed himself with pride at his conscription.

"Nothing to worry about." Heywood's voice carried that tone used to calm small children. Nash didn't know how Mama could stand it. "We don't do the battling, only send the troops out. If need be, of course."

Miss Wetherby's steady brows pinched in the tiniest bit. "Manchester has so many criminals you must call out an army?"

His pride sank to his shoes.

Wetherby answered his niece. "It's the lower orders. They seek to break machines and steal from better men than they."

Heywood held up a hand. "Too strong."

"Is it? Looks like a return of the risings of Seventeen."

"Which were put down quickly. And only the guilty workers were put down," Heywood soothed Mama.

Put to death, he meant. The bite of turbot lay like ashes in Nash's mouth. He swallowed it down. "I heard it was spies for the crown that started the tinder."

"Whyever would they?" Deacon's brow knitted.

"To earn their keep," Nash bit out. "No revolt, no pay for spies." He'd known some spies in the Navy, nasty buggers.

"But it isn't spies inciting these blighted meetings spreading across Lancashire." Heywood pointed his fork at Nash. "Ten thousand at the one in Manchester this past winter alone."

"I observed that meeting, and while the words were strong, the people didn't appear violent," Nash said.

"Perhaps the spies were away that day?" Wetherby's baiting skills needed work, though they made Deacon smile.

Deacon looked to Heywood. "But still you formed a committee? Sidmouth must be quaking."

"Trumped-up aristo." Wetherby dismissed the chief of the country's Home Office with a flick of his twice-ruffled wrist.

Deacon signaled for the next course. "I for one don't wish any trouble. The last thing I need is my tenants up in arms. As Nash is forever reminding me, I am responsible for them. *Noblesse oblige*, and all."

"Nonsense." Wetherby straightened his cuff. "*Noblesse, c'est toute.*"

Mama clapped twice in appreciation of his witticism, but her smile did not reach her eyes. As her gazed traveled the circuit from Wetherby, Deacon, Heywood, Miss Wetherby, to him, her expression clouded.

"I must admit, I did not arrange this supper, nor was I consulted on the guest listing. Shaftsbury drew it up himself, and Perkins did the favors. I cannot fathom why we all are drawn together tonight."

"It's for me, isn't it, Mama?"

"Of course, Deacon dear. But Mr. Heywood, while a very old family friend, has no special connection to you. He's been closer to Nash these past years." She pursed her lips, looking at Wetherby.

That man tittered, an oddly feminine sound in this room of solid timbers and armaments. "Too true. Your husband, rest his soul, did not invite me to ordinary events. Why should I be here now?" He was so magnanimous she patted his hand in praise.

Mama continued down the table. "And you, Miss Wetherby?"

Nash felt the lady stiffen, her hands quickly dropping below the table to twist at her napkin. She must have looked to Deacon, for Mama flicked her gaze in that direction, mouth thinning in calculation.

"Miss Wetherby has aspirations to join the family, Mama. Sadly, father neglected to inform us of that fact."

Everyone at table and standing around it turned to stare at the lady. She looked into her lap. Then snapped her head up, resting her gaze on Mama.

"Impossible," Wetherby declared.

Mama only sighed. "I wouldn't put it past him. Poor George."

Nash felt compelled to correct their impressions. "She has letters from father, Mama. Letters that reach back a decade or more."

"I don't doubt it. The man took an unhealthy interest in

you from the start. Apparently, he always wanted a girl. Obstinate creature."

Wetherby finally cast a glance at his niece. "Why ever would a peer choose to correspond with you? You're nothing to him. Less than nothing."

She opened her lips, but no sound emerged. She closed them again, swallowing hard, her hand reaching for her throat protectively. "He called himself my godfather."

"So he was." Mama turned to Wetherby. "A quiet affair, at the chapel at Wetherby. She was a bit older than she should have been, or bigger at least."

Miss Wetherby's voice was stronger now. "The earl—the previous earl—arranged for my schooling. After my parents' deaths. His influence helped turn me out as a lady."

"What do you know of being a lady?" Wetherby's anger took Nash by surprise, but did not rattle Miss Wetherby.

"I was born one, and raised one. And nearly always act as one."

"Hear, hear." Deacon raised his glass to her.

Wetherby scowled. "Don't encourage her."

Her gasp knifed Nash's ears. He couldn't let that pass. He'd had well enough of Wetherby.

"What do you mean by that?" His protest drew all eyes to him: Mama's confused, Deacon's amused, Wetherby's infuriated, and the lady's prepared for more pain.

Wetherby shrugged and turned his attention back to Mama.

Deacon tried to smooth things over. "Not just family. It seems she's to be my wife." He tossed the word out lightly, as if marriage were the biggest joke in the world.

Wetherby burst out laughing, the sound ringing to the

candles above their heads. "A marvelous joke. Did your brother set it up?"

"My first thought, too. But no, it was my dear papa's doing."

Wetherby sat up straight, choking off his laugh. He stared at Miss Wetherby a long moment, and then turned away in dismissal. "She does her family proud."

Mama set her glass on the table with an audible clink. "Lord Wetherby, I must protest. How could you say such a thing of your brother's child?"

"She isn't my brother's child."

Miss Wetherby's hand went to her throat again.

A clink of silver on plate reminded them that theirs weren't the only ears listening in the room. No one spoke until the young rabbit had been served, and Mama sent the staff from the room.

"A by-blow?" Deacon's eyes lit up, as if the circumstances of her birth were the only thing that could interest him about Madeline Wetherby.

"Worse. The daughter of no one."

"Explain, if you please." Mama tapped her mouth with her napkin, and then rested her hands in her lap, as if to give a lecture—or receive one.

Wetherby obliged. "As you know, Lady Shaftsbury, my brother's wife refused to whelp him the requisite pups."

"She didn't refuse, she miscarried. And speak of the dead with more reverence, if you please."

"Beg your pardon, ma'am," Wetherby drawled. He looked pleased that he had their undivided attention, and spoke loud enough that those servants listening behind the doors could easily make him out. "The lady finally did bring a child out into the world, but sadly he did not last a week. Shortly after, while riding back from town, the family carriage ran over a farmer's daughter. Those sort like to walk in the roads as if they own them, you know." He shrugged.

"This woman died on the spot, but the babe in her arms was tossed free, and unharmed, they say. My lady sister-in-law took that child as hers. This Madeline."

"That poor Lady Wetherby. To keep such a secret."

"What about the babe's other family?" Deacon leaned forward, rapt.

"My brother paid them handsomely. I'm sure they didn't miss her."

Nash was sure they did, and their mother more.

Deacon's eyes flashed with his mind's humming. "So they adopted the girl, and then had a boy of their own. Isn't that always what happens?"

"Exactly. *Nihil et nemo.*" Nothing, no one.

Madeline Wetherby lurched to her feet, swaying. The four men at table scrambled to their own feet. Nash had no doubt all were wondering the same thing: Does one stand when a lady does if she's suddenly no longer a lady?

Mama rapped her knuckles on the table. "Sit down at once. Don't you dare faint; it's been done already once today." The girl sat down, her breath escaping in a gust, like a sail pulled too fast on the line.

Nash didn't like the looks the others were giving her.

"She is still a Wetherby." He wished he could stretch his arms across the table and slap some sense into Wetherby's too-fine façade.

"Not by blood."

Mama's hand fluttered over her chest. It was her reaction Nash feared the most, he realized.

"This changes nothing," he said, rather too forcefully.

"I don't know, dearest. What could Shaftsbury have been thinking?"

He had to wonder the same thing. His father had been a stickler for "pure blood," critical of any news of a dilution of the peerage. Or was he? "I suppose that is why he felt responsible for her."

"He needn't." Wetherby sliced a bite of the tender rabbit and ate it. "Her kind always lands on its feet. Look how high she's risen."

"Take care, Lord Wetherby. My father was in trade as well."

Both her sons turned to their mother in shock. Deacon recovered first. "So the old codger did have something of the democrat in him."

Miss Wetherby held her hands in her lap as if squeezing coal to make a diamond. "I don't believe you," she said, looking directly at her uncle. If he was her uncle.

"Careful what you say, girl. Accusing a peer of lying is a transportable offense."

Heywood seemed to rouse himself at last. "Now, now, we're all friends here." He drew his hand down the length of his beard, a sure sign of nerves. "In fact, I now know why I was invited tonight."

Deacon's eyebrows arched. "I hardly know if I can stomach another surprise."

"Nothing like. In my earlier days, I served as solicitor for the great families, you'll recall. I drew up the adoption agreement for Miss Wetherby, and served as parish witness at the christening.

Madeline wasn't your first name, you know." He wagged his head slowly side to side.

She slowly mirrored the movement. "You don't say."

"Right. So I'm here as confirmation, so to speak." He patted her arm, an Iago to her Desdemona.

She started at the touch, and pulled away, toward Nash. "She wasn't my mother? My mother was dead? I have two dead mothers?"

"They adopted you, and my father stood up as your godfather. So he approved."

Wetherby dropped his silver onto his plate, the crash a signal that the course was over and the servants should come in and clear away. "If you say so."

FIVE

Maddie followed Lady Shaftsbury upstairs to her cozy sitting room, behind the minstrel's gallery of the banqueting hall. Supper had continued for another three courses, but she could not remember if she even tasted them.

Adopted! She'd never heard of such a thing. Children were taken in, and some eventually adopted, but never in such secret. Her mind skittered around the thought. To light on it for any length of time made her stomach lurch.

The lady seemed to have no such troubles. She steered them into the small room with painted paneling and a roaring fire. Directing Maddie to a small settee too close to the heat, she deposited herself on the large upholstered sofa behind it. This odd arrangement placed their heads at the same height.

"Unusual fabric, don't you think? It's Indian silk. We're becoming quite the cosmopolitan establishment." Lady Shaftsbury seemed content to natter on, maintaining both parts of the conversation on her own. Grateful to be relieved of this social obligation, Maddie found it gave her thoughts too much space to roam. Still, she didn't trust that her clenching throat would allow her to speak.

Adopted. What did that mean? She had precious few memories of her childhood, little bits of treasure. Mama and her roses, Papa's booming laugh, baby George who liked to drool. She didn't remember the overturned carriage that took their lives while sparing hers, though she'd heard the story enough to picture it in her mind: tumbling over a soft embankment, rolling, spilling her clear before coming to rest upside-down in the tumult of the spring-swollen river. The dazed outriders, also spun free, had found her at the edge of the river, watching the axle drop below the water line.

Lies, all of it. She'd been unconscious when they found her, her Nana had said.

Did her Nana know about her? Adopted. Did everyone know? Maddie shivered, even with the burning fire. It was as if she had been stripped bare for all to see all this time, and only now discovered it.

"Not listening at all, are you, dear?" Lady Shaftsbury patted the seat beside her, bidding Maddie move. The sofa was softer than it looked, but the world seemed so much harder. She tried to force the words out, the simplest phrase, "Thank you, ma'am." But the sound she heard was completely different.

"Oh my Lord."

"My sentiments exactly. What a pickle for you. But it answers a score of questions for me." She held her hands out toward the flames. "I always wondered why your mother— pardon me, Lady Wetherby—didn't accept the usual bedside callers after you were born. You weren't born, were you? Well, you were, but you understand." She patted Maddie's hand, branding her with the heat.

"I'd heard she'd had another boy, and we were all so glad because the first one hadn't lasted. But then you appeared. First-born girls aren't preferred, of course, but a healthy specimen did promise that a living boy might be forthcoming. And so he was."

Except that boy hadn't lasted either. And instead there was Uncle Cecil.

Maddie shook her head slowly, trying to keep the tears at bay. How could the lady act as if everything were normal, when the whole world had changed?

She was not a natural Wetherby. Everything her parents had told her was a lie. They weren't even her parents.

She was no one.

No wonder Uncle Cecil didn't care for her—he wasn't her uncle. She had no family. What would happen to her? What would she do? Whom could she ask for help? Who would deign to help her, a girl of no family?

"What will happen to me?" She didn't know she'd spoken aloud until Lady Shaftsbury answered her.

"Your uncle will find you something, I'm sure."

"I think not. He would prefer me dead."

"A bit extreme. But then, it might have been better, were you dead, than all this hullabaloo." Lady Shaftsbury's limpid gaze suggested she had no depths. Her nearly unlined face, with its touch of powder, bespoke a nearly worry-free life. But Maddie knew better.

"Your husband once wrote me that you were the smartest person he'd met in the flesh."

Her expression changed in an instant. Her jaw tightened, revealing the sharp shadows of cheekbones. Her gaze shot toward the door, as if to assure herself that no one had overheard.

"How he hated that. Men do, you know. But no, you haven't yet learned it. Deacon said you argued quite persuasively."

"He was not persuaded."

"He nearly was, to his terror. You mustn't frighten my boys. They'll run away."

"His father wrote that I could confide in you."

"More fool him. Why should I help you, who were too fine an infant to have poor me as your godmama?"

Maddie bit her lip. The iron taste of pain stemmed the confusion of her thoughts. "I'm sorry?"

"Don't I sound the petty one. Must be talking about my late love that does it. Or that Lady Wetherby." She rolled to her feet, smoothing out her skirts. "It's late. I believe we'll do without tea tonight. The boys will drink hearty to Deacon's majority. They won't show their faces up here."

Maddie's legs wobbled but held as she rose. She wanted nothing more than to escape into a silent bedroom and sleep this nightmare away.

Nearing the door, Lady Shaftsbury turned back to look at her. "You're certainly a pretty thing. And well-trained. Perhaps one of my friends will take you on. Companion or governess?"

Maddie fell mute in shock.

"Think on it, but quickly. I'll start writing the letters in the morning."

Then she understood.

Like a silk dress from the wrong provenance, she was no longer marriage material.

"A RIDDLE: When is a Wetherby not a Wetherby?"

Deacon tilted his head, the better to gaze at the rainbow created by his snifter of brandy. The colors shifted prettily, far finer than Nash's thoughts had run these past few hours. He'd never think of his brother as Shaftsbury.

"She still is." His voice came out a growl. Refined folk, his ass. These fine folk beside him cared for nothing but themselves.

"She never was." Wetherby had kept the decanter for himself, sharing only with Deacon, since the ladies had left the table.

Heywood seemed to find some pleasure in his cigar. "She is, in the eyes of the law." Heywood should know; he'd done the paperwork all those years ago, back when Madeline Wetherby was but an angelic face on a doll's body.

Deacon shifted his already wobbling gaze to the older man. "But then, why did we have the care of her?"

Heywood's gaze flicked to Wetherby. Deacon's meandered after him.

Wetherby made a pretty moue with his mouth. "Shaftsbury said he wanted it so. Who was I to argue? I needed his support with my tenants, and that was his price."

"A little girl?"

"Useless, I know. Shaftsbury sold himself cheap."

Nash had never met such an ass. "What help did you need with your tenants?"

"Can't rightly recall. Some talk of an uprising. Always happening in these parts."

"Not at Shaftsbury, nor Middleton," Nash said.

Heywood tapped his pipe. "What the master is, that will his men be."

Deacon laughed. "I should hope not, if Wetherby's their master. The countryside entire will be a'wenching, without the benefit of Maypole Day. Still, the girl is beautiful. I'm surprised you gave her up."

"Quite the anomaly, a rose born among the mandrakes. But then, there are plenty of pretty girls, even among the low folk. The old man told me to forget her, and I did obey."

"Everyone obeyed the old earl."

"Except Nash," Deacon said, and then pursed his lips, as if he would take the words back. Instead, he plunged on. "Did you get me a gift?"

"You want another silk suit?" This time his brother's eyes laughed with him.

"Something far more precious. Your time." Deacon mustered up his lost-little-boy voice. "Stay on a day and help with the accounts? You're so good at it."

Nash's mood dropped on the words "stay on" and sank into shadow on the word "accounts." He was not his brother's keeper, nor his lackey. "Do your own accounts or remedy this problem with Miss Wetherby. I don't have time for both." He didn't have time for either, in fact.

"What problem? Just toss her out." Wetherby waved his drooping hand as if shooing a dog out of the room.

"As her own family did?" Nash could not let it go. "She's a Wetherby, yet precious little blunt is settled on her. If Deacon doesn't claim her—"

"And I don't." Deacon pushed out his glass for Wetherby to refill it.

"Then she has no family to go to."

"She can stay in the hovel that sprouted her." Wetherby slammed the decanter onto the table.

"Enough." Heywood rose to his feet, stamping the cigar out on the plate as if it were an asp's head. "She was raised a gentleman's daughter, and that is what she remains."

"In the eyes of the law, perhaps," Wetherby said. "But what will happen when all the society mamas hear of her lineage? I don't see them lining up their precious little boys to match with that pedigree."

"Whoever would loose that rumor? Surely not us." Deacon loved gossip, but hated being the subject of it.

Wetherby chuckled. "Who could ever keep such a juicy item to himself? I'll wager it already has traveled two or three miles down the road just since the cheese course."

Heywood's jaw worked silently, as if it were arguing in pantomime. Finally, he gave a short nod. "It's late. I'll leave you to it."

Nash pushed back his chair as if to leave as well. But he paused, thinking. "If that's the case, then we should settle something on her right away. Before her reputation is ruined."

Deacon raised his hands. "I'm not marrying her, no matter

what those letters may say. The last thing I need now is the nagging burden of a wife."

Wetherby tipped his head up to catch a last sip of brandy. "How about this? You call for another bottle and I'll take the girl. She's our family's scandal; I don't see why you should worry in the least about it. I'll see she gets all she deserves."

Deacon seemed to consider it. "A nice farm, perhaps. A landowner, of course. Though she'd make a lovely milkmaid."

"No." Nash's ears were pounding. "We'll take care of it. Our father set up a plan, and if we don't follow it—"

"Which we won't," Deacon cut in.

"We will find another way."

Wetherby shrugged, as if he couldn't care less. But Nash saw a predatory gleam in the man's eye. "As you wish. But I'd advise a tight leash. You know how those country women can be."

"Wetherby." Deacon sounded seriously tired of this topic.

"I mean, really, even when she was that angelic four-year-old you said you loved, remember that? She needed to find out who was the true leader of the pack."

"And how did you do that?" Nash snapped, his temper fighting at its leash.

"How do you train any puppy?"

SIX

N ash wasted no time following Heywood out the door. The mystery of Madeline Wetherby lay in wait for him in the library.

She certainly hadn't wanted to give up those letters. She'd handed them over peaceably enough, but when he gave them to Emmett, he'd thought she would chase the poor man down and grab them back. But she remained a lady, instead chasing them only with her gaze.

Spreading them across the desk, Nash combined the correspondence into order by date, a regular back and forth every six months for fifteen years. Arrayed down the length of the table and back again, it amounted to thousands of words. His father had probably spent more words on this stranger than he had on his own son. Second son.

Nash swallowed the iron tang of his jealousy, and it soon gave way to curiosity. It was not her fault his father never spoke to Nash, but what hold did she have on him that he did speak—

and write—to her? Something in their exchange that would explain why the old earl, who held himself aloof even from his family, had maintained a strong bond with a young girl from the neighborhood who wasn't even who people said she was. Why his father, who would not deign to speak to strangers, had adopted one, in the eyes of the church.

"Start from the front or the back?"

Nash's head snapped toward the open passage from the library, where Deacon grinned at him. His big brother had always walked like a cat, insinuating himself into a room. Nash expected Deacon found it harder nowadays, with everyone's eyes out for the new earl.

"Is it wise to leave Wetherby alone with the help?"

"He prefers it. Doesn't like me to poach. And wenching in one's own garden feels a tad incestuous to me." He shuddered, but delicately, as only Deacon could.

"You trade gardens, then?"

"I tried. But Wetherby's pile doesn't attract the pretties. Speaking of lovelies, how do you find the resurrected Miss Wetherby? Good length of limb and fine face, but pushy. Trying too hard." He drifted over to the desk.

"A fine caricature, but more important is whether she speaks true. The front." Nash scooped up half the letters, the earlier ones, and pushed them toward his bother. Deacon took the first of the stack, Nash the last of the later stack.

From Miss Wetherby to poor Perkins, it confirmed her intention to arrive at the castle yesterday. So she hadn't lied about that. The letter was dated a few weeks after the old earl's death. An earlier card from her regretted that death, calling the old sod "a great gentleman and the finest friend a lady could hope for."

"She's adorable. 'Thank you much for placing me here. Miss Marsden is so strict—strict is crossed out and replaced with kind—I know I will work hard here.'"

Nash looked up from his father's final letter. "He's parroting himself. 'Deacon is to marry at twenty-five, and sire a child at twenty-eight. Three years should be plenty for you both.'"

"Bully. I like him better here: 'You are not to worry about what happened at home. Of course, you may feel sad from time to time. But you will always remain the strong, cheerful girl I know you are inside.'"

Nash leaned back in the chair, now rather enjoying its swivel. "What did he know of how we were inside?"

Deacon glanced up at him as he was pulling another letter open. "He wrote all of us. Everyone else at college received letters from their mamas, but I got them from him. Quite the coup, even among the heirs. And he wrote to Mama, too, whenever he traveled or stayed in London for long."

Nash's stomach ballooned with bile. "He never wrote to me."

Deacon measured him with a glance, uncovering his pain in a moment. Then he shrugged, as if he hadn't just seen into his brother's twisted soul.

"He wrote you by proxy. Look again. Navy seal."

The ones he'd seen earlier. He took them up, the paper nearly cardboard. Quarterly updates on Lieutenant Nash Quinn, from his first voluntary impressment through his discharge from the *Nisus* as acting captain.

Nash read through his own history as recorded in the

cramped hand of a Navy secretary. His medal for valor, his near court-martial, and a complete listing of all prize-money earned. The conniver had known all this, and not said a word.

He slapped the chair arm. His father had known how he had proved himself over and over, even learning that damned algebra to graduate to officer. And not a word of praise, not a word of understanding, not even a word of welcome home when Nash had returned a decade later. But then he'd known his son was coming home. The Navy had told him the month before.

The old man also had known that Nash didn't need the family's stipend, didn't need to show up at the castle once a quarter and grovel to obtain it. Yet he'd played along with Nash's pretense, which let him see Mama and yet remain at odds with his father.

Only his father had not been at odds with him.

His eyes stung, and he blinked rapidly. Deacon chuckled. The bastard had been watching the changes on Nash's face the whole time. Nash pinched the space between his eyes, as if it was his head that ached.

"You had to like the man, in his correspondence. In the flesh, well, wasn't that another story." Deacon unfolded another letter.

"The girl enjoys English and French classes, but finds figures a bore. And did you know a cold could cause one's spelling to suffer, at least as recorded on the quarterly test. But nothing about friends, and nothing about coming home for holidays. That's all I ever wrote about. That and for another advance."

Nash returned his attention to the Wetherby letters. "He may have been the sweet patron when she was a babe, but he's up to his old tricks later. A commandment to learn about sheep and dairy. And corn blight, lord help her. And here he's telling her to learn to keep books 'as if you were in trade.' Not ladylike at all."

"But undeniably useful. Little Maddie goes on and on about how she wants to be useful, especially to the Quinns. The perfect serf." Deacon's brow drew down, and he quickly reached for the next letter.

"Find something?"

"Nothing good. Shaftsbury paid for a good family to take her in one winter's holiday. Friend of the girl's."

"He bought her a friend?"

"Wasn't she the ugly duckling? Here she gushes at the experience; it's full half the next letter. I feel like blubbering."

The event was not repeated, that Nash could tell. His heart hurt at the image of a little girl, alone with the help in midwinter, and all summer long. Small wonder she had to be reprimanded for spending too much time with the help. Small wonder she hired herself out as a tutor as soon as she turned sixteen.

Madeline Wetherby had been earning her own keep for the past few years, though she had spent half of it on the specialized coursework his father had recommended.

According to her teachers, she was an apt pupil, a quiet girl, eager to please. They said nothing about her dreams or her fears; they seemed not to know her at all.

Were all women raised to be such blank slates? Madeline had reacted so badly to Deacon's refusal, and said it was because she had trained herself to fit with only him. He should remind her how apt a pupil she was. Surely she could fit herself to any man. Perhaps she'd suit a tradesman in town.

But the idea left a sour taste in his mouth. Shaftsbury had offered his heir, and here they now sat contemplating foisting her off on a soap maker or manufactory man.

"Here we go." Deacon waved a letter in his father's handwriting. "It was you who were the intended spouse. Until you up and deserted us. 'Nash has a good head on his shoulders, for all that.' I'll spare you the earlier part; we're none of us without faults, especially at eleven or twelve. Seems the old dear expected to find you a living, and make her a rector's wife. Or perhaps an advocate, like Mr. Heywood. But he prefers the church. A good living—he underlines it."

"Wonder how long it took him to give up that dream?"

"Who says he ever did? You'd make a stellar Reverend Honorable. You have the sanctimonious prose down already. You were ever holier than thou."

"And you the unrepentant sinner. He's promised you to her these past ten years."

"So unfortunate that you were 'lost to the sea,' as he so poetically puts it. That could have solved all this trouble."

"By laying it on my doorstep."

"You always were the responsible one. But it's I who have all the responsibilities now."

Deacon swept the letters into his arms, snatching one out of Nash's hand. He turned toward the fireplace, embers only but still hot.

"You wouldn't."

"It solves the problem." He waved a letter over the embers, which caught up a glow again.

For a moment, Nash sat frozen. Even with this correspondence, Deacon could still argue against the match, especially on grounds of false promises. They could pay Miss Wetherby for her silence. It was the easiest solution.

But it wasn't right.

The old earl had made a family promise, in writing, and repeated it. Should the letter disappear, Miss Wetherby's legal standing would weaken. But she could call on her teacher, on Perkins, and perhaps others, who would argue in her favor.

But she would need funds for that. And the Wetherbys had left her nothing, the earl, pitifully little. Because he'd offered something more.

Now Nash understood why she was so agitated at handing her letters over. The Quinns might not be trustworthy.

Deacon let the letter float onto the embers. It caught, an orange blaze. He let go another.

"Don't!" Before Nash could push his legs around the desk, Deacon had sacrificed more than half to the flame. Nash wrenched the rest away from him.

"You have a better idea? I thought not." He grabbed them, pulling Nash's hands toward the flames as well. Nash was forced to let go. The paper caught, and flamed high.

"Damn it, Deacon, I gave my word."

"What of it? I never gave mine."

"Idiot. That doesn't change anything."

Deacon clapped his hands as if brushing away soot—or a young woman's dreams. "Now let's see what mettle she's made of."

SEVEN

After a quick course through the close shrubbery, Nash decided that wild hair and wet cuffs were perfectly adequate for an early morning breakfast table. But as he strode into the small dining room, he immediately regretted his carelessness.

Miss Wetherby jumped up from her chair, spoon still clutched in her hand. He couldn't go forward, as that would be rude, but he couldn't retreat, as that would be ruder still. She saved him in that way women do—with conversation.

"A fine morning for a ride, Mr. Quinn."

Magically released from his invisible bonds, he surged into the room. It had once been a type of greenhouse, until some ancestor had allowed vines to cover all the windows. It still received plenty of light, but of a greenish cast guaranteed to make even the most hale of visitors look sickly.

It certainly paid no compliment to its current occupant. Her dark-blond hair had gone drab, her rather pretty face waxen. It did inflect the green in her eyes with something, not fire exactly, but the light cast even darker shadows on the bags under her eyes.

"I apologize for my state of undress, Miss Wetherby."

"I thank you, but there's no need. I understand habits in country houses are different."

"I am no slothful part of the landed class, I assure you." He called for coffee and toast with egg, as she was having, and sat opposite her. This table was a petite version of the giant banqueting monstrosity; it seated only twelve. She had taken a spot on the bench along the side, leaving the ends for the hosts.

"I apologize for implying so."

Nash sipped his blazingly hot coffee. "Apology accepted. So neither of us has slept."

She stirred her cocoa, avoiding his gaze. "A lot to think about."

He could well imagine. Yesterday, she had been a Wetherby, today she was not, some would surely say. Did that change anything? Not in his mind. She had been raised a lady and she behaved like one. A lady without a title. And a bit too high in the instep for him—seven trunks, by god—but fair enough for her station in life.

But what was her level? Was it the station she deserved, though she had not the blunt to pay for it? Or was it the station she had been born to, apparently a tenant's cottage somewhere in Lancashire?

"Might I ask you a question?" he said. "You needn't answer."

She raised her moss-eyed gaze to his, and waited.

"I know you are not well set up, in terms of funds, yet you

have nearly as many traveling trunks as Mama." He trailed off, shrugging.

"Why do I have so many clothes?" He instantly felt an idiot for asking. She was a woman—would she not spend all her pin money on raiment?

She touched the collar of her silk dress, a darker gray than yesterday's version. "It's your father's doing. He allowed me five new outfits a year, and as I stopped growing quite a while ago, they have added up."

"Fifteen years times five is 75 dresses." Far more than seven trunks.

"They weren't all at once, of course. And it was a good idea, when I was growing like a weed. I'd get two in winter and three in summer. There were always girls who didn't have enough, so when I stopped growing I would take one of them with me to share the bounty. Your father was a generous man." A small smile stole onto her too-wide lips at the memory.

Nash restrained a scowl. He had no such illusions of the man. But he shouldn't begrudge her hers.

"I suppose I will sell them," she said. "But in Manchester, no one will buy my cloth, will they?"

"You believe we will cast you out?"

She said nothing. The shadows along her jaw deepened. She was clenching it tight enough to break teeth.

His hand ached to brush the side of her face, smooth away her worries with a stroke. But he could think of no force to bring on his brother that would lead him to accept this lady as his wife. She wouldn't be happy with the likes of him, either, no matter that their bodies looked as if they would fit lock and key. Deacon lived on the surface, happy enough. This

Miss Wetherby had depths Deacon wouldn't even know to look for.

But would she marry a merchant, such as him? Another idiotish thought, Nash berated himself. Ladies with creamy skin, handsome manners, and seven traveling trunks would not stoop to bunking in his cozy hovel, especially when they had been promised a castle. All women want to be princesses.

This would-be princess, perfectly turned out at six in the morning, lifted her toast to her mouth. But her hand shook. She put it back on the plate, and spoke the words he had been dreading since he woke this morning.

"Did you read the letters?"

"They were as you say." A wave of anger sent spikes down his chest and into his belly.

"I'd like to re-read the correspondence entire, if I may. I'm rather interested in myself as a child."

His throat seized. Nash held the coffee to his lips, trying to fool his gullet into releasing a swallow. "It's not pretty," he croaked out. As her face pinched in at the nose, he tried to repair the damage. "No, that's not what I mean. I mean—"

He watched the change come over her features, the smooth skin taut, the wide eyes closing to almond shape, the full lips pressing themselves compact. The lady from the crossroads.

But she wasn't as skilled at it yet as she should be. He read doubt, despair, and even hope arguing for purchase under that glassy lady's mask. He didn't want to see how they were hurting her. He didn't want to feel that he was to blame. There was no profit in it.

The truth of the letters danced on his tongue. He swallowed it. And tried to meet her gaze.

Maddie looked into his eyes and knew he was lying about something. His shoulders hunched, and his long hands didn't seem to know what to do with themselves. But his face was still, and his eyes calm. Clearly, he made a good man of business, able to bluff and throw smoke. He certainly did not have the gift of tongues, though.

"I understand your meaning," she said into the silence his last bewildering statement had created. The space between his brows puckered. Could he not be as sure of his meaning as all that?

She wished sleep had come last night. Her years of training had not prepared her for the explosion of events yesterday. But today Lord Shaftsbury must say yes. She must be persuasive, no matter that her thoughts were as muddled as the baths at Spa.

Who was she? The daughter of an earl, or of a common laborer? Should she be birthing and training up the next line of great men and fine ladies, or the next shepherds and farmer's wives? What if the Quinns sent her away, to live with the cottagers, could she even bear it?

Of course she could. Anything, except perhaps returning to Wetherby. There were far too many hurtful memories there.

"Why did you not return home for holidays?"

It was as if he'd read her mind. She shivered inside. "The new master would not have me."

"This Lord Wetherby? Surely you mistake the matter."

"He did not invite me, in word nor deed. He never wrote." He'd made it quite clear that he considered Maddie no family of his. She had thought he blamed her for his brother's death, though how a three-year-old could be to blame for a carriage accident she couldn't fathom. But his reason was entirely different. Adopted! Sharing not a drop of blood. And with the gentry, blood was all.

In her imagination, even in those of her dreams that hadn't been nightmares, Maddie had the arguments that would magically remake Deacon Quinn's mind into her image of it. He would read the letters, recall himself to his duty, and get Mama launched on the preparations for the wedding. But even in the half-light of early morning, Maddie knew it would take more than that. She would need to be persuasive. Back in Bath, all her arguments had seemed so strong. But here, in this mountain of a castle, they seemed gossamer. If only the previous Lord Shaftsbury had lived just six months more.

And this Quinn, the one opposite her, was the least likely to help her stake her claim, no matter his words of comfort the night before. He'd read the letters, and likely found some loophole, some alley through the words to help his brother escape her clutches. And could she blame him?

They heard the murmurs of men approaching. Mr. Heywood turned into the breakfasting room, while the butler, Emmett, continued down the hall.

"Can't stay. Just a bite." But the sturdily proportioned man took three slices of toast and the pot of preserves to himself. He had a fast, neat style of eating, no wasted time and no crumbs, on cravat or beard. Still he touched a napkin to the corner of his lips.

"Early day, Heywood?"

"Late already. Ellspeth's like the dead to raise in the morning. Says she wants to come home for the week. Told her she'd need to rise at dawn if she wanted my carriage. Now she says she's nearly ready. Women." He poured a half-cup of coffee into the cup a maid hastily provided to him. Taking the precaution of blowing over it, he downed it in one draft. He patted Mr. Quinn on the back, a punch, really.

"A shame about the letters."

The younger man's mouth pinched, as if he'd drunk a lemon. "Shaftsbury told you?" he finally said.

Maddie's heart lurched into her throat. She shot a glance at Mr. Quinn. "What is the matter with the letters?"

His gaze shifted away from her, and then away from Mr. Heywood, who was downing another half-cup of coffee. What was he hiding?

"No matter." Heywood set the cup down with a crack. "You couldn't have counted on them to save you, Miss Wetherby. We Mancunians shift for ourselves. I have a proposition, for you. I'm needing another bookkeeper, for the venture I'm starting with Nash here. What do you say?"

For a moment, Maddie could say nothing. What about the letters? Was this an alternate offer? Could he possibly be serious? Had she fallen so far as to need to become a working girl? But then, who was she, really? And she would need an income, as well as a place to call home, if these Quinns played her wrong.

"We've a dormitory for women, a fine place. Probably like enough to your school days."

She couldn't say no to a guaranteed home. But she couldn't bring herself to say yes, either. Not yet. She took a deep breath, forming an answer.

Mr. Quinn jumped in first. "You'd make a working girl of her?" His fair face reddened, even in the green light of this odd solarium. The color also called out the red tinting hidden in the brown of his wayward hair.

"She won't get a better offer. Even this is more than she warrants, if one were to go by connections."

By connections? Maddie knew he couldn't mean the viscount. Did he know more about her family—her true family? Would he tell her?

"She warrants far more than that, in my father's eyes. You dispute him?" Mr. Quinn's words seemed to push him to his feet.

They looked at her, awaiting an answer. "It is a generous offer, sir." She ignored Mr. Quinn's snort. "But allow me time to think upon it. Just a day or two. So much has changed, I'm afraid I need time to sort myself out."

"Understood." Mr. Heywood happily punched the younger man on the shoulder, not seeming to notice the glare he received in return. "But a good businesswoman knows when to reel in an opportunity. And when to cut bait."

"We'll take care of her."

"Nothing is sure in this world. But Miss Wetherby, if the Quinns do desert you, don't return to Wetherby. Come to town, to me, and we'll sort you out." He tipped his head to her and grinned at Mr. Quinn. "Magistrates' meeting on Thursday. I'll see you there, won't I?"

"I'll remember." Mr. Quinn remained standing, staring at the open doorway. He was as tall as the new earl, but looked stronger, his forearms testing the seams of his simple shirt. She wondered what it would have been like had this man been born first. She wondered if he ever wished it, too. She could not afford to care.

"What happened last night?"

He turned back, his face a careful mask. Maddie's mind raced. Had her earl lied to her? Was it all one horrible mistake? Could she have been wrong all these years? Had he truly not known who she was? Had he rescinded his offer on his deathbed? Why didn't Mr. Quinn just say something?

She could not wait him out. "You've found something ill."

He shook his head. He started, stopped, reconsidered, started again. The suspense was strangling her.

Finally, he spoke. "My brother burned the letters."

She shot to her feet, her head spinning. "The earl? Why? My letters, too? Those were mine."

"Please, sit. You look about to faint."

She wanted to hurl herself across the table and strangle him. Instead she sat, hard. She put her palms on the table, hard. The cutlery clattered. "You promised," she said, her voice dripping venom.

Mr. Quinn froze where he stood. "He did it so quickly. I know it's no excuse. We did read them; your claim is true."

"But I have no proof, thanks to you. It's my word against that of an earl." She'd lose. She'd lost.

He seemed to recover himself after a long moment, rubbing at his eyes and sinking back onto the bench. "Don't worry. Whatever happened last night we can still make it good. Make you whole."

No one could do that.

EIGHT

Nash paced the house, read the papers, and paced the house again until the clock at last struck eleven, the earliest Mama ever rose. It was always a danger bearding her in her den before the coffee had kicked in, but he checked with her maid of chambers, who declared it safe.

She'd already ceded the earl's chambers to Deacon, but even in the generous north light of her new rooms, she looked worn. Father hadn't lingered, and his death was mercifully brief. But she had grown weak these past months. He should convince Deacon to take her to London, or Plymouth, or Spa. Society and sea air might do her good. It was foolish to think the absence of the canker that was his father would cure all her ills.

She sent for another pot of coffee, and watched him carefully as he sat in the chair opposite hers at the tiny boudoir table.

"So it's to be an interrogation?"

"Mother."

"I remember when you would sit at my feet, your head on

my knee, eyes closed. Why, I would ask. Just happy, you would say."

"A long time past."

"But not so long a mother can't remember. Dear heart, when was the last time you could say you were happy?"

So she was going on the attack. He could beat this back. "Friday, Mama, before I remembered I must attend Deacon in all his state and finery."

She laughed. "A chance to visit me does not make up for the distaste you have for your brother?"

"It isn't distaste, and you know it. Deacon cares not for what he should: the land, the people, the future."

"So you are disgusted with me."

"With you?"

"For not having birthed you first."

Her tone was light, but Nash frowned. He hadn't thought of it that way. "I do not mean to cast aspersions on you in any way, Mama."

"No need for the formality, sweeting. I merely tease. You used to love that, too."

He stood and walked to the window beside her. "Time has changed me. Not all for the good."

"Was it really so hard in the Navy? Shaftsbury said you suffered terribly."

"He told you that?"

"He truly was not the tyrant you boys paint with such relish. Oh, he could be hard, but deep down he was a good man. And he cared for nothing more than family."

Here was his opening. Nash banished the stray feelings his mother's words conjured up.

"Why was Shaftbury so interested in Madeline Wetherby? One, he was her godfather, and no one else's."

"Yes, while I wasn't pure enough to stand godmother." Her bitterness led him to turn back to look at her. She tilted her head, her long natural hair swinging in its tail. "She looks nothing like him, if that is what you are implying."

"Two. When she has relatives of her own, he is the one who paid for her to go to school, and for far longer than he paid for Deacon's schooling."

"Deacon came home on his own. I'm sure Shaftsbury would have loved having him continue to Cambridge. Even Oxford."

At least she was talking. He pushed on.

"Three. He maintained a steady correspondence with her. A regular exchange of letters, like clockwork." He found it hard to swallow.

"So that's it. You are jealous of the little orphaned girl."

"I'm not." But he was. He could at least admit it to himself. He dropped back into the chair, running his hands through his hair. He'd forgotten to do up the band in the back properly.

"You look a positive scarecrow. My brush is over there."

He did as she bid, and sat cross-legged in front of her chair the way he had when a brutish boy. She brushed through his hair, none too gently. He winced and pulled away a bit. She harrumphed.

"Were you my man, I'd have barked at you already, Mama."

"Your man, had you one, wouldn't touch you, seeing this rat's nest. Did you sleep at all?" The pulling gentled, carrying his thoughts into a slower rhythm.

"I believe father intended to settle money on her, but it was to come with the marriage."

"You learned all this from the lady's correspondence?"

He stiffened, remembering the scene at breakfast. Miss Wetherby was contained, indeed, but not without passion. He sighed under his mother's hand, relaxing again. "No, I've learned it from you."

She brushed the last, now smoothed strands into her hand, and tied the bow a shade too tight. "She was a beautiful child. A green-eyed angel. Lady Wetherby was giddy over her. And Deacon."

"Why don't I remember her?"

"We kept you boys apart at that age. Deacon wasn't ready for a brother then."

Nor ever. Nash rolled his eyes behind closed lids.

"Don't be so hard on your brother. It takes more than three generations to make a true peer. Cecil Wetherby is only the second, you know. Your father and grandfather took to it like fish to water, but our Dee has yet to find his way. Why make it harder for him?"

"Shaftsbury wanted this match, and he knew all about the lady."

"Even wise men make mistakes."

"Has she truly changed from yesterday to today, Mama? Did you?"

"Don't be daft. Of course she's changed. Everything has changed. And thank Providence we dodged that bullet. Can you imagine the scandal?"

"The same scandal as when he wed you, a tradesman's daughter?" He tilted his head back. In reply, she kissed his forehead. "Has your mama slipped from her pedestal? I suppose your argument has merit. You always were the little debater. If the girl is a squire's daughter, she might do for the likes of you, perhaps. Deacon, never."

"What if her father isn't even a squire?"

She rested her hand on his shoulders. "So strong." Her touch melted some of the stiffness. He rolled his head to ease the tension in his neck. "This has nothing to do with you, my sweet. Don't vex yourself. You have enough to worry about, with that monstrous warehouse and all your men scurrying over the seven seas."

He allowed himself the luxury of a moment's relief. His mother's voice could always soothe him. It was good to know that, at least, still held true.

"After all," she said in that honey voice, "this is family business."

Nash shot to his feet, chest burning.

"You seem to forget, ma'am, that I am part of this family too."

"I have not." Her voice was nothing soft now. "You were the one who deserted us, and who kept away. You always make it so clear how unhappy you are whenever you deign to make an appearance."

"I will not argue with you, Mama."

"Because you haven't the standing."

"No. Because family is a birthright. Regicides still have families. It seems that only I do not." And Miss Wetherby, he suddenly saw.

She frowned, a paper subterfuge. As he walked away, she called after him. "Make peace with Deacon."

"I have no argument with Deacon." He could not keep the anger out of his voice.

"Then you should have no problem with it."

Nash had just enough control to keep from slamming the door.

MADDIE REMEMBERED the castle as a medieval palace, but the truth was it had been built only a century ago by an earl whose chief image of a castle was square turrets and walled gardens. The entry might have a weighty iron drop-gate, but the outer walls had wide windows, difficult to defend.

Its name, Shaftsbury Castle, had captured her imagination. At school, during gusty winter afternoons, she would conjure up a vision of her life-to-be, queen of the castle. Its king, the new earl, had been no more than a dark shadow at her left as she walked the corridors or welcomed guests to the many evening entertainments at which she would be the perfect hostess. She sat through countless fine concerts in Bath's upper Assembly Room, transposing them in her mind onto a stage somewhere in the castle, with herself the proprietress. She would host singers and harpists especially.

Now, on this very real day in late May, Maddie wanted only to escape the castle, to be free of this tangle if only for an hour or two, to be somewhere that made sense. The walled gardens, which rambled alongside the south wall, were the perfect choice. Her traitorous feet took her in the opposite direction, though, toward the castle's working side. She passed the kitchens, their animal pens just below the hill. When she saw the two-storey horse barn, she knew why her steps had brought her here. This was where she'd hidden on that long, fretful, summer's night.

At the side entrance, her hand reached down for the latch, not up as she had then. As she passed through, her shiver was memory, not terror. Just as on that night long ago, no one saw her.

She trod carefully through the tack rooms and skirted the stalls, her quick breaths pushing the strong animal scents out as fast as she took them in. The ladder was in the same place, leading to the loft.

This time, she had to climb it one-handed, her other hand managing the folds of her grown-girl skirt. Ladies did not climb ladders. Still, she didn't hesitate, drawn forward as if she were a pilgrim only steps away from Mecca. She stepped onto the platform, amid barrels of oats and bales of hay and straw. The window in the far wall was square and paned, but now only as high as her waist. Her sturdy boots made little sound as she walked toward the glass, but her steps slowed nearly to a crawl. Now that she was here, taking the last steps was almost too much. Even her shallowest breaths stung.

She touched her necklace, stroking the length of its tiny cross with her thumb. This was foolish fancy, not the sort of thing ladies engaged in. If she were truly a proper lady, she would be concentrating on the wreckage that was her future, not trying to recall that of her past. Maddie stiffened her shoulders and nearly ran the final few steps to the window.

Heedless of her hem, she sank onto her knees. The view out the window was the familiar green of the meadow beyond the walls, but it failed to soothe her. She rested her fists on the bottom edge of the frame. It was still loose. She pushed it aside to reveal a leather necklace, and the key. It fit easily inside her hand now. Before, she'd had to wear it under her dress to hide it.

Back then, she'd stand, back to the wall, as she'd seen the servants do, and he would walk down the hall, passing her, and then snap his fingers. "Mouse!" If she did not scurry fast enough, he hit her. Then he would hand her the key. "Get my tools ready."

SCURRY AHEAD OF HIM, to his dressing room, where the dark oak chest lurked. Twisting the key in the lock, and pushing with both hands, she could slowly, painfully, open the lid. On one side were his tools. She didn't look at them as she pulled them out. Because on the other side were Mr. Bun-bun and all the rest of her toys, taken one at a time as punishment for her infinite misdeeds.

She had no toys now. She didn't want them anyway. They had chosen My Lord Viscount.

How she wanted to burn that chest, burn the whole house down. But the one time she'd tried she'd only spilled hot tallow on her arm, burning herself.

My Lord forever promised to return Mr. Bun-bun, once Mouse had learned her place, but she never could. And she was always caught when trying to run away. Four-year-olds are easy to run to ground.

Finally, midsummer festival arrived, with a huge moon to light her way the long, long way to the castle. It had taken her all that long night; she'd tucked herself away in the hayloft just as the groomsmen were stirring. She hid that damned key where My Lord would never think to look for it, and then slept like the dead until it grew dark again.

By the time a groom discovered who she was, it was too

late to send her home. Lord Shaftsbury himself decided against it. "When they ask us, that's when we'll tell them you're here."

No one ever asked. After a few days bedding down with the housekeeper, she saw My Lord's carriage pull up. She made herself so small no one could see her. Later, when she turned up starving for supper, the housekeeper brought her up to the earl, who told her about her new life, as a boarding-student way away south. It sounded marvelous.

Maddie saw she was swinging the key like a pendulum. Now it was just a key, one that likely didn't fit in any lock. He'd likely changed the lock, all those years ago. Nothing to fear. And if school had not been completely marvelous, it had not harmed her, either.

The slights and fears that stung in those early forms were gnat's bites when seen through the eyes of adulthood. The terrors she'd felt at Wetherby House were likely the same, just childish fantasies. What had Lord Wetherby done to her that lords hadn't done to poor relations for ages? Her case was common enough, now that she understood more of the world. Then, she'd thought him a cruel, cruel tyrant; now she saw him as an unmarried man saddled with a traumatized, nearly wild infant. Small wonder he thought to take her to task; small wonder he did not know how to treat little girls.

But had the Lord Shaftsbury done any better? He'd had her raised to expect the world, or at least a peer as a husband, when the truth was she was more likely to be the governess than the lady of a great house. The disappointments of childhood paled in comparison with this latest letdown. Who had done her the most lasting harm—the lord who pretended she was a princess when she was a pauper, or the one who took pains to remind her how pauperish she was?

She'd thought Lord Wetherby was in the wrong all this time. Now she had to admit it was she. Without an alliance with the Quinns, or Wetherby's support, she was nothing, no one.

She had adopted the Quinns as her secret family all these years, hiding from the fact that she had no family. That mirage may have comforted the child Maddie, but it was high time the adult Madeline put away her infantile fancies and dreams.

Maybe little Maddie still hoped that Deacon Quinn would see his proper duty, marry her, and make everything right. Grown-up Madeline knew the new earl's duty was to marry a true lady and continue a clean line of peerage, and she didn't signify. The letters meant nothing, less than nothing now that they were ash.

She dried her tears and flexed her knees to stand, the key swinging on its brittle strap in her hand. Tomorrow, she would take Mr. Heywood's offer, and learn not to shudder at being thought a working girl. Her grand schemes as lady of the castle were done.

Beggars couldn't be choosers.

NINE

As soon as he recognized the clack of billiard balls being racked up, Nash knew where Deacon was. Why on earth had his ten o'clock scholar of a brother chosen today to become an early riser? Why ever did he blab to Heywood about the letters? Come to that, how could he have burned them in the first place?

Nash rolled his shoulders as he crossed the hall to the game room, trying to loosen some of their tension. Shaftsbury raised a brow in greeting; his opponent, Wetherby of course, had his back to the door, lining up the break shot.

"Heard you were in early with Mama. Brave little brother."

"Heard you already spilled all and more to Heywood."

"Trump to you, then." Deacon pouted as the balls, hit too soft, clumped in the middle.

Wetherby leaned on his cue as Deacon took the table. "The prodigal returns."

Nash's shoulders stiffened again, but he would not rise to

the bait. Instead he dropped into the overstuffed chair made from his grandsire's best jumper. "Saw your niece this morning."

Wetherby's whole body went stiff. "She is not my niece."

"Poor lost Wetherby." Deacon sank two, but missed the third.

Wetherby turned his attention back to his opponent. "Half-mourning, Shaftsbury? I thought those days were done."

Deacon shrugged, puckering the shoulders of his charcoal velvet coat. "Habit, I suppose. I certainly don't feel even half-mournful." He walked to the sideboard and poured out what looked like a fingerful of brandy. Perhaps he also had not slept well? "Listen, Nash. I've had an idea."

"The heavens ring," Wetherby quipped, and sank a ball.

Deacon ignored him. "What if I gave you that loan? The one for the Netherlands deal?"

What the hell? Nash willed himself not to rise, not to sound the rabid hound. "Heywood talks out of school."

Deacon shivered elegantly. "Stand down. It would be better to keep it in the family, wouldn't it? And I don't know how many more bolts of silk we can absorb."

"You think my situation that desperate?"

"I don't know, really, do I? Just that you grumble and grouse, night and day, about outlays. Or outliers. Damn, you made me miss the pocket."

"You'd make a beggar of your own kin?" Wetherby smirked far too much.

"What are you trying to say, Wetherby?" Nash had not thought he could dislike the man more.

Deacon jumped in before he could answer. "I'm only saying, perhaps the family could help you, if you help the family. Plus,

plus, plus?" His voice lost steam as he noticed the fire of Nash's glare.

At last Nash blinked. "If you will not do your duty in marriage, My Lord Earl, you should take Miss Wetherby to London, with Mama and Miss Heywood. You don't want either of the ladies, and they both would do well on the marriage mart. And I would have Mama safe from whatever marching and mayhem the radicals plan this season."

"I heard of the seditious talk in Oldham." Wetherby at last decided on his angle, but failed to sink the ball.

Deacon groaned in sympathy. "Two young misses is one too many. One is one too many. And I should be here if there is riot, shouldn't I? I need to keep my people safe."

"Keep them in line, more like. Wouldn't you say, Quinn?" Wetherby pulled back his lips in a painful looking grin.

Deacon muffed his shot into the edge of the felt. "Right. What I mean is, if you take this Miss Wetherby, then father's promise is kept."

"He promised her you."

"He promised her you first."

Wetherby avoided the safe shot and took one at the far end of the table, not taking his gaze off Nash. "So you did not honor your father's intentions?"

"As you did not your brother's? To his sole surviving child?"

"Boys, boys." Deacon stepped between them, though there was a good ten feet between them.

Nash couldn't let it go. "At least I did not leave a family member to fend for herself at four years old."

Deacon snorted. "No. You left when I was thirteen."

87

Wetherby's grin crept back into Nash's view. "We are more alike than you'd like to admit."

"I'm nothing like you."

"Second son, something to prove, on the outs with your patriarch. Has a familiar ring."

"You are the patriarch now, though."

"And isn't it marvelous." Deacon took advantage of Wetherby's oddly weak shot and sliced his own lie, knocking in his final ball. "Game."

Wetherby shook his head. "You must have a touch of the faerie in you, with that luck."

"Skill, my good man. Care to have at me, Nash?"

"With that skill?"

"Sod yourself. Nash is the true luck in the family," he said to Wetherby. "Even the Navy couldn't kill him."

"Not yet." Wetherby posed *en garde*, pool stick like an epée aimed at Nash's heart. Nash, sprawled in the chair, didn't blink. Instead he stretched like a cat, drawing his chest an inch closer to the blunted blade.

Wetherby spun the stick in his hand until the back end was toward Nash. He bowed, as if presenting a scepter to the king.

"How very kind," Nash drawled.

"It's no joy to be defeated twice in a row. You should have to take some blows, as well."

Nash took the stick, unbent his legs and stretched, rolling his shoulders again. "And you'll just watch?" He didn't like the looks of that grin.

"Mayhaps. I might go a'wenching. I know a certain wench newly up for grabs."

Nash let go one end of the stick. It swung bare inches from

Wetherby's shoulder to point to the ground. "She's your niece, man."

"Not in the eyes of the law."

Even Deacon couldn't let that one lie. "Damned bad form, man. Even the suggestion."

"She could always say no. A desperate woman, in desperate times. What think you?" Wetherby sketched a bow and rolled an expert saunter out of the room.

"The man's poison," Nash ground out. "Why do you tolerate him?"

Deacon dropped the first shot, and swore under his breath.

"And I'm the one with the temper," Nash said.

"So they say. Will you not consider marrying the chit? You do like her, I can see it."

"Your castoff."

Something constrained Deacon's usual easy form. He blew his ball entirely. "But she suits you. She likes to argue, and talk about duty and contracts and all that, just like you. And you did stare at her all through supper."

Nash waited.

Deacon stepped into the breach. "And I would have her happy. She does seem to be the only one who met our father's expectations. I suppose she deserves something for that. Not me, of course."

"Why has anything changed? Shaftsbury had held his tongue all this time, as has Wetherby. If you marry her, who would speak nay to a newly minted countess?"

"That's nonsense and you know it. And when did you learn to slice like that? You're a positive shark." Deacon sighed, ceding the game. "Not a loan, then. What if we call it a dowry?"

"That's medieval."

"That's Society."

What was a lady worth? What was a fair price? Why was he even considering it? He wasn't, was he?

And after the scene at breakfast, it seemed very unlikely she would even have him. Worse, what if she thought she could do no better, and accepted him despite her own opinion? He'd been told before that he wasn't the most romantic of men.

He glared at Deacon. "Five thousand or five hundred thousand, I'll not take a woman to wife for money."

"And you call yourself a man of business. Marriage is the oldest money transaction there is, save one."

"Then consider my refusal a business decision." He dropped the stick on the table.

"But if you would just do this, think how much the family would owe you." Deacon was starting to wheedle. Nash knew they were in the home stretch. But the win didn't taste as sweet as usual.

"What makes you think I care for the family's favor?"

"That's all you have ever wanted, baby brother. Here's your chance. Take it."

It was tempting. But the woman was flesh, not commodity, and he would not be pushed about, no matter how tasty the offer—and the woman—might seem. Nash looked at his hands, his knuckles braced hard on the table, and then back up at his brother.

"No. I won't dance to your tune."

AT THE ENTRY to the stables, Maddie stopped short. Nash Quinn stood on the other edge of the courtyard, speaking to a laborer and pointing at the gables on the roof of the kitchen. The last person she wanted to see. He stood so straight, scowled so manfully, and had failed her so severely.

Why had she even put her trust in him? Men were so selfish and unreliable. Miss Marsden might never have said so outright, but she surely implied it. Maddie herself had a ream of experience that proved the truth of it. Hiding would not solve anything, though, and might get her trampled. At her back, she could hear a horse being prepared for riding. Maddie stepped out, into the sun, heading for the fountain in the center of the yard. She had half a mind to throw the key into the water; it might bring her good luck. Before she could, a voice at her shoulder stopped her cold.

"Such a pretty picture. The country girl at home." Lord Wetherby grinned, the silver thread in his robin's egg coat twinkling in the half-light.

Maddie's face and throat burned. Must she always appear at her worst in front of this man? No, instead of meekly scurrying away, she stood her ground. As he gave directions to the groomsman, she smoothed her skirt and straightened her shoulders. When he turned his attention back to her, she nodded gracefully.

"Uncle Cecil."

His fine face pinched. "I told you never to call me that." He strode past her to the step-up and then turned back, striking a pose she'd seen in the pages of *Le Beau Monde*. From his well-oiled hair to his well-oiled boots, he brought the caricature to life. A flyaway cut to his coat set off the bright yellow of his frilled shirt and matching cravat, surely China silks. She didn't dare do more than glance at his fawn breeches, so tight she wasn't sure he would be able to ride in them.

"You look well," she said.

"Weeks out of date. Country living, I can't stand it."

Maddie stood, quiet, hands clasped, waiting on him. He'd opened the conversation, and she had continued it. Now it was his turn again. Everything proper.

He fingered the intricacies of his cuff. Was he nervous about something? Warm empathy washed through her. She could see now that he was no black monster, only a man like everyone else. How childish she had been. Perhaps this family separation had all been a simple mistake. Imagine if she might put it right again in a moment. Return to a family. Her heart skipped a beat in anticipation.

He spoke. "What's that in your hand?" He straightened his arm to shake the cuff out.

"Your key. Do you remember?"

A smile slithered onto his lips. "Of course. You went missing, and so did my key. A key is easily replaced." As were you, his eyes implied, but she knew that wasn't true. No other young girls had lived at Wetherby after her. She had it on authority from Emmett. "Give it back." He held out a hand. His other held his riding gloves. She lifted her arm to match his gesture, but her glove fisted over the key. Her jaw clenched against a rising tide of unwanted feelings. She did not want him to have it, even if she had just thought to drown it in the water. She frowned and fought her imaginary fears. He didn't need it, he said so. Why should she give it away? She didn't want it, so where was the trouble?

He dropped his hand, annoyance flitting across his too blue eyes, quickly replaced by a look of unconcern. He had a very pretty mouth for a man. "I know you have no love for me, and if I thought of you at all, I'd have none for you. I see you're at a bit of a loose end, though; no one will have you. So why don't I take you up?"

Maddie's dreams collided with her hopes on the way from her heart to her head. "You would be my uncle in truth?"

"Listen to yourself, all breathless. Of course not. This would be a business transaction like the one you were kiln-hot to settle with Shaftsbury."

Marriage? That seemed too far beyond possible. He'd already declared his lack of love. But society weddings were contracts, not love-matches. Did he mean to marry her? She shuddered. What did she possess that he could possibly want?

"I suppose, because you think we're unrelated," she started, but he cut in.

"We are not related."

"I don't understand."

"Still the simpleton, after all those years at school. Must I write it in chalk on your slate?"

That certainly didn't sound husbandly. She took a step away from him, out of the range of his grasp, and looked around her. Mr. Quinn was struggling with some vines around the kitchen door. Was there no one else who could help her? She stared at his back, willing him to turn and look at her.

As if by magic, he did. His features hardened as he caught sight of her partner. He nodded to the worker and strode across the cobbles toward them. His boots were scuffed, his coat shone only at the shoulders and elbows with wear.

"Wetherby, leaving so soon?"

Her uncle rose to his full height, which matched Mr. Quinn's, but the merchant had bulk and heft enough to dwarf him.

"I think Lord Wetherby has asked me to marry him?" Both heads snapped to her, mouths slack. Wetherby recovered first.

"She lies. I've done nothing of the kind."

Maddie's cheeks burned as if he'd slapped her. Confusion fed her anger, stanching the pinpricks of tears tugging at her eyes.

"Is that true?" Mr. Quinn stepped closer, taking her elbow. His face showed too much kindness. She could not hold back the tears, though she fought them every inch of the way.

"He said he'd take me up. A contract. Like with the earl."

Wetherby snorted. "A contract, to be sure. For marriage? My god."

The grip on Maddie's elbow tightened painfully. She tried to shrug his hand away, but it would not let her go.

Wetherby rolled his eyes. "It's nothing. I merely offered shelter to your wayward ward."

"Shelter, my ass. You wish her on her back."

"Crudity does not become you. I merely offered a business arrangement, the same as thousands of others enjoy every day. If she doesn't wish it, she is free to say so."

Maddie closed her eyes to stop the landscape from shaking. The tilting did not stop; it was she who was out of balance. A stranger's hand was all that held her together. She was so stupid, just as her uncle said. Not a wife, a mistress—a whore. He wanted her to say she agreed, for all the world to hear. For the good man beside her to hear, to judge.

Never.

Someday, she might need to stoop to selling herself for money, someday soon perhaps, but never be to that man. She'd tried to give him her love, all those years ago, and he'd slapped her face with it. He would never get another chance.

Her thoughts racing beyond her, Maddie didn't see her hand lift. When the key and its tail hit Lord Wetherby's shoulder and fell to the stones, she was as surprised as he was. So unlike a lady, but for once, she did not feel ashamed.

The hand on her elbow slid into an arm across her shoulder blades. She sank into its strength.

"You have your answer, Wetherby."

He did not stoop to pick up his key. "We paid for you. You are just another piece of Wetherby furniture."

Her throat thickened with suppressed sobs. Mr. Quinn's throat had no such trouble. "I see now why father took her away from you."

"He paid for her, too. She's your family's furniture now. And well-used."

Her companion growled deep in his chest. "You've said enough."

"There's no tax on speech."

The security of his grip disappeared. She felt raw there. Mr. Quinn stepped forward.

Wetherby's facile expression dropped as he saw what was coming, but wasn't fast enough to prevent it. One blow knocked him to the ground, holding his nose.

"But there is." Mr. Quinn turned back to Maddie. She could see blood on his knuckles. Wetherby's blood. She blinked slowly, as if her vision had deceived her. This was not real.

"Are you hurt?" he said.

She didn't understand the question. He seemed to be always hurting her, by his very presence. She stepped back, back, away from the bloody vision. In coming to her rescue, he'd assaulted a peer. He could be hung, or transported.

She'd killed him.

"Let her go. She's not worth losing your life over, Quinn." Wetherby spat blood onto the courtyard. "You are your father's son, all right. Right down to his way of settling an argument. Too bad your roundhouse is so much weaker than his. And of course, you're no earl."

TEN

N ash fought to control the rage and panic tightening his limbs. He had to quit this courtyard before he made any more fatal errors. Where had that come from? He'd never been so out of control. He'd frightened the lady, and he'd frightened himself.

Wetherby spat a second time, still sitting in the dust in those dancing tights he called breeches. The sound startled Miss Wetherby, whose eyes had taken on a terrible blankness. She turned away from them, walking and then running for the door leading to the outside gardens. With movements so stiff, and gait so broken, she looked as if she'd been shot, not merely spoken to.

Nash reached a hand out to Wetherby, who used it to lever himself upright. A stable boy was leading his mount to the ladder. Nash wondered who else had seen the fracas.

He hadn't seen anyone but the lady and her uncle, locked in what looked like some mummers' show repeated from their past together. Nash couldn't shake the impression that the lady had changed into an automaton, a puppet, something not entirely human. Well, if she had, this Wetherby had made her so. People were as well as they were treated. Obviously, Madeline Wetherby had been treated very ill.

Wetherby mounted easily. His lip had stopped bleeding but it and his nose were already starting to swell. "We'll not mention this to Shaftsbury." Taking Nash's silence for agreement, he gave his horse her head and departed.

Nash had dreamed of the day he would take that impudent jackass down a peg or two, but the reality lacked the sweetness of his fantasy. For all his rescue of the damsel, he couldn't undo whatever blows she had already received. He had been estranged from his family all his adult life. But he never doubted that they were his kin, and if worse came to worst, they would take him back in. And never as a servant. He could barely imagine how it would feel to be told your family was not yours—that you were of no family—as a child of four. Would she even have understood?

And who would blame her for jumping at the chance to join with the next family that came her way? One with a golden little boy who thought she was an angel?

"She was just the sunniest child," Mama had told him this morning. "Until her parents died. We didn't see her for a while, and then one day she just appeared, in the stables. Looking for Deacon. Apparently, he had promised to protect her and marry her one day. Must be where Shaftsbury got the idea. The fancies of a child."

"Did you see her? What did she look like?"

"Heavens, I don't know. I was with you, remember? That was when you had the scarlet fever. Shaftsbury said Wetherby had frightened her. He was a stranger, and she'd been through so much already. He sent her straight off to school, and that's the last I heard of her."

Nash washed his hands at the pump and headed back inside. He needed a drink.

He knew that some in the peerage thought of people as possessions, as objects. He had seen enough grooms whipped for their owner's carelessness and heard of maids sent from service for showing signs of babes their masters put there. But he had not thought much on it, assuming people would start acting better in these modern times.

Now he felt shame that he had not spoken out about it. It was a slippery slope from the thought that a person could be whipped like an animal to the thought that a person was an animal.

How could such people still keep on about maintaining lines pure of taint? Their own behaviors put the lie to the very idea of "purity." What was in their blood that made them any more pure than their servants, than their tenant farmers, than the weavers? This last line of thought was dangerous. It was the very argument the weavers were using to demand suffrage. If men were created equal, as the American declaration put it, should they not vote?

He had seen many terrible things in the Navy, and even signs of abuse among the younger boys. But to call an infant furniture, tell a child who depended on you for everything, for her very life, that she was nothing to you? And he was sure Wetherby treated her as the lowliest of servants as well. The cock-of-the-walk would enjoy that. He'd probably even beaten her.

Deacon had taken the horsehair chair, and had two glasses and the decanter ready beside him on the table. "I do hope you have spent your untoward aggression, dear brother." So much for his non-promise of secrecy.

"It was as well meant as it was deserved."

"I suppose I must agree. Where is the chit now?"

"She ran off." He didn't blame her. There was nothing he'd like more than to gallop hard away from this place. "Perhaps I'll follow her."

"I think you should." Nash speared him with a glance. Deacon held out a glass. "Truce, brother. I simply meant that she needs rescuing, and as you are the resident knight in the family, it's only appropriate."

"I might marry her, you mean?" The idea should have appalled him, as it had earlier, when Deacon first brought it up. But instead his breath quickened, his mind sharpened. Did he like the chit? Not a chit, a lady.

"Always at the extremes, aren't we? I meant go and fetch her back. We don't want her to miss tea time."

Nash rolled the idea about in his head, the way he rolled the deep brandy over his tongue. Looked at in a certain light, the woman might be an asset. Excellent manners in company and an understanding of business that would lead her to accept his being away from home. She was not encumbered with odious relations he would have to kowtow to. She was beautiful in a tragic way, not an Aphrodite but a Helen.

He suddenly saw the appeal of it. She did need rescue; she surely would see him differently now.

Something about her called to him, stirred his blood: those sharp eyes and that husky alto, scared and strong, hummed like bee-filled honey in his mind. He could protect her; offer her shelter from her stormy childhood. She would be grateful, perhaps passionately so.

She did need a rescue. And then there was the money. "Were you serious earlier? About a dowry?"

Deacon sat up and set his glass onto the table, its contents pushing first to one side of the rim and then the other. "Are you?"

"I could use the five thousand. And I'd prefer not to be beholden to Heywood, especially as there's no hope for you and his daughter."

Deacon tapped his lip, thinking. Nash held the glass to his own lips to disguise his fraying patience, always bad during negotiation. A man should never prefer that a deal go through—the least-interested bidder got the best deal. But he found this simple subterfuge almost impossible at the moment. Stalking about punching peers was hard on the nerves.

Deacon pursed his lips. "She'd never take you. Would she?"

"Why ever not?"

"Don't jump down my throat; I'm just thinking aloud. I admit, it would neatly solve our puzzle. But now that it's in the air, I confess I'm a bit queasy. I wouldn't want to see you made unhappy."

Deacon's voice carried such a note of wistfulness that Nash took a deep look at him. His brother did his best to shrug in that stylishly pinched jacket, and his thin lips trembled toward a smile. His brother wanted him happy. Nash's ribs felt tight.

He might do this. Not just for the family, but for him. It would free him from the town biddies and their grasping, graceless daughters. And he liked the shape of this Miss

Wetherby, the warmth. She fit his hands. She'd fit his bed, too.

"I'll be happy enough." He cleared his throat. "Just keep that idiot Wetherby away from me."

Deacon sighed, but not unhappily. "It's not fair, it never is. You gain a wife, and I must lose both capital and my boon companion?"

"You should choose better friends."

NASH SPIED Miss Wetherby on the far side of the artificial pond, the castle between her and the Wetherby lands. Through the quarter-hour it took to round the water and reach her, she sat against a downed tree trunk, her bonnet in her hands, watching him.

Taking bad-tempered Roanoke out on this mission might have been a mistake. He'd chosen the beast to beat out some of his own pent-up energy through its pounding stride, but that wasn't quite the thing for a tender young lady in fragile spirits.

With the light dappling her tousled hair and fancy-tucked dress, she looked far better suited to Regent's Park than this northern land. She had nothing hard-edged about her, nothing forged or seared strong. How would she survive this new world? His heart ached to help her. His head asked, how far would you go?

He should concentrate on his own troubles, Nash told himself for the dozenth time this afternoon. He was doing his best to keep his men employed, but the market for their cloth and goods was running dry. And with the government stoking its tinder, a mere spark might set the whole town off. Adding a wife to his roster seemed less than seaworthy.

She rose as he drew near, and came to the head of the horse as Nash dismounted.

"Coming to my rescue again?" Her voice was ragged. Trails of tears traced the planes of her face. Since when had women's tears had such an effect on him?

"Nothing of the sort," he said, and immediately regretted it. The flimsy mask of sociability she wore crumbled. She dropped her head to study the dead leaves and new grass at their feet and struggled to catch her breath.

"No one wants me." She said it not with anger, or despair, only bone-deep grief. It cut him to the quick. His mind skittered away from the pain.

"That's doing it too brown," he said teasing, as if she were a moped-up ensign. He took her elbow, but she didn't shift her gaze. He slid his hand down to her palm, and tickled it. The shock of contact startled them both. She blinked, and tumbled to the ground.

He'd hurt her.

"I'm sorry. I turned my ankle a little, before." She pushed to her hands and knees, and gingerly rolled up to a stand, clapping the dirt off her hands. The dress already had more than one stain; she must have done this before. He was a blind fool not to notice it earlier. "You see, I was, rather, hoping for a rescue. At least from these woods."

"I'm your man. Can you sit the horse?"

She eyed the stallion, whose shoulder reached past her head. "Sit, but not control."

"We'll band forces. He's plenty long enough, and strong."

He made a step of his twined hands, and lofted her up to sit sidewise ahead of the saddle. He vaulted into place behind her.

Roanoke was on his best behavior, and after only a few hundred yards of stiff riding, Miss Wetherby relaxed her chilled shoulders into his chest. A strange weight, but not uncomfortable, and she quickly recovered her warmth. He'd guessed right —she would be a perfect fit for him. She'd need new soap though; he hated lavender. As they passed from the loamy chill of the wood to the breezy sun of the meadow, only a mile from home, she let out a great sigh.

He scrambled for a topic that would divert her from thoughts of Wetherby or Deacon or Shaftsbury or what all. "Have you read of the reform meetings? It's all the talk."

She took the bait. "Can the magistrates keep the peace?"

"Depends what peace means. Most on the committee take the part of the manufactories. The yeomanry—shopkeepers, thieves, and other brigands volunteering to spy on their neighbors—are a wild card. Wildest card of all, though, are the craftsmen. Do they seek to form unions of trade to improve their lot or destroy ours?"

"If there were a union, what could it do?"

"Organize an attack on the new machines stealing their livelihood, I suppose. But that would only delay the inevitable, not to mention send the breakers to Australia or the gallows."

Nash wasn't sure if the magistrates had the right of it. What was the difference between profit and livelihood?

At Shaftsbury, Deacon was responsible for the well-being of his tenants. In town, who was responsible for the well-being of the manufactory workers? The owners didn't claim it. Would the government step in, or the church, with its almshouses and orphanages? Would Parliament build laws to protect people or to protect commerce? If it were a choice between the paltry taxes the workers paid and the chunks of blunt the manufacturers paid, Nash knew who would prevail.

She shivered in his arms, and he cursed himself for not thinking to bring a blanket. Even in May, the woods weren't warm. He pulled her closer. She wasn't wearing a corset today. He shifted slightly in his seat. She should try honeysuckle. What were they talking about?

"But aren't you a magistrate?"

"I'm on the special committee, yes. Lucky to be chosen. I run a warehouse and sales concern, so I understand the claims of the manufacturers. But I also trade with their workers, and have tradesmen working for me. Silk weavers."

"I must arrange for new clothes." She picked at the fine dyed silk. He wondered where she had found straw in the woods.

"Might not. I'm trying to convince Deacon to take Mama and you to London. Would you like that?"

"I can make the best of it."

"You don't like the city?"

"It's kind of Lord Shaftsbury to consider it. I owe your family a great deal."

Nash wasn't sure what came over him then. Was it passion, the shock of holding a lovely young thing in his arms for a half-hour? Or simply that her flat statement of debt called to his love of negotiation? She held the weak position; he could get the best deal.

"Let me offer a proposal."

"First politics, and now business?" She was warming to him. He smiled at the patterns of sun-warmed curls in her hair.

"Here in the North we do business at every meal and even on the church steps." He took a breath, air mixed with her soft scent, and unfurled the spinnaker. "Miss Wetherby, would you consider an alliance with me rather than my brother?" He rushed on. "It would fulfill the letter of your contract, er, letters." He winced at the reminder of his perfidy on that account. "They did say 'my son,' after all. And you cannot care so much for a title and all the trappings. It seems to me you're rather a quieter mouse than all that. What do you say?"

She turned in his arms, forcing him to loosen his grip on her. Her deep gaze searched his face. He held his breath. Frowning, she turned back to face front, but she rested her head back against his collarbone. "Exchange an earl for a man in trade?"

"Don't be that way. We might rub along well together. Far better than ever you would with my dandified sibling. He'd steal all your lace."

"What says he?"

"He's all for it." Nash couldn't stop some of the bitterness from seeping into his voice.

"You don't think much of him."

"Deacon is a good-enough brother, I suppose. But as Shaftsbury, he's been a poor earl. At least he's not like the old sod—he's not the sort to haul off and slug someone to end an argument."

She stiffened, and he suddenly remembered he had done exactly that, just this afternoon. Could he be like Shaftsbury in other respects, as well? It didn't bear thinking about. She sat silent the whole of the quarter-mile ascent to the castle. Standard tactic, but it got under his skin nonetheless. He would win this negotiation. He needed another argument, one a woman would accept.

Instead of turning toward the stables, he rode down the central courtyard. She stirred under his arm, and he knew he had her. Leaping down first, he caught her by the waist as she slid off the stallion, slowly settling her on that tender ankle. Then he swept her off both feet, and carried her up the stairs. Depositing her into a chair in the main hall, he called for Emmett to round up men to take her up to her room, as well as a cold bucket of water for her ankle.

"Well, Miss Wetherby, what do you say?"

"You don't abhor me and I don't dislike you."

He didn't have her.

"Please, Mr. Quinn, that's not what I mean. I mean, I shall consider your proposal, and give you an answer at supper. Agreed?" They shook hands on it, Nash holding hers a shade too long. He wanted this deal closed, now.

He spent the next several hours closeted in the office, deciphering its tangled ledgers, but left early to dress for supper. He wasted a ridiculous amount of time on his cravat, second-guessing what sort of look she might prefer. This was a business transaction, he reminded himself, unwinding the damned neck-wrap once again. Commerce, not frip-frap talk of love, drove this assignation.

He needn't have bothered. Only Deacon noticed his plumage, the better to taunt him for it.

The lady stood him up.

ELEVEN

Maddie didn't know how long she'd been tucked into the window seat in the castle's blue bedroom. Maybe an hour, maybe a lifetime. At first, the afternoon light outside was too bright, so she turned her gaze to the reds and oranges behind her eyes. The pain she found there was deeper, stabbing, a wound that only ever scabbed over, never knit.

She had never felt so out of control. Others had always decided her fate, and she'd more or less eagerly made the best of it. Now with all of it fallen apart, and her very name in question, she was asked to make her own choice, and she had no idea what to do.

So she did nothing, hunkering into the seat cushion, behind bolts of silk curtain that still smelled slightly of indigo. A wounded fox in the bushes, hoping the hounds would take their baying elsewhere. Of course, they never would. This was their bush, their lovely blue bedroom, their castle, their country.

When she heard the tip-tapping on the door, she thought it only the long-faced maid, come to check on her yet again. But the footfalls carried more weight, and a man's scent, and Nash Quinn's shape. And as he had just broken a prime rule of decorum—his presence in a private chamber with a lady not his wife with the door closed, was scandalous—she knew he would not be so easily dismissed.

It didn't mean she had to look at him, though.

He paused, perhaps to grow accustomed to the gloom. Her ears strained to know where he was, but her gaze didn't leave the branches of the oak outside the window. At his movement, though, they too shifted, converting the glass into mirror. She watched him approach, blinking slowly.

"Missed a fine pork loin. And cherry sauce." He leaned against the wall, arms crossed. Even from the corner of her eye, even in the gloom, he cut a fine figure. Long legs, strong hands, and that tousled hair that made one want to fix it for him, just for pleasure. She'd heard Byron worked for hours to attain just that bounding insouciance; she suspected this man spent one-sixth the time.

"You came to lecture me?"

Face frozen in half-smile, his calm eyes weighed her. She couldn't rise even to this challenge, and simply sat, waiting. He would come to his point soon enough, then leave. Everyone left. They hurt her, and then they left.

She shivered, and drew her arms closer. He pushed off the wall and strode away. She let out her breath, surprised at the easy victory. But he stopped at the foot of the bed and picked up the shawl she had thrown there. He draped it over her pulled-in knees and returned to his spot by the wall.

"You could ask for a fire."

She said nothing.

"You were missed at supper."

Silence.

"Is this your answer for me?"

She closed her eyes. At last, he fell silent, too. The night, and the room beside it, grew dark and darker, until she could pretend she didn't see him at all. Didn't hear his steady breaths, or the subtle shifting of his weight as he went to light a candle by the bed.

Though her arms were wrapped tight around her, a soft sob escaped, and another. Yesterday, she had spent the night watching her castles in the sand, her hopes and dreams for the future, wash away.

Tonight her very presence was dissolving. By tomorrow, she would be as empty as a babe in swaddling clothes.

She was nothing like she thought. Her reflection in the window wavered in the single candle's light, her darkened hair down and far more wavy than in the daylight mirror. Her eyes looked huge, as if she were a wraith finally exposed to view.

She was a pale shadow of a pale shadow.

She closed her eyes again. She could feel her heart pumping, pounding rather, the shudder of her breath, the sway of her hair along her shoulder blades. So parts of her were still solid. Corporeal.

She lost her balance, and had to open her eyes. But her thoughts still looked backward, to the parents she barely remembered. Mama, talc and cinnamon, soft and warm. Papa, well, papa looked rather like Nash's father. Somehow she had overlaid her own father's face with the old earl's.

Except he wasn't her own father. She wasn't a true Wetherby.

Maddie's gaze shifted back to wind toying with the tree outside the window. Out there, her father might still be living. Might still be missing her. Longing for her.

She had to find him, before she could do anything else. He would take her in; he would have to. Then she remembered. He had given her away. He hadn't wanted her when she was a blameless child, there was no way he would want her now, her head full of useless knowledge, her hands empty of skills, her sensibilities honed to razor sharpness.

How could she live in a cottage? And what if her family could not afford even a cottage? What if next month it was she who begged at street corners and the entryway of the theater? Or, failing at begging, would she be forced to do worse?

If only she could fly away. The window's glass let so much of the night in, it must be wafer thin. She pressed her palms into the cold. Perhaps she should jump through. Who knew? If she could fly, she would leave this place. If she could not fly, her problems would still be over.

"Get down. Now." His hand was warm on her ankle. Maddie found herself standing, her slippered feet sinking into the padding of the window bench. She knelt down, and then dropped to a seat. Her mind sent the signal to kick his hand away. Her foot did not respond.

His hand was gentle and warm. But she did not wish to be gentled, or warm. She would kick it away. She would kick him away.

Still, her foot did not obey.

He pushed his way to sit beside her, pushing the stray folds of the shawl into her lap. She drew her knees closer to her chest, blocking herself nearly into a ball. Her knees protested at the tight stretch, but she ignored them. They were connected to her rebellious feet.

He let go of her foot on his own, replacing his hand on her knee. She was glad her knee hurt. He would not comfort her.

"How about we talk. Just a little." He would not stop looking at her. She didn't know where to look; anywhere, only not at him. She dropped her forehead to touch her knees. His hand was in the way. He slid it up to palm her cheek. She tilted her head to rest it in his hand.

He brushed her temple with the tip of his finger, and as if he had tripped a switch, the tears started to flow. She couldn't even feel ashamed. After all, he'd done it to himself. He reached around and pulled her into an embrace. His hand guided hers to his sturdy shoulder. Even through the thick shawl and thicker tears, she sensed his warmth, drawing her in. His hand stroked her back, again and again. His voice, silent, left her to her thoughts. Her thoughts, silent, left her to her despair.

She was no one, nothing. Just as her slippery, false uncle had said. His words echoed through her head, a deep and familiar refrain lying in wait to be rekindled. This was her truth. This was the story of her. These people who thought they meant well, her false parents and her legions of instructors, why had they done this to her? She didn't belong in their world, and they had raised her to look down her nose at what should be her own.

She hated herself, this new, nobody self. She hated this new, nobody future. Hated it. He whispered shushing sounds. The soothing on her back did not leave. She felt her body ease, her spine melt toward him.

Madeline wasn't even her name. A poor woman walking by the side of the road was her mother. Was she a weaver, a worker, a farmer's wife?

Was she a whore?

Maddie's lungs stung as she sobbed. The harder she cried, the closer he pulled her. If only he could pull her all the way inside him. She could hide there, if she could not sprout wings and fly away.

The pain eventually spent itself. Emptied, even her thoughts went quiet. She counted her heart's beats. She counted the click-clack of the timepiece on the bedside table. She counted their matching breaths.

When she woke, it had gone almost black inside the room.

"You've put my arm asleep." His voice carried humor, not anger. He pushed her gently to sit up beside him. She swayed, dizzy, and he pushed her a bit farther, to rest her back against the wall of the window. He rose and stretched, then went again to the side of the bed. He poured a glass of water and re-lit a candle. But he returned to her in the safety of the dark.

"Where are you now?" His eyes were shadowed, but his mouth was soft, as if he might smile.

"Here."

"With me?"

"Of course."

"There's my snappish girl."

"I am not your girl." She sniffled, and he leaned back and pulled out an ivory linen handkerchief. She felt a twinge of compunction using it.

"What do you think?"

"I'm too tired to think."

"Right." His hand was on her knee again.

"You are very forward."

He nodded but didn't move away. "So, how about Tuesday?"

She frowned at him. "Today is Sunday."

"Monday is a market day, so I'd be a bit pressed for time." He shrugged.

She shook her head. Did he still mean to marry her, then?

"You cannot be serious." She tried to make it sound firm, but her voice wobbled.

"You still won't have me? After I defended your honor and rescued your maiden self?"

"I did not ask you to rescue me." She was growing used to his lopsided grin.

"The petulant princess." He seemed to fall off the bench seat, onto the floor. Then she saw he'd taken the medieval swain's position, on one knee, one hand on his heart, the other stretched toward her.

"How about this? O tender mistress of the night, fiddle-dee, fiddle-dum, folderol, and let us be one. Marry me." He must think his face properly swainish, but instead it gave the impression he had indigestion.

She coughed out a laugh. For a moment, her ribs did not hurt.

"That bad?" He pushed up and sat beside her again. "Accept me now, or I promise it will only get worse." He gazed at her, eyes so calm she felt sure he could read her mind.

"You know I cannot marry."

"Whyever not?"

"I don't even know what my name is." Her spine started to waver, her eyes to leak again.

"Madeline." He reached for her.

"No! I don't even know if my name is truly Madeline. I'm nobody. Nothing."

She started to crumble, she wanted to collapse onto the seat and sleep her life away. But he put a palm on her chest, over her wildly beating heart, and pushed her upright against the window frame.

"Listen. I saw your documents; I'll show them to you. You were baptized Madeline Wetherby, and that is who you are."

"Not by birth."

"So be it. Soon you'll be Madeline Quinn. Not by birth." He stopped, as if struck by an idea. "Though other births may follow." His grin took on a roguish cast.

"Nonsense. You shouldn't throw yourself away. What would your fiancée say?"

"Clever. But, as she is a figment of your imagination, we'll give her a long-lost beau who has just returned from a shipwreck in the Bahamas. She has her own wedding to plan."

"Fanciful."

"Pragmatic. Handsome, or so they say."

She was running out of arguments, and he could see it. They fit together on this seat too well. What choice did she have, really? A merchant's wife, a manufactory's day worker, or a viscount's whore.

"How long would we stay together?"

"I don't understand."

"To establish the marriage. A year?"

"Madeline, the marriage is established at the signing."

"So, only a week or two?"

"Until what?"

"Until you send me away."

He tilted his head, his expression reminding her of his brother. "Why would I send you away?"

"Why would you keep me with you?"

"Because we are wed. We will be wed."

"But you don't want me."

His eyes hardened, and despite the shawl, she shivered. "You think I care only for money."

The desperation simmered to the top again. "You can have it all. I'm sure I can live on an hundred a year. I can take on pupils, live cheaply."

"Madeline nee Wetherby. I intend to marry you and I intend this marriage to be a true one, in all senses of the word." He took her by the shoulders. "Do you understand?"

She didn't. He must have seen it in her face, for his hands tightened. His gaze dropped to her mouth. Hers fell to his.

He pulled her toward him. Their thighs met, then their lips. His pressure certainly didn't hurt her. As he wrapped an arm around her back, she awakened into his kiss.

He pressed the small of her back, which somehow opened her mouth, and their tongues met.

Maddie gasped, mesmerized by the sensation. He seemed to be everywhere, behind her, before her, inside her. The heat of him singed her skin through the layers of cloth between them.

When he let loose her lips, she was panting. A storm was brewing inside her, warm and pleased. She wanted more of this, more of him.

He replaced his lips with his thumb, pressing on her lower lip, as his own lips pressed on one of her closed eyelids, then the other. His breath teased her lashes. Her hands were twined around his neck, she discovered as he tilted his head back a bit. He didn't fight her confinement, but instead rested his forehead on hers, chuckling. She opened her eyes into the depths of his gaze.

She smiled tentatively, not sure whether to laugh or cry. Could this be true? With a finger, he traced the edge of her face, down her neck, across the dip in her throat. He plunged lower, to nearly between her breasts.

A sudden wave of disgust and fear washed through her. Maddie shot back, away from him. Her spine struck the window frame.

His hand hung there in the air, finger out, like a gun with a crooked barrel. He turned it to palm up, a gesture of surrender.

A splash of light startled them both. The maid stood in the open doorway, a candle in her hand, mouth agape.

"Miss Wetherby needs a fire, Mary. And some of that stew from supper." The girl shut the door, and the room fell back into dusk.

"You, my dear, are compromised. Carry on this way and we will need to marry tomorrow."

"You did it on purpose?"

"No. Well, maybe. It couldn't hurt." He kissed her again, a slow, gentle promise. She tried to relax again, but failed. She knew he could feel the stiffness in her limbs, her failure to enjoy the moment. He pulled away, but still his smile held. She shuddered in relief.

"You're right. No need to rush." He brought the finger to

his lips and kissed its tip. Then he touched her lower lip, transferring the kiss.

"After all, we will have a lifetime. Won't we?"

She would marry, after all. She would marry him. She could make this work. She *would* make this work.

"Yes," she said.

TWELVE

Nash missed the crisp orders and tight command aboard ship. Even on the ships of the line, the jawboning diplomatic officers rarely surfaced to muddle the crew. Here on the Manchester Select Committee in Charge of Keeping the Peace, he sat among some half-dozen of their ilk. And there were only eight of them sitting around the dark oak stretch of the Star Inn's banquet board.

Heywood took the center of the table, facing the door and anyone who might enter. "You're to be my support in this," he'd told Nash, "against the tide of fools." Nash didn't know that they were fools, but they did enjoy hearing themselves talk.

Hugh Malbanks, sitting at the far end of the table, owned the most profitable cotton mills in town, though he had just passed thirty years of age. Gray-lipped and stern, he drove the hardest bargains and wasn't above threatening his workers if it would get the job done. His trading with Nash was fair enough though, and he was one-third partner in the consortium Nash had drawn up to bid for steady work from the Netherlands. The first, trial, supply was due to ship in less than two months.

William Clayton had some two decades more experience than Malbanks, but his cotton operation was only half as extensive. Heywood had introduced him as "the professor," and he did carry a rather abstracted air behind narrow-rimmed spectacles. He sat to Malbanks's right, but lost his seat to a new arrival when he got up for another draft.

The others on the committee Nash knew by name or sight, excepting the Reverend Ethelston of Cheshire. Four of them seemed to be taking their afternoon doze.

Heywood cleared his throat, a mighty roar, and they staggered awake. "Old business. I see the ban on singing has been proclaimed."

The recitation was a formality, but Nash couldn't let that one go. "I do feel safer now."

"You weren't there." Malbanks spread his palms on the table. "Those men stood one step away from insurrection. We don't need a reprise of the business of Seventeen." Like then, Manchester's workers were grumbling strike, and the manufactory owners needed to nip that in the bud. As a supplier, Nash's livelihood depended on steady need. Even a week of work stoppage would overflow his warehouses. And if the ship from Boston made Liverpool on Thursday, as expected, he would need to erect a new warehouse out of thin air by week's end.

Heywood stroked his beard. "I don't recall song being part of the incitement to riot in Seventeen. Press the men down too hard, and they'll rise up out of plain orneriness. We do have your fine yeomanry to keep the town serene, after all."

"The workers are girding for battle," Malbanks said. "I see it in their eyes."

"When do you get close enough to a worker to see his eyes?" Clayton shook his head, and then had to readjust his glasses. "Someone is going around painting frightening pictures, but they don't represent our town men."

Nash's ears pricked up at that. "Saboteurs?"

"Don't use those Frenchified words at me, sailor boy." Clayton winked. "Aye, Trefford's house had mud thrown on it. But was it the men, or merely their children?"

"His workers are merely children," Nash said.

"We did have to raise our first workforce." Trefford seemed little taller than a child; seated at the far end of the table, his legs didn't touch the floor. "But they've all grown up now. Adults make better workers."

Malbanks lifted his hands and crossed his arms. "But they surely aren't as docile as children anymore. What we need is a constabulary force, a standing police."

"You can't be serious. A standing army of policemen? In Britain? Never been done." Heywood had to take a drink just to stop his flow of talk.

The man from Cheshire piped in. "We have a standing army, potential policemen, just miles out of town. What is the difference?"

Malbanks glared at him. "We would have control over a civilian policing force."

Nash crossed his own arms. "Who is this we? The merchants? Or would London step in again and order us about?"

"If London will not pay to help us, I don't see how they can give the orders," Malbanks said.

"What we need is representation," Nash shook his head. "Who argues for the interests of industry? No one. We need a member of Parliament from Manchester."

"Two members!" Clayton's shout did not help Nash's argument.

Suffrage had not kept up with the times. When boroughs had been assigned, Manchester was merely a meadow by a river. The two members of Parliament from Lancashire, more than fifty miles away, represented all the people of the county, and did a ramshackle job of it, in the opinion of Manchester's men.

"We need the help now," Malbanks said. Heads nodded, and he continued. "I propose calling up special constables. We would disband them, Mr. Heywood, when summer marching season is done."

"See that you do."

Malbanks nodded. "I know many of the innkeepers, bakers, and the like, eager to ensure the peace. If they can't afford the horseflesh to join the yeomanry, this will do for them."

Nash wasn't convinced. "An armed, untrained military force, charged with keeping the peace?"

"At least we'll know innkeepers won't be as drunken as the yeomanry," Clayton said, glasses precarious on his nose. "They won't care to deplete their wares."

Heywood rose, and the meeting was ended. Nash followed him down the stairs and grabbed a pint. They settled at a table by the only window in the place.

Nash couldn't keep quiet. "Why didn't you knock them down? Constables. What idiocy."

"It's a distraction and a comfort. These are trying days for men who aren't fortunate enough to have contented workers. Let them have their toy soldiers. It will keep their minds off greater mischief."

"I can't like it. We need to steer clear of smelling like an army. My own men seem happy enough, but for my going missing in the middle of a working day. Why have this meeting at mid-day?"

"Because that's when the owners are at leisure. That is, the ones who can ever afford to be at leisure." Heywood quaffed his half-pint and smacked his lips. "Speaking of mischief, I hear congratulations may be in order."

"You disapprove?"

"You're free to marry any girl you fancy. A mighty short fancy, I might notice. I hear that money may have sweetened the deal."

"I do not marry for the money." Nash sat back, frowning. How did Heywood still know so much of his family's business?

"Strong protest indeed for a man newly endowed as partner in our new enterprise. I must remind you, the woman brings nothing to this marriage, no connections save those that could harm. You could do better."

"You know of her family?"

"I wrote the contract, remember? I know they agreed never to claim her, nor seek her out. In exchange, we agreed to keep her out of their way. The mother is buried at St. Mary's, of all places. He wanted her interred, and I knew the vicar there wasn't so choosy."

"Is the vicar still there?" Madeline might wish to speak with him. "Perhaps he could perform our ceremony."

"Too late for that; he's gone to his maker. I'm still a deacon there, though; if you want it, consider it done. I must warn you, Quinn: A bad wife is far worse that a bad business deal. Don't do this out of some false vision of family honor."

"It isn't false."

"It isn't honor. Setting up some chit to marry Shaftsbury. What was the old man thinking?"

"Perhaps that the girl would be a good match."

"Didn't he choose his own bride, and that fell out poorly? Why did he think he could choose any better for his sons?"

Nash frowned. "Sons? Do you think there is some young thing training herself up to be my bride?"

Heywood laughed, the roar streaming out the door and echoing into the street. "A bride for the lost little lamb? I should say not. We all thought you would come out of the Navy buggered."

"Blasphemer."

"That's not blasphemy, it's slander. But tell me true, do you feel anything at all for this woman?"

Nash tried to sound out his feelings. Dormant so long, they were hard to read. "There is something between us, something that could be kindled. I intend to kindle it."

Heywood lifted his mug to him, and drained the last of his bitters. "I'll tell my lady wife to set up a decent supper for her, then. She'll need all the help she can get."

❧

MADDIE PACED the small track from bookshelves to window in the small study. She'd spent much of these past three days here, finding an outlet for her nerves by organizing the chaos of the castle's accounts and paperwork. Shaftsbury found her just as she was turning away from the cloud-soaked view outside.

"Thought I'd find you here. The carriage is come round." Dressed in hunter and gold, Lord Shaftsbury looked like a Gainsborough painting come to life. His smile was wider than Mr. Quinn's, or what she could remember of his. She hadn't seen him since the morning after she'd accepted his offer. He'd returned to town for some meeting and never come back. At least he'd sent two letters, short as they were. In one, he'd made the biggest concession she could imagine.

He'd written that he'd found the churchyard in Manchester where her mother was buried, and that if she wished they would wed in that church rather than the castle's. Her mother's name was Mary Moore. Reading the words, Maddie had nearly fainted, right there in the chair in her bedroom. It was surprising enough that he would seek out that hallowed ground, but that he would both consider her wants and dreams and place them ahead of the raft of his own family's traditions made her head spin.

As it did his mother's. At news of the engagement, Lady Shaftsbury had first sulked, but relented under Shaftsbury's gentle prodding. She'd even offered to allow Maddie to wear her own wedding shawl as the "something borrowed." When the venue changed, so did Lady Shaftsbury's mood: She had refused to attend.

"Looks like rain," Maddie said. "Your mother made the right decision."

"It will hold off. It's been such a sunny spring. I've seen you enjoying the gardens; aren't they grand? As for Mama, she's changed her mind again."

"She's going to Manchester?"

"She's taking my place. Says that's more appropriate. She's such a stickler for everything proper."

Was it proper that an earl not attend the wedding of his only brother simply because he was marrying a nobody? Maddie held her tongue.

Shaftsbury turned to the shelves. She'd made short work of the ledgers, which hadn't been touched since Perkins left four months before. "Hard to believe you did all this in a matter of days."

"I like doing the accounts, making the columns come out right." Tidying up the world, at least the arithmetical part of it, as Miss Marsden put it.

"Might I offer you some advice? As well as your license, since Nash never showed up to take it off my hands." He pulled out the folded paper, signed by the local archbishop, and handed it to her; without it, they would have had to wait weeks before marrying. "You know you don't need to wed so quickly. For as much as he despises autocratic behavior, my dear brother practices it almost daily."

"I do want this." She saw him staring at her hands, which were crushing the vellum. She loosened her grip, and tucked the license into her bag.

"Rushing you into a hastily planned wedding is the least of it. Stand up to him from time to time, if you're able. You might suggest you help Nash with his accounts, as well."

"He has trouble with maths?"

"Not with maths, no. With making space for people in his

life, yes. My brother tends to forge ahead and forget to look back to see if you're following, if you get what I mean."

She wasn't sure she did. Shaftsbury's smile grew crooked. "Not too clear, am I? You'll figure it out. And you might see if he'll release Perkins. The castle needs him. I was an idiot to send him away."

"A generous admission, my lord."

"Merely the sad truth. But I must say you look beautiful this morning, a radiant bride. Look, you even blush. No, no, somebody needs to fawn over you. Nash will forget, and Mama," he paused, "well, she's probably at the carriage now so we'd best make haste."

As he handed her into the carriage, and she settled next to her soon-to-be mother-in-law, Maddie finally felt her heart ease. So much had happened so quickly, but it was turning out all right. Perhaps even better: There would be no extended engagement, as she'd expected when she believed herself the earl's bride. She would be a married woman—part of a true family—far earlier than she'd dreamed.

PART TWO

Thirteen

It was supposed to be a mid-morning wedding, but that was before the sudden downpour, the trouble with the front axle, and the driver's having forgotten that Saturday was produce day, plunging them deep into the throngs along Market Street.

Trying to avoid the crowd, the driver got turned around again, taking them on a sodden tour of Manchester, a dank town reeking of wet cinders. Already, Maddie missed the open, warm fields of the country. When they finally landed at the church, shortly after one o'clock, Nash's face wore a rictus welcome. Of course, he'd been on time.

He'd said not a word to her on the church steps and even in the sanctuary, even during the ceremony his "I do" was more a grunt. He'd even signed the register in silence. Finally, outside the church, he spoke. "I must return to the warehouse. Mama will escort you home."

To say Lady Shaftsbury was displeased at that information was an understatement. She did not hide her further displeasure when Maddie did not immediately follow her into the carriage but instead sloshed about the cemetery in search of her mother. She could wait; Maddie wasn't about to leave empty-handed.

Back along the far wall, she found it a simple white slate with *Moore* in capital letters, and below it *Richard, 1777—* and *Mary, beloved, 1780—1799.*

No death date for her father meant he must still be alive.

She touched the stone. Cold and slick, it offered little comfort, it was solid, and permanent, and she had found it at last. Her secret mother. At least there could be no more surprises now.

She unclasped the gold necklace her Wetherby father had given her. Kneeling, but careful not to soil the dress, she tucked the gift into the clay dirt beside the marker. It was all she had to give. She'd received a new one from Nash as a bride gift, a single black pearl on a white-gold chain.

She turned away from the grave. It needed ornament, perhaps some lilies. She'd arrange for it. She needed to arrange for pin money and discover how Nash managed his household's expenses.

Trudging across the muddied path, she smiled grimly to herself. She'd need to learn to live at the whim of another stranger. It wasn't as if she'd never done it before.

Lady Shaftsbury had spread her skirts across the entire bench of the carriage. "Found your old Mama? I'll be your new Mama now."

Maddie settled on the back-facing bench. "I appreciate any advice you wish to give me."

"Ask away. But be quick about it. Deacon tells me we depart for London on Monday next. Of course, you may write me. Once a week is plenty."

Maddie touched the solid band on her finger, a slight weight that suddenly seemed to grow heavier. "What would make him happy?"

The duchess didn't smile, but her blue eyes shone kindly. "Don't aim too high, my dear. He's chosen to live in this noisome, sooty town, amongst its poorly dressed, ill-mannered citizens. The best you can hope for is contentment. Relieve him of his worries and cares. He always chooses the heaviest burden."

Like you, Maddie heard, though the the lady hadn't say it aloud.

MADDIE HAD NOT SEEN many detached houses as they drew into the town. Most of the folk in this gloomy, wretched place seemed to live in a darker cousin of the rowhouses she'd grown up among in Bath. But there were no seaside prospects here, and precious few hills. As they turned away from the river, the stench from the tanneries beside it seemed to chase after them. They had passed the worst of the smell by the time the coach came to a stop.

Lady Shaftsbury rolled down the glass on the carriage door to get a better look, and shuddered. "As I remembered. I'll say my farewells here. I'm sure you'll wish to have your new home in order before playing the hostess."

Maddie's throat burned. The woman was deserting her on the doorstep, like an unwanted infant? As the outrider turned the latch, Lady Shaftsbury leaned over to pat Maddie's knee. When the door opened, she leaned back quickly, pulling a handkerchief out of her sleeve to drape against her nose.

Maddie stepped from a spray of the lady's talcum powder into a sooty drizzle. The red-brick house before her had at most three stories, two main floors, a cellar kitchen, and perhaps an attic. At least it was on the end of the terrace, so the door could be set to the side, allowing the windows to be in alignment. Maddie wasn't sure what she'd expected, but it certainly wasn't this.

The slick cobbled street was quiet at mid-afternoon, save for the Shaftsbury coach clambering away back to its gargantuan home. Maddie stood at the base of the five steps leading to her new front door, and turned away. This prospect was slightly better. The soldier's row of housing did not face another regiment, but a small meadow housing a miserly flock of sheep. The roadway was not dirt but stones, and there was a sort of walk on the side for pedestrians.

This would never be mistaken for a neighborhood of great houses. Nash Quinn was not the man high in business she'd been led to believe. And Mrs. Nash Quinn, while not a nobody, was not so great a somebody, either. She would need new clothes.

She heard the door open behind her. "Mrs. Quinn, ma'am?"

"Mrs. Willis?" The housekeeper, small and tidy, carried a worried frown, but at the sound of her name, the creases beside her eyes and mouth deepened in displeasure.

"Oh, dearie, come in. Just like him, that is, depositing you like a bag of grain. Mr. Willis said a carriage come, but I was up in the back with your trunks. You'll be used to his ways soon enough, I expect. Oh." As if she'd just remembered, she bobbed a proper curtsey for someone who had rheumy limbs.

The dried-apple face pursed its lips and scanned her as she came up the stairs. Maddie imagined her counting the extra hours it was going to take to keep her linens white. Mrs. Willis wore cream and gray. "We'll be sending out to laundry, I expect."

It took less than a half-hour to view the entirety of the estate: Two rooms on each of three levels, plus an attic room for the Willises, though Mrs. Willis often stayed in the larder off the kitchen when her joints were acting up. She slowed more with every stair step they took, and Maddie's spirits sank in proportion. After managing a staff of eighteen at the girls' school, she wouldn't need more than an hour or two a week to manage a steady two lodging and one day-worker. She'd need to find something beyond this home to be of service to. She hoped Shaftsbury had the right of it, and her new husband would not mind taking a wife to work.

Showing Maddie the outbuildings in the minuscule yard took less than five minutes. Everything seemed to be run on a rigid scheme, or what Maddie had started to refer to as ship-shape. No room served fewer than two purposes, aside from the water closet, which while one could scent its purpose was so bright and clean, with a manner of window in its roof, that Maddie rather suspected it was also used as a reading room.

Nash Quinn had taken the lessons learned in his majesty's Navy to heart. She wondered if she would be made to serve multiple purposes, as well.

Returning from the attic, they stopped at the second-floor landing. The front room held a rowboat-sized bed, but had only hooks on the wall, no presses for clothes. He apparently kept most of his apparel in a battered sea chest. Was she expected to do the same?

She trailed Mrs. Willis into the smaller room, off the tiny hall. Maddie's trunks, doubled up, crammed the space to the fireplace. The men had moved the writing desk downstairs this morning. The dormer window gave on to drizzling rain.

"We'll need a press, and a bureau. We can squeeze in with the linen closet for now." Mrs. Willis went to the first trunk on the right, lid open. She pulled out Maddie's winter cape, and shook out the folds. Maddie sank onto the lid of the trunk closest to the door. This was too impossible.

Mrs. Willis turned at the sound, and nearly dropped the cape. "Poor dear, you must be famished, and here I prattle on about presses." She patted Maddie's shoulder. "I'll just go down and do up some tea."

As soon as she heard the older woman's careful tread on the step, Maddie buried her face in her hands. Her eyes and throat already burned from the foul air of this town. She was acting all missish in front of the help, and it was so clear to her, and surely to Mrs. Willis, how poorly she would fit into their ship-shape lives.

She had too many clothes, and yet not enough. Nothing of hers was appropriate for either this town or her new station in life. But how did one go about obtaining presses, and frocks, and matronly hats? She had no capital, and her husband's interests all lay elsewhere. Not a fortnight ago, she had thought her possessions perfect, herself exactly what was wanted—even what was needed. Now, she was a wife, as she'd expected, but of the wrong man, in the wrong place, for the wrong reasons. Forever after.

The heavy step on the stair reminded her of Miss Marsden's. What would the headmistress say if she were to look at her now? "Tears are fine in moderation, but deciding what to do will help you more." Maddie smiled at the memory, at the idea that Miss Marsden's lemon-sour face could bring her solace.

She sat up straight as Mrs. Willis came in with a tiny tray laden with pot, saucers, and a plate of scones. "Very nice. Thank you, Mrs. Willis."

"Don't I remember my first day away from home." She sat the tray on a small foldable stand Maddie hadn't noticed before and started the tea steeping.

"No need to unpack all these. We'll take just what's needed and sent the rest of it back to the castle for storage. My wardrobe was rather—ambitious." She didn't wish to face that mistake every morning as she walked into her new boudoir.

Afternoon stretched into dusk, and then evening, and Maddie was still alone with the help. She had her books, and letters—the few still remaining. She'd written to Miss Marsden with all her news, as promised, already. She convinced herself that she was not lonely, but the truth was she'd thought the castle a bit bare of people. She missed the bustle of the girls' school, and the chatty ways of small-town Bath.

This was just her first day here, she reminded herself. Of course she would make friends. Who would those friends be? Gentry? Wives of men of commerce? Working people? She must take Nash's lead. She was an extension of him, in society's eyes at least. Where was he?

At the warehouse, Mrs. Willis said, always at the warehouse. He might then go directly to some merchants' meeting scheduled for tonight. He could have sent a message. He might have called for her to come and meet him. Why had he insisted they marry today when he had no time to spend with her?

What performances would he force upon her, when he did arrive home? Her wifely duties, of which she had heard much but understood little.

By eight o'clock, despite her best intentions and the best efforts of the ghost of Miss Marsden, Maddie had built herself up to a fever pitch. Nonetheless, when she heard the outside door open and his voice in the hall, she forced herself to sit still, not to run to him. Surely she was stronger than that. When he passed by the half-open door and went upstairs, though, she cracked. By the time he returned, and did open the door, greeting her with a grin and some faded bloom of a compliment, she barely heard it.

"I didn't realize you wanted a potted plant for a wife."

"What is wrong?"

"Why am I here?"

"This is your new home. Supper at nine?" He sat in the armchair opposite her, eyes wary, and then straightened out the afternoon newspaper and started reading.

Maddie bit her lip. Her hands busied themselves twining in her lap. Why wouldn't he understand? Her foot stomped softly.

He looked up. "Do you wish to read the paper first?"

"No."

"I should have brought you a posy?"

"No. Yes. No. I don't know. I need something to do. A place."

He sighed. "An assignment. You consider yourself an employee."

"You are master and commander."

"Do you believe that?"

She didn't, but she was beyond thinking clearly and wouldn't be made happy. "I don't know."

He stood and sat on the armrest of her chair, taking one of her hands in his.

"You're freezing. You should have called for a fire."

"It's nearly June. I'm just an ornament, I don't require accommodation."

"Nonsense, and you know it. What is really wrong, Maddie?"

If she knew, she would have told him. All she knew was she was full up unhappy, dissatisfied with the mess she had found herself in.

Nash absently rubbed her hand. The rhythm of the touch sent soothing waves up her arm, calming her stupid nerves. Still, the thought niggled: Why hadn't he been here to do this earlier?

"You wanted me home to welcome you."

"I felt like a stranger."

"I apologize. I intended to, but there was a problem at the 'house, and I thought I needed to fix it. But you are right, there are often problems at the 'house, and a man brings a wife to his home only once in his lifetime. I should have been here."

Maddie's shoulders eased. She leaned into his side. Who knew the power of his touch, his scent?

"Could I help you fix the problems? I'm a quick study." *Please*, she almost begged, but held herself in check.

His hand stopped a moment. "I see I have been remiss. Give me a day or two, and I'll rustle up an invitation or a concert. Tonight I'll write introductions to two of the wives of men I do business with. You'll be thick with friends and acquaintances in no time. You'd like that, wouldn't you?"

She had one answer, at least. She was a merchant's wife. She'd known few of their sort, but those at least had some schooling. She prayed it was true here in the over-practical north, too, or whatever would they have to talk about?

FOURTEEN

After a quick, nearly silent supper on her new, folding dinner table, which might be pressed to seat up to six, Maddie retired upstairs and dressed for bed. The maid-of-all-work needed to return home for the evening, and Mrs. Willis wasn't sure her fingers were nimble enough for the hooks at the back of Maddie's dress. She would need to order dresses that hooked in front, dresses made of good Mancunian cloth.

Nash had agreed to the purchase of two dresses, with three more after she'd had time to discover which styles would suit her. He had not agreed to the clothes press and cabinetry, saying he'd see if Deacon had castoffs first.

"We'll not live here forever," he'd said, as if that were an explanation. She couldn't foresee living in any place that could not use a good press or bureau. Even ships must have presses, if ladies were aboard.

Her head ached from learning about the house and fretting

over everything else. Her back ached from the interminable carriage ride in an over-tightened corset. Despite it all, she could not bring herself to just tuck into her new husband's sleeping area.

The bed looked rather like a landlubber furniture-maker's image of a ship. Dark mahogany sides curve slightly inward, gripping the mattress at the edges. The posts held curtains that were little more than canvas, which would be good to keep the light out but bad for air circulation.

The maid had not let down the curtains. Maddie loosened one of the ties and a trickle of dust drifted down. Apparently he did not need the privacy.

Well, she certainly did. She pushed the panel down, casting dust into the air and down the floor, and then jumped back away from the worst of it. The canvas was lighter than she expected.

Each of the three sides exposed had its own curtain, stopped by the mast-like posts at the corners. By the time Maddie had all three down, the air in the room was cloudy. She went to the window and opened it. The temperature was a little cooler, soothing, but the consistency was much like the inside—except the outside air carried that blackish soot from the chimneys of the manufactories. She trusted the soot would drop and the air here on this floor, well off the ground, would be clearer. A light breeze fanned the curtain in.

She missed the smell of the sea, the shadow of salt she used to taste on her tongue from the air in Bath. Here, the air had a vague metallic finish, sharp but in a different way.

She was surprised that the master bedroom faced the street. But also glad, for she could see a dark figure walking with Nash's long stride down the street. He'd gone to check on something at the warehouse again. It looked like she would be forever competing with that building for her husband's attention. If only she could enlist its help.

She pulled back from the window so he wouldn't see her, and continued to observe him. From his slouch hat to his multi-pocketed coat, he looked the moderately prosperous merchant. His sloping step was not as bow-legged as many of the gentlemen who rode every day, and he had lost much of that shuffling gait sailors used on land.

She heard him turn the key in the door's lock—another difference from the country—and step inside.

A shiver of fearful excitement swept through her. They had performed the public ceremonies to become man and wife. Now they would perform the private ones.

She wanted his hands on her, his solid warmth, his lips. Oh yes, those lips.

He opened the door, a candle in his hand. He looked at the canvas curtains, and then saw her at the window. She felt naked under her night rail and wrapper, and tucked her arms around her waist.

"Don't be nervous." He set the candle on the stand beside the bed away from her, and walked to the chest in the corner opposite.

"Do you need your man?"

"No man. You could help me with my boots?"

Maddie found that small domestic chore eased her nerves. Until he spoke again.

"Is that a new wrapper? It's quite sheer. I believe I can see your shadows."

She looked down. The hint of dark at the tips of her breasts was obvious. She watched in shame as the pale skin around them flamed pink.

"I don't want you wearing that around the house."

"Of course not." She wouldn't dare. She tried to cover herself, but felt the heat pink her chest and wash up her face to the roots of her hair.

"Good." His voice roughened. "I don't wish to share you with anyone."

She looked up, startled. He took her elbow and pulled her toward him. She settled carefully onto his lap.

"Can you feel how much I want you?"

The ridge in his pants burned where it touched her thigh. She could hear his quick breaths.

"I want you, Maddie. Are you ready for me?"

She frowned. "I don't understand."

He sighed, a cross between a chuckle and a groan. "You're not, then. Help me with my shirt."

His shirt had more buttons than she expected. "I thought most shirts had ties."

"They do. I'm wearing my inventory, as they say. We have far too many buttons on hand. Why not set a trend for the men?"

She undid a button at his cuff, her finger running along the pulse point in his wrist. He inhaled sharply. "Should I wear buttons, too?" They might be easier for Mrs. Willis, as well.

"I should think so," he said, capturing her hand and pulling it up to his mouth. He gave the palm the gentlest of kisses. She closed her eyes and forgot about Mrs. Willis.

The kisses continued down the inside of her arm, past the indent of her elbow. They paused as he pushed her wrapper off her shoulder, and then continued on the prickled-hot skin of her upper arm. With his other hand, he massaged across her shoulder to her neck, pulling her closer to him. She pressed her hands into his chest.

Her head fell back, her neck aching for his favors. With his thumb, he teased her lower lip. By the time his lips replaced his thumb, hers had already swollen with promise and an ache that was starting to grow familiar.

Maddie opened her mouth eagerly. She loved this part, when their breaths mixed, their tongues joined. The movement took all her attention, the loneliness and worries of the day washed away.

She wished the kiss could go on forever, but too soon Nash broke it. They sighed in harmony. His chuckle drew a small smile from her. She liked the deep dimple on his left.

He pushed a stray curl back from her forehead. "Shall we dispense with the rest of my clothing and try the bed? It's a dashed sight more comfortable than this chair."

He gripped her under the knees, his other arm behind her shoulders and stood, lifting her easily. As she turned her head to see where the edge of the curtain was so she could pull it aside, he kissed the tender space along her neck under her ear.

She pulled the curtain back slowly, opening the bed to the moonlight from the window. He bent and gently lay her on top of the covers. "Stay there," he said, and then shrugged out of his shirt. His chest was wide and strong, as if it were he who carried the bolts and bales in the warehouse. Small wonder he'd had no trouble toting her.

He turned a bit to push his pants down. His rounded buttocks and powerful legs shone in the bluish light. He was just as magnificent without clothes as in them. He turned and stepped into the bed so quickly she got only a glimpse of his manhood. But that quick peek told her he was ready for plowing, as the farmers put it.

"I don't wish you to be frightened." He sat at her hip, his bent leg hiding his manly tool. "I want you to enjoy this as much as I do. I understand that it may not be so the first few times."

He reached out, running a palm down the side of her face. She breathed him in, wanting him closer. Wanting to please, to not disappoint.

She took his arm to draw him in. He pushed up to his knees and settled himself to her side, pulling her to her side. She wanted to look down between them, but her gaze skittered away. He smiled, and taking her hand, pulled it down to his center.

"It's nothing to be frightened of." He pushed her hand onto his shaft. It was warmer than she expected, pulsing with life. She kept her hand still for a moment, and then wrapped her fingers along the thick width of him.

He groaned, moving his hips. A shock of elation shot through her. She moved him with just a touch. Surely she could do this.

Then he was kissing her again, faster and harder. She could feel whispers of an echo of what their tongues were doing in the movements of his shaft against her hand. She nipped at his tongue with her teeth, and the shaft jumped.

A dark flash of imagination cut through her mind, and she gasped, drowning.

She'd heard this before, and it was bad. A bad thing. She was bad. A bad thing.

Before she knew it, she was all the way off the bed away from him, on the floor. The closed curtain surrounded her. She scrambled to slide under the bed, but the wooden sideboards went all the way to the ground.

She was in a pit, with snakes all around. Warm pulsing snakes. They were huge and growing larger. She was small and shrinking. She cried out.

"Madeline!"

Something grabbed her shoulder, a python ready to bite. She shrieked and tried to get away, but it held her in its hard jaws.

"Maddie!"

Someone whispered her name. A good voice, strong. She shuddered, and the snake's head on her shoulder melted into a warm hand. The legion of vipers on the floor slid away until all that was left was the dust of the curtain and her nightgown, twisted around her.

"Come back to bed."

Nash's arm slid under her armpit, pulling her up. Once her hip hit the bed, he pushed to embrace her.

"What happened?"

"A nightmare. Was I sleeping?"

"Not exactly." His voice carried concern, and not a little bit of ruefulness. "I've never experienced that reaction to my love-making before. I must be out of practice."

"I'm sorry."

He pulled away, and gazed at her face a moment. "Why?"

"It's my fault. I ruin everything."

"Who told you that?"

"Just look. You aren't even excited by me anymore."

Nash chuckled. "Hearing your partner shriek in terror is not the best aphrodisiac, true. Maddie, I want you. I like your smell, and your taste." He bent down and licked her exposed shoulder. She froze, and then forced herself to relax. "I like the sound of you and the look of you. I never meant to frighten you."

"You still want me?"

"I do. But I want you to feel the same. If you can."

"I can. I was. Then." She shook her head. Where had that image come from? Nothing in her life had been remotely as terrifying as that nightmare.

"It's all that fire and brimstone they feed you at church. You'll find it's not at all like that." He pulled the covers down and she wriggled into bed. He slid down beside her.

"Don't you wear anything to bed?"

"I haven't. I can change if you wish it."

"Must I be naked, too?"

"Only if you wish it."

"Do you wish it?"

He turned her on her side away from him. Wrapping his arms around her, he pulled her into his front, as if they were spoons. "Does this frighten you?"

She listened inside. Where had that screaming bit disappeared to? "No."

He sighed against her neck. He kissed the lobe of her ear, and then whispered, "I would love to have your skin next to mine, in passion or in sleep, but only if you, too, wish it."

"I like this."

"Then I like it, too. Your hair smells of honeysuckle."

They lay together, and gradually the muscles in her legs relaxed. Her shoulders eased. Her breathing became more regular. Her zigzag thoughts started to slow. It had never been so easy to fall asleep.

Nash did not fall asleep. When he was sure Maddie was deep under, he gently pulled his arms back, pressing the covers in place around her. He rolled over and up to sit with his back against the headboard, his knees up.

What the hell?

Having a wife was already more work than he'd expected. He'd hope his bride would shriek, true, but with pleasure. This one's voice held pure terror. He devoutly hoped the Willises hadn't overheard.

Something had hurt her, something fierce. Had she spent years at the feet of some vicar who equated pleasure with sin—or death? Had her headmistress been a secret sadist, teaching her poor charges how filthy they were? She'd read too many of the wrong sort of books?

He'd seen the terror well up, her gasps for air forcing her eyes wide and dark. She'd fought to find her breath, to warm to him again, and she had—until another wave knocked her away and out of the bed. She had passion enough. He grew harder at the memory, and shifted his position. But then—the abyss.

Nash cursed himself in a whisper. He had worked so hard to pull this wedding off quickly, but had forgotten that marriage followed hard upon it.

His wife had no idea of Manchester, no friends, no relations. He did not know her habits, her likes or dislikes. Would she enjoy a concert or a poetry reading, or was she a dancer and gossiper?

He had not known her a week, and not even seen her half those days. He did know that she was cut adrift, looking for purchase, and he had failed at anchoring her. What had Mrs. Willis said? He'd dumped her on the stoop like so much cabbage. His housekeeper was kindness itself, but perhaps a bit fearsome looking to a stranger.

What had his new bride thought to see this house, when she'd dreamt of castles all her life? Had he been in the same position, he might have had the same snappish feelings, too. In fact, he was lucky she'd only bitten his head off this evening. She should have punched him. He would have. He'd acted worse than Deacon.

She deserved better than him. At the least she deserved a decent home, with dress-presses and cupboards and what all. In that nightdress, her hair in loose braids, she had glowed. He liked the heft of her, the shape of her here in his bed. He hadn't even minded that the canvas was down. With a finger, he kissed her neck, the lightest of caresses. She sighed in her sleep, and something locked tight in his chest released. He traced her shoulder, then over the blanket covering her hip. This part he could get comfortable with. If only she were this pliable when awake. Or in heat.

That shriek had been raw fear. Whatever had installed the fear wasn't going to have to clean up after its mess, Nash was. He wasn't sure where to start. He didn't know if he had the patience. He only knew that if he did not do something to repair the damage, his own sad cock would be sorry indeed.

FIFTEEN

The next afternoon, Maddie turned her new key into the lock and let herself into the hatbox that was her new home. Sitting through the sermon at St. Mary's, and simultaneously pondering whether her vicar of old had planted that seed of terror in her mind, had worn her out, but her first encounter with her mother's resting place in full sunlight brought some peace. The air was lighter when the mills were closed.

She dropped the key into her reticule and took the stair to her boudoir to hang up cloak and bonnet. At least they had places now. Even at church, she'd felt singled out, and not because she'd come without her family. That would have been true in Bath. Here most of the parishioners looked like working women and their children; both groups stared openly at her. The rector hid his surprise with more skill.

His sermon, on doing one's duty, only served to vex her further. What was her duty now? Follow the lead of her husband, but he didn't appear to want much of her, and what could she rightfully demand of him? What he had wanted, last night, she'd failed to give.

Some of the women followed her same path home, over Shude Hill and through Thomas Street. They didn't speak to her, but nodded amiably enough. Two stopped to watch her enter this house. She was the news of the neighborhood by now. She hoped their stories reflected well on Nash, despite her soft Southern accent and foreign-made cloth. By what else could they judge her?

She found him in the main room, reading yet another newspaper. "More protests?"

"Not in London." He set the paper on his lap and rubbed at his brow.

"I missed you this morning. When did you leave?"

"Shade past six. Weavers are an early crowd."

"On Sunday?"

He shrugged. "They wanted to deliver today. I'm told there's a rally in Oldham tomorrow. You've missed dinner. Churching takes so long?"

Maddie glanced at the clock on the mantle. Four o'clock. The half-hour she thought she'd spent clearing her mother's place must have been twice that long. "I visited my mother's grave again."

It felt so strange, having another mother. She'd already been to Mary Moore's graveside more than she ever had that of Lady Wetherby. It was not thought proper for a child to haunt her parents' grave; the new viscount had forbidden it. She sat sidewise on the chair in front of the folded-out writing table.

"Why so far away?"

Butterflies, suddenly awakened in her stomach, raced toward her throat. She gulped them back down. "I apologize for last night," she said formally, as if distant words could mask the immediacy of her emotions.

His face stilled, his expression intent on her. He didn't say anything. No longer butterflies but bees of panic shot out to her limbs. He patted the chair beside him, offering it to her. Maddie scolded herself for jumping to conclusions as she sat down. Her rotted imagination ruined everything.

"I do not believe an apology is necessary. You obviously could not help what you felt. I did not realize how repellent I am." He softened his words with that self-deprecating half-smile, but his indigo eyes were sad. She wanted to reassure him, but didn't know how he would take to reassurance. He seemed a hard man.

"You must know you're catnip to the ladies."

"Now I know you taunt me." But he laughed, and Maddie's buzzing bees settled back to sleep. He took her hand, stroking it, over and over. But soon enough his thoughtful frown returned. "Last night, it frightened me, as well. What could have caused it? Has it ever happened before? You looked scared to death."

She shook her head.

"Something that happened only once, perhaps, but now you avoid the activity, or the color, something, that caused it. Anything?"

Maddie was sure she didn't know what he was getting at. Then she did remember something. A scent.

"The barbershop."

"The barber? When would you ever go there?"

"Never, except for the once. We girls wished to buy a gift for one of our teachers, who was returning to the continent. We collected money to buy him an aftershave, because he often smelled of mothballs and we thought he might have more luck with the ladies if he carried a sweeter bouquet."

She had gone to the busiest barber on High Street. The man had been kind to a rather nervous young miss. She hadn't been afraid at all of him, until she nearly fainted.

"I see now it wasn't the barber that frightened me. It was the scent."

After she'd explained her errand, the barber had opened up a small bottle of powerful perfume. He hadn't even told her the price before she had run out of the store feeling as if she were chased by hounds.

"All this time I thought it was him. I even whipped up a tale of terror for the girls. Another girl went to a different barber. He must have given her a different scent, for when Mr. Purdy dabbed it on, I didn't need to run."

"A scent."

"That can't be it. You weren't wearing anything last night. Besides, I like your smell."

His eyes sparkled, and she realized what she had said. The bees painted her face hot red. "That's a comfort."

The blush burning her cheeks reminded her she'd missed bathing this morning. "Do you think there's enough water to bathe today?"

"Aye, but not enough hands. The Willises are off until tomorrow. Didn't you have a bath yesterday?"

That was only a sponging wash, barely enough to signify. She needs must wash once a day. It was part of her, part of Godliness. Bathing was not negotiable. She would have put it in the marriage contract had she known she'd be living in a house that had to collect the rain for bath water.

"Don't worry. I'm sure they refilled the pitchers before they went. I had to push Mrs. Willis out the door. They with a new grandchild to see. All she thought of was you."

He leaned in. She held still as he kissed her temple. "I like your smell, too." She blinked slowly, the bees settling down, sated.

He leaned back. "I've arranged for us to be invited to sup with the Heywoods. She can introduce you to the crowd, and then you can begin making calls. How do you like that?"

She'd like rather for him to give her more of those kisses. "I'd be grateful to them."

"Heywood has been a mentor to me. We've joined in a fabric scheme that could bring steady work to Manchester. Now that Deacon has put off the daughter, your being on good terms with his wife could mend things."

"I'll do my best."

"The dinner's not for a few days, though. So what do you say to a tour of the warehouse tomorrow?"

The secret sanctuary?

He grinned at her expression. "Monday's are a bit slow. We could wait until Tuesday. That's a market day."

"Tomorrow is better." And perhaps she could return on Tuesday, and Wednesday, too. If she could convince him to share this part of his life, maybe she could convince him to share more.

"You don't seem as fearful tonight."

Nash undid the hooks at the back of his wife's dress. She'd already sent five of her trunks back to the castle, a good sign. At dinner, she talked about the household budget, and how it would need at the least an incremental increase. Painful, yet also a good sign. Plus, she wasn't screaming in fear. Yet.

He tried to remember which touch, which sound, had set her off. Was it her thigh, her hip, her belly, her breast? He ran a finger up from the base of her spine, bare now but for her shift. She shivered and leaned into the touch. *Good.* As he neared the nape of her neck, she pulled away, turning so fast he caught a glimpse of giant green irises before they shrunk back to normal. What could have happened to her neck?

He knew she wanted him to say *I'm not going to hurt you.* But it galled him to be distrusted so. He turned away from her, silently cursing the man or beast that had wrecked this moment for her. He prayed the damage wasn't permanent.

She laid a hand on his shoulder, stopping him. "I'm sorry. Please."

"Come to bed."

When she slid in beside him, she wasn't wearing anything but gooseflesh. "I'm not afraid." Her voice shook.

He pulled her into an embrace, his chin at the top of her head. At first, it felt like hugging a female scented tree trunk. Soon, her arm eased, and wrapped itself about his waist; her hummingbird heart slowed to a steadier rhythm.

He skimmed his hand along the side of her face, up over her ear, over and over, always avoiding the neck. Her breasts caressed his chest, but the nipples weren't hard. He was, though. He hadn't had a woman since he returned to town, first simply to make sure he was still clean, later because he spent himself on his work. Perhaps his cock had had something to do with this sudden interest in securing a bride.

She didn't flinch as his hand dropped to the rounded corner of her shoulder, but she did pull away. That frightened look was in her eyes, like a cat unsure if you are going to stroke it or strike it. But her mouth was firm and practical. He wondered if he could kiss it soft again.

She clamped her jaw shut and rolled onto her back. "I'm ready."

"For what?"

"It might be better to do it quickly." Before the screaming started, she didn't need to say.

Her eyes big and water-bright, her mouth a straight line, she looked as terrified and as brave as a sailor facing his first gale wind.

"So you are a virgin." He traced her brow.

Fear forgotten, she glared up at him.

"Forgive me." He kissed the line he'd traced. "But I've never seen a naked woman in bed less ready." He couldn't take her like this, no matter how hard his body ached for it.

"When, then?"

"Tomorrow, or tomorrow, or tomorrow. No rush, Em. We have our whole lives together." He pushed on her shoulder, and she rolled onto her side, like the night before. He slid his arms around her middle, under the soft weight of her undertouched breasts, and pulled her close.

"I like this." She sighed into him, wriggling her buttocks deeper into his groin.

"Me too," he said, lying only by omission.

"I like Maddie. Not Em."

"Maddie, then."

He'd nearly nodded off when she spoke again. "We're a family, aren't we?"

He wasn't sure what she was asking. "We make up a household, yes."

"I had a family, once. Father, mother, brother, me. Like your family."

"I should hope not." She stopped cold. Nash felt his shame wash over him. Here she was talking fondly of her dead family, when he only pretended to want his dead. "Do you miss them?"

"Every day. But I don't remember them. I wasn't yet four when they all died. I'm haunted by ghosts of memories."

"Shhh. Why tell me this now?" His eyelids were so heavy. He blinked hard to stay with her.

"I want to find my family. My real family."

That woke him up.

She sighed. "My father must be alive. Richard Moore, Seventeen seventy-seven, but no date of death. He might be in this town, tonight."

This was a bad idea, but Nash couldn't quite put his finger on why. He sighed into her honeysuckle hair. "Let's talk about it tomorrow."

She quieted, and quickly fell asleep. He felt he'd dodged a bullet that he hadn't known to watch out for.

Perhaps she would forget by tomorrow. He would make her forget. He had an entire warehouse with which to distract her.

SIXTEEN

The warehouse, just off the newly widened Market Street, resembled nothing more than a defunct opera house. More than four stories high, its front had once been a warren of windows. Now the window frames held dingy canvas tarps, giving the impression the building was a sleeping spider.

"Had to cover the panes to avoid the window tax." Nash handed her out of the hack coach to the neatly swept courtyard. "Boards would have been cheaper; we have to wash the canvas every few months. But the fabric lets in some light, at least. Some of the rooms would be caves without it."

A handful of people, most carrying bolts of cloth, were making their way to the front of the building, marked *Quinn & Sons* in four-inch-high letters. He saw her staring at the sign. "It read *Brown & Sons*, and I was too cheap to paint over the whole sign."

"Or optimistic. These are all your workers?" Both the men

and the women dressed in simple cloth, their clogs clacking on the cobbles as they walked.

"So to speak. They are hand-laborers, spinners and weavers. They do their work at home, in Middleton, Ashton, and Oldham. They bring in finished work and take the raw materials, cottons and some silks, home to finish."

"It was weavers you came to trade with yesterday."

"This crew must not be going to the meeting."

Maddie wanted to hold his hand, but held back. Just to be allowed to see the warehouse was a treat, Mrs. Willis had told her. The housekeeper herself had only been once, at Christmastide, and that was only to hand out gifts of food.

The courtyard looked quiet enough, but when they walked around to the side, she saw a line of horses and carts and young men darting to and fro.

"These are come to deliver Saturday's orders. Customers come in a few hours, order their goods, and by the time the carts return, they are loaded up again. On a good day, we finish with less inventory than we started with."

"Do you ever run out?"

"Better to run out than sit on an inventory from quarter to quarter. Although there's not much one can do when the winter-weight fabric doesn't arrive till spring, or a packet of intricate buttons during a workers' strike."

"There is no strike yet."

"Just the threat is enough to stop a manufactory from buying. They can always pick it up at the last moment."

"Unless you are out."

"Right. Then they are shut down again, and blame me."

Men carrying oversized bales of tightly packed cotton made a steady stream out the barn-wide doors. Nash directed Maddie to a smaller door to the side.

They entered a wide, deep, open space, bathed in brackish light from the canvassed windows. Wooden crates taller than she was lined the far wall, with those of assorted sizes marching toward the front.

"We keep the most perishable items closest to the doors, and the most popular."

"What is moving today?"

"New cotton from Virginia. Many of the manufactories want the cotton already spun, so I've had to engage the work of spinners. The spinning machines aren't dependable."

They skirted around the crates back toward the front of the building. Nash must have a dozen people working for him.

"You are a large merchant?"

He turned back to wink at her. She blushed at the double entendre.

"Just a supplier, but I'm the largest in town, by volume. The manufactories are king, though. I'm but a prince."

Up the stairs at the corner, and they were on a balcony that ran the length of the warehouse. The wooden rails were swept clean.

They paused in its center. Nash leaned his elbows on the railing. Maddie gripped it with both hands.

"Afraid of heights?"

"Prudent is all."

A man passed behind them, carrying jars of some sort. "We keep small batches, oils and perfumes, up here. Careful, man," he called out. "You're spilling some."

"You carry oils and perfumes?"

"Very little. Overseas trades often are uneven, and rather than cash or receipts, which aren't easy to exchange, the difference is made up in other items. Once I received a family of monkeys."

"They were part of the trade?"

"One was; it was caged. The others were a surprise. Perhaps a family that didn't care to be separated."

"What did you do?"

"I gave them to the London zoo."

"You sold them, you mean."

"Gave. And they inveigled a donation from me for their upkeep, as well."

"A merchant with a soft spot?"

"Don't let it get around."

As the lean man passed by again, Nash stopped him to ask about the oils.

"Mebbe hairline crack. Checking t'others."

They followed him into a small room lined with shelves of coarsely hewn planking. Strong scents fought for dominance of the air; cinnamon seemed to be winning. The floor under the set of urns was slick. Nash found the culprit, a jar on the top shelf, and handed it to his man. "Olive oil. And good, too. Take it down and see if we have another pot for it."

He hoisted it onto his shoulder and turned to go.

"Hold the handrail," Maddie couldn't help but exclaim.

Nash chuckled. "Want to smell the perfumes?" He led her across the way to a shelf of mismatched glittery vases and pitchers. "None carries much value."

She reached for a deep emerald jar, like one she'd pictured with reading the Arabian Nights. "Are they all perfumes?"

"And potions, and magical creams. We don't usually sell them, although some do go to perfumeries. I mainly use them for gifts."

"You give a lot of gifts?"

"To customs agents, merchants' wives, magistrate's daughters. They buy me a bit of goodwill in a country where businessmen who trade overseas are looked at askance."

Before Maddie could ask more, they heard a breaking like crockery, then a shout and a sickening thud.

"Man overboard." Nash ran toward the door. Maddie followed, but crashed, softly, into his back at the doorway.

"Stay still. The walk is slick."

"Where is your man?"

"Fell. I'm going to go the other way. You stay here."

He turned and ran to the other corner of the building, taking the stairs two at a time. Eyes on the boards, Maddie stepped onto the walk, reaching for the rail and gripping it hard before she looked over.

The image swam before her eyes, then she swallowed her vertigo and the edges sharpened. The man lay on the floor, his eyes closed, face drawn up in pain. One of his legs was bent the wrong way, and the white of bone peeked through a tear in his pants.

Maddie's vision blurred again, but she forced herself to be strong. Nash and another, older man had reached the porter. Nash patted down the man's arms and good leg, and then touched the broken one on the thigh. The man's soft groan echoed through the warehouse. All other activity had stopped.

The gray-haired man stood and turned so fast he almost dislodged his spectacles. Nash looked up and called for water.

He bathed the man's face, and then started talking to him in a matter-of-fact tone.

She couldn't hear the words, but his voice seemed to carry a dull magic. The porter's moans grew softer, his eyes fluttered closed. Two men carried up a folding cot. Nash hoisted the lanky porter, who though thin must weigh ten stone, as if he were nothing, setting him gently on the cot.

Not two minutes later, the spectacled man returned, with steaming water and cloths, and a doctor. Maddie strained to hear him. She followed Nash's path down the stairs, though far more slowly and carefully, and was soon at the scene.

The doctor stood, his handlebar mustaches drooping. "Have to amputate."

Nash crossed his arms belligerently. "There's little chance of gangrene. Why don't we set it first and see what occurs?"

"Longer course of treatment, and it still may not work. You'll pay for the upkeep?"

Nash nodded yes. Maddie hated that medical care was always a question of who would pay.

"Then find me two sturdy pipes and binding cloth."

Nash nodded, and his men scurried to search out the tools. He saw Maddie by the couch and scowled, but didn't say anything.

He did take her arm, though, and none too politely. "You know what to do, doctor? Splinting, not amputation."

"As you say."

Leaving him to it, Nash pushed Maddie under the walkway and through a door into an office, and then kicked the door shut.

She spoke first. "Why didn't you listen to the doctor?"

"Why didn't you listen to me, when I told you to stay put?"

Maddie huffed. "You don't always know what's right." She hadn't hurt anything or interrupted anyone.

"But I am the master here. In the warehouse, you do as I say. Understand?"

His eyes were stern, mouth set hard. He was serious, Maddie realized. He wasn't just playing the merchant while his men ran the business, as Deacon had told her.

"Understood," she whispered.

He pushed out a breath and released her arm. She rubbed it absently.

He touched her hand. "Sorry if I bruised you."

"I'm not that fragile," she shot back.

"Right. About the doctor, his answer to nearly every ailment is amputation. I think he would have had my head off last winter when I had the cold, if it wouldn't have killed me. And losing a limb is just about as fatal, for a man who earns his living as a porter."

"Why does it cost more?"

"The physician will need to return, and there are more supplies to purchase. But the end result can be far better."

He set his hands on his hips. "That railing was supposed to hold. Jem must have had oil on his hands, so when he grabbed for the rail, he slipped under." He sighed, running a hand through his hair. "At least we didn't lose him."

"You know the names of all your workers?"

"I try. I can't pay top wage, but I try to treat my men fairly. Jem took a pay cut to work for me. He said it was worth it to know he was guaranteed work at least forty weeks a year, and to be treated like a man."

"Will you pay for his care?"

"Aye. Once he can maneuver again, I'll set him to work in the office until he returns to full strength. I'm lucky, for he can read and cipher a bit. Unlucky for you, though."

"Why?"

"I was thinking of offering that bit of work to you. You said you wanted something to do."

"Wouldn't that hurt your reputation? In Society, I mean?

He tilted his head, considering her. She liked the way his hair swung over his eye. "I thought you wanted to be a useful wife. Not just ornamental."

"I do."

"Then who cares what Society thinks? You're a wife helping her husband. What is more natural than that?"

Maddie looked about the office, a counter and two stand-up desks with tall stools, a window with a view of the courtyard. She could be here with him? Wanting shimmered from her belly, rising to her throat.

She swallowed it back down. She would never want to take the food from a working man. "Does Jem have family?"

"A wife and two babes. Perkins is going to collect her and prepare the house for the invalid. It's bad news, but it could have been worse."

The spectacled bookkeeper had returned. "The wife is weepy but ready. Did we lose much inventory?"

"Damn the inventory. Sorry, man," Nash put a hand on his shoulder. "Perkins here is supposed to ask that sort of question. No, just a pot or two of olive oil."

"At an hundred pounds a pot."

"What is it, compared to a man?"

"Depends on the man." Mr. Perkins's face creased into a grin.

"For Jem, threescore pots of oil." Nash said, matching his grin.

For the next few hours, Maddie sat in the corner watching as Nash and his bookkeeper sorted out the bills and charges. This part was both familiar and strange. At the girls' school, she'd had the books to herself. Here they seemed to need to talk about the transactions. She ached to be the one Nash had to talk to.

She remained within the office as Nash went out to treat with the merchants arriving to buy his bales and bolts and jars.

He seemed to be friendly with everyone, from the driver coming to pick up a missed box to the owner of the biggest manufactory, a Mr. Malbanks. Through the open doors, Maddie watched a slice of life she had never seen before. It was a man's world. The only other woman she saw inside the warehouse was the cook who had brought the bandages for Jem.

Too soon, Nash declared it was time for luncheon. "Sales are done. When we return, we'll package the items for tomorrow, deliver the ones for today, and call it a day."

"How often do you get a shipment in?"

"Every day, small shipments. A big one once or twice a month, depending on the seas and the speed of trade in Liverpool."

They left by way of the front door, avoiding the horses and hubbub. "Thank you for showing me this."

"I'm sorry you had to see Jem's fall. We haven't had such an accident before. The last thing I need is a reputation for careless-ness and danger."

They walked home, which Maddie discovered was less than

fifteen minutes from the warehouse. The hack ride had taken nearly that long. "Why didn't we walk this morning?"

"I wasn't sure you could take such strenuous activity." She cast a sidelong glance at him. He shrugged. "We don't know much about each other, do we?"

"I know I could do what Mr. Perkins was doing," she ventured. "And that he would rather be at the castle. Where Mrs. Perkins is."

"You know all that?" He took her arm, protecting her from a less-than-cautious curricle.

"Take me on as a test. If I pass Mr. Perkins's muster, would you consider it?" She held her breath.

"A wife in trade? Heywood's lady might think less of you. Then again, she might not." He rubbed his upper lip with a knuckle. "Why not?" He held out a hand for her to shake, all official. "Welcome aboard."

Despite the growing overcast of the day and the usual dingy air, in Maddie's vision, there were sunbeams.

SEVENTEEN

Over the next few days, they started to build a steady pattern to their lives. While Nash rose at cock-crow, Maddie slept another hour, her eyes protected from morning's light by the loosely tied bed curtain. At mid-morning, she joined him at the warehouse, easily stepping into Mr. Perkins's shoes. The man already was talking about returning to the castle by Pentecost.

For Maddie, the bustle of the warehouse, as seen through the open office door, wasn't so different from the humming of a well-run school. She knew she should soon be forced to cut her afternoons short to start paying her afternoon social calls, but as she had no society to speak of, she hadn't started doing it yet. That would change tonight, when she attended her first formal supper in town, hosted by the Heywoods.

The hack carried them on a roundabout route. Market Street and Deansgate bustled even at night, rows of small theaters and halls brightly lit. Most of the houses, though, were two-storey or three-storey, similar to theirs. They turned a corner, and she saw a stretch of homes palatial in comparison.

"Mosley Street. Many of the manufactory men, mill owners, and advocates have homes here. The richest also have home farms outside town."

"The magistrates, as well."

"No. None live in town."

"Will we ever live here?"

"Do you wish it?"

Her first impulse was to say yes. Who wouldn't want to look out the window to a lovely park across the way and another mansion beside it? But she paused. "What would I give in exchange?"

"Freedom, for one. This is a closed society, even more than a girls' school. Flexibility is the other. If I wish to gamble on a ship from the Indies, but I know I have the weight of a household such as these, I'd think again. That is, were I a rational man of business."

The houses, with their manicured lawns and large-paned windows, seemed to wink at her. How hard could it be to gain one?

"How do these men do it?"

"A few, like Heywood here, married money and use the wife's portion to run the household. I used your dowry to seed the Netherlands deal. It wouldn't have brought much more than the outbuildings on this property, though."

"The others earned their places?"

"The majority fell in love with the pomp and circumstance. Their homes are the spoils of mercantile wars."

"So long as they are happy at home."

Nash laughed. "You're right to sound doubtful. One of them told me he must keep a large property simply to be able to avoid his wife in its halls."

He sobered as they stepped up the stair to the door of the middle house in the row. "That is also why some of them are so dead set against any of the workers' demands. Any slice taken out of their pie puts them at risk."

"And you?"

"I can withstand most troubles, I believe. Anything that lasts more than a month or two would set me back."

The largesse of the exterior was matched by the interior, with its vaulted entry hall and candles in sconces that it would take a ladder to reach. The underbutler had an underbutler, both in the multilayered uniform better suited to a duke's residence. But their shoes were wrong, not dainty slip-ons but sturdy heeled shoes.

"Nash, darling, we had all but given up on you." A pretty woman with upswept hair and a voluminous carat-folded gown called down to them from the balcony. Twin sets of stairs wound up from the edges of the hall to meet in a rounded balcony.

Nash followed Maddie up the stair. She slowed at the top, and he stepped easily to stand beside her at the top.

"Mrs. Heywood, allow me to present my lady wife, Madeline."

Maddie dropped into a curtsy, and then raised her eyes. Mrs. Heywood had her arm out, as if she had expected to shake hands. Maddie wavered, then mid-bend, stuck her own hand out. The woman took it, smiling as she pulled Maddie gently back up.

"We're nowhere near so formal as all that. And we are so louche as to drink ale with our cheese course."

"I hear the Duke of Bedford does the same. Perhaps you set the trend."

Mrs. Heywood patted her arm. "Nonsense, love. We are safely a step behind. Let the tall men like your husband blaze the trail. Those buttons are lovely. I see he's already made a merchant's manikin of you." She winked.

Mrs. Heywood crinkled as she led her into a sitting room drenched in yellows. "Like my crinoline? My William has a stake in the manufactory that makes all the lady's drawers for miles around."

"But he only ever wants to get in yours." A hatchet-faced woman rose to greet them. "I can see why, with all the folderol the young misses think of to talk about."

"Mrs. Quinn, this is Mother Blayney, my parent. Mother, Mrs. Madeline Quinn." Maddie didn't know whether to curtsey or hold out her hand, so she did nothing. Apparently that was what the lady expected, for she continued without censuring Maddie.

"Your maiden name was Wetherby, if I am not mistaken."

"Yes." Maddie paused, and the lady's gray feathered brows shot up. She knew she should say more, but what? Yes, but they weren't my parents? Yes, they were my adoptive parents?

Mrs. Heywood stepped in. "Such a tragedy. I mean, to lose both parents at once like that, and a brother. You must have been heartbroken."

"It did change my life."

"And Ellspeth's. Let us hope this trip to London sets her straight. An earl! The presumption."

"To be sure." Mrs. Blayney scowled. Maddie reflected for the first time how fortunate she was that Nash's mother was neither harpie nor virago, and how perhaps her having no living relations might be seen as an advantage to a prospective husband. Perhaps that's what sold him on her.

"Look about you, Mrs. Quinn. Do you catch my meaning?" Mrs. Heywood waved her hand, gilded by a white gold bracelet. "There is Mr. Malbanks, whose cravat is the finest Mancunian lace, and his coat a coarse but more expensive weave. Mrs. Clayton, there, shows on her sleeves and that lovely front panel the best Mr. Clayton's mill workers can do. As for me and Mother Blayney, it's crinolines and leathers."

"Your boots are gorgeous. Such a rich color." Maddie had never seen boots dyed to match an evening dress.

"My father's shop, rest his soul. Blayneys are boot makers to royalty. You must allow my brother to make you a pair. He measures your foot in six places."

Mother Blayney harrumphed. Now Maddie could see the odd thick ribbon trimming her dress was superfine strips of leather. "You, Mrs. Quinn, had the good fortune to marry a man who trades in all goods. You'll never grow tired of just wearing leather."

"Nor find yourself unable to sit because the style is to over-starch one's crinoline."

Maddie held out her arms. "Today it's buttons." She plucked at the pearled ornaments running along the underside of her lower arms.

"They make the sleeve look the part of a fancy lady's glove. You might start a trend."

"I believe that's the idea." She was glad she'd talked Mrs.

Willis out of sewing them up the back of the dress. Not only would they have competed with the laces, but she would have had to turn her back on everyone to show them to advantage.

"Your new husband also makes a handsome manikin."

Maddie followed her hostess's gaze to the knot of men beside the tall front windows, and caught her breath. Nash had looked well in the simple dark suit he wore for their wedding, but in his dinner finery he shone. His smart midnight blue jacket, and a lighter blue vest, complemented her dress. The crisp white of his shirt and deceptively simple cravat offset the dark browns of his already curling hair and steamed brown of his eyes. His dark trousers slid into a pair of what must be Blayney short boots.

"Lucky woman," her hostess breathed. Then, at a signal from a servant, she clapped her hands to call them all to supper.

They did not follow any precedence Maddie understood on their way into the dining room. What was the proper precedence here?

Everyone talked across the table, and Mother Blayney seemed to talk down to everyone equally. Maddie felt the loosening of proper society's strictures as a form of freedom. When the conversation turned to business and politics, she listened attentively rather than making small talk with quiet Mrs. Clayton. Mr. Clayton noticed her attention, and turned to her, his spectacles sparkling in the good candlelight.

"So, Mrs. Quinn," He twirled one of his moustaches. "What do you think of our Manchester?" Maddie weighed her words.

"I have seen only a little, but I do rather like it. It does seem odd that Mr. Quinn must cover the windows of his warehouse, though."

Clayton laughed, hiding his mouth with his hand. "Don't get me started on the follies of London, ma'am."

"London?"

"We are the biggest manufacturing city in the nation, but have no direct representation in Parliament. So we must solve our troubles on our own, with our hands tied behind our backs. Inane machinations and unreasonable taxation are inflicted upon us by Government and Commons alike. Taxing a man's windowpanes! Incredible."

"Come now, Clayton." Mr. Heywood signaled for the next course. "We all support the Government here."

"To be sure. But who speaks for our interests? And don't men of business always shoulder the blame for all manner of ills, from childhood deaths to bad water?"

Mr. Malbanks set his fork down and cleared his throat. The shortest man, and the finest dressed, he seemed to command their attention at will. "They blame manufactories for the smoke in the air, when everyone cooks with coal. And the measures to prevent it only succeed in making criminals of all the owners. No one can follow the law, or he'd be out of business in a month. And now we must work in the dark, or pay a tax on the sun."

"Is that why the workers must see their pay cut?" Maddie's skin goose-bumped as the air in the room seemed to ice over. She wished she could take the words back. One did not speak of cutting pay, but reducing costs.

Before she could incinerate in mortification, Nash spoke. "The problem isn't capital, it's trust. Government and manufactories. Merchant, master, and man. How does one build trust where none exists? It's hard enough man to man. Between classes of men, it's nigh impossible."

Clayton nodded. "Yet it must be done, or we'll all sink. These are hard times."

"I'll not sink, and I thank you to leave my men out of this." Malbanks took a moment to drink from his wine glass. At the fourth course and on at least his fifth glass of the stuff, his cheeks blotched tomato. Maddie hoped the Heywoods had not adopted the society habit of offering a full ten courses.

Clayton pounded him on the back as if he were choking. "Think you're safe from the strike? Yours is the only trades group that has even set it to vote."

"To vote, as if they were deserving of suffrage." Malbanks rolled his eyes. "*Habeas corpus* was reinstated. More than they deserve."

Maddie frowned. Clayton leaned closer to her, his moustaches dancing. "Means the government cannot hold a man as long as it likes without trial. Suspended this winter, that and the meetings act stopped both workers and owners from gathering in groups larger than us at this table. The Government feared the mob, as if English peasant stock were no better than the French. Nothing came of it, nothing but the odd riot foisted on those soft-minded weavers who fell for Oliver the Spy."

Nash nodded. "If the crown had not planted the spy, it wouldn't have had its foment, its blanketeers, its cries of revolution. A more cynical man might call it a presumptive attack."

"Prevention is nine-tenths of the law," Clayton quipped.

"Radicalism is treason in disguise, whatever shape it appears in." Malbanks nearly slammed his glass down. "If we cut it down as the snake is a'borning, we need not fight it when it's a full-grown adder."

Mrs. Heywood tapped her own glass, a bell. "Peace, Mr. Malbanks. You'll spoil our taste for the next course, and Cook is rightly proud of her eel pie."

Maddie didn't feel as out of place as she had feared. If these *nouveaux riches* liked to behave beyond their station on the social ladder, why not? These people lacked for nothing. Their want was not intellect, energy, or even education. It was only standing, under the feudal system of government they had all inherited. And if they did rattle on about commerce, who could blame them? It made for interesting conversation.

After dinner, the men did not leave the ladies for long. Soon, it was time to take their leave.

"We married men can't stay out too late," confided Mr. Heywood in a loud voice to Maddie.

Mrs. Heywood took the bait. "Married to the manufactory, more like. That's why you need rise so early."

"I thought you liked my rising early, Mrs. Heywood."

"It's whether you can stay up all day that's the question."

Maddie tucked her arm into Nash's; the Heywood's ribald laughter followed them down the stairs and onto the street.

"I like your friends."

"They will make a good start for you."

They found a hack immediately, and were soon home and washing for bed. This part of the day was becoming a comfortable habit, as well. Maddie washed her face, neck, front, back, arm, arm, midriff area, leg, leg, feet, and hands. The well-choreographed routine took about ten minutes.

Nash spent the last five sitting up in the bed watching her.

"Did you not wash this morning?"

"I get dirty during the day."

"How? You barely go outside." He pushed down the sheet so she could get in. She slid on her backside and down before he could grab her. He slid down to meet her.

He kissed behind her ear, then lower, near her neck. She sighed into him.

"You're tired."

Her spine stiffened. Did he want more? He should. Could she give it to him this time? What if she couldn't? How could she call herself wife, if she denied him his rights as husband? Mrs. Heywood kept her husband happy, all too obviously. Could they tell that she was failing at this?

He blew warm air down her neck, tickling the tiny hairs and easing her thoughts. "I'm not complaining. I'm a bit tired, too. And I like to hold you like this."

She sighed, snuggling deeper into him. A living blanket, his warmth stirred peace into her skin.

"I don't know why you are afraid of me, Maddie, afraid of what we might do in this bed. It is wonderful, nothing at all to fear. But we will wait until you feel it's right." He chuckled. "For my sake, though, don't let it be too long."

EIGHTEEN

Not everything in Manchester was new plate and flash. The church that guarded Maddie's mother was a vertical gothic structure, stone walls and razor spires. Protected by a wrought-iron fence and a small lawn of headstones, it looked out of place, as if the bustle of town had surprised it sleeping.

Maddie went through the gate and took the roundabout path, lazily twining through the graveyard. Nash didn't know about these regular visits, on her way to the warehouse. He turned cool whenever she spoke of her first family. She couldn't help herself, though. She had decades of proper daughtering to catch up on.

The church clock read five of ten; already she was late to the warehouse, and she'd do anything not to lose that position. She loved working with numbers, but it felt so much better doing it for him. Even when the figures showed ill for the day, he smiled when she served them up to him. She was the prettiest bookkeeper he'd ever had, he'd say for the dozenth time, and still it would set her insides glowing.

She carried that glow through their genial walks home, as they read each other parts of the day's papers, as they went to bed and he continued his gentle lessons in the mysteries of their bodies. Far and away, the best was the sleeping. Most nights now she slept without those awful dreams, and without waking. Something about Nash set her soul at rest.

It couldn't be his body, all strong lines and sharp angles. Nor the musk of his arousal. Perhaps it was the sound of him, his regular breathing, the soft murmurs he made when she started to wake, shifting position in the night. She prayed she kept him half as content.

The path took her to her mother's grave from the back. Maddie touched the curved headstone, sending a prayer to heaven for her mother's soul, and for the souls of the Wetherbys, her families forever tangled in memory. It wasn't until she'd raised her eyes again that she saw the flowers.

Three daisies and two ferns, tied with string, at the foot of the front of the stone. Maddie nearly dropped her own small bouquet, a half-dozen lilies.

Somebody had been here. On purpose, to visit this grave, this one alone. She saw no other posies near any other marker. Could it be a friend who remembered Mary Moore's birthday? Maddie had no idea what day her mother had been born. Was it a child playing a game, choosing a pretend lover to mourn? She never saw children in this garden.

Or could it be her father, truly, who still mourned his wife, taken from him too soon?

Maddie swayed on her feet, dizzy with imagination. She

scanned the yard again, but she was still the only living soul. The flowers had wilted, as if they had been left yesterday. It had been a working-man's holiday; perhaps that's why he had time to come. He might want to visit every day, as she did, but was prevented by work. If he was a worker, that is.

Mr. Heywood would not tell her of her father, saying that no contact was the terms of the adoption agreement he had signed. She had signed no such agreement; she never would agree to such a thing. She could contact him.

Once the idea came to the front of her mind, it grabbed her with talons. He might come back. She would need to change the timing of her visits, to see if he came at different hours. She would alter her habit of taking walks at mid-day, and take them throughout the day instead. But Nash would notice that, and Mrs. Willis would worry.

Perhaps she could hire a boy to stalk the graveyard. But what boy would wish to do that? Nonsense, she scolded herself, she had no proof he came regularly. She should learn the workers' calendar and plan her visits around that timetable.

The ground-thrumming of the morning bells made her jump. Ten o'clock already, so late she would need an explanation. She'd need to work hard to hold *I've found my father! He lives!* behind her lips.

She laid her bouquet behind the smaller one, nesting like spoons. As she hurried down the straight path she thought her lungs would burst, or her heart. She had never felt so happy.

Something good would come of this. Something wonderful.

It must.

THE STARR INN did not improve on acquaintance. Nash inhaled the bitter foam of his ale to mask the sour-mash odor of the place. He should be at the warehouse, where Maddie was, not jawboning again with these special-committee blowhards. Nothing had changed but their tempers.

"We need martial law," Malbanks declared. "After Oldham and Stockport, there can be no doubt we have revolt on our hands."

"Nonsense." Nash set his ale down on the mightily scored trestle, trying not to inhale too deeply. "Peaceful marches, both. A day of speechifying and no mayhem—unless you count our volunteer constables."

"They were right to take offense at talk of sedition."

"Again, there was no loss of life or property." Clayton took off his glasses to clean them on a none-too-clean handkerchief. "Even the letters from London say watch and wait. If London does not fear imminent revolt, why should we?"

"London is days away," Malbanks said. "The battleground is here."

"There's been no violence here, despite the talks of strike, and the hungry men," Clayton said, resetting his spectacles.

Heywood held up a hand. "Malbanks, you are close to the constables. Do Nadin and his crew see trouble brewing?"

"Not directly." The man looked angry at his admission.

"Not at all, you mean." Nash tried to tamp down his own anger. Why had they all been called in just to argue this point yet again?

"No, there is some evidence." Malbanks pursed his lips, as if having to explain himself left a bad taste in his mouth. "Many of the villages have trimmed the size of their rushcart parades, siphoning money and attention to flags and carts for these public meetings."

"I would think you'd approve of that," Nash said. "Fewer drunken bumpkins on carts on Sundays." While the purpose of the rushcart parades was to bring clean rushes to line the floors of parish churches, they also included a weeklong pageant of revelry that could get out of hand.

"Instead they preach sedition at one another. Scarcely an improvement. And Nadin says they are far better organized than back in Seventeen."

Clayton rubbed at his spectacles with a finger. "And how does our chief constable know that?" Malbanks's glare sliced through the grime on Clayton's glasses, and the other man flinched.

"The question is a good one." Nash easily countered the man's grimace with one of his own. Their gazes locked with a near-audible click. Malbanks looked away, back to Clayton.

"The meetings are public, and these so-called reformers let anyone listen."

"Even our spies? Brave men, after Seventeen." Clayton patted Nash's hand. "You were at sea then, but those poor reformist souls stood no chance. The crown knew their every step, and swept them up and off to prison like leaves."

Nash never took his gaze from Malbanks. "I heard that most of the brouhaha was fomented by the spies themselves."

Malbanks shrugged. "What if it was? They would have done it anyway; we just set it up that they did it on our schedule."

"Gentlemanly of you."

Malbanks returned Nash's glare with new ferocity. "This

radicalism is no mewling cry for reform. It's a cloak for conspiracy and rebellion, and we must stamp it out."

"To be sure." Heywood's soothing tone acted as a balm, easing them all back into their chairs. Malbanks even took a sip of his claret as Heywood carried on speaking. "It is telling, though, that there has been no voice of rebellion in these meetings. That is unlike Eighteen seventeen."

Malbanks choked the wine down. "It merely means these rebels learned their lesson. They've gone further underground."

Nash had had enough. "So having no proof of rebellion is now proof of rebellion? Your evidence of conspiracy is a complete lack of evidence?"

Malbanks pressed his fine lips tight. His man, Trefford, spoke up. "They outsmart us, is all."

"Unschooled weavers and spinners, outsmarting the cream of Lancashire? It's laughable on its face."

Heywood rapped the table. "Enough. I do not see agreement at this table to declare martial law. We'll meet again next week. I hear there is to be another meeting in your town, Trefford. Perhaps you will have a clearer reading for us then."

Malbanks pushed to his feet, a bantam used to outpunching his weight class. "The longer we dawdle, the more the danger builds. I might point out to you, Mr. Quinn, that with this new consortium scheme of yours, any delay at all would sink you." He strutted out of the room.

Heywood leaned back in his chair. "You took that round, boy. But the spread is growing tighter. Watch that you don't drop your guard."

MADDIE LIKED WORKING with Jem Smith. The warehouseman's leg was much improved, though he still needed the crutches to walk. To appease Lord Shaftsbury and please Mrs. Perkins, Nash had sent Perkins back to Shaftsbury Castle, leaving Maddie to manage the bulk of the office bookkeeping, with Mr. Smith standing in on those afternoons she paid her social visits. His hand was as neat as hers on the ledger lines, a relief from Perkins's hen-scratches.

With Nash out at another committee meeting, Mr. Smith was back in the warehouse proper, overseeing the loading and unloading. His time in the office had shown her husband Mr. Smith's qualities. She hoped Nash would make the warehouseman his second in name as well as deed. With another skilled overseer to hand, he might allow himself a day off.

Maddie needed less than a week to comprehend the general operation of the warehouse. An astounding amount of materials came in and went out, and very little was retained as profit. The intricate balance between suppliers and customers was difficult to maintain, especially as the stock was so changeable. She didn't know how Nash managed smiling at men who would badmouth your product just to buy it for a few pence less.

He was a natural salesman though, able to talk with anyone. He couldn't have learned it at the castle, or even aboard ship. Perhaps he was just born with it. She wondered what she had just been born with. Certainly not the gift of conversation. Those social calls were draining. Nor a love for figures, despite her fondness for them now. Perhaps her imagination, though it, too, brought her little profit.

She caught herself dawdling, staring moonstruck out the small-paned window. He was late. The shadows halved the courtyard. If he did not come soon, she would need to call Mr. Smith to take the receipts to the banking-house. Nash never liked to keep much paper overnight, saying if they were known as a cash-poor 'house no one would think to rob them. He had a man in overnight, to guard the contents. And, of course, he paid the constables the donation they expected to keep a sharp eye out.

Finally, she saw him striding across the yard. A loader ran out to meet him, agitation in his step. He nodded and followed the man toward the side entrance, but remembered to look for her at the window and wave. She turned back to her little counting-desk, smiling. He'd want the receipts soon enough.

She didn't look up immediately as the door opened, its tiny bell ringing. It wasn't Nash, though, but someone with a cough so painful the sound of it pinched her lungs. A young man, grizzled before his time, and spitting into a filthy rag.

"Spare a cuppa water fer'n old man?"

He wasn't old, but there was no doubt he needed the water. She poured him a glass from the pitcher at the sideboard and walked to the front to hand it to him.

He grabbed her by the wrist, spilling the drink. "No screams, clear? Where is your blunt?"

"At the bank."

"Not seen him left yet."

Maddie flicked her wrist hard, fingernails talons as she turned. He let go her arm with a yelp.

"No need for that, miss."

"Get out." She stepped away from him. He pulled a knife out. The flash of its blade mesmerized, the thought of its power scared her. The man might be scrawny and sick, and smell of an ash heap, but he could still cut her bloody.

"Not without the blunt."

Panic raced her heart, and sense fled. But anger remained. She would not be pushed about so, and by a stranger whose breaths were shorter than her own.

"You know so much, you find it. You know so much, then you know you haven't seen me before. I don't know where the strongbox is."

"But thee know it's a strongbox. Give it me."

Never. Nash would be livid, and he wouldn't let her help him anymore. What was a small cut compared with spending the rest of her years shut out of his life? "Follow me, then."

"Tell me where it is, and you can run out the back." He was softening to her, or at least didn't want to cut her if he didn't have to. As coughs racked his chest, he brought both the knife and his grimy cloth to his mouth.

"But that's where it is, in the back. He keeps it where he can see it, he does."

"No good for the clerks."

"We don't handle much coin here. Mostly receipts." They paid out more in coin, to drivers and delivery men, than they took in. Were he clever, the man would have known that the time to hold up Nash was on the way back from the bank in the morning.

Although he did seem to know that the time to hold up Nash himself was never. His feverish gaze flicked from her to the back door, to the front door again.

"Do you wish me to lock the front? So no one disturbs us?"

"Aye. Bonny day." He dropped the point on the knife, and

she slipped past. The tumbrels in the lock clicked, and she pocketed the key.

"It's just beside the door." She gestured behind him, as if she wanted him to go ahead of her.

"You first."

She slid by him as far away as she dared. As she neared the inner door, she started to run. She slammed the door shut and began to scream, letting loose her anger and fear in sound.

Within seconds, a half-dozen men ringed her, with Nash panting up behind.

"There's a man inside wanted to take your money."

"He threatened you?" Nash's voice was ground glass, dripping menace. "You two, around to the front." They took off at a run.

"Wait." Maddie gave Nash the key.

"You took the time to lock him in?"

Maddie said nothing. They could talk about this later. She moved away from the door, gesturing that he could enter.

Nash nearly broke the hinges opening the door. Maddie saw the rail-thin thief in the center of the room, his head snapping from one doorway to the other, eyes wide.

Nash closed the door behind him.

NINETEEN

N ash could barely see the scarecrow of a man in front of him for the screen of red shading his vision. The idiot thief had his hands up already, in complete surrender. It would be unmanly to strangle him, or even to punch his face into pulp. Nash did not trust himself not to do either.

"Jem, get between me and this—this—"

Jem did as told, his hobble slowing his progress long enough for Nash to regain some of his composure. Now he wished only to rip the man's face off.

"Why did you make the lady scream?" His voice held only a quiver of anger, yet it was enough for Jem to slide closer to the scrawny criminal, as if to protect him.

"She did it of her own. You know how women are."

Nash waited. The truth often took its own time. He was rewarded less than half a minute later.

"Wasn't nothing, guv. A short blade, is all."

"You held a knife to her throat?"

"Not her throat." Another pregnant pause. "More her middle, like. She weren't afraid at all. She were quiet."

Nash's hands were so tightly fisted the nails drew blood. A low rumble started at the base of his ribs, reverberating past his heart, roaring out his mouth.

"You thought to stab my wife?"

Jem started to move toward the front door, pushing the man ahead of him with the crutch. "I know this man. Part of the union Malbanks turned out."

"Mill-breaker?"

"No, a union man. Cowper, is it?" The tone of Jem's voice had shifted. Nash pulled his gaze away from the idiot scarecrow trembling before him.

"What of it?" But the man's voice burbled, and he spit a bolt of phlegm onto his sleeve.

"This is no place to tumble, man. Quinn here isn't a man to cheat. Best you go."

"A mistake is all. Just a mistake," the scarecrow choked out. But he added, "No harm done, eh?"

"Step over here and say that." Nash looked at the floor, as if he were a bull getting ready to charge. No harm? Maddie could have been hurt. She could have been killed. The thought sent spikes through his belly. No harm? He was never letting her out of his sight again.

"Quinn." Jem's voice startled him. The man never addressed him by name. "I have this here. The lady, might she be needing your help?"

Maddie. Nash pressed his palm to his overheated forehead. She was all alone while he was thundering on about how he'd keep her safe. He was an idiot.

He turned on his heel and had a hand on the door's knob when Jem spoke again.

"Be needing the key."

He tossed it to his man, glaring so hard at the scrawny piece of thieving humanity beside him that the coward visibly wilted. Then he pushed the door open.

Maddie was there, by the wall. He barely registered the handful of men around her, just the worry on her face. He took her by the arm. "We're leaving."

"Is the man all right? You didn't harm him?"

They were all the way out into the side yard when the gist of her question registered in his overdriven mind. He pushed her toward the shade by the wall.

"Harm him? I should well have done, for his harming you."

She rubbed her arm where he'd grabbed onto her. "You are the one to draw a bruise."

With a fingertip, she wiped a bead of sweat from his brow. At her touch, his anger receded, washed away by a flush of relief mixed with pleasure. She worried over him.

Then the anger rolled back in. "He threatened you. You'll never feel safe here again."

"Nonsense." Her other hand framed the side of his face. "I may not be so eager to give glasses of water to strangers, but I cannot say I will be frightened."

"Of course you are. Women always are."

Her touch drew him closer, until they were chest to chest. She kissed him on the lips. It was the first time she had ever just chosen to kiss him, and it was sunshine sweet.

"With you as a protector, how can I fear?"

She kissed his lips again, gently. Too gently. He took the back of her neck and plunged his tongue into her mouth. The unrelieved anger still pulsing through him transformed to an aching need for her. He needed to taste her, to have her.

It was the thought of her gone missing that dug the hole in his heart when he'd heard her scream. He'd dropped everything and run. He couldn't even remember what he had been doing before her voice shot panic down his spine.

Already, Maddie had laced her way through his emotions. Who would have guessed he'd fall for his own wife? He had never needed anyone so much. Seeing her, talking with her, touching her, sleeping with her, gave shape to his days.

His hand slid down her lightly corseted back and over her non-corseted rear. She hiccupped, and then moaned into his mouth. The sound enlarged his heart—and his cock.

There was a shuffling behind him, and someone cleared his throat. Nash turned to clock the noisy bastard, and then realized he was standing in the loading area of his warehouse. A yard full of men pretended not to be watching him manhandle his wife in public. He let her loose, a little bit.

Again, Jem was the brave soul bringing him back to earth. "He's gone, and he'll not return. And his wife and child live in your debt."

He'd been acting to save his own family, but Nash was beyond caring. "Then he shouldn't have threatened mine."

Jem nodded. "Thinking you might be taking the lady-wife home. There's a cart to spare."

"There's not. We'll walk." Though Nash had to wait a moment before he was ready to present front to the world at large.

Maddie looked like she needed the time as well. Her eyes were wide and dazed, her lips luscious from his kisses. He'd damned well do more than that, but Jem was right. Better to do it at home.

&

MADDIE'S HEAD was spinning as she raced to keep up with Nash's long stride. Was he angry with her? Should she not have screamed? How could she have known he'd go rabid?

She came up beside him at a corner when they had to wait for a farrier's cart to cross. He took her hand. She had forgotten to put her gloves on, or her coat, but the rush of blood after her encounter hadn't settled, especially with this pell-mell scurry home, and she was in danger of overheating.

"You'll not be going back there." His voice was oddly low and tight. Its timbre so distracted her that she did not at first understand the meaning of his words. Then they only made her blood race faster.

"One mistake and I'm out?"

"First, Jem breaks his leg. Then, a robber threatens your life."

She tried to follow his thinking. "One didn't cause the other, and neither has anything to do with me."

"If you weren't there they wouldn't have happened."

Insufferable man. "Do you blame me for the dip in the calico trade? That happened this month, as well."

He shot a sidelong look at her. "I wouldn't put it past you. What's true on the seas must be true on land, too. Women are plain bad luck."

Maddie had never heard anything so inane, or at least not since grammar school. She said nothing, but her anger simmered for the final few minutes of their sprint.

How dare he accuse her of wrecking his business? As if women never came to the warehouse. She knew of at least two who had come to buy, and more who had come to sell, just this week. He was being irrational, and because he was a man and especially because he was her husband she must allow it. It wasn't fair, or right, or even proper. The very idea set her blood to boil.

By the time they arrived at their doorstep, she had had enough of him. Nash pulled the door open, and nearly dragged Maddie through.

She wrenched her hand from his grip, and they stood there, panting from the forced march, glaring at each other. Maddie massaged her wrist as she took stock of her husband.

He had a wild look in his eyes, which stared straight ahead, not even casually scanning the room the way he usually did. His hands were fisted, punching rather than resting on his hipbones. The front packet of his trousers was starting to bulge out.

He snatched her wrist right out of the hand that was massaging it, and started up the stairs. She heard Mrs. Willis trundling up the basement stair. "We need nothing," he called out. Maddie could say nothing, as she gasped for the breath to pump her legs fast enough to keep up.

"Dinner?" Mrs. Willis's voice followed them, surprised.

"Supper, later."

She had barely made it into their bedroom when he kicked the door shut. Her skirt, caught between the door and its frame, ripped as he pushed her back against the wall beside the door.

Maddie was through being manhandled, and put her hands on his chest to push him away. But she misjudged the strength of his movement. Her hands were crushed between their bodies.

Then his mouth demanded hers.

Her anger spent itself in dueling with his tongue. The tingling in her limbs grew from distracting to pleasurable, the skin of her fingers sensitive to the pounding of his heart.

When he let her go, it was with such force her head bumped the wall. He wrapped a hand around the spot, as if to protect it, and with gentled kisses traced the line of her jaw to her ear. Then he tucked her head in the bulk of his shoulder, gripping her tightly.

"I thought I would lose you." His whisper carried enough pain to sink the world. "How could I have put you in such danger?"

Maddie felt the anger in his muscles, and smelled the fear. He had been afraid for her, not angry at all.

He cared for her.

She smiled into the warm musk of his jacket, and slid her hands around his back, meeting at the join of his spine. She didn't want to lose him, either.

They stood still, together, in the quiet of the afternoon when everyone else was working. Maddie wanted to trap this moment, to hold it in her hand if she could, store it in her heart.

"Come to bed," she whispered.

"You're sure?"

"I need you."

He loosened his grip, and pulled the kerchief away from her neck and out of the cleft of her breasts. As the cool air touched her warm flesh, she sighed.

He lifted her arm, kissing the inside of her wrist. The pulse welcomed him with warmth. He smiled and undid the six buttons holding her sleeve, then did the same to her other sleeve.

This was slow torment.

"Who put all these buttonholes in your clothing? Dashed inconvenient." Maddie hummed in agreement and kissed his cheek. The impatience in his voice turned her senses on high. In a flash, all her skin wanted to be free, to be open to his touch. He turned her around, reaching for the buttons up the back of her dress.

"Cursed ornament," he muttered, but now he didn't seem in quite so much hurry. Each button undone, he slipped his finger under the fabric to reach for the next one. Each feather touch set another little patch of her spine on fire. She shivered happily.

He undid the last button, near the base of her spine, and pushed the sleeves of her practical cotton morning dress down to her elbows, trapping her gently in its folds. He made quick work of unlacing the half-corset, until all that was between him and her flesh was the thin cotton shift. Dispensing with his own coat and shirt, and pulled her to him, her back against his chest. Her skin rippled as it met his, her neck tilted, pleading for his kiss. He swiftly complied, one hand reaching around to embrace a breast, the other wrapped around her hip, drawing her even closer to him. She felt the hot demanding readiness of him, and the mild echo in her core raced to match his. He ministered to her breast, and then nipped at her neck, and she moaned. Everywhere was new sensation, everywhere wanted more.

He pushed her sleeves down, and then lifted her by her elbows out of the dress. She kicked away the skirt as he swung his arm down to scoop up her legs. He carried her to the bed, setting her as if she were riding the bed sidesaddle. He didn't join her there, though. Instead, he knelt and took her foot, removing the shoe, and then sliding ever so slowly up her calf, over her knee, to the edge of her stocking. Would he ever stop?

Heat pooled only inches away from his fingers. He must know it. She ached for him there. The fingers stopped, waited agonizing seconds. Then they started back down, dragging her stocking with them. She tipped over to lie on the bed. She couldn't hold back the groan.

"Want to try again?" He grinned at her as she lay sideways looking down at him. "Roll up. There's another leg."

She rolled onto her back as he slipped her other shoe off. He sat at the foot of the bed taunting her other calf, her knee, her thigh. She wouldn't fall for it this time. Still she felt every whisper of movement, every wisp of his breath. The fingers stopped, and bent around the edge of her stocking. The muscles in her hips melted.

The fingers did not go down.

Her whole body went electrically still, snare-drum tight. She felt his thumb sliding up, up, yet her stocking was also sliding down.

He had two hands.

It was too much, too much. She had to fight to keep from writhing, her breaths too fast and shallow. Would he touch her there? Would she die if he didn't?

He did, thank heavens, a gentle press of his palm through the cotton over her warm curls. She arched into him. He groaned, and took his hand away. She reached blindly for the hand, as if to put it back, but he grabbed hers instead and pushed it onto the bed. He was directly over her now, still touching only her hands. He dipped his head for a kiss, which she met and matched.

His breathing was not as fast as hers. For just a second, she was all over shy. Then she went mad to make him feel the way she felt. Slipping a hand free, she reached between them for the waist of his trousers. At her touch, he jerked his hips away, and deepened their kiss. She was not completely distracted, though, and reached again.

She had never felt this way. Out of control yet safe, dangerously powerful. She wasn't even ashamed of how much of her body she was showing him. She wanted to show him all.

His hips settled down, and she fiddled with the front placket until he reared back. "You drive me to distraction."

"I'm not left-handed. It's hard."

He had the placket open in one second and his clothes entirely off in two. "That it is."

She reached for his member, swollen for her. Just as her fingertips sensed the heat of him, though, the familiar dread crept up her arm, toward her heart. She shouldn't be doing this.

He didn't seem to notice, busy pushing her shift up to her hips. She dropped her hand to the comforter.

"May I?" His hand, resting on her hipbone, held the fabric of her shift.

"Yes." She held both arms over her head, as if she were one of the littlest girls at school waiting for the housemother to pull her shirt off. Instead, it was Nash pushing the fabric up her sides, onto her arms, and over her head. There he stopped, trapping her face in a white cotton mask. She gasped, a flash of panic. He leaned over to lick her lower lip through the fabric. He bit her lip, gently, and then kissed it, pulling off the mask, setting her breath free.

Her arms were trapped again, but she couldn't think of that now. She had to make him love her.

"Beautiful. Face to feet, inside and out. I'm so glad we waited for this."

She pulled her arms out of the shift and reached for him, for the warm touch of his reassurance. They embraced, breast to chest. Nash ran his hand down her spine. "So smooth, so perfect." He rolled her onto her back, traveling with her until he was on top of her, their bodies touching everywhere.

"So mine."

Something, the word, the feel of his cock, the throbbing of her heart, set off alarms in Maddie's head. She gasped, clenching her fingers into the fine hairs on his chest. Panic started to swell, from her hips, through her belly, warming her heart.

"Maddie?" Nash's smile faded. His hips, which had started to rock, went still.

She couldn't do this. She couldn't go all cold on Nash again. He didn't deserve it. She had to master this. Here. Now.

Or he would leave her.

She pushed her lips to smile. "Touch me. There."

"You're not ready yet." He reached down and feather-stroked her. His hand between her and his cock gave her the space to give herself a stern talking-to.

This was Nash. He wasn't going to hurt her. He couldn't. She was going to perform for him, as a good girl did. She was a good girl. Slowly she relaxed into his touch.

"Good girl," he whispered. "So lovely, see? So beautifully wet. Ready now?"

She sighed, thinking of a certain warm meadow in springtime, an image she hadn't called up in a long time. "Yes."

He touched her lips with his wet fingers. She licked them, salty sweet. "That is you. All you."

Then he replaced his fingers with his lips and tongue, and this time when his hips moved, she could move hers in matched time. She'd heard copulation was pleasurable, and it was all true. The rocking built a warm glow in her middle.

When his fingers touched her there again, she was ready, arching into them. When they slipped out again, and were replaced by his man-rod, she took herself far away into the clouds. This had been quite nice.

He didn't seem to notice her absence, growing more and more distracted, until a wave of rumbling ran through him, the rod flipping and flopping inside. Then he rolled off her, his hand on her hip.

She closed her eyes so he wouldn't see her disappointment.

She had worked so hard to make it so he wouldn't see her fear, she should rejoice in her success. Instead, she felt sad and angry, and somehow cheated.

He hadn't noticed.

They never did.

TWENTY

The shadows crept up the bed, covering first her feet, then her knees, and still Nash breathed like a metronome set at lento. Maddie didn't wish to wake him, but she couldn't stand to be in her skin one minute more. And what if he woke and saw her like this?

She rolled, dislodging the log of an arm he had draped across her waist, but he only murmured, settling deeper into the mattress. The planes across his cheekbones and jaw softened with sleep. With his eyes closed, he looked a boy, but the shading under them spoke of a man's cares. She so wanted to please him.

His shout of release had startled her. Who knew men could contort their faces so? She grinned. That complete surrender of his body, he called it "spent"—she had done that. He couldn't find fault with her now.

She pushed fully free of his arm and the sheets. Silently rolling up to her hands and knees, she stepped backwards onto the floor. Another adjustment, and the metronome started up again. The hair on his forehead fell away in that odd side parting. She wondered if he had been cut there, falling out of a tree or perhaps in a pitched battle. While Deacon's hair marched perfectly across his forehead, Nash's was a less well-trained regiment.

Her parts down there ached, shortening her steps. The lid of the chest squeaked as she pushed it up, looking for her wrap.

"Come back to bed." His voice was slow and thick.

"In a minute." She swung the wrapper around her, tying the belt loosely. She had her hand on the doorknob when he spoke again.

"Where are you going?" He sat up, eyes sharp. The sheet slid to a pool about his waist. His body was perfect, solid and strong. The scent of him drew her despite herself.

She was filthy, not fit to touch. "I just need a word with Mrs. Willis."

"Why?"

"To ask her to run the water."

"Another bath? He slid out from the covers, six feet of obviously virile male. "What was last night?"

Why didn't he understand? She was dirty, she must wash immediately. There was nothing to explain. She shrugged, praying he would step away. Praying he would not look too closely at the sheets.

Fully erect, he walked toward her, his lips shaping that limb-melting smile. "And who is to say we are finished here? You don't want to waste a whole tub of water."

She couldn't allow him to touch her now. She couldn't bear to see that smile drop away, replaced by the twisted mouth of disgust. She backed into the wall so hard her shoulder blade protested.

"Why is wasting water so important to you? Manchester has plenty."

"The Willises have plenty of other duties. Wait until tomorrow." He took her hand, playfully swinging it.

"No."

The swinging stopped. The smile faded. His other muscles seemed to relax as well, all except his eyes, tight on her. "Yes."

"I can't."

"Can't? I repel you that much?" His lips flattened, his gaze accusing.

"Don't. You don't understand." She blinked back stupid tears.

"Stuff the dramatics." He leaned against the door next to her, crossing his arms, casual in his nakedness. She knew he didn't see the sense of it, and she wasn't sure she did, either. She loved the smell of him, clean or covered with their lovemaking. It wasn't the same for her, somehow. She simply could not stand one more moment of filthiness.

What if he refused her? What if he pulled her back into the bed? As a husband, he had every right. Her skin started to burn with itching. Thousands of gnats biting, clawing, scratching. She gulped so hard for each breath her body shook.

"You are serious." His voice went flat, as if it were something he could not believe.

"You don't care."

"Nonsense."

"Then move."

He frowned, and didn't budge from the door. Maddie's desperation grew, a monster starting to eat her insides.

"Let me go!" She heard the taint of hysteria in her voice.

He grabbed her to him, his voice a tight buzz in her ear. "Maddie. You can't keep doing this. It's not healthy."

She pushed him away, trying to slide between him and the door. She had to get out. He'd never understand. No one did, not even Miss Marsden. The headmistress had found a way to solve her problem, but a school always had pots and pots of water hot and handy. Here it was all the poor Willises could do to keep up with pumping and carrying enough for cooking and drinking. Maddie knew she was a burden here, but what could she do about it?

Nash had to listen to her. She could compromise, she just couldn't give in.

"I could have one pail of hot water to four pails cold."

"You'd catch your death."

"I've done it before."

He rubbed a hand across his face. Not only his face, but even his manhood was disappointed in her. She wrapped her arms around her.

"Choose: Bath or supper."

She didn't hesitate. "Bath."

"And no supper?" She nodded. He dropped his hand, staring at her as if through force of vision he could change her mind. He reached a finger to stroke her face, but stopped in mid-air.

"Now you flinch from me?"

He shrugged himself off the door, but instead of slipping

through and running to Mrs. Willis, Maddie stood there, a manikin, shocked by her body's own response. "I'm sorry."

Nash already had pulled his shirt over his head. He over-stretched his stockings and yanked his trousers on. He stood, shoes and coat in his hands.

"I'll inform the kitchen, ma'am. Good evening."

He walked past her without looking at her, opened the door, and passed and through the doorway. He closed the door again with such force the wall shook.

Maddie sat on the bed, relieved and bewildered and just a little furious.

What had she done?

Nash found both Willises in the kitchen. Their picture of domestic harmony slapped him in the face. Even as the scent of the chops set his stomach growling, he scowled.

"No need to fold out the table, Willis. The lady will have no supper."

The couple exchanged a look. "She'll be wanting the bath sooner, then?"

"Aye. But finish your barm cake first."

Mrs. Willis stood up from the cook fire, tapping a ladle on the iron pan. "And who will eat these chops? Fine pieces, they are."

"Leave two for yourselves, and pack up the rest. I'll take it to Jem Smith's family." They could certainly use it, with his father on half-pay and his wife out entirely.

Again the Willises exchanged a look. Willis shrugged, but his wife spoke. "Half of it is already marked for them. Mrs. Quinn sends food over most every other day." Her steady stare somehow felt a rebuke.

"Our food?"

"We found some savings, and I believe she uses a bit of her clothing allowance. It's no burden." She turned back to the pot. "Do you think to set and eat with them? I'll pack a bowl and spoon."

"I don't need to be reminded that their house doesn't brim with plate. And stop looking at each other like that."

They turned to him, matching looks of shock in their gazes, "like what?" in the arch of their brows. Like a couple. Like people who cared for each other. He was an idiot.

"When can it be ready?"

"No time at all. Have a barm." Mrs. Willis set a plateful of the buns on the table with a bit too much force.

Nash sat himself with too much force as well, the simple bench creaking in protest. He set a hand on the edge of the table on each side of the plate and glared at the buns. Willis drained his tea and rose, head down so as not to be accused of looking at his wife. He took a bucket and left the room, going to fetch Maddie's blasted bathwater.

After a minute, Nash picked up a bun and bit into it. Still warm, it melted a shard of the ice over his heart. Mrs. Willis set a mug of tea in front of him.

"A lady likes to be clean."

"It's unnecessary. Expensive. Unreasonable. It's too much work."

"A lady won't pay social calls when she knows they'll not be returned." To a house like this, she left unsaid.

"The house is plenty."

"And ready water. And where will we put the bairn, when he does come along, God willing? And his sister, praise be?"

"I'm not a family man yet." But he may have started one with their gymnastics upstairs this afternoon. Then how much wash-water would they need every day? A bit of bun lodged in his throat. He choked it down with the nearly scalding tea.

How had things come to this? Not two months ago, he'd never heard of her. His biggest problem was he was running out of his supply of calicoes. Now his place of business was dangerous and crime-prone, his house was too small, his staff overworked, his rod underworked, and his wife unsatisfied.

That last grated on him, worse than a razor-toothed rasp on standing rigging. What had she to complain of in his bed? It was as if she were afraid of him, and forcing herself to overcome it, ordering herself to submit.

He didn't want her to submit to him. He wanted her to want him, to come to him of her own accord. To show he was as important to her as she was to him.

"Tell Mrs. Smith she needn't return the crockery. Mr. Willis will fetch it when next he comes by. Or Mrs. Quinn." She handed him the pot, cool but warming with the food inside, and a box with buns and a bowl for him.

"No one needs a bath every day." His voice sounded petty even to him.

"Not everyone is afraid of the water." She gave him that hateful, pitying look that made him feel five years old again. He should apologize. He was out of line. Instead, he stomped out of the kitchen, likely in the same way she'd seen him do it dozens of times as a boy.

He'd given them a good roof over their heads, and they all needed to learn to appreciate it. He blamed Mrs. Heywood and her new supper table that didn't fold, just took up space all day long in that blasted "dining room" of hers. A bad precedent. It was not his fault if Maddie grew up expecting a castle. She should be content with what she got, and the incredible forbearance he'd shown her, as well. He'd waited all this time, hadn't he?

Why wouldn't she want him? He shifted the pot in his arms and stepped around a puddle in the street.

Perhaps that was a useless wish. Perhaps no one had such a connection. His parents had not, nor his grandparents. Still, he thought he saw it in the Willises, and among the flock at church. Perhaps they were better at pretending in public. He could imagine Maddie acting the good wife in church, while at home it was something different.

Or was it? Was she acting this afternoon? Her body wasn't, at least at first. She had wanted him, with her pounding heart, her wide eyes, her grasping hands, her heat and wet.

But he'd also felt her go stiff, in that awful way, and then relax. That was when the acting started.

He was too far gone to stop, and he took her. He disgusted himself. He knew she had no experience and he'd raced her along to the finish line anyway. He was the household boar, just as his father used to say.

Next time would be different, he promised himself. She would be as satisfied as he.

But what if she wasn't? What if she was always cold and frigid and this was the best she could do? She hadn't turned away from him, like the other times, or screamed, like that first night. She swallowed her distaste, her bile, to allow him entry.

How lowering.

When he had pictured his married life, Nash had rather glossed over the physical aspect. He'd assumed he'd be attracted to whomever she was, and the rest was understood. The questions in his mind revolved around where to live, whether to move, how many children to have, whom the woman would befriend, and how it might affect his business prospects.

He had pictured the woman herself as some shadow, he realized, less a human being than an additional appendage. This view guaranteed that he would be the one to set the rules, and this shadow-creature the one to follow them.

Sad to say, his marriage was nothing like that.

Along River Street's blocks of back-to-back rowhouses, the one held by Jem Smith and his family had pride of place. At the street edge of the narrow, dark court, the stacked single rooms had two windows each instead of the one sported by the other dozen or so dwellings in the ring. And if the air were ever sweet, it would be sweetest here.

Mrs. Smith did her best not to take fright at seeing him, but Jem came quickly to her side to take the heavy crockery. He invited him in, but Nash hesitated on the threshold.

"It won't cause you trouble, having a master in your home?"

"Nay. All know I'm a master's man." He grinned and set the package by the hearth. "As well they know the difference between a Quinn and a Malbanks. You'll stay to sup?"

"If I may. Mrs. Willis said she packed extra."

"Not extra. Double." Mrs. Smith raised her dark-rimmed round-rabbit gaze at the news. "You such a big eater?"

As his eyes grew adjusted to the dim, Nash saw plenty of mouths to feed. Jem introduced him to his in-laws, the father chair-bound, and his two boys, a spiky lad of six and a roly-poly toddler. If they could stack six souls in two coal-scented rooms, what did Maddie have to complain of? At least the charred-wood smell covered the other, less-pleasant odors.

They had no table. Mrs. Smith scooped the chops and greens into bowls and handed them around. They ate where they sat, the missus and her parents by the hearth with the boys, Jem and Nash on a bench by the street-view window.

"Food gives heart, my folk say." Jem ate quickly but neatly. "We also say eat like the wind or there'll be no seconds for you."

"About this afternoon. Does that man live around here?"

"Across the Irwell, in Clayton's housing. He were run off for drunkenness. He sobered up, but all he could find was piecework with Malbanks. That wage will starve a man slow. More?"

"You take it." Nash leaned on the bricked wall, no plaster here. And no wood on the floor. But Mrs. Smith kept a neat house, and she served her man his seconds with a slow but honest smile. He thought he saw something pass between them, but couldn't read it.

"She wants to know if you'd take tea after. The boy can run across and borrow a dish."

"I thank you, but no. I should be getting home." He'd been too hard on poor Maddie, taking his frustrations with work out on her. What was six buckets of water a day, compared with the chance at a comfortable hearth and a smile just for him? What could he say? She'd see him as a tyrant, and if he waltzed back and charmed her, she'd see him as capricious. Perhaps he could build her something, but what? A blasted bathing chamber, floating in thin air?

"Give our thanks to your ladies. Mrs. Willis's chop may be better than her brisket, and that ain't nothing to scoff at." Jem set down his bowl to lift the toddler onto his lap. The boy held some sort of wooden puzzle toy he slid apart and back together, chirping in his own child language. Nash saw the grandfather had a similar piece, unfinished, in a basket beside him.

A part fell to the floor, and Jem leaned down to pick it up, giving it back to the boy. "We can play this game for hours."

Now that he'd said he needed to go, Nash's bites grew smaller and smaller, stretching out his supper to hold onto an excuse for staying. For the first time, he considered how his life would change if Maddie gave him children. Not the sort that run into the wheels of carts and frighten the horses, but the sort who delight in the toy a grandfather makes him. That sort might not be bad at all. Might actually be quite fine.

An unfamiliar feeling burned at the top of his chest. Perhaps Mrs. Willis's chops were too spicy today.

Jem shifted the boy to sit sideways across his legs. Nash's legs moved to make the same shape, as if readying themselves. "About this afternoon. You're on the committee, so better I might tell you."

"The meeting in Middleton? You're going?"

"Aye, but not that. Here. I think there's something up."

"A strike?"

He shook his head no. "Most thought it better to hold the reform meetings than go out again."

"Good."

"But there's too much ill-caring toward the Malbanks mills.

The wage cut on top of losing all that broadcloth work to the machines. A hard man, he is, and not fair."

"Striking wouldn't break the machines."

"Nothing will. We're none of us Luddites here. And yet." At Nash's blank look, Jem mimed striking a match and flinging it. Fire.

Uncontrollable, unpredictable, fire was the biggest bugaboo in town. One building could set others off, and if it got hot enough, even brick would fall. And here they were in July, with the Irwell running low and the ponds gone dry.

Nash jumped to his feet, startling the baby into dropping his pieces. His wail started low but continued to rise.

"I must warn Malbanks. Do you know when?"

"I don't even know if, if you take my meaning."

Nash nodded. He bowed over Mrs. Smith's hand, and nodded to her parents. Setting his hat back on his head, he headed downtown.

No one wanted a city in flames.

TWENTY-ONE

Master Hugh Malbanks first erected a monument to commercial progress, the largest spinning and weaving mill in Lancashire, and then one to his family, a six-column mansion, appropriately enough near the bank of the river. Built on a plan by Wren, or rather one of Wren's acolytes, the edifice did impress on one's approach. To Nash's eye, though, the monstrous house looked orphaned and crowded, without an estate of rolling hills and gentle valleys cradling it. Malbanks did hold a home farm, out past Bolton, but he wanted his house to have a view of his domain, which stood at the south end of town. If the day rooms also had a view of the fortresslike New Bailey jail, well, the man might equally well enjoy that prospect.

Malbanks kept Nash cooling his heels in the stately entry hall. He wasn't surprised—the doorman seemed nearly faint with shock that someone would be calling.

Nash didn't know much of the man beyond general

rumors. Malbanks worked hard, played little, endowed a Methodist church in his mother's name, and acted the aggressor in negotiations, even when it wasn't necessary. He took overmuch care with his dress, a sign of foppishness or new money; Nash suspected the latter. Still wearing his workday uniform, a jacket losing some of its blocking and good-enough trousers, Nash could pass for the oldest of old money—or no money at all.

Malbanks had learned the manners of polite society, as well. He was at table, finishing what looked to be roast pheasant, when the butler showed Nash in. Malbanks nodded and took another bit of the fowl, failing to offer his guest either refreshment or a seat.

This was standard treatment for petitioners and other poor folk, but it took Nash by surprise how small it made him feel. If he'd had a cap in his hand, he might have twisted it between his hands in that nervous way he'd seen the tradesmen do so often at the castle. His blocked hat sat on the stand in the hall, so instead he stood at parade rest. He was an uninvited guest at an odd hour, and Malbanks could do as he liked. They might well have sent him down to the kitchens, the highest floor the "lower classes" were normally allowed in the rare event they came calling.

At the far end of the eight-foot table sat a well-dressed, exhausted-looking female. The rumored Mrs. Malbanks, who was said to be continually pregnant yet had not offered any offspring to public viewing. Deliberately breaking the unwritten rules of decorum, he openly analyzed the lady. Watching her quick peeks down the table at every sound, the way she looked at him in glancing blows, and the tiny bites she took, only made

Nash grimmer. When Malbanks set his silver down, ending the course, she jumped.

"Mouse, this is Nash Quinn, merchant and lately magistrate. Mr. Quinn, my lady, Mrs. Malbanks."

Nash half-bowed in her direction, and thought he heard her squeak. Hadn't Wetherby called Maddie mouse, as well? He'd obviously never met this lady.

"Malbanks, I apologize for calling so late, but I've just heard information pertaining to your mills I thought you might want to hear immediately."

"No need for formality, we can talk freely here." The servant carrying the soup course stepped neatly around Nash to deliver the tureen.

"As you wish. One of my hands has heard of trouble brewing."

"An old story. They decided not to strike. Didn't get enough votes 'aye.' A rebellion felled by democracy. Choice, isn't it?"

"Not a strike. A fire-set."

All motion in the room stopped, save for the flat clang of the soup ladle dropping into the tureen. Mrs. Malbanks's breathing grew audible, rapid and shallow. She started to rock, forward and back. Her chair was unusual, higher than the others.

The mill owner scowled. "Enough, mouse. They wouldn't dare." He turned his attention back to Nash. "How good is your information?"

"Second-hand, but I trust the source."

"All talk. That's all these Mancunians are good for. Talk and half-work."

"It's dangerous talk. No one wants a London Bridge."

Mrs. Malbanks moaned softly; Nash winced at the sound.

"And they won't have it. Mouse, leave us." A servant rushed to pull back her chair. She didn't rise, though. The chair had wheels at the bottom. She gripped its arms as the servant pushed her from the room. After the door shut again, Malbanks spoke.

"I'd thank you not to speak of burning things before my wife. She has bad memories of fire, as you see. But I do not. As you know, the river runs through the main mill, and a holding pond sits beside the other. I'm in no danger."

"Even a small fire, easily doused, would stall production. We need your mill at full output to make the Netherlands deadline."

"Is that what you're fretting over? That deal may mean everything to you—it's your entire stake, is it not?—but it is small change for me. We'll get you our portion well in time to meet your ship."

Nash knew it for a lie. The man's portion was half the cargo, and the order hadn't yet been started. "Your spinners are back to working again, then?"

Malbanks looked to the window, swallowing quickly. Then he slowly lifted his glass for a servant to refill it and drank half before setting it down. "Consider it done. Now if you are through terrorizing my household, I'd like to enjoy my soup before it congeals."

"Three weeks."

"It will take two. Good night, Quinn. I believe you can show yourself out."

At least the fool didn't worry he'd steal the silver on his way out the door.

ALL MADDIE WANTED WAS to be a good wife, a good Mrs. Nash Quinn. She did not dispute her husband's right to set the house rules, though it was unusual. Man led, and woman followed.

The walk to church did not soothe, the streets bustling more than usual during work hours. She'd fallen asleep, clean but fitful, in the new sheets Mrs. Willis had thoughtfully put on the bed as Maddie soaked. She knew he'd come home because the bed was warm and rumpled there when she woke. Plus the note he'd left ordering her not to come to the warehouse.

He could do that, and what could she do? If he pressed the point about bathing, what could she say? What if he were so angry he sent her away? He might have her transported to Australia as a bad wife. No one would gainsay it. She'd argued with her husband—they'd say she brought it on herself.

By the time she reached the gate to the churchyard, she was panting as if she'd narrowly lost a race. Even the sight of her mother's resting place could not calm her. She paced the length of the path it stood by, fifty steps back and forth, and again, and again. The July sun shone bright but cool; by midday it would be scorching, drawing away the loamy scents of the grounds.

Of all the things Maddie imagined could put a wedge into their closeness, bathing had never made the listing. For the hundredth time, she thought about her father, his family, her real one. Why shouldn't she try to find him? Surely they would love her, want her. They would have to.

How could she even start to look? Mr. Heywood had fobbed her off, and if she pushed him he might tell Nash. Nash seemed to have little enough use for his own people, how could he understand this crying ache to find her own?

If only it were easier to procure a bath, if only it didn't take an hour of heating water and carrying it, no one would gainsay her. At school, the bathing chamber was next to the kitchens, and she could always be sure of getting one pot of hot water. She'd mix it with the cold herself, and after she grew strong enough to carry it, she would replace what she had taken, bothering no one. Here it seemed she had unbalanced the entire household, right on up to its master.

She couldn't rely on him. She had to have money of her own. If she had funds, she could hire another porter, half-time. Or even build a bathing house, with its own fire that she would tend herself. It would be a tight fit in the tiny space behind the house, and close on the night-soil and cinder boxes, but it could work.

If Nash didn't want her at the warehouse any longer, perhaps she could hire herself out to Mr. Heywood. She might teach, or tutor. Her needle skills weren't what they ought to be, and besides, they were masters of the cloth here. She might find a place back at Miss Marsden's school, if he deserted her completely.

At that thought, she had to slow down. No, she couldn't go back. And she didn't want him to desert her. She wanted him to love her, treasure her, and not always find her so wanting.

He seemed pleased enough with their coupling. Perhaps if she found more ways to pleasure him, he would overlook her oddities. At least until she had enough saved to feel secure. Men owned women's money as well as their bodies, the law said, but that rule was not as fiercely attended. Perhaps Mr. Heywood would act her legal guardian. It was all so difficult. Why couldn't she just make herself suit?

Turning at the end of the path, she saw what looked to be her shadow, only it was moving toward her. Brown curls sneaking out of a plain bonnet, open oval face topping a printed dress in browns and greens. Maddie dropped her gaze. Her own dress was green and cream.

The other woman's purposeful stride didn't catch; she hadn't seen her. When she paused at Maddie's mother's grave, Maddie retraced her steps, and stopped an arm's length away.

It was no shadow, but a young working woman, beautiful in her strength. They stood silently, staring at the simple stone.

"She'd have been forty this week, had she lived." The woman set three daisies banded with yarn on the top of the marker. She glanced at Maddie, a flash of blue diamonds, and then looked out at the nearby stones. "Is your Ma here, as well?"

Maddie couldn't speak, the words stuck in her heart, not even reaching her throat. She gasped a breath out, then in, pushing, pushing.

"Are you my sister?"

The ice blue gaze snapped back to Maddie's face. "I had a sister once, when me Ma was living."

"What happened to her?" Maddie pushed out.

"Emily? We sold her to the nobs what killed our Ma."

Maddie's head felt too light, toppling her balance. She set a hand on the top of the grave marker to steady herself. The daisies tumbled. The blue-eyed shadow took a step toward her, arms rising as if to push her away from the stone. Then her eyes widened.

"It be you?"

"I was Emily Moore. They gave me new names."

"Sounds about right. Well, I'll be." She shook her head hard, as if to settle the thought in her mind. Instead of pushing her away, the woman reached back to touch her own bonnet near her temple. She ran her finger down the side as if to trace the edge of Maddie's face. Maddie's skin sensed the touch as if it were real.

The woman smelled of new cloth out in the sun, fresh dyes and smoke. She stood Maddie's height and had her proportions. Except for those eyes, they might be twins. They might be sisters.

Maddie pushed her lips into a wobbly smile. "I never knew I had a sister. Are there others?"

The woman flinched hard, as if Maddie had struck her. Her lips twisted down in a way that Maddie would ever remind herself not to emulate. "What do ye want?"

"Nothing." Everything.

The woman crossed her arms tight, frowning. "We thought they might throw you back on us when we heard as how the nobs was killed. Proper way to go, we thought."

"I was sent away to school. Just came back, just found out I was adopted. I was about to marry, and—"

"And so he deserted you?" The woman didn't seem to think much of men.

"No! Well, yes. But his brother didn't. He married me."

She quickly scanned the cemetery. "Does he know you're here?"

Maddie shook her head. "He knows I come here."

"Looking for us?"

Us? Maddie's mind went blank with pure joy. Only the woman's quick grip on her forearm kept her from fainting away. She pressed all her hope into words. "Our father still lives?"

Her sister's mouth pursed as if she would spit. But she thought better of it, and relaxed her lips. "He's a top man, now, in the trade. Master weaver."

Maddie skirted around feelings too strong to bear, retreating to the comfort of conversation. "And you, you are a weaver, too?"

"I work the mills. But I spin for Da, too. This is our work." She pressed down the skirt of her dress.

"The colors are so rich."

"Good weave, aye. But if I'm wearing it, that means we couldn't sell it. The mills are the death of us, he says. You can stand now?"

Maddie nodded, and the woman took her hand away, leaving what felt like a true hole in her arm. "I'm called Madeline Quinn now. Mrs. Quinn."

"Kitty. Miss Moore, if you please." She held out her strong hand, a Mancunian woman of business. Maddie took it carefully and performed the odd pumping motion. Kitty let go first. The touch failed to satisfy, but Maddie didn't dare ask this stranger-sister for an embrace. She wouldn't risk anything that might make Kitty disappear.

"I saw your flowers, last month."

Kitty stared down at the stone. "I've seen yours, as well. Must have been. I don't come by so much. When times are hard, I find myself here more often."

"Times are hard now?"

Kitty frowned at her as if Maddie were simple. Then she shrugged. "Wages be half what they was when I started at the mill, now a dozen years past. Bread is a shilling a loaf. The men talk reform, when all that will get them is prison. And then where will we be?"

"You can't have been ten years old when you started. You look so young."

"Ten exact. That were old."

"I don't know much. My husband is in trade." For the first time, Maddie didn't feel that little twinge of shame at the word. The open space set loose her tongue. "Would you introduce me to our father?"

Kitty's eyes narrowed. "Why?"

How could she not understand? "I lost the only family I thought I had when I was four years old. Now I find I might have had another family all along. Wouldn't you want to find them? To know them?"

"Depends whether they want to find you, don't it?"

"I ache to see him."

"I ain't so sure he aches for you."

Maddie's skin chilled, choking her bones.

Kitty pressed on. "Didn't think on that, eh? He did sell you once. Mayhaps he regrets it. Can he want you standing there reminding him of it?"

Maddie tried to collect herself. Of course her father might never wish to see her. After all, he had washed his hands of her decades ago and here she pops up like a bad apple.

"Don't start blubbering. I may be right off. Let me gets to asking him, like, before I make any promises."

"May I see you again?"

She frowned. "Aye. Don't know how much I can look on you. It's not like I ever expected it, you see? And you the spitting image of me Ma. Our Ma."

"So are you, then. We share the same features."

"Nothing like. It's like looking at a ghost. Only Ma never looked so rested and plump, begging your pardon." Kitty shook her head. "I'll have to warn Da about that, too. A ghost risen, he'd call ye. Holy hell."

"Can you go to him now?"

"He'd slap me silly. He's trying to get the last load of weaving done before the meeting. I best be off. My lunch hour is far gone. Ain't you going to be missed?"

Maddie looked at the church tower. One o'clock already. Mrs. Willis would be missing her, indeed.

"How may I reach you? Where might I send a note?"

"None of that. You're Quinn, of the warehouse? I'll come round, when he's ready."

Maddie couldn't help it. One more time, she grasped Kitty's calloused hand in her soft one. "Sister. I am so blessed."

"Don't know about that." Kitty pulled her hand away, but a smile tipped her lips. "Seems to me you was a right ornery baby."

TWENTY-TWO

In the nine days between her banishment from the warehouse and the Heywoods' monthly supper, Maddie and Nash exchanged barely an hour's conversation. He stayed away from home, running between the warehouse, his consortium partners, and the recalcitrant magistrates' committee. When he was home for supper or before bed, his lips were pressed tight, the dimples at their corners crevasses. She could watch the sharp line of his cheek muscle snapping as he chewed —and as he sat silent, thinking.

Maddie herself had never been so frustrated. Knowing she shouldn't try to contact Kitty but wanting to, so much, she haunted the graveyard in the mornings and early evenings, but her sister did not return. Maddie felt if she could just stretch her arms a little further, she might touch upon her father, but her arms stubbornly remained too short.

She had nothing to do. She was dull company during afternoon calls, and her attempts at charity work were met by angry stares and the advice that the poor would prefer wages return to normal than a hand-me-down shawl or lessons in their letters from the likes of her.

Even in church, she felt divisions growing. Women with plain bonnets did not step aside for those in decorated bonnets, but glared at their owners, who had done nothing but dress up to seek salvation. On the streets and in the market, Maddie saw jostling, muttering, and just plain rudeness. Mancunians already were a busy, brusque people. Now they seemed ready to come to blows.

If this was the face the people showed in front of their wives and mothers and daughters, what must Nash be facing? His big order was due to the ship next week, and from what she could tell from his single-word answers and grunts, it would be a close thing. Even Mrs. Willis tiptoed around him lately.

That was the excuse Maddie gave herself for not telling him about Kitty and her father. He didn't need more to fret on, and wasn't she fretting on it enough for the both of them? But while she was used to keeping her own counsel, this time she thought she might burst with its telling. But what did she have to tell? It had come to nothing, hadn't it. So far.

The trees swayed in the heat-edged breeze as they walked through Mosley Street to the Heywoods' residence. The great houses stood solemn in the cooling dusk. Nash stopped at the base of the stair, waiting for her to catch up.

"I'm sorry I set such a breakneck pace. I'm not looking forward to this tonight." He took her hand. She covered her surprise by pretending she was merely catching her breath. He set his foot on the first step, but then paused and turned back to her.

"I'm sorry our house isn't fit for proper company."

His sable eyes were windows tonight. She could read his care-worn heart, ever striving to make things right for his warehouse, for his workers, for her. Her heart unfolded in response.

"I found my sister," she blurted out.

He brought his foot back down to the cobbled street. He blinked, his brows knitting, the two vertical lines between them angry welts. "You have family? I thought your mother was killed."

"An older sister. At the graveyard. We met."

"You met. And was she delighted to see you?"

"Suspicious. We agreed to meet again, but she has not returned. I don't think she trusts me." Maddie's stomach heaved, and she put a hand over her belly in protection.

Nash squeezed her hand. Even his grip seemed tired. "Maybe it's for the best."

"No. She was going to speak with my father, and I was going to see him."

"How can you know she is your sister, in truth? People see what they want to see."

"I shouldn't have told you. She said you would be mad."

"I'm not mad." He blew out a breath, puffing his hollowed cheeks. "I just don't want you hurt. The man sold you, Maddie."

"Perhaps he had no choice."

"Don't be a fool. Why can't you be content with the love of the people in your life now?"

She cast about for a better argument, but her hurt feelings distracted her. Why did he call her names? "Do you love me?"

"How can you doubt it?"

"It wasn't part of the negotiations for marriage. I am not so sure I love you."

As she watched, his eyes shuttered, breaking their connection. The loss was a blade in her chest. She was, indeed, a fool.

He rolled back on his heels, away from her, dropping her hand. Then he looked up and down the street, as if to see if any passers-by had observed them.

Light splashed across them. The Heywoods' door had opened.

"Come in, come in, don't stand there." Mrs. Heywood herself manned the door. They must have been seen, arguing. Maddie wilted inside from the shame of it.

Nash turned and raised a hand in greeting. "We'll talk about this later."

She knew they never would.

"Lancashire? Never." The words burned down at her as Maddie and Nash entered the hall.

"You're late. The swords are already out." The cheer in Mrs. Heywood's voice rang false.

"Malbanks intends to win by force of volume, I hear." Nash's voice rang equally jovial, and equally false.

"Mr. Clayton has his match. My poor Heywood suffers from a summer cold." As Nash took the stairs two by two, perhaps thinking to rescue his mentor, she smiled at Maddie. "You look lovely, dear." Maddie almost burst into tears, gulping air to keep her equilibrium.

"That bad? You're not with child already?"

Maddie, startled, shook her head. She might have been with child, but no. "It's that time."

"We all take things too much to heart then. A woman's weakness, one of our many. Shall we see if we can use our beauty to distract these beasts?" She took Maddie's arm, and they ascended the stairs together.

The men were not distracted, and they drew the women in after them. Even quiet Mrs. Clayton, so often preferring to affect a supreme indifference, watched the men as if she were watching tennis.

Mr. Clayton sat beside her on a gaily decorated seat for two, a jolly old soul beside his Jack Sprat wife. But tonight his ruddy cheeks sagged a little more, and his horn-rimmed eyes looked as stern and dangerous as even Mr. Malbanks's did. That man stood in front of the closed fireplace, as if conducting an orchestra. Mrs. Heywood motioned for Maddie to sit beside her on the fainting couch opposite the Claytons. Heywood moved across the room to stand behind his wife, and Nash followed suit. Mrs. Heywood raised her hand to her shoulder, and her husband touched it with an absentminded fondness. Maddie didn't dare raise her hand, fearing Nash would not mirror that movement.

"Oldham, Salford, with their bloody *habeas corpus*, they'll march into Manchester next." Clayton threw up his hands.

Nash jumped in. "The workers can do just as we do." She wondered if the others could hear the spent string in his voice.

"They demand franchise." Clayton shook his head, dislodging his spectacles. "We don't even have that to speak of, and do you hear us caterwauling about?"

Malbanks barked a laugh. "I hear you wailing, Clayton.

Laws made at a distance, meddlers wrecking our plans and profits."

"These chaps, they demand what they're owed when they haven't earned the right to be owed anything at all." Clayton's face flushed dangerously. Mrs. Clayton reached into her husband's pocket and pulled out his rather large handkerchief. He took it from her in exchange for his near-empty tumbler of spirits, and wiped at his ruddy forehead. "The right to air their grievances should be enough to satisfy them."

Nash cleared his throat. "Up to a point. Airing one's grievances is hard enough, for people so proud. If no one listens, how does that ease their minds?"

"What can you mean?" Heywood turned to him.

"To speak, there needs must be a listener. Who is listening to the people?"

"Why should we listen?" Heywood shrugged. "We know what they are going to say."

"Do you?" Nash countered.

"And even if we did listen, what then?" Malbanks slapped a hand on the mantle. "They might expect us to do something about it."

The men laughed. The women sat silent.

Clayton's color had subsided. "So, Malbanks, how do we put an end to this frenzy of meetings?"

Heywood stepped in. "They can't be stopped, if they are in good order."

Malbanks nodded. "So we put them on notice to follow every rule, with our yeomanry ready when they don't. A show of force will always frighten a coward."

Heywood snorted. "The yeomanry? Merchants, shopkeepers, the chandler—a fearful lot, indeed."

"You forget the pawnbrokers and publicans. And the fact they sit on stomping horses. Quite menacing, I should think."

"Manchester's workers don't need menacing. We beat them down plenty enough already." Nash's words carried the weariness of constant repetition. This time, though, it had a singular effect. Malbanks stood rigid, anger vibrating from his limbs.

"This from the man who ran into my house in the dead of night panting that the chaff were nigh upon revolt. I've slept at the manufactory all week—and nothing. Now they're a docile bunch?"

"Not docile. Downtrodden." Nash nearly spat.

"Balderdash."

Maddie found her voice. "I spoke with a woman who said her wage was half what it had been a decade ago. When she was a child."

Malbanks voice could cut glass. "We don't hire children any longer."

"Now they've grown, you mean." All heads turned to Mrs. Clayton, who raised her hand to her mouth, equally surprised that she had spoken.

Mrs. Heywood cleared her throat. "I see children younger than our own come out our manufactory every day. They are not workers?"

"Of course they are. But there are fewer now. Ever fewer. No one needs Parliament to tell him that grown men and women are better workers."

"Now that we've trained them up, you mean." Heywood let go of his wife's hand. She smiled sadly at Maddie.

Clayton looked at Heywood. "Nonetheless, what they're contemplating is sedition, isn't it?"

"As a lawyer, I tell you they've skirted to the side of it. Marching and meeting and airing perceived grievances is not against the law. We have nothing to fear. The magistrates have this well in hand. Did they not force that Orator Hunt to behave this past winter? He'll rouse no rabbles here."

Nash tried again. "The reformers who are local men, we might listen to them."

"Cut them off first, you mean?"

"No, I mean hear them out, and tell them what we mean to do."

Malbanks spit into the fireplace. "Tell them our business?"

Nash looked at the man. She hoped he held less tension in his eyes than in the hand gripping the couch behind her. "If they knew about the contest for the Netherlands trade, would they not willingly cut their rates to secure themselves continuing work? As it is, they see us earning riches from last year's good season and turning around and cutting their wages."

"Tell them our trade? These clods wouldn't understand the business behind it."

Heywood pursed his lips. "They might tell others who might, and would undercut our bid."

"Who would that be? Plymouth? Bath? They know already, and already lost their bids. We keep secrets unnecessarily and to our detriment." Nash looked to Clayton, who was again rubbing his overheated face.

Clayton failed him. "I have to agree with Malbanks. These workers wouldn't understand."

Mrs. Heywood leaned into Maddie, bumping her shoulder

gently. "I heard there are some women reformers, as well." Though she spoke softly, Malbanks snorted.

"See how far this has gone?"

Maddie heard a low growl, and realized it was coming from her. Neither Malbanks nor Mrs. Heywood seemed to notice, but Nash put a hand on her shoulder and squeezed, a warning.

She ignored him. "I fail to see why, if women can work, they cannot comment upon their work, just as men do."

Malbanks turned the flash of his gaze toward her. "If the men are idiots, what does that make the women?"

Before he could say more, Nash laughed, its honeyed ring carrying a brittle edge. "This woman managed to get you to argue with her. What does that make you?"

Malbanks locked stiff gazes with Nash as if dueling, but Clayton's face grew animated. "Suffrage for women, as well. Wouldn't that be interesting."

"You have no representation yourself, Clayton," Malbanks said. "You'd hand power to the landless masses? First thing they'd do is take your land. Then perhaps your property, if not your life."

"No need to exaggerate, my man. No one wishes death on anyone." He made an abridged sign of the cross on his chest. Maddie was surprised he practiced that faith.

Malbanks turned to Nash. "Nash Quinn of Shaftsbury castle. Do you believe your great brother represents your interests?" Malbanks tilted his head, a caricature of royalty.

"Leave my brother out of it."

"And the gob-ment?"

"He won't even take his seat." The look on Nash's face

matched the bitterness of his tone. His eye was twitching; he must be close to his limit.

Malbanks pounced. "So, no one needs any representation, he thinks."

"That's not what he said." Maddie stood, as if to block Nash from his attacker with her puny woman's bulk. Malbanks's gaze simply flicked over her head, taunting Nash.

Nash grabbed her elbow, a sharp shock. He must think she'd made him look weak. "And you, what working woman do you speak with? I'm surprised you could stand it. Did you need to wash after?"

She jerked out of his grip. His face went slack with surprise. He couldn't know how much he'd hurt her. They stared at each other, not wanting to reveal their hearts, and not wanting to see the other's heart now, either.

Clayton cleared his throat, and started on about volunteers versus trained soldiers, but Maddie could barely distinguish the words. How could Nash have aired their dirty linen in public? His eyes carried regret, perhaps, but she knew he would never apologize, not here.

She wanted to scream at him, push him, punch him, and cut his heart out. Instead, she walked to the window with all the deliberate grace she could muster, away from all of them.

She crossed her arms to corral her racing heart. At first, all she saw was her own reflection in the glass. Her eyes glittered, but she would not cry. She watched the shape of Mrs. Heywood heading toward the hall, heard her voice say something about calling for supper.

She heard Nash's voice rejoin the conversation. Though it

was the end of July, her bones went cold. She had to find her family. She had to find a way to be safe.

"You could join the yeomanry, Quinn." Clayton called after him.

"And drink all day? I've a business to run."

"So do we all," Heywood said. "And we need to keep the workers laboring."

"And the rabble-rousers out," Malbanks seconded.

"Else we'll all be in the poor house by winter," Clayton finished.

Outside, the blocks around the theater stood out, light against the other districts' dark. Except beside the river, where a large building was rather too well lit. Maddie twisted her neck to get a better look. She tried to make sense of it. If only it were daylight.

She felt Nash at her shoulder. "Maddie," he started.

"Look. Over there. Is it the sunset edging that building?"

"The sun is long gone." He opened the window and leaned out, and then snapped back into the room.

"Malbanks, your mill is on fire."

TWENTY-THREE

While Malbanks rode ahead on his roan, Heywood, Clayton, and Nash followed in the older man's sideboard, carrying every bucket the servants could find. Mrs. Heywood forced a quickly packed basket of food on them, choice cooked morsels that wouldn't last an hour. But the cook also packed two loaves of bread and bottles of water underneath.

"Hell of a way to break up a party, Quinn," Heywood muttered, his concentration on the team of horses. Clayton, squeezed between them on the bench, nibbled at a leg of pheasant.

Nash couldn't eat. Even the smell of the bird turned his stomach. How could he have said those things to Maddie? How could he have said them in mixed company? In any company? If a person could melt, she would have melted in front of all of them, he was sure of it. And that look—not angry, that he had been braced for, but deep green pools of pain.

And for what? For standing up to Malbanks, a feat which in all rights should have gained her praise. And now he'd left her, with those rigid shoulders aching for a touch, with the sniping biddies of Mosley Street. He was the worst husband, the worst lover. No wonder she couldn't say she loved him. After that performance, he couldn't even love himself.

The gray-orange bloom of the fire lit the sky but darkened the streets they traveled. It was slow going, though Clayton had taken to calling out a warning, fire-truck, make way. They looked very little like any fire-truck Nash had seen, but the calls did have some effect. They turned into the lane leading to Malbanks Mills less than twenty minutes after Maddie had sounded the alert.

Flames danced from the last of the three seven-storey manu-factories, the newest one. A blessing, as that one was farthest from the others, separated by the two-storey warehouse and counting house; even if it went, the others might be saved. Some two hundred people scrambled about, lending an odd sense of day to the night-dark scene. But something else was odd about the picture.

Clayton caught on first. "Why is no one going to the river?" The people, shadows in their dark clothing, congregated in front of the new mill, facing away but keeping a good distance from the flames.

"Blast it all!" Heywood snapped the reins, and the wagon lurched. Nash made out what he'd seen: Malbanks holding his horse, on the wrong side of the road, with a crowd of work-ingmen on the right side, arrayed to block his way toward the cindering building. As Malbanks turned his back to tether the stomping horse, a stone flew at him from the other side. It missed him, striking the horse's head. It reared in fright, and the man, suddenly dwarfed, jumped back. He turned to face the crowd, and Nash saw the rifle in his hands. Malbanks hadn't been merely tethering the horse, but arming himself.

Another stone flew past him. He lifted the gun to his shoulder. Now they could hear hissing, an hundred voices like steam from a kettle. Then all seemed to hear the sound of the cart; at once, all heads turned.

Heywood stopped the cart dead in front of Malbanks. "If you shoot, shoot through us."

Nash waved at the workers, some so near they could have easily pulled him out of the cart. Even with the smoke filling the air, he could smell the mutiny in their ranks. He had to distract them from that idiot owner and his weapon.

"Your homes, there. Your family." He swept his arm across his body to point past the warehouses, drawing many of their gazes with it. Two-storey cottages backed directly against the manufactory's wooden fence.

"Think the flames know to stop at the property line?" He could feel their pause, a mass intake of breath. "Take this bucket. You," he pointed at the largest man he saw. "To the river. I'll take the front." Not waiting to see if they'd follow him, he scrambled onto the back of the cart and started throwing the buckets up over the crowd.

They did follow, and quickly. Shouts, murmuring, and then Nash heard nothing but the dry roar of the blaze. Malbanks's screech and Heywood's rumble were no match. Hoping Heywood had the man well in hand, Nash dropped to the ground.

Clayton stood beside him, breathing hard. "Storehouse is a

loss, but if we keep that side damp it might not spark the other workrooms. I'll take that."

Nash turned to the building before him. The roof glowed reds and oranges, but the flames clawed on only the top two floors. If they concentrated on the third and fourth, perhaps they could save the foundation.

As he neared the entrance, workers unbolted its doors and freed Malbanks's foreman and a few of what looked to be yeomanry, who rushed out and toward their boss. For a split-second, Nash thought he saw Maddie among the crowd making way for them, her face in a black bonnet as determined as when she'd argued her case for Deacon. His guilt made flesh, but he couldn't take time to dwell on it.

The foreman agreed with Nash's plan, and with the bucket brigade already in motion, they stepped into the heating building and up the stairwells. Nash took the fourth floor until it grew too hot, its walls first warming, them buckling. They didn't save the third floor, either. But on the second, they battled to a draw with the relentless, fickle flames.

As the first purple-blue of dawn touched the sky, the ground floor foundation remained, untouched. The walls held only cinders, as if the building was naught but a giant fireplace. It would take weeks to clean out.

Nash walked out the door, stamping at stray cinders on the ground outside. His shoulders ached, and his throat screamed for water, even though he'd splashed some on himself from the buckets whenever he remembered to. The hundreds of hands they had started with had dwindled to a bare two dozen of the strongest men, now all sooty black, as if made of cinder themselves.

He found Clayton sprawled out asleep in the back of the wagon, Heywood upright but dozing on its seat. Malbanks, sooty as Nash but with his clean rifle now slung over his shoulder, paced back and forth in front of the wagon.

"Could have been worse," Nash said as he came up beside him. He reached into the wagon, finding a bottle still filled with water, and draining half in one gulp. He held the bottle to Malbanks, who shook his head no, then handed it to the man's foreman, who knew better than to refuse it.

"Not a total loss," Malbanks said. "I must thank you."

"Fire is everyone's foe."

"Not the fire, the mob. Should have had more of my yeomanry in, but I just didn't believe they had the balls." Malbanks spat, another black mark on the ashy ground.

"We've pushed them to the limit." The water had dislodged some of the grit in Nash's throat, and he spit it out, another slash.

"They cut their own throats with this."

"At least you have the Netherlands order. Quick turnaround; good dose of capital return. You hadn't started yet, you said?"

Malbanks kicked at an ember, once his building or one of his machines. "And I won't." He glared at Nash, bloodshot eyes in a hollow face drawn by soot. "We're shut down until autumn, at least. I'll not endanger myself, or these workers here. See how they like that."

Nash had no energy to argue, but forced himself to. "That puts two thousand souls out."

"Closer to three thousand."

"And their families. You know the rest of us can't absorb that. The men need to work. Especially now."

"The men would rather throw stones at their betters than give a good day's work. So be it."

It wouldn't be only the workers sunk if this deal fell through. Nash might be able to keep bread and butter on the table come winter, but precious little else.

❦

FROM THE HEYWOODS' bowed window, Maddie watched the orange rays stretch through the purples of daybreak. The dark scar of smoke from the manufactory, slashing into God's display, also grew lighter with the day. Lack of wind must have helped Nash and the others to fight the blaze, but it also meant the smoke lingered, a wide, wispy cloud over the town.

"Did you sleep at all?" Mrs. Heywood looked ten years older in this light, or perhaps it was just lack of rest. She joined Maddie in looking out the window, and frowning.

"Some. I thank you for allowing me to stay." She'd slept in her loosened stays and undergarments, to be ready when he came to fetch her. The buildings had burned all night, the underbutler said, but the fire hadn't traveled. She felt bruised and tired. Nash must be dead on his feet.

"I was glad for the company, especially after Mrs. Clayton's dramatics." She took Maddie's arm, linking it with her own, bumping her softly on the hip. They stood the same height. Mrs. Heywood porcelain with dark hair, Maddie creams and browns.

"A woman fainted on my first visit to Shaftsbury, as well."

"Don't blame yourself, dear. Cecilia Clayton is a country girl, you know, she was raised in the south. Lived here twenty years, and still she's always on about the noise and the bustle."

"The town has changed quite a bit in that time, Nash says."

"We've reaped the benefits of it. Your Nash, why he's built a small empire just since the war."

Maddie tried not to think about Nash, and his unreasoning expectations, and his hateful words, and how she'd failed him, and what if he never came back. Mrs. Heywood studied her a moment, and then looked out the window again. She squeezed Maddie's arm a shade tighter.

"I remember when he arrived on our doorstep, mariner's bag in hand—and with a full beard! The maids were quite afraid of him, and I admit I didn't know what to think. He cleans up well, I don't have to tell you that, and in a day or two he'd quite won us over."

Maddie didn't trust her voice yet. She closed her eyes, and prayed for the lady to continue.

"He was in funds, from his prize-ships, and he had ideas, but for an earl's boy he was shockingly direct, even to the merchants. Heywood sorted him out soon enough. On a magistrates committee already." She pinched Maddie's forearm gently. "Catnip to the ladies. No one knew about the Navy money, but once it was clear he would do well in business, I had all the proud mamas begging me for invitations to our suppers. Like everything else, he decided on a bride in his own time and in his own manner."

"I think he would have preferred to be always on his own." Maddie cringed as she heard the words, lingering in the breath before her face like smoke. Hadn't he cast her out of the warehouse on the smallest of pretenses? Hadn't he continued to find fault with her ever since?

Mrs. Heywood stood quiet a long time. At last, she rummaged in her pocket with her free hand, pulling out a handkerchief and handing it to Maddie.

"What puzzled us was why he didn't go to his family first. Heywood would say the word Shaftsbury, or merely mention him in passing, and Nash would bite the conversation off before he could finish it."

Maddie wiped her eyes and sighed heavily, finally able to turn her thoughts outward. "Then why return here at all? On his ships, he must have found plenty of likely spots to settle on."

Mrs. Heywood patted her arm. "His heart might know the right direction, but his head will fight it every step of the way. Look, is that them? They look veritable chimney-sweeps."

Nash's hair had turned gray with ash. His hands held the reins so loosely the team kept sliding off the track of the road, then he'd snap back up and they'd roll right. He'd spent himself helping a man he did not care for. Longing surged through her. She wanted to be right for him, whatever right meant.

Mrs. Heywood pulled away, calling for the butler. Maddie gripped her arm, not releasing her. The butler on his course, she turned back to Maddie, a question in her gaze.

"How do you do your plumbing here? The baths, are they downstairs? Might I see them?" Maddie winced at the screech of desperation in her words.

If she thought the question odd at a time like this, Mrs. Heywood made no mention of it. "They'll wash at the pump, I expect. But we might meet them there. Your Nash might not wish to come in, as he is."

"No. I mean, what do you do? For proper bathing?" She trailed the lady down the two flights of servants' stairs to the back of the house. More than anything, she wanted an answer. More than anything, she didn't want the lady to know why.

They stepped outside, on the path to a small garden. "There," Mrs. Heywood said, pointing to a pump with a trough. A man pumped the handle quickly as Nash and the others splashed their heads and hands. Once the bulk of the grime had rinsed away, they disappeared into a small brick cottage behind the pump.

"There's a boiler in there, fed on the outside. I had it started last night. It's usually good for the lot of us, but will get a serious test this morning." She called for clean clothing to be brought for all the men, and motioned for Maddie to follow her to a bench under a wide elm.

"Our yard is too small." A bathing room that size would fill it twice over, not to mention their distinct lack of an army to do the pumping.

"I hear you do have a water closet, which is more than we had until we heard of Nash's. He must have brought that fastidiousness back from the Navy—I hear he has one even at the warehouse."

Maddie was still puzzling out the bathing cottage. "It must need a cistern."

"No, we have an excellent well, which is what you lack, in that neighborhood of yours. At least you're downwind, so the air doesn't smell, but if you want more, you'll need to convince him to remove to better ground."

More likely he'd remove her from his home than spend all

his capital on a wasteful mansion like this. Maddie frowned as Mrs. Heywood mused aloud.

"That unlikely, is it? Water, water. You send out your whites to the washerwoman, right? And the closet uses catch-water, I understand. So, what's left is only..." She stopped. Her gaze seemed to draw the blush out of Maddie's skin. The lady looked away. "The ash makes the air sparkle, can you see it? The whole town will be dusted in it."

Maddie watched the air between her and the pump. Tiny shards of mirror floated by in air still cloudy violet. True sunlight hadn't yet reached the garden. She hoped Mrs. Willis had shut all the windows at home, or it would be a day of wiping with the damp cloths, another use of scarce water.

"You've heard about the Roman baths?"

Maddie frowned. "Are they outside town? I don't remember seeing any ruins."

"He hasn't told you? Center of town, and not ruins, working baths. Whole rooms of water, running water, over beside the Infirmary. Marvelous thing, really, like a tiny sea under a roof and four walls."

"And one gets clean there?"

"I'll take you. Not today, tomorrow, that's a ladies' day."

"The ladies have their own day?"

Mrs. Heywood stood up. The men were coming out. Nash looked an overgrown boy in Mr. Heywood's trousers, too wide at top and inches too short at bottom. He wore the shirt loose.

"It's a subscription, like the lending library. Nash, dear, why haven't you taken your wife to the public baths?"

He stopped, thunderstruck, as if she'd asked him how was their trip to the moon.

"Don't bother the boy, Penny. Can't you see he's exhausted?" Heywood bent to kiss his wife on the forehead. Nash watched them, and looked at Maddie, his eyes swollen and red. He made no move toward her.

"The fire is well out?" She asked the easiest question she could think of.

"We're here, aren't we?" To Mrs. Heywood, he said, "I'm sorry Madeline has troubled you with our affairs." Now his face was cleared of soot, Maddie could see how drawn it was, how exhausted.

Mrs. Heywood's mouth pursed. "Perhaps she sought kinder counsel, is all."

"I'm not following." Heywood rubbed at his eyes, displacing the tangle of bristles that formed his brows.

"We're all overtired, dear." His wife rested her hand on his shoulder. "I thought I might take Mrs. Quinn to the baths this week."

Heywood's grunt sounded more like a snore. "We all need a trip after last night."

"Not all of us," Nash muttered.

In their bedroom, Nash peeled off Heywood's clothing, but instead of hanging it neatly as he always did, he draped the pieces over the trunk. His best suit of clothes, in a sack by the entry, now were fit only for their own burial. He shuffled his feet and dropped onto the bed. The room smelled of ashes.

"Guess I needed a wash, eh, Madeline?" His voice sank in sad resignation. She sat on the edge of the bed as he pulled the sheet over his nakedness.

"Let me rub your shoulders. You've worked them so long."

"I'll not bother you."

"It's not a bother."

"But it is, wife. You bother the entire household."

"Rest now. Should I go to the warehouse for you? It's not a market day, but—"

"No." He waved her away as if she were a buzzing fly. "Nothing from you. I just want to sleep."

She couldn't think of anything to say. Even if she could, there was no air in her lungs to push the words out. She held in what little breath she had.

He turned his head to look at her, his lids so drooped she wasn't sure he saw anything. He let out all his breath in a sigh, then took it in again. "I like your scent. Honeysuckle? But I'm beginning to think we won't suit." His long exhale ended in the start of a snore. He was dead asleep.

Maddie sat still, barely breathing, making sure he slept. He rolled onto his back, one knee bent, its foot in the crook of his other knee. His arms crossed at his breastbone, as if he were a living corpse.

Even sapped of energy, his skin shone with health in the new day's light. Ruddy brown beard shadowed his cheeks and lips. His lashes were too long for a man's. His breaths were elastic, pulling at her heart, and then pushing her away.

She tugged the sheet away. His strong chest tapered into sturdy hips, which split into the thighs that had ridden her—was it only last week? Her own thighs throbbed at the memory.

His cock, asleep, was as long as her hand. She longed to cup it. Her hand reached out at the thought, but froze in midair. She shook her head in frustration. He was asleep. Where did this fear come from?

She reached out again, just a finger to feather up his shaft.

The hot panic swelled from her belly to her forehead, as if her body were fighting her mind. But she was in the sun, safe, and slowly her finger started to move again. She stroked up his shaft, the lightest touch.

He stirred in his sleep, rolling away from her. She considered waking him by doing that trick with her hand he always seemed to like. But he was exhausted. And unpredictable. And he couldn't have made himself any clearer.

We don't suit.

Twenty-Four

The streets reminded Maddie of Christmastide, the soft snow blanket today sharp ash. Her half-boots kicked it up no matter how carefully she walked. She'd lain in that bed for an hour, wide awake, before giving in and getting up. Even in the downstairs drawing room, she'd felt suffocated. Mrs. Willis thought she was going to church to give thanks the blaze had claimed no lives, but Maddie was more selfish than that.

The flakes of gray-black floated like oversized dust motes, and just as elusive. When she reached for one, it seemed to pulse away, but as she walked, more and more fixed on her. The parasol protected her head and shoulders, but her skirts slowly turned from blue to light gray, streaked with black.

After all this time, she knew not to expect Kitty would be there. When her sister came up beside her as she paid her respects at her mother's grave, she could not feel surprise. Today was already too much.

"You be persistent." Her bonnet and skirts, already black, took on sheen from the soot. She was coated in it, even her sharp chin streaked. Maddie wondered if her own chin could take on as hard an aspect as Kitty's. Her lids were half-closed, her blinks slow, but her eyes carried that same unearthly crystal blue.

"You could not sleep, either?"

Kitty shrugged. "No work today. Any cloth as goes out of doors is ruined for sale."

"Did you see the fire?"

Kitty's gaze tried to read her. "Did your husband tell you so?"

Nash had said nothing at all about the fire, Maddie realized. "Were you there?"

"Heard it first, nothing like that sound. Then the light, pouring down our streets. You don't see that but once a lifetime." She tapped their mother's grave marker as if for luck.

"A blessing no one was killed."

"But no one will be working there no more, either. More like a slow death for some."

Not her! Before she even thought of it, Maddie reached out to touch her sister. She jerked her hand back, but not before Kitty had taken a half-step away from her.

"Don't worry for us. We've some saved. Hard times are forever on the way, you need be ready. Besides, this month it gives me more time to help with the banners for the meeting."

"The reform meeting? You know the reformers?" Maddie couldn't hide her shock, or her interest. Nash and the others were always going on about them as if they were devils, and Kitty might have spoken to one.

"I'm one myself. Treasurer of the Women's Reform Society,

allies with the Manchester Patriotic Union, although we have far more cheer than coin."

This time, it was Maddie who took a step back. Knowing someone who knew of a reformer was one thing, consorting with one herself was another.

"I won't infect you, if that's what you think. Especially seeing as your master is one with the magistrates. Da said to stay wide of him."

"Did your father agree to see me?"

"Not yet. He's thinking it over, though." Kitty's voice rang carefully neutral, but her words sent Maddie to the depths and heights alternately.

"Truth is, he doesn't know what you want."

"Only to meet him once. Perhaps to see him from time to time. I could help him."

"That's the part worries him."

"Why?"

"We don't need your blunt. He's worried of what you might do to him."

"What could I do to him?"

"Why, you'd unman him, wouldn't you? Make servants of us. We earn a good living, most times. We do fine on our own." She was nearly shouting.

"I have no thought of that, I swear. I might help you, if you need it, but I would never force you to take anything. I would never force him to do anything. I would rather hope he might, he might..." She couldn't get the words out.

"He might love you?"

Maddie nodded, her heart almost too full to speak. "I don't expect it."

"You do hope." Kitty looked out toward the street. Through a slow drip of tears, Maddie watched her sister, her face so like, mirror the same shifting emotions that buffeted her. Fear, joy, terror, dread, anger, pain, loss.

"I hope, too," she whispered.

Maddie grasped at this lifeline. "I don't expect it."

"Well you shouldn't." Kitty's gaze sharpened, and she drilled it into Maddie. "Still, I don't see why you shouldn't give us a hand, now and again. Quiet-like."

Maddie nodded. She could help her father, and he wouldn't need to know.

"What sort of straits are you in?"

"Same old." Kitty's legs twitched, as if she was tired of standing. "I have an idea, though, how you could help, and not just our poor, piteous family. Can you pay a call in two days' time?"

"To your home?" Her hopes were a rising balloon burst by another of Kitty's sharp glances. Maddie's throat burned with ash.

"No, an inn. We're holding a sort of a meeting there." Kitty's hands grew animated. "A charity sewing party. Help some of the folks put out by the fire."

"I would be honored to help."

"And you'll say nothing to your Mr. Quinn?" Maddie shook her head no, not really a promise, more an intention.

Kitty nodded. "Then come by the Black Tulip, up Long Millgate at Millers, around four. Can you do it?"

No one wanted her at home, and here was an opportunity to do good for others who needed it right now. A Christmas sewing circle come early. Maddie didn't think twice.

"I'll be there."

"Sidmouth's mouthpiece calls it sedition." The boyish committee man from Ashton pounded the table at the Star Inn. Nash tried not to roll his eyes. He was losing a lovely Saturday afternoon to this?

"Sit down, Mr. Trefford, thank you." Heywood's crisp diction washed the spirit out of Malbanks's lackey. Nash was surprised to see Malbanks seated in his usual spot. With his manufactories boarded up, the man could go on holiday. Heywood jostled his arm, reminding him to take the floor.

"Mr. Trefford and I have differing readings of the current instruction from London. The Home Office, you'll remember, including Lord Sidmouth, advised to arrest the Oldham delegates and prosecute the speakers at Ashton, and we did neither."

"How could we?" Malbanks glared at him. "Sacrifice our spies to prosecute some low-lying fruit?"

"As you said at the time. The meetings here and at Stockport came off with no loss of life, property, nor apparent sedition. The latest meeting, in Birmingham, also was peaceful, though Wolsey's nomination worries London."

Clayton snorted. "I should say so. Electing a legislatorial attorney, my ass. It's pure National Convention, and you know how poorly that served the French."

Malbanks stood, leaning over the table toward Nash. "I tell you we have revolution on our hands."

"And I tell you we don't. London agrees with me. Look at the instruction: 'Watch and report.' Nothing of arrests; nothing of sedition." Nash leaned in, glaring at the man. Why wasn't he in Bath? Or Plymouth? Or Spain, which would win the Portuguese trade now that he'd toppled Manchester's chances.

Heywood nodded. "We should have started arresting the rabble-rousers in Oldham. Now we're deep into marching season. There's no stopping them." Silence settled as each of the dozen men considered his personal stake in peace and order.

Heywood turned to Malbanks. "What do our spies tell us?"

"Our men see conspiracy, but they can't put their finger on it."

Clayton patted the man's hand, not unkindly. Malbanks stared at the hand, then the bespectacled man, with something like wondering disgust in his face.

Clayton lifted his hand. "Spies are paid only when they discover conspiracy. It's in their interests to push one along."

Nash still stood. "Or create it wholesale, as did our friend Oliver."

Malbanks turned back to him. "Oliver didn't create the Pentrich rising. That was local men, acting alone."

Clayton gave the man's hand one last pat. "Then why did Oliver have to flee?"

Nash tapped the table. "Gentlemen, please. I've heard that plans are under way for another meeting, here in town, even bigger than February last."

"Who's your spy?" Malbanks pulled his arms in and crossed them.

"No spy, a young man who attended an open meeting up in Middleton. He says organizers sent an invitation to old Major Cartwright, but he's ill, and now they are asking Hunt."

Clayton tapped his chin. "Hunt was well-received last winter. In summer, he could easily draw thousands."

"Cut them off at the root," Malbanks urged. "Nothing good can come of thousands storming the town."

Nash pushed off the table, disgusted. "You put thousands out of work. They 'storm the town' every day now."

"It's too bad about your precious merchant cartel, but true gentlemen need to do what's right for England."

"Our men need work." Nash closed his eyes. He needed this man's agreement, or at least his neutrality, to make his plan real. "Listen. I can set up a parlay, a meeting between some of us and some of the more-moderate reformers. Perhaps we can agree to delay the meeting, or kill it outright."

Nash could sense their interest. No one had pitched this idea before. Even old Pedersen, nodding off, shook himself awake.

Malbanks crossed his arms. "What man would parlay with us? Seditious bastards, all."

"Bamford, from Middleton, Knight you know. One or two others."

Clayton puffed out a chain of smoke. "The older crowd might listen to reason. What would we give them in exchange for their docility?"

"Information. We tell them why wages are depressed and agree to revisit the issue come winter."

Clayton nearly dropped his pipe. Malbanks laughed out loud. "You mistake them for rational creatures." Pedersen smiled, and then nodded back off. A few others snickered behind their hands or their pints. He was losing them, but he had to keep trying.

"They see us making profit now, while they suffer. Even an irrational man can see the imbalance."

Heywood rapped the table. "I agree that to tell them our

trade is foolish. Simply sounding them out might serve us as well. At the least we know how they will argue their case and we can prepare a good defense of our position."

Malbanks waved an arm wide. "So we parlay. Let it be not some token group, though. Let all of us stand before this rabble, and see how bravely they come to meet us then."

Nash could just picture it. Not a cordial introduction, laying the groundwork for a continuing conversation, but a parade of battleships meant to awe and cow. Malbanks had twisted his plan to sink it. The man would put his own pride ahead of an entire country's livelihoods.

Nash wished he'd never come up with the idea. Of course, it might still work.

Just as there might be another virgin birth.

THE ROMAN BATHS were all Mrs. Heywood had promised. A city block long and wide at Piccadilly and Portland streets, the series of baths weren't even a decade old, yet their style called to mind the aqueducts in Bath. Mechanical rather than natural, they were far more reliable.

The whitewashed stone walls gleamed even in the dusky haze of a heavy manufactory day. And they were full of lovely, steaming bathwater. Of course, she couldn't have it all the time. Ladies and gentlemen took turns, morning shift or evening. Pay the ten-shilling subscription fee, and come as much as you like.

Once she'd seen how delighted Maddie was with the place, Mrs. Heywood had paid her first month's subscription then and there. "No need to bother your busy husband about it just now." Maddie could have kissed her.

Even the prospect of attending the baths on her own didn't frighten her. Mrs. Heywood came only rarely, with that cottage bath of hers. Once Maddie made acquaintances, she wouldn't feel so lonely, either. Even if she did, it was so, so worth it.

On her second visit, she nearly skipped the eight blocks from the cemetery and still had plenty of wind to greet the baths' proprietress, a tall no-nonsense woman wearing a practical cotton dress and Roman sandals. Of the four styles of baths, Maddie preferred the swim pool, which ran nearly the width of the building.

After a quick rinse and in her new swimming outfit, a woolen singlet, she stepped into the rooms full of waters, humming with the sound of their movement. She'd forgotten the taste of the waters at Bath, its murmurs and gurgles. Only a handful of other women lined the edges of the pools, most content to float, eyes closed, or chat in whispers. Once their hair had fallen free or been tucked into neat caps, she couldn't tell which were the great ladies and which the merchants' families. Did workers come here, as well? Kitty would love this.

Maddie spent two entire hours in the baths, first a cool, bracing one. Then she slowly swam lines in the larger pool, reveling in the sleekness of her body as the water rolled around it. Finally, she soaked in the warmest bath, relaxing muscles just starting to feel the strain of her new exercise.

She could be clean every day, clean down deep. It was a dream come true. Best of all, it cost Nash nothing, just the pin money already allotted to her.

After the serenity of the baths, the streets seemed to shout with activity. Nash would be at the meeting all afternoon, so there was no need to rush or take a hack. Maddie glided through the halting, teeming stream of human beings, seeing them as flashes of gray, brown, blue in the heavy afternoon light. There were always more people milling about now, walking slower, as if they had lost their purpose. After months in town, her own steps had taken on a force and direction that matched the flow of traffic, but now her steps seemed too fast. It was summer, and there was little work.

Crossing Piccadilly, she wondered whether Jem's family might enjoy a visit. She was empty-handed, though. Perhaps she should first go home to pick up some of Mrs. Willis's fresh-baked bread. People in good times should share with those in need. She didn't see the wiry man in her path until he spat on her.

She stopped, raising a hand to her chest. For a moment, she wasn't sure she'd understood what he had done, and then she saw the trail of brown spittle leaching down her shoulder, toward her hand. She swallowed the bile back down to her stomach.

Not a large man in size, but his face was red and raw. In rough homespun, he stood feet splayed, hands on hips. "Wear Frenchie cloth in a good English town, do you?"

He was right. She'd somehow chosen her favorite dress from school days, simple spun silk in a sea-foam green near the color of her eyes. Her chest thickened, heavy with shame. How could she have forgotten, after all this time?

"It's folk like you put us out of work. You're as bad as the masters." His breath reeked of homemade ale and cabbage. He turned, as if he would call the street's attention to them. She had to say something.

"I am sorry you have no work."

His head snapped to look at her, mouth softening. "A southern girl? Don't know no better, I expect."

"It's not like a girl can swap out her wardrobe every time she moves to a new town."

"Would be for the best, missy. Sell 'em or burn 'em, don't matter much. Hard times, these is, and a body's looking for a fight. Begging your pardon." He touched his cap.

She knew better than to offer him money. Mancunians wanted to earn their keep. Best to simply watch him go and swallow the tears.

No one showed weakness in these streets.

TWENTY-FIVE

Ll the talk in and out of the Exchange and about the warehouse carried the same overtone of hysteria Nash remembered from the eve of a major sea operation. Once the crew saw the enemy ships, all set to, determined and unyielding. Beforehand, it was as if nearly every hand had turned into a fishwife.

He closed the account books and set them on the high shelf. When Maddie was here, he'd set them lower, so she could reach. His workers would not riot in the streets, and what befell Malbanks was of his own doing. So why couldn't Maddie come back to work? Because her husband was a hypocrite.

Most women didn't mind being left alone to play all day and visit their friends, he'd always heard. What utter nonsense: His own Mama managed a large household, and Heywood's lady oversaw the busiest charity in town, the widows and childrens' fund. Why wouldn't Maddie wish to be of use?

Somehow, she'd grown too precious to endanger by

exposing her to the rough ways of the warehouse. Idiocy. He'd seen women at Malbanks's 'factory, helping their men, as well as the wives of the spinners and weavers; surely they were just as precious to their husbands. Maddie deserved the chance to be useful just as he did. More, probably. If she chose to serve in trade, what of it?

It couldn't be worse than her behavior when he forced her to be a hothouse flower, all dainty and fragile. This obsession with water, when would it end? How he tried not to look at her when he left after luncheon, the longing in her face unmasked. The sound of a rushing skirt as he opened the door, only to see her sitting noodling at needlework on the seat farthest from the window. She waited for him, because that was all he'd allowed her to do.

Nash left early for home, but opened the door to silence. Maddie must still be with Mrs. Heywood, at those blasted baths. Nobody needed to bathe every day. If only she had more friends. No, as Mrs. Willis had pointed out, Maddie couldn't very well entertain here. These were Spartan single man's lodgings, not the gracious home of a fine lady.

A letter stood on the sideboard in the hall. Nash hung up his hat and took the starched vellum piece into the drawing room. Sitting down, he noticed with surprise how calm he was, how regular his heartbeat, despite the fact the letter carried the Shaftsbury seal. He didn't dread what Deacon could write to him.

They had both lived in terror of their somber, stoic father, but now Nash wasn't sure if that hadn't been all their imaginations. The man had been gruff, sure, and a heavy sort, but he never struck them, except with a glance or a word. Nash had experienced far, far worse in the Navy, but never the lead-belly dread as at Shaftsbury. And if anyone should have felt their father's wrath, it was Deacon, nearly drummed out of college for failing to attend to his studies.

Instead, the old sharp had found another answer—a woman who would undertake Deacon's studies for him. He hadn't sought to break his boy and re-form him into the earl's own image, but left Deacon to grow into what manner of man he would.

The old earl's best correspondent, by far, had been Maddie, and her view of the old man matched Mama's. Perhaps he had been mistaken about the man. Perhaps Maddie had the right of this, as well.

He had just finished reading the short note when he heard the turn of her key in the lock, the swirl of her skirts in the hall. He was on his feet and in the hall before she had turned back from pulling the door shut. He nearly stroked her shoulder, but she was turning, pulling on the ribbons of her straw bonnet and stepping into him. They bumped hip to leg, and she stopped short. The bonnet slid down. Her face was full of tears.

Iron panic washed over him. Heart playing a tattoo, he touched her shoulders, gripped her waist, twisting her side to side. Nothing bloody, nothing obviously broken. Then the rushing in his ears stemmed and he could hear her breaths, regular and easy. Not wounded, sad.

He pulled her close, removing the lump of a package in her hands and setting it on the sideboard. She smelled of fresh sea, and the mild dyes of the south, and somehow of tobacco. She felt right, tucked into his chest just so. But her tears didn't stop, and were joined by hiccupping sobs.

He heard a tread coming up the kitchen stair, and pulled out of their embrace, still holding Maddie in the circle of one arm. "Some tea, Mrs. Willis, if you please." The tread descended, and he drew Maddie into the sitting room and onto the bench beside him.

"I knew you would despise the baths. That's why I didn't bring it up. Damn Mrs. Heywood for frightening you. You never need go back there again."

She wrinkled her face. "The baths?"

He smoothed her brow with his finger, and then kissed her forehead, running his hand through her damp, selkie hair. "You don't have to explain it to me. That water is too wide, too deep. It's not natural. Man is meant for land."

She closed her eyes, her brow softening, her lips slipping into a smile. Something eased in his chest, as if a boulder he'd forgotten about had suddenly dislodged. He would have her forever making that half a smile, just for him.

"You are afraid of the water." She opened her eyes, teasingly triumphant.

He sat back, but she leaned into him, closing the gap. "Not afraid. Prudent. Respectful."

"Respectful." The way she said it made it sound like the excuse it was. "You didn't tell me about the baths not because you thought I was a silly woman but because you thought I'd be afraid."

He wished she would stop using that word. She didn't need to sound so blasted pleased about it. Wasn't she crying not a minute past? "Then what has upset you?"

Her gaze dropped to her lap, or perhaps it was his lap. He shifted a bit, and tipped her chin up with a finger. She wasn't going to distract him that way.

"In the streets, there's so much anger, so much shouting. It's a giant steamkettle, and we're all too close."

She'd caught the stench of discontent in the air. How could she not? "We're all of us out of gearing, not running smoothly. Soon enough, we'll slide back into place. We always do."

"I need some new dresses, and to sell these old ones. They aren't right to give to charity."

He frowned. She wore his favorite of her southern frocks, a green calico that sharpened the cat's-eye flecks in her eyes. It did carry a stain on the shoulder, and he had to admit it was a debutante's style. "Heywood's wife looks the part. You might ask her to recommend a seamstress. 'Here's something that might cheer you up now. How about a picnic?"

The flat doubt on her face surprised him into a laugh. "You have time for such frivolity?"

"You know, I don't think I've ever heard that word applied to me before. I might cultivate it." She matched his smile with a sideways grin of her own. "Truth, it's not my idea. Deacon plans a lawn party for his tenants and neighbors. The meetings have eaten into the rushcart parades and fairs, and he wants to restore some of their fun."

"A day in the country does sound nice. It's good of him to think of it."

"And good to keep in his people's good graces. My brother may yet step up to his role. I might have underestimated him."

Her touch on his knee surprised him. Was she promising more later? "Might I invite a friend of mine?"

"Jem's family?"

"Someone I met at church."

"Why not? Deacon's lawns are large."

§&

IN A PITIABLE ATTEMPT at neutral ground, the meeting between the magistrates and special committee of Lancashire and the town's workingmen took place in a second-floor room at the Exchange. Nash expected that none of the workers had ever been there, and that first view, of the cacophonous floor devoted to commerce, was as likely to tie their tongues as the most hell-fire sermon on Sunday. By the time they climbed the two sets of stairs, open and edging the trading hall, they would be as cowed as any royalist magistrate could wish. Watching the men called the leaders of their group—don't dare call them a union—shuffle in wearing their odd clomping sabots, Nash caught a whiff of the same stubbornness. Not a penitent among them.

Coarse cotton arrayed itself in a row facing fine linen and ermine—Heywood wore some hoary piece from the days of the seigneurs, complete with gilded necklace—and no one took a seat. If it would not be a successful parlay, and Nash knew now how truly foolish a dream that had been, at least it would be short.

He had had to suggest that they introduce themselves. The working men were reluctant: "If you make a listing of us, suddenly we are without all work." The magistrates were just as bull-headed, and so the speechifying began with no one having any idea whom they were dealing with. Nash knew from hard experience what an ill start that was.

Heywood's opening gambit, ten minutes of *let's all return to the earlier, happy days*, didn't persuade even his own side.

A middle-aged man, a weaver, took it to pieces in a bare minute, but at least he carried a smile in his voice. History-wise, he rightly pointed out, nothing had changed. "It's your part to beat us down like plate, to swell your fortunes. It's ours to stand up for our families and demand justice and fair play. We make your profits, and we should help spend 'em."

Could this be the Sam Bamford Nash'd heard of? It must be; his phrasing was direct from the pamphlet the workers' reform committee published arguing in favor of the meeting. A formidable foe, but he could be just the sort of man who could listen as well as argue. Of the half-dozen workingmen, two looked bulls, no chance of changing their minds. Two looked wary, gazes circling from the dozen scowling magistrates to the closed doors. One was the eloquent speaker, and the last a mere boy, still wearing the red spots of youth. The magistrates shared the same proportions: one-third bull-necked and bull-headed, another third terrified trade would suffer, and a bare two or three willing to listen even a little.

The men wished to hold a public meeting in just a week, the ninth of August. The magistrates couldn't say no exactly, as it was legal to meet, but they could stand in the way, by denying petitions to use the space or declaring the meeting illegal. Under law, a meeting couldn't be called illegal until something criminal occurred at it. He could see Malbanks's eyes shuttering and shifting, trying to find the loophole that would give him sway.

As both sides sidled along the path of reasonableness without stepping directly upon it, business was, indeed, transacted. The workers agreed to reapply "properly" for permission, delaying the meeting by a week, and the magistrates agreed to allow it to take place. Nash suspected Malbanks and his crowd wouldn't be satisfied until all the workers were in jail, though it would sink their own profit.

The meeting lasted twenty minutes. Nash followed the workers out the door, managing to catch the sleeve, and the attention, of their main speaker.

"You're Bamford?"

"And you're Quinn." The man turned, framing up into a fighting stance, but his gaze was more interested than belligerent.

"I thought your rebuttal in the papers a piece of work. Good work. Might you be someone I could talk with privately? Where might I find you? An alehouse? Somewhere public."

"The Black Tulip. Let it be known you're looking, and one or t'other of us might be found. Mayhaps even your father-in-law. He's one of us, you know. The tall one."

Nash reeled back on his heels. "You know my wife?"

"Only by reputation. A fine lass, if a bit dressy. Aren't they all." Bamford winked. "The Black Tulip. Miller Street."

Maddie's father was a radical? Should he tell her? He couldn't. It would cause far more problems than even he could manage this summer. Later, when tempers cooled with the autumn, he might mention it. Suddenly, he burned with curiosity about the man, Moore. How could a father have given up such a treasure? He didn't have time to do more than wonder. As he turned back toward the meeting room, he could hear the angry rumble of voices. Entering the room, he found he needn't have hurried. No one had changed his mind.

"If they protest, it's on their heads. Any violence, and their leaders are in the poke before they can finish their dinner." Malbanks smacked his lips, salivating at the prospect.

Nash interrupted. "I should think that would push them to

keep their men in line. No one wants to spend an evening in the New Bailey."

Trefford's shrill tenor broke in. "These men don't share your sense of logic. Their only sense that is developed is of entitlement."

Malbanks nodded, turning to Nash. "Did you hear that weaver? 'All's we want is what's fair.' How is it fair for us to work so hard, and they skim all the profit?"

"Those men work hard for their wages. Wages, I needn't remind you, that are significantly reduced from last year, while the price of wheat has doubled."

"Let the parish take care of the starving."

"We are the parish." Nash bit his cheek to prevent another outburst. A more pig-headed bunch he had never met, unless one counted one's relations.

"So we do nothing?" Trefford's voice and hands trembled at the idea.

"Nothing we can do, more's the pity," Heywood said.

"We could arrest Hunt, when he comes to town," Malbanks said.

Nash unlocked his jaw. "On what grounds?"

"Incitement to violence."

"No. They'll have their meeting," Heywood said. "That is the law."

"So's they say," Malbanks said. "You heard what happened in Birmingham. They won't get away with that rabble-rousing here."

Heywood shook his head, his necklace clanking dolefully. "I don't see that we can do anything. We must trust that they value their good word." He held up a hand to forestall their protests.

"Nay, Manchester men are strong and proud. They won't fall in with these radicals from London. They are what makes us strong."

Malbanks huffed, his peacock chest swelling. "Sooner we replace them with machinery, the better."

"Listen to yourself." Nash couldn't hold back. "Without wages in their pockets, who will buy your broadloom cloth?"

"Parliament may, and hand it out to the parish poor."

Heywood laughed, breaking some of the brittle tension in the room. "Now you want government in your business? Backing the smokestack tariff now, too?"

Malbanks would not be silenced. "This will come to a bad end, believe me. There can be only trouble when the lower orders collect in one pen."

TWENTY-SIX

{ 2 ^{6}} The Black Tulip did not smell like a coffee shop. The well-made sign over the door was plain enough, though. Maddie stepped over the threshold on the fumes of her courage, and stopped.

A crusty bar stood to her left, an orchestra of mismatched tables and chairs to her right. A half-dozen drooping men in 'factory smocks sat scattered about, though the day's dismal bells had not yet rung closing. Overpowered by generations of beers spilled and baths skipped, she held her breath to regain her balance.

One by one, heads perked up at the sight of her. She shouldn't have worn her new dress, a robin's egg blue from Clayton's mills. She clutched the pocket holding her purse. The money was for the women's society, for the out-of-work families; no one else must take it from her.

This was all fancy. Kitty wouldn't have led her to a place where she might be robbed. Maddie pushed her feet to step to the bar. The keep, a woman of faded brass, blinked slowly at her, and then tilted her head toward the far wall. Stairs rain up the wall to a sort of balcony; beside the stair an open doorway led to another room.

Skirting the tables, she was rewarded by the sight of her sister seated in the small room. A well-dressed older gentleman, seated to her left at a round table, rose as Maddie entered.

Kitty rose, as well. "Told you she'd come."

He bowed so gracefully Maddie curtseyed before she thought better of it. In blue lapelled coat, light waistcoat and wool trousers, he seemed overdressed for a Manchester summer. Perfectly proportioned to his six feet in height, he had only one flaw—a tightness about his thin lips. Even his gray-brown hair, brushed forward onto his forehead and cheeks in the London style, was his own.

Henry Hunt, "The Orator" to his detractors, a prince to the radicals. She'd seen his likeness in the papers, though he presented even better in person. His white top hat, a symbol of the reform, hung on the hook beside her at the door.

"You've found me out," he said, looking in the direction of her gaze.

"The papers say you are in the south." The royalist papers also said he was inciting sedition across the country, and warned that his coming to town would endanger all Christian folk. To look at him, though, was to see the truth of it. He was just another politician, only of the "broad cloth" people rather than the "narrow cloth" ones, as Jem's wife would put it. And, no doubt, Kitty.

"I find it's best to stay a step ahead of the press."

This must be one of those committee meetings, those formerly clandestine affairs now merely shady and unsavory, according to the *Observer*.

With a shiver of anticipation, she sat down in the chair Hunt pulled out for her.

"I'm ringed by beauty," he said in silver tones. She smiled, shy at the compliment, and then froze. Small wonder Kitty had made her promise to say nothing of this to Nash. He would never want her here.

She wasn't doing anything wrong. Wasn't he himself at some sort of committee meeting over at the Exchange? She was merely exercising her right to talk with whomever she pleased, and who could be more intriguing than Orator Hunt? Still, Kitty had been sly. She looked past Hunt to her sister. "A knitting circle?"

"We'll get to that after. Mayhaps."

"Tell her the truth, Miss Moore. We're here to plan the largest collection of the disenfranchised this country has yet seen."

Maddie's heart thudded in her chest. "You mean to riot Manchester?"

"Exactly the opposite. We mean to show that the good denizens of this town can meet and petition a redress of their grievances without resorting to violence of any kind."

"Is that possible?"

"Not only possible but probable. Surely you saw our request for a permit in the papers. The magistrates cannot deny us a meeting." He looked to Kitty for confirmation, and she sat up a little straighter.

"Aye. That's what we're waiting on—our men to come back from the parlay."

He nodded. "Like the promising citizens they are, they're man to man with the leaders of this great town."

Nash's committee. Well, if he could stick his nose in the swirl of the most interesting event in Manchester this summer, she could stick her toe in. After all, she wasn't a member of this committee, just an observer.

Hunt leaned toward her. "What does your husband have to say about the rally?"

"I'm sure I don't know." He frowned. Maddie searched for something to please him. "He is at the committee meeting."

Hunt brightened. "Then when we see you next we can have his version of it, as well as that of our men. They'll be here soon."

Not a minute later, she heard a murmuring grow louder toward them, and a trio of men entered. Maddie was reminded of the three pigs: One was older and gruff, one barely past his childhood, and one just right.

Could he be Richard Moore, her father? Her throat swelled as if to burst, and she had trouble swallowing. But it was the older man, his black eyes blazing in a pale face fringed by a thin wreath of hair, who couldn't stop staring at her. And when his gaze snapped to Kitty, who nodded yes, Maddie was sure of it.

"Linen, or cotton?" His words rasped, as if his throat were sandpapered.

"Cotton, of course," she said. Linen in this style would mean it had been made overseas, a slap in the face to these men. After her encounter on the streets, Maddie had sent all her offending dresses to Shaftsbury, destined for dusters or charities in the south.

At the sound of her voice, the other two men looked at her dress, then her face. They snapped their heads around to her sister, and back to her. The young man whistled.

"Quite the likeness, Kitty."

"Nothing like, George Swift, you're barely off your mother's teat and blind as a babe."

The older man hadn't stopped staring. But it was the other who came to sit beside her.

"Sam Bamford of Middleton, weaver and seeker of justice, ma'am." He held out his hand and she remembered to shake it this time. "It's been a long time."

She dropped his hand in her shock. "You knew me?"

"A speck of angel's hair, you were. And just as lovely now you're grown." He patted her hand where it had fallen to the table. His deep-set eyes and forgiving mouth appealed to her, even as his diminished hair and bulb-tipped nose offset his general good looks.

Kitty spoke up. "Sam, how go the rushes?" She motioned to George Swift to sit beside her, leaving the place opposite Hunt for her father. Maddie's father. She concentrated on the set of his chin, as high as she could trust herself.

Finally, his gaze slipped away from her, chin wobbling. The arch of his eye matched Kitty's. He hadn't acknowledged Maddie.

Her heart sank to her knees. He didn't wish to know her. How could she have been so foolish? She didn't belong here, this was all wrong. Her breath raced away from her, but Bamford's second touch on her hand brought it back.

"A cheap season this year, I'm afraid. Saving the blunt for the meeting. New banners, new sashes, and the rushcarts will go to good use then."

"No rushcarts." Hunt tapped the table with the edge of his hand. "This is to be a simple march and meeting. That is, if it is allowed. What did you hear, Moore?"

"Allus the same. They'll consider it 'til they deny it." He sucked a tooth, as if to prevent himself from spitting.

"They can't. It's not illegal."

"Magistrates say as what's legal here. Arrest today and let the courts decide tomorrow, they say."

"They did suggest we wait a week." Bamford shrugged. "Put a new announcement in the papers, and do it proper."

Hunt nodded. "A good plan. We must be in everything peaceful and legal. On the day, we'll start first thing in the morning to head off any unnecessary imbibing. We'll wear white and carry nothing."

"We need a few pikes. Cudgels, of course." Kitty's voice sounded shriller than usual. "Streets aren't too safe even on fine days."

"Nothing. Just a spirit of peaceableness, the likes of which this town and its people have never seen."

Bamford grimaced. "I don't know as I like the idea of having nary a tool at hand. What if the good volunteers of the yeomanry take affront to my behavior?"

"If your behavior is gentlemanlike, they'll have nothing to criticize," Hunt said.

"That's putting a barrel of faith in a bunch of drink-heavy layabouts," Bamford retorted.

"My faith is in the Crown and her laws. We will be yards within the law."

George Swift cleared his throat, but his voice still squeaked. "Will we elect an MP? Like Birmingham?"

"Gods no," Hunt said. "This town is not ready for such a thing. We need to prove our peaceable intent. Manchester will be a model for the country. To those who say we're nothing but a muddy, unkempt rabble that don't deserve the rights of suffrage, we'll present a clean, sober, respectful disproof."

Maddie tried to listen, but it was all buzzing to her ears. She sat only a foot or so from the man who helped make her. Her eyes soaked in every detail, from the slouch of his posture to the toughness of his fingernails. He did not look at her again.

"No pikes." Bamford scratched the calluses on his hand. Maddie thought she saw the same calluses on her father's hands, until he snatched them off the table and rested them in his lap. "I'll present it to my committee. I may need you to explain it better to them, though. It might fall hard on their ears."

"I am at your disposal."

"Also, one of the coves at the 'Change wants to act as parlay with us." Bamford leaned toward Maddie. "Your husband, ma'am. Quinn?"

Her father slammed the table with a fist. "Parlay? Spy, as more like."

"We can meet him and judge for ourselves," Hunt said.

"Do it in the wide open, and be bloody chary what you say." He pushed up to his feet so quickly he was nearly to the door before the others could react. He didn't spare her a glance as he stormed out of the room. Soon after, the meeting broke up.

"That went well," Kitty said, taking her arm as they left the room.

"How's that?"

"If he met you here, he couldn't well pitch a fit, could he? Worst he could do was walk away."

"Which he did."

"Aye, but he finished his business first. I call that a bloody good sign."

MADDIE COULDN'T CONTAIN HERSELF. She couldn't sit still to read the *Register* and the pamphlets Mr. Bamford had pressed her to take. She certainly couldn't simply go to sleep, with all these feelings and thoughts swirling about. Could she confide in Nash? Their days lately had been temperate, their nights calm. Dare she try him on her family again?

What sort of rickety bridge of a marriage would it be if she could not? She had to try. She also could try to stack the deck in her favor.

That night Maddie was the first to initiate intimacy. Pressing herself along the length of him in their bed, she started in. "I have something to tell you."

"You need me primed first?"

"It would help."

He groaned. "Fire away, before I do."

She looked into his eyes, a glint in the shadow. No help there. Her nerve faltered, and she tucked her head into the crook of his arm.

"That bad?" His whisper singed her ear.

"I met my father today."

It was as if his body had turned to stone. Maddie curled up tighter, wrapping her arms around her knees. Finally, he took in a long breath, let it out slowly, and squeezed her tight. "As did I. Where?"

"My sister told me to meet her for a knitting circle."

"Sister? Surprise, surprise.. She took you home?"

"A coffee shop, she called it. The Black Tulip."

"The radical hole. You talked sedition?"

"Is that what your committee was talking about?"

Nash turned her to face him. "My committee?"

Maddie flashed fear. But he wasn't hurting her, just searching her with his dark gaze.

"I think so. Some of the men had just returned from the magistrates' caucus, but they had precious little to report."

Nash pushed away, falling to his back on the mattress. "Wasn't my doing. I said we should tell what we could, if we couldn't tell all. Bloody idiots in charge."

"Who is right?"

"The men have a point, but the manufacturers have a better point. Thing is, if they worked together, they would both get what they wanted."

"How?"

"This isn't pillow talk."

She leaned over him, taking his mouth in a slow, languorous kiss that stole the breath from both. She pulled away, and sense returned slowly. Nash stretched an arm out for her, but she leaned out of his lazy reach.

"How?"

"Wench. Everyone has problems, see? The men need steady

work at good pay. The manufacturers need steady orders at a good price."

"Sounds like the same thing."

"Nearly. But what they both need, more than anything, is a voice in government."

"Suffrage."

"Without that, we'll keep snit-snatting over pennies while our rivals in the South and in Europe steal our pounds. London is jealous of us Northerners."

"Or frightened."

"Surely not."

"Aren't the manufacturers frightened of the workers? And vice versa? Seems like everyone's first response to strangers is fear."

"Such the expert." He pulled her down to nuzzle her neck.

"An expert stranger." She leaned toward him, ready for more kissing. He held a hand at her breastbone, gazing at her.

"My beautiful stranger." He wrapped his arms around her. She sank into his embrace, into the mattress as he turned her and pushed onto her.

This time, the wall of fear was easier to cross. Every time it grew easier. Nash's hands now triggered pleasure more than fear. She could even wait half a day before the urge to wash him off her grew too strong.

"Sweetest. Someday I'll show you ecstasy. You'll forget everything from before."

"Promise."

"I swear by my sword. My little radical."

THE NEXT SATURDAY, rather than counting out the bales of cotton Clayton wanted, Nash stood in chest-deep bathwater at the Roman baths, cursing Heywood, his wife, and her balmy ideas. He was not getting his head wet, no matter his mentor's taunting.

"Don't tell me you can't swim, man. You're Navy."

"Navy men think water is for transport, not dunking."

Heywood performed some sidelong stroke that took him around Nash in a lazy circle. He found himself spinning on his feet to keep the man in sight. He stopped, planting himself facing the door.

"Not leaving already? You haven't gotten your money's worth." Let the man laugh. Or don't—Nash was finding it difficult to know where to look to avoid seeing a flash of cock bobbing about as his friend rolled onto his back. He did not wish to know so much of the man. Heywood seemed oblivious to how unmanned he appeared. It was all Nash could do not to cover himself, but his hands were needed more to protect him from going under. Whose blasted idea was this, anyway?

He tried to look at the overlarge pond through Maddie's eyes. She, apparently, loved it, coming home damp and with a clear expression of joy. If this were a vice, he had to admit it was a mild one. The subscription fee filtered out the riffraff, and if the men were any indication, no one even smiled at anyone else, much less made inappropriate acquaintances.

Heywood appeared again in his sights. Nash had to look away, to the replica of a Roman mural on the far wall.

"Saw the new announcement in the papers. Not much to gainsay." The advert took full half the top of the front page, requesting "the borough reeve and constables call a public meeting a week Monday." No mention of electing a shadow representative, nothing about forming a new government. Nash leaned back a bit, trying to discover which part of the movement had drawn that grin onto Heywood's face. The mural on the ceiling showed the swan taunting a rather buxom Leda.

Heywood stood up beside him, splashing warm water in his face. Nash rocketed to vertical, sputtering. The man patted him on the back like an infant. Nash was never doing this again. Heywood looked away, shaming him further. Maybe talk would distract the man.

"You do still think we should allow the meeting."

"What choice do we have? Let them walk and talk, nothing will come of it. We can't very well give the men suffrage when we don't have it ourselves."

Nash leaned back to take another look at the ceiling, careful of the waves he made. "But can we count on the committee?"

"Not bloody likely. Malbanks is glad-handing the army encamped outside town. He says they will have our backs if the riffraff start to rabble."

"The army? Who will protect us from them?" Nash sat up, pushing the water off his chest and arms.

"Exactly. That militia—shopkeepers all. Pretend soldiers."

Nash crossed his arms. "Might be wiser simply to create a police."

"If you can convince them of that, I'll owe you a three-chop dinner. I'd throw in the whole hog if you could keep the army out of my brickyard."

"Or it's Eighteen seventeen. I've heard it before."

"You weren't here, boy. Armed rebellion, blood in the streets. The wife had to go to her mother's. Nothing but evil."

"I've heard nothing like that this time."

"From the moderates. Believe me, these radicals, whatever they say, are just a cloak for conspiracy and rebellion."

"I'm going to talk with them."

Heywood scrambled to his feet, water sluicing from his hair and the clefts in his beard. "Alone?"

"They wouldn't harm a committee man. If I can understand them, I can help them to understand us. We shouldn't be on the battlements. We want the same things. Safety, security, prosperity. Love."

Heywood's eyebrows arched. Nash shook his head. So much water must have addled his brain. "Think the army would come if called?"

"They did at Plymouth."

"Bloody hell."

"Does your wife approve of your language?"

"Her father is a weaver. She's probably heard worse."

His friend stopped shaking the water from his hair to look at him. "I thought she'd not met her Da."

Nash couldn't very well say she'd done it behind his back, though she had. "Why shouldn't she?"

"I can think of a dozen reasons why. The man's a rebel. He was at the 'Change, for god's sake." A red flush rose from Heywood's white-furred chest into his face. "He is whom you parlay with. Does she know?"

"She's met him. Once only," Nash added, as Heywood's face rounded and reddened like a beet.

"Listen to me, Quinn. We promised, your father and I, to keep the girl away from Moore. She's had trouble enough, hasn't she? You'll not go against a promise." He whispered, but Nash felt the blade behind his words.

He didn't understand it. "How does a stranger's promise weigh against Maddie's chance to know her last living relation?"

"I've heard enough." Heywood pushed himself through the water toward the shelves of stairs at one end. Nash stumbled toward the stair, but wasn't fast enough to avoid being left alone in the deep.

TWENTY-SEVEN

Kitty arrived early to the house on Stevenson Square, but Maddie had expected that. She answered the door herself, and had spirited her sister up the stairs before Mrs. Willis reached the ground floor landing. "I've picked out the perfect dress for you," she said.

"You don't have to do this."

"I want you to feel beautiful today. Don't you have beaux to impress?"

Kitty actually blushed. "Nay. Men are dolts, only wanting one thing from a lass. They'll not get it from me." She'd screwed up her face so tightly it looked as if it would crack. Maddie had to laugh, and in a moment, Kitty did as well. "True, it ain't that bad, and I have walked about with a few likely lads. These days, though, I want a man that can take care of himself, and me, too, in a pinch. Even the master weavers are hurting for work."

"Then a farmer it will be for you." Maddie pulled the blue

twill from its peg. "Plenty of hog-men and corn-men at Shaftsbury."

"Best be a red dress, then, to catch the bull-men." Kitty started to laugh at her joke, but stopped when she saw the dress. Her eyes widened.

"See, blue. Lustrous, like your eyes. Turn around," Maddie said bossily, "and I'll throw it over your head."

Kitty did as told, and the rounded dress draped her shoulders and hugged her hips like a glove.

"You're thinner in the belly and bust than I, but the dress has tucks there, see? So it's not so noticeable."

Kitty turned to see herself in the half-glass. Her hands traced the lace around the modest squared collar, then down the row of buttons closing the sleeves. "This is too fine."

Maddie, busy closing the buttons, looked up, catching Kitty's glance in the mirror. "You are just as fine."

"My hands are rough, and my hair–." She touched at her braids as if they were thistles.

"That's what gloves are for, and combs. Will you let me do your hair?"

"Like yours?"

"Is that how you would like it?"

Kitty chewed her lip. "No. More swept-up, like in the pictures. Yours looks like your husband had his way with you this morning."

Maddie patted her own wayward curls. "He may have." She loved this. Kitty was beautiful, so strong and so sure, the very model of the modern Mancunian. Maddie would do anything to be like her.

She had no trouble sweeping her sister's hair into a proper

style, anchored with combs at the back. Maddie was seating herself on the stool, just to do a touch-up, when she heard Nash's voice in the hall. He was back from the warehouse sooner than she expected.

"Quick, stand by the door."

"Why?"

"See if you can fool Nash."

"In your hair and your dress?"

Nash knocked, Maddie answered, trying to throw her voice the way they had in school. She watched in the glass as he came in and stopped short, gazing at her sister. He blinked once, and then extended his hand.

"Nash Quinn. Brother-in-law."

Kitty's pout was not as practiced as her own, and was gone in a flash when she realized Nash was serious about shaking hands. She pumped his arm up and down, laughing.

"Thank the lord I don't look like my older sibling."

"I hear the new Lord Shaftsbury is a looker."

Nash shrugged. "If you prefer blond boys."

"So happens, I do." Kitty winked at him.

Nash did the double-take Maddie had expected him to have done earlier.

"You'll not dare to aim that high?"

"Ain't aiming at nothing. Just want to see how the nobs do it. Before they kick us all out."

"They can't kick us out." Nash held his arm out for her to take. "My brother owns that town."

Maddie breathed a sigh of relief. Nash had taken immediately to Kitty, as he should. His approval could only help them when they arrived at the castle.

They were still a quarter-mile from the main house when they met the line of carts and coaches parading toward Deacon's grand affair. It was rare that an earl reached his majority and rarer still that he threw open his doors to masters and tenants alike. Nash had called his brother's idea clever, replacing the tenants' shortened celebration with this one—and brilliant to do it when Mama was away and couldn't faint over it.

Kitty gasped when they finally past the gate into the castle proper. They were fashionably late, for Northerners, the sun's mid-afternoon slant outlining the full-grown wheat in the fields in orange and red.

"I never thought to see this." Kitty's smile was infectious, her laugh a joy.

"Why not?" Nash looked past Maddie to her sister.

"Country folk and town folk don't much mix. Country folk are clannish and distrusting of strangers."

"And town folk aren't?" Sparing a moment from the horses, he winked at her.

"May be so." Kitty touched her hair for the dozenth time, as if she still did not believe she was so *à la mode*, either.

He checked the reins again, and then looked at Maddie but spoke to Kitty. "You did not invite your father?"

Kitty's face turned crafty. "He wouldn't have liked it. He's a hearth-and-home sort."

"Who has no room for Maddie." Nash's voice dripped disbelief.

Kitty looked at her gloves. "It's the shock, I'll tell you. After he saw you at the meeting, he didn't say a word to me for two days. I don't know what he is thinking."

"It may be unfortunate that you look so much alike." Nash's gaze passed from one to the other and back.

"Maddie is the likeness of our Ma." Kitty's mouth turned down. "Might be hard for him to even look upon her. Aye, and worst is the days around the wedding date. Now."

Maddie, who still marked the death of the Wetherbys every year, knew how an anniversary deepened one's sense of loss. "It sounds like they deeply loved each other."

"Aye." She sighed.

"Will you...will you like being here, Kitty? Will you be comfortable?" Maddie knew they were the wrong words, but her nerves overpowered her.

The smile drained from Kitty's face. "You're ashamed of me?"

"Of course not." Was she? So much was expected of Maddie at the castle, and she wasn't sure she lived up to it. How could Kitty, with no experience at all?

Kitty frowned.

Nash touched Maddie's arm. "I know that look. Stubbornness runs in your family."

"I can enjoy myself with the nobs as well as with anyone else."

"Good." The relief in Maddie's voice surprised her, and by the look in Kitty's face, surprised her sister as well. "I mean, I want you with us."

"You need ammunition?"

"Support. I was raised with this sort of people, and I know what they must think of me now." Just the thought set her belly churning. She set her palm against her dress as if to calm it.

Kitty saw the movement and nodded smartly at Maddie. "I'm here now."

Nash turned onto the inner drive. Cottagers and gentlemen, cobblers and clergy milled about the lawns and gardens outside the walls of the great house. Ale tents and the sound of fiddles edged the woods, and games for children and their parents claimed the wide meadow. No one in the county had missed this invitation.

"There must be whole villages here." The castle wasn't exactly dwarfed, but for once it had to compete with the noise and energy of humanity for pride of place. Maddie had forgotten how clear the air was here, and the rich smell of turned earth and fresh-cut grass.

Kitty whistled. "Here I thought there won't be room for us all."

"The old castle has some thirty rooms and the two additions another twenty."

"Just your mother and brother racket around in all that?"

"Along with their phalanx of servants. Actually, I do believe it is close to an hundred. I'll have to ask Deacon."

"One hundred twelve." Maddie smiled at his raised eyebrow. "According to the temporary bookkeeper."

"Remind me to hold my accounts with you. Such a precise memory."

A groom took the reins, and Nash walked the ladies through the inner courtyard and up the stairs to the main entrance. Maddie was surprised to see Deacon himself in the shade of the hall. They stepped in and performed their courtesies.

"Welcome, my dears. You'll stay to supper? Cook is rabid that the courses won't stretch, but I told her I would skip some if worse came to worst." Deacon's eyes darted from them to the lawn to the drive to them again, frantic. This day involved so much planning and organizing, and he'd done it all himself. So he would think, when Maddie knew Mr. and Mrs. Perkins had it all in hand. His hand was clammy in hers as he bent to kiss it.

"You're doing too much, my lord. Enjoy your day. I'll check with cook; she likes me. You and Nash might give Kitty a quick tour."

His shoulders dropped an inch as he let out a great breath. "You're a saint. Talking to Cook is like speaking French to a German." He stopped short, staring at Kitty. "This is the sister? She is very like."

Kitty curtseyed carefully.

Deacon gave her a gallant bow. "How do you find Shaftsbury? Miss Moore, is it?"

She glanced past him, at the castle. "Fine and all." Deacon started; Kitty was shouting. She softened her voice, if not her tone. "It's hard to favor fat priests and gentry who sit on their arses—begging your pardon—while the likes of us break our backs merely to make them rich."

"You're a rebel?" He grinned at her.

"Reformer," she said.

"Radical reformer," Nash said.

Kitty turned to Nash. "Did your Maddie tell you, I'm officer in the Women's Reform Society?"

"Women need reforming?" Deacon laughed. "I had no idea."

"You know they don't," Kitty rolled her eyes at the earl.

"Right. It's men that do." Deacon nodded like an Old King

Cole, making them all laugh. Maddie breathed easier. This afternoon would go well.

"Make fun all you like, Sir Earl," Kitty put her hands on her hips, grinning. "I helped design the flag we'll carry to our meeting next week. It's to be the biggest yet."

"So I heard. And you'll be dreaming big—wanting the franchise, too?"

She frowned, really more a scowl. "Your women ain't even got that. The men can have the vote. They'll do by us."

"Just so." Deacon waved at the entrance to the main house. "How about a tour?"

Kitty dipped another curtsy. "Begging your pardon, sirs, but I'd not say no to a pint of something first."

"A woman after my own heart," Nash said, taking Kitty by the arm. "We'll meet you down at the tents."

Maddie watched as they sauntered down the stairs and across the lawn.

"They make a handsome couple, do they not, sister-in-law?"

Kitty was a head shorter than Nash, but they did seem to proportion up right, somehow. "They do."

"That's how you look, too. A right couple, shaping up nicely. Are you?"

Maddie had not yet grown used to her brother-in-law's style of interrogation. She puzzled on her words a moment. "I believe so."

"Nash seems as settled as a Navy man can be. He even stepped into the castle without growling. A miracle." They turned into the cool of the castle. Deacon took her hand. "One has only to glance at Nash to see your influence. The man went through an entire conversation, short as it was, without scowling once." He put his arm around her shoulder. "I need someone like you, reliable, temperate, and smarter than I. Blasted if my old man hadn't had the right of it after all."

At first sight of them, Deacon's beefy cook threw both her bread-loaf arms in the air, crying, "I give up." Deacon matched her expression, and Maddie sent him outside for good. Ten minutes of wailing and whining on one side and gentle persuasion on the other, and cook was back happily stirring the soup-pot where she belonged.

Maddie felt that, perhaps, she just might belong here, too.

NASH FELT an odd combination of comfortable and awkward with his sister-in-law by his side. Especially as she was in Maddie's frock. He caught himself leaning too close to tell her something about the castle, then pulled himself back suddenly. He hoped she didn't take affront.

"Already used to having a wife around, aren't you?"

So, she had noticed.

"I'm an easy touch." Surprisingly easy, where Maddie was concerned. When she screwed up her courage to spill the news about meeting her father, he could have hugged her for her bravery. She should never be afraid of her husband. As mad as Nash could get, he would never go back on a promise.

"Are you such an easy touch for the pints? I don't have much coin."

"This is no festival, this is a party." He saw she didn't understand. "The beer is free. Ale. Even lemonade."

"Lead me on."

Kitty took two mugs of ale, and handed one to Nash. She drank her own with gusto, but then seemed to remember where she was. She looked around furtively, as if to gauge reaction to her behavior, but no one was watching.

"Enjoy, Miss Moore. That's what the drink is for."

"Which is why the true ladies don't drink it. Kitty is all you need say." She finished the pint in smaller sips as they left the line at the sideboards and headed for the trees.

Nash wondered how many times Maddie had stopped herself from pleasure in the same way. He'd seen her hesitate, during a savory course at table, and once during the harpist's performance at Heywood's. She certainly held herself back in bed.

"Kitty, you're a woman."

"What of it?" She flicked a speck of foam off the top of her lip. If Maddie had done that, he would have bedded her right there, damn the sun and the crowd. Kitty might look the same, except for those blue eyes, of course, but she did not move him at all.

Could he make Maddie happy? How did he make her love him, the way he had started to love her? "How do I persuade Maddie that she might show pleasure?"

"She sure don't laugh enough now. I thought that's how ladies was."

"That's how they are trained up to be, but I don't believe she is like that at all. I see hints, suggestions, that she is enjoying herself, but only a small smile, or a light laugh."

"You want her to guffaw."

"Actually, I want her to scream."

Kitty coughed, covering a laugh and nearly spilling her half-empty pint. "Might be your method has something wanting about it."

The hairs on the back of Nash's neck rose. "My technique is fine."

"Judge by the results, my lord."

"Nash is enough."

"Does she trust you, now? Did she tell you she how she wanted to meet her Da?"

"I told her no."

"Judgment falls. What will she take from that?"

"That I care about her and don't wish her hurt."

"Could be, or could be that she'd better darn sure do as you say or you'll toss her out."

"My love is not contingent."

"You sound so sure. What if she really did disobey you?"

"I don't force her to obey," Nash sputtered. He hadn't considered it, and now that he did, he was not sure what he would do.

"You look to me like a fair-weather friend, Master Nash. I might not put my trust in you, neither. Hiding her away in a cottage when all the others like her sit high on the hill."

"She thinks I'm unreliable?" Nash's shoulder blades stiffened. She shouldn't be judging him that way. He never would judge her. Wait, wasn't he doing just that here and now? Demanding that she expose her feelings to him, as well as her body? Who was he to demand anything?

Her husband. Nash disliked the philosophy that woman was owned by man, be he father, brother, or husband, but apparently he still subscribed to it. It was bred into his bones, but wasn't it bred into hers, as well? They might fight their training, and succeed, but first they had to realize that it was training, and not nature.

"You look as if you have an itch, and you need our girl Maddie to scratch it. Where is that one?"

"Let's go find her."

"Nay, I'm after another pint. Or the sack races down the hill. Looks to be some fine man-flesh on display."

Nash nodded. He did need to see Maddie. Could she truly think of him as Kitty told it? He had to change her mind, and now.

He watched her saunter back to the line for ale. There were plenty of other village women around for comfort—and to keep their men safe.

He headed back to the house. He had philosophies to expound. And Maddie had better listen.

TWENTY-EIGHT

Maddie saw Nash coming toward the kitchens and hurried out to meet him. There was a grim set to his mouth that hadn't been there before. Had something happened?

"Maddie, I need to talk to you."

"Where's Kitty?" The rivulet of worry in her voice seemed to stop him. He frowned, and then turned to look back down the hill, holding up his hand to block the sun from his eyes.

"She said she was going to watch the races. This way." He dropped his sun-kissed hand and held it out to her. She took it, warm and welcome and a treasure, indeed. When she had first met him, she'd never have dreamed he would be so affectionate, and in public. They started tracing a leisurely path down the grass toward the crowd framing the contestants.

"Listen, Maddie. Do you think I'm unreliable?"

Where had that come from? Maddie stopped, but the pull

on her hand was steady and she came to herself enough to keep moving. "I think you are very reliable."

"Not like that." He swung his free hand wide. "I mean, do you think our marriage is a trial? No, that's not what I mean, either."

She tried to guess what he wanted to hear. "You're a good man, Nash Quinn, and I do my best to live up to your expectations," she said.

"That's what I mean," he said, stopping a ways away from the crowd. Nearly everyone was watching or running in the races. Contestants for the three-legged race were lining up: She thought she saw a pair of young lovers, another team of siblings, the sister nearly half again as tall as her little brother, and some strong-looking farm hands. "My expectations. What about your expectations?"

"I don't understand."

"Which are we, Maddie," he said, looking at the racers. "An evenly matched team or an ungainly one?"

"The lovers, there, by your brother."

She waved toward the far end. Shaftsbury himself was officiating; nearest him were the young couple, the woman laughing so hard her partner had to hold her up. Shaftsbury raised his arm to *set* and dropped it for *go*. The lovers were the first to stumble, the farm hands the first to fight. The ungainly siblings loped in for the win.

"Or perhaps not," Maddie amended.

Nash smiled despite himself as the crowd roared its approval. "You mean the world to me," he said. Taking her hand again, he swung their arms a little as they joined the crowd.

Shaftsbury soon spotted them and sauntered over. "A good

contest, that one. Next up is sack-racing. May everyone retain their teeth." He smiled at them, and then looked down at their hands, entwined. He looked up at Maddie and grinned. She couldn't help matching his smile.

A cloud passed over his countenance. "Word of warning. Wetherby's here."

A chill started at the base of Maddie's spine and sped toward her neck. Nash squeezed her hand, and the cold seemed to recede.

"My god, man." Nash's voice was rough. "You invited him?"

"Had to, didn't I? Couldn't very well invite the men and not their master." Shaftsbury shrugged apologetically. "At least I didn't have to invite the army."

"What army?"

"He's bunking a regiment, or some such, on his lands. Better him than me. Worse than rats in the kitchen, the army. They just sit and eat."

"They shoot, too," Nash said. "Those must be the men Malbanks was on about. So close to town?"

"They're not at Shaftsbury. I told Wetherby to give you wide berth, too. He's easily enough avoided. The only one here in bloody orange. More princely than Prinny."

Maddie stood on tip-toes, scanning the crowd. Nothing orange. Still, her heart would not calm. "Seen Kitty?"

Nash understood immediately. "He'd have to be a blockhead to go after her."

There she was, at the race's finish line, a parade ground's distance. The blue of her dress, Maddie's dress, nicely set her off against the stand of trees behind her. It was so strange to look at her, like looking at a moving mirror. Maddie loved Kitty's smile.

She hoped hers was as fine. Then she saw who her sister was smiling at.

Maddie's shout came out a strangled sob, but Nash heard it. He pulled her closer, bumping shoulders as he reached around her waist. "What is it? Take a breath, Maddie."

Wetherby was offering Kitty a mug of ale, holding it out and then lifting it up, out of her reach, and taking a step back, making her follow. Maddie had played that game with him, too. It never ended well.

Did Kitty not see that he was driving her into the woods? Away from the people? Maddie stumbled out of Nash's arms and ran a little up the hill. Kitty might see her better that way.

She did, thank the Lord. Nash joined Maddie on the hill. "By the trees." She could barely get the words out, her throat was so clenched. "Wave to Kitty to come over here."

He followed her gaze and stiffened. He shouted and waved, Maddie waved, come here, come here. Kitty lifted her hand in greeting, looked at that man, and then back to Maddie.

Kitty grinned, and turned back to the man.

She wasn't coming. She was following the man in orange into the woods.

Maddie started to run. They couldn't be alone. She had to stop him. It was wrong. It would not be well.

Nash didn't catch up to her until they were nearing the edge of the woods. Together they crashed through the underbrush but didn't see anyone at first. She knew the man usually took his victims deep.

She heard a dull thud, there, over to her right. Kitty, hair wet, dropping to her knees, a whoosh like clothes falling from a hamper. He had hit her with the tankard.

Closing in, they could hear his voice. "Back where you belong, little mouse." One of his hands held Kitty by the back of her neck, the other was undoing the front of his trousers.

Maddie felt Nash's hand pull her back, behind him, as they reached the couple. She tripped, and hit the ground hard on hands and knees. The tankard lay on its side in front of her.

Nash grabbed Wetherby by the collar and yanked him back, away from Kitty. "Give me one reason I shouldn't knock your teeth out here and now."

Kitty lifted her hand to the side of her head. Her gaze was off, but she wasn't bleeding. Maddie picked up the tankard.

Maddie's lungs were bursting as she pushed herself to get up even as her fears fought to slow her down. The bright dots in her vision flashed into a tapestry of memories.

His hands on her skin, on her belly. Inside her. His face, too close. His slicing sneer. "Good girls don't cry."

Good girls don't lick their uncle's cocks, either.

Maddie blinked hard, trying to come back from the shadows of her mind. She saw him true now, a stoop-shouldered, balding viper.

Against Nash's pull, Uncle raised his hands in surrender. "I'm a peer, I'd remind you. And besides, didn't I train her up well for you?"

He should not have smirked.

Maddie swung the tankard up as she rose to her feet. It connected hard with Uncle's cheek, knocking him out of Nash's grasp and back onto the dirt. She sank onto her knees in front of him, just as he always liked. Hands fisted one inside the other, she lifted her arms and slammed them down on his pretty face. And his shoulder, and his leg, and back to his face.

She had been a good girl, all along. It was Wetherby who had been bad. *Very bad. Not again. Never again. Never, never, never, never.*

"Maddie?" Nash knelt on the other side of the body, which had stopped groaning.

"I won't be his whore anymore." Her tears softened his face, but not the shock upon it. She had shocked him. She had shamed him.

Maddie shrunk back from the body, from Nash's outstretched hand. She was unclean. She would be forever unclean.

She had to get away, run away, hide. He sometimes got tired of looking for her when she hid. *Down the path, strange to be outside. There was a pond here somewhere.* She needed to wash, too, and find a place to hide.

He was calling her name, angry. She must get away. She was still sore from the last time. She needed to rest.

Her breaths pounded in her head. The pictures wouldn't stop. Now she could sense the smells, too. And the sounds.

"You are nothing, you hear me? This is all you are good for. And you're not even good at this. I should keep you in the sty with the pigs, you're so useless."

"Give me that bread. You know to take crusts only. And stay upstairs, out of sight. Don't let the clean people see you."

"Swallow, bitch."

Maddie pounded at her head, but nothing blocked the river of memories. Her eyes were cloudy, and the path she ran was narrow. A wild-pig path? Exactly where she deserved to be.

She heard his voice calling, too close, and ducked under two crossed trees lying on the ground.

He'd never find her here.

NASH COULDN'T HOLD HER. Maddie had pulled away from his outstretched hand as if it were on fire. By the time he was on his feet again, she was at full run, deeper into the wood.

Bloody hell.

But before he could go after her, he heard Deacon stumbling into the chaos.

"Bloody hell, Nash. Not again." He knelt beside Wetherby. "The coat is ruined. What have you done?"

"Maddie did that, and from what I heard he deserves a damn sight more. He...he...my god, Deacon. He was having his way with her, and her but a child." His mind skittered away from the picture, it so disgusted him, but his heart wouldn't hear of shrinking back. "No wonder Father sent her away. His goddaughter." Nash looked at the prone form on the ground. He should be under the ground. "Bastard."

"Nash! Step back from him. And the sister?" He looked at Kitty sitting still against a tree.

"I'm fine," she said. "Bit of a cracked head."

Nash would not be distracted. "Wetherby attacked her. He was forcing himself on her."

"And your bruiser? Where is she?"

"She ran." He had to find her, now. His red-hot gaze pleaded with the cool of his brother's.

"Leave it. Go."

Nash ran, glad to put space between himself and the man he

longed to slaughter. The bastard betrayed a little girl. He probably broke her little body.

His Maddie.

Wetherby deserved to be shot, or castrated, or both. But as a peer, he was nearly untouchable, unless he attacked another peer.

He hadn't, had he? He'd attacked a defenseless girl, an orphan, looking to him for solace and safety. *Fucking bastard.* No—it was precisely because he was not a bastard but a titled heir that he could get away with this.

Nash ran past the broken branches he could see she'd crashed through and up the trail, but Maddie had simply vanished. He retraced his steps. *Gone.*

He pounded down on a young ash in frustration. Its snap back nearly beheaded him. How could he have been so blind? She could barely speak to the man back at Deacon's birthday supper, and they'd all thought her shy, overcome by the long-awaited reunion. Overcome, true, but by loathing and disgust.

And that scene in the barnyard. Hadn't Wetherby actually touched her? Lucky she merely fainted, or whatever she did. Run away. Well, he knew all about that move, too.

And Heywood's face at that first supper. He must have known something of it, as well. His friend had kept it damned close to his vest, if he did. Small wonder Heywood offered her work rather than return to Wetherby.

With clues so obvious, the Quinns were but three blind mice, and him the blindest. Lord, she flinched at his touch. The barest stroke brought her to tears. The miracle was that she did join with him, forcing herself to submit for the sake of—what?

—propriety? Wetherby had trained her to submit, but he couldn't train her to like it.

Nash tripped over a root, sprawling into the grass along the path. He lay, dazed, unsure where exactly he was in his family's own damned play forest. Maddie must be completely lost. The trees canopied, spilling fresh green light through the air. He sat up, head reeling, hands gripping the cool sod as if to pull up the earth itself and look under it for her.

He knew Maddie had a history, a sad story indeed. But it was easier to blame himself, for lacking some critical skill to please gentle ladies, than to consider that something that had happened so long ago could leave a trace in the adult mind.

It had; he couldn't deny it now. Just as, if he would but admit it, his own childhood terrors and longings diverted the currents of his thoughts.

The look on her face, green flecks giant in her rounded eyes. Her mouth, drawn down at an impossible, a painful, angle. The arch of her back as she raised her fists, rounding as she brought them down, her body a guillotine.

She would turn that force on herself. She mustn't be alone. The very moment she needed a loving hand, she stole herself away. Didn't that sound familiar, too. Just what one would do, if one believed love brought only pain.

He had to find her. He pushed up to standing. He was just south of the castle. Where was she? She wouldn't leave the safety of the woods, surely. Only an acre. He'd already crossed and re-crossed it twice.

Maddie held joy in her, he was sure of it. She must have learned to protect herself inside, tricks to keep her sane. She hadn't attacked Wetherby when he propositioned her, but when he threatened Kitty. Why not? It didn't make sense.

And then it did. Kitty was new, untouched, at least by Wetherby. Maddie might save her sister, if she could not save herself. Kitty was clean.

What did Maddie say, sometimes? *I'm so dirty*. She'd call for yet another bloody bath. The iron fear turning in his gut melted into leaden dread. She'd find her way to the pond, sooner or later. He had to get there first.

TWENTY-NINE

Maddie floated back to life, the speckles behind her eyelids resolving into sunlight through dappled leaves.

She lay on the dirty ground, the dead tree above her dropping shards of bark onto her dress. She was just as filthy inside, far beyond redemption.

She was nothing human. She'd been sold as a pup, coddled like a pet, used like a dishrag, and then discarded as trash. She didn't know for what use the old earl had intended her, but the present one had the right of it. She was not marriage material.

Worse, she had lied to Nash. She hadn't saved herself for marriage, yet had pretended to be a fragile virgin, even to herself. The truth was she was a filthy manikin, not a God-loved human at all. Not even the biggest ocean could wash away all her sins.

Or perhaps it could.

She crawled from under the tree, and sat upon it. Her vision was still spotty, the trees looming close, and then fading away. The air tasted of metal.

She would try the pond. Perhaps it would be large enough to wash away some of the dirt. But it would keep collecting, attracted to her, knowing her. She could never hold the blackness back.

Her feet moved after a fashion. Her toes dragged, and she had to keep reminding herself to pick them up. It was quiet here in the woods, empty, even the animals had fled from her presence. She heard a crashing on her left, as if a family of deer were bounding away from her. *Wise deer*.

She wiped at her eyes, and her vision improved somewhat. She was so tired. How could not remembering something be so exhausting?

She heard the soft rustle of wind on water, and in a moment the edge of the pond drew close.

Maddie slid in the mud, and stopped as the water caressed the toe of her boot.

A shiver of a breeze pinched ruffles into the surface of the water. Its familiar agitation warmed her. The water was as restless in its thoughts as she. As hungry to be saved.

She slid the boot deeper, lifting her skirt dry. With the next step, her arms were too tired, and she let the pretty, ruined fabric go free. Nash said the green brought out the color in her eyes. He was so pretty.

If the water caressed her ankles, it slapped her shins with cold. But soon enough she was used to it, and in a few more steps she was in a patch of sunlight. Her shoulders warmed as her hips drew in the cold. She might crack in half, but it would be pretty symmetry.

"Maddie." The wind whispered her name. No, that was Nash's voice. She looked back. He stood on the bank. His chest filled and emptied so fast.

She turned to face him, and stepped back. Her belly chilled, the butterflies inside slowing their wings.

"Wait." He reached for her.

She took another step back and slipped, arms pinwheeling before the water pushed at her and she righted herself.

Nash's face flashed anger. He splashed two steps into the water and stopped. His rapid breaths seemed to add a counterpoint of ripples to the surface of the water.

What could he want? Not her. She turned away from him, toward a bigger patch of sun.

But he made so much noise in the water, with all that breathing and thrashing about. She pushed deeper, away from his flurry, water to the top of her corset, and then over. The chill stole her breath for a moment. It could have it all.

Her arm jerked back, and she turned. He held her by the wrist, water sluicing off their arms.

They stood, her chest deep, him legs splayed, waist under water. His cheekbones cut against the pale of his skin. His eyes burned and bruised as if he'd never been so angry. But his jaw was set, stubborn.

It took her a moment to notice he was reeling her in, so slowly she made little ripple.

She wrenched out of his grasp so hard she lost her footing. Her knees buckled, and she tumbled under the surface. The cool on her scalp was bliss.

But the skirts got all tangled, or he tangled them, pushing into her. She felt his fingertips on the skin of her neck, and then he had hold of the corset and was hauling her back into the air.

She spluttered, hot with shame, anger, and the blinding pain she'd run from for so long. She pounded on his arm, but he didn't break his grip. With his other hand, he pushed the hair from her face. His gaze burned her, accusations, recriminations, hate. She gasped a breath deep, hurting her chest, reaching for the words, pushing them out.

"Let go."

His look said she was a fool. "Not again." He pulled her closer. She pressed her hands against his chest, but he pushed them away as if they were gnats and trapped her against him, sealing her cage with the staccato beat of his heart.

"Come inside. I'll make a bath. I'll bathe you."

He was so solid, so warm. She felt herself melting into him. All she wanted was his arms around her and no thoughts at all. But she didn't deserve him. She was a liar. He would despise her if he knew all she'd done. He'd leave.

"Don't cry like that. This isn't you, Maddie."

"You can't see. You don't want to see."

"Maddie, love." The heat of him crept past the chill and the wet. He ran his fingers into her hair, and she gasped at the pain as he pulled the wrong way.

He undid the combs holding her hair. The release unlocked something deep inside her. It welled up through her heart, past her soul and out her throat, deep sobs wracking her like a rag doll in a hurricane.

This time Nash didn't tell her to hush, he simply held her, stroking a glowing path down her back, for hours or minutes or even until the end of days, it felt the same.

At last her sobs ebbed, but her body kept shaking.

He had not left. He had not deserted her. But his body was shaking now, too.

"You're chilled through. Will you come with me?"

She would.

THIRTY

Nash supported Maddie's dragging form along the cart-path that snaked around the back of the castle, past the stables, away from the hubbub of the lawn party. Deacon must have been watching; he met them at the door to the kitchens. A quick conference, and he went down to the kitchens to commandeer hot water.

Nash and Maddie managed the servants' stairs. He set her on the stuffed chair in the blue bedroom, the one most comfortable for her.

Even under Deacon's order, there was nowhere near enough hot water to spare for a bath. Still, he did wrest a large soup-pot's worth from the much-put-upon cook. Nash took it from the servant at the bedroom's door.

"All they could spare," he said, setting it near the hearth. He quickly built up a blazing fire, and fetched the sheets and toweling, pan and pitcher, from the washstand. He knelt in front of her, his hand gentle on her knee. She'd been broken the last time he took this pose, and now he knew why.

"May I wash you?"

Maddie's gaze was locked on some interior world, but he thought she nodded yes.

He rose and locked the door. Pulling her to her feet, he quickly stripped off her sodden clothes. He did the same for his own, wrapping a towel about his hips.

He laid two folded sheets on the carpet in front of the fireplace, and she laid herself upon them. Two pillows from the bed propped up her head.

Her hair was tangled as Medusa's, so he started with her feet. Dipping the washcloth first into the steaming water, then in the cool in the washstand basin, he created the perfect temperature for her.

He picked up her foot, the toes bluish, and stroked up her sole. He ignored the tears rolling down her face as he ministered to her arch and ankle, and every little toe. Her second toe was longer than the big toe.

"Can it be Maundy Thursday already?" she said, her voice so soft.

He rinsed the cloth, and then took up her knee, and sluiced warmth in and dirt out of her well-formed calf and shin. Her sobs began to quiet, her breathing to ease.

He repeated the pattern with her other leg, monitoring the water levels. He didn't dare run out.

But she would not stop crying. Tears streaked the streaks of earlier tears. It was killing him.

"Talk to me, Maddie." He kept rubbing her calves, lazy eights, not looking at her tears.

"I lied to you."

The anger shot out before he could stop it. "Don't say that. You are not to blame yourself for any of it. Not when you were a babe, not when you were a child, not now."

"I married under false pretenses. You should have it annulled."

"Why ever would I want that? I want you, Maddie, only and ever you. You had trouble in the past, bad trouble. It's no secret now. And it's too bad. Or maybe it is good. You can cry and grieve out loud, instead of locking it deep inside. Let go of it, and perhaps you'll have room for more. Room for me."

His voice cracked on the last word. He ducked his head, warming the cloth. His tears were just more warmth. He set to work on her arms, and her beautiful hands. Her eyelids flickered, her breath slowed.

He rolled her onto her right side, toward him. With the warm, wet cloth, he slid his hands down the tempting curve of her side, sliding past the breast, along the waist and down the hip to the knee. Her skin was so pure, as if it had never been touched or seen by anyone but her maker. If only that were true. He leaned in and planted a kiss on her hip, as his hand slid between her hips, rinsing clean that place that had seen so much pain.

He swept up her belly and around her breasts and breastbone, and did a quick pass by her face. He'd return to that for a more thorough cleaning later.

He admired the shape of her curves, so exactly woman, while he mourned for the child she had once been. How could any man torment a child? There could be no grace in marring such beauty. "I'll kill him," he said.

"You would hang. I'd rather you be safe."

"Kitty is a pistol. She looks so like you. Wetherby must have pissed his pants in surprise when she slugged him."

"We're not alike. She is strong."

Did she truly believe she was not? "Kitty did not survive all that you did. And she had the constant guide of a parent."

"She would have fought."

"You fought."

"Never succeeded. Not strong." All the breath sighed out of her, a doleful breeze.

"Strong enough to run away and walk ten miles in the dark. Strong enough to plead your case to my demon of a father. And succeed." The more he thought on it, the more he admired what she had done. He had run away, true, but at twelve, and toward something else. At four he was probably bawling in the garden with Nana.

"Madeline Quinn, you are a marvel. But you'll have to help me here. What is the best way to wash your hair?" She rolled onto her back and stretched her arms over her head, weaving her hips to carry the stretch down her legs. Nash was instantly erect. He silently cursed himself. Now was not the time to be attracted to his wife. He shifted up to crouch on his feet, turning away from her and tightening his towel. Her eyes didn't open.

"It's damp, so that step is done. Just rub a little soap in your hands and run your fingers through it. Pour the basin water back into the pitcher. I lean over the basin and you pour the pitcher."

She opened her eyes, dark pupils ringed in greens and browns. She rolled up onto her knees, and then sat on her haunches, her back a clean curve. He poured the still-clean but cool basin water back into the pitcher and set the basin on the towels. She put an arm under the hair at the base of her neck and leaned forward, flipping the bulk of it over to cover her face and fall into the basin. He ran his fingers carefully through the tangles in her hair. Once she winced.

"Sorry," he said.

"It always pulls. It's the curls."

"You have beautiful hair. Why keep it so short?"

"It reaches nearly my shoulder blades," she protested.

"I suppose hair that falls below one's rump must be hard to care for. I am glad my first time is with you."

She pulled away, turning her head to look through the tangles at him. Her gaze was here, with him.

"You don't think I've acted the ladies' maid with all the women about town, do you? Lean over." He pushed her shoulders down to get more hair into the basin, and then lifted the pitcher and rinsed the soap out. She braced herself with her left hand, using her right to help push the water through her thick tresses.

This was bliss, just the two of them without interruption. Passion was wonderful, and ecstasy celestial, but such quiet intimacy held marvels of its own. Setting the pitcher down, he watched her push onto her knees and reach two hands to her hair. She twisted the length of it, squeezing water out, and then sat up.

"Towel."

He reached behind him for another dry cloth, and handed it to her.

"Smaller." He chuckled and gave her a smaller one. She did some sort of special folding, and fashioned a turban of it over her head.

"How did you do that?"

"Ladies need some secrets," she said, his nude goddess, shining and sparkling in the firelight.

He draped the bigger towel around her shoulders, pulling the ends to him to bring them closer together. He kissed her brow, each eyelid, and then the tip of her nose. Her lids flew open again, her eyes sparkling.

"Checking to see if your face is clean enough. I see we still have some work to do."

Her expression fell so far so fast, Nash was taken off-guard. Idiot. He had worked so hard to help her feel clean, and he turns around and tells her she's still dirty.

"Just one last, tiny speck," he said, trying to salvage her pride. He wiped the warm cloth in feather motions from her nose onto her forehead, then around her cheeks, chin, and finally her nose.

He kissed her again, slower, savoring her soft scent hidden under the mild soap smell. He lingered on her cheeks, and then the corner of her lips, slowly moving toward the center. He pulled her lower lip a bit, and her lips opened a crack.

He took her mouth in a demanding, forgiving embrace, a kiss that carried all he had to give. His passion, his understanding, his hopes, his love. She responded to his gift in kind, a sweet return.

On their knees, hip to hip, chest to chest, their tongues entwined, Nash remade his marriage vows in his mind, promising her no one would ever hurt her again.

In the eyes of the law, she belonged to him, his proud, careful, broken wife. But law or no, he belonged to her, as well.

And God help anyone who came between them.

PART THREE

THIRTY-ONE

"Is there nothing we can do?" Even the committee men who agreed with him winced at the whine in Trefford's voice.

Nash gripped the arms of his chair, hidden under the table, one nail tapping a tattoo on the hoary wood. He was sick of Trefford, disgusted with Malbanks, wary of Heywood, and terrified that Maddie was sitting home alone for the first time since the dread day at the castle.

She must be home by now. Nash had insisted she sleep, and that she and Kitty eat a decent meal before they left Shaftsbury this morning. His brother's care and compassion had surprised Nash, and reminded him of the many times Deacon had acted the elder brother when they were boys. How could he have forgotten? Today Deacon hadn't said anything directly, but his attentions to Maddie and her sister spoke volumes. He might grow into a fine earl. He might be one already.

Nash had to leave before she woke, to get to this blasted

meeting in this deuced tavern. The stale smells turned his stomach—as did the conversation.

"I don't see why we have to approve it." Trefford's voice was nails down a chalk slate.

Nash pressed his temple for a moment, gathering his patience. As no one else seemed inclined to speak, it fell to him. "Again, the petition is not illegal. They are within the law. Well within, as they have agreed to the terms we demanded, including changing the date."

"But the meeting itself is illegal," Trefford whined.

Heywood rapped the table, finally asserting his authority. He hadn't met Nash's eye when he greeted him. Had he gone turncoat? "Home Office advises that we cannot stop it."

"Home Office deludes itself." Malbanks flicked a speck from his coat, a shade of orange that reminded Nash of Wetherby. Nash closed that door in his mind before he lost his concentration.

"Perhaps," Heywood said. "If they do speak sedition, we're to arrest this time. If they riot, we use force."

"Riot or immediate incitement to riot." Malbanks tapped a page of vellum on the table in front of him. "That is the phrase exact. How do you think calling thousands of angry layabouts together, to hear a series of harangues over how ill their fortunes are and how we are to blame, will not incite riot?"

Nash tapped his own piece of paper, the *Observer*. "It hasn't yet. Read the advert: *A public meeting to talk about reform.*"

"I did read it. It also says because the magistrates declined to call the meeting, they are doing it anyway."

"You know that is play-acting."

"So is the phrase *public meeting*."

Nash scoffed. "Now you think they are clever. Before you thought they were dolts."

"Only one of them need be clever to write an advert. Surely you can find one clever man in a town full of dolts. They probably imported one from London."

Heywood rapped the table again, as tired of this argument as the rest of them. "The odd thing is that they seem to be making some effort to stay within the law."

"Smoke and mirrors. Our spies haven't found the conspirators, but they will." Malbanks rapped the table himself, once.

Nash pushed his back into the chair. "What if there is no conspiracy?"

"Nonsense. You've been spending too much time with the under classes."

This was a new tack. Nash stared Malbanks down.

The man looked to Trefford, shrugging. "Didn't you just marry one of them?"

"Madeline Wetherby?"

"Her surname was Moore, I hear," Malbanks said. "Family will out."

How dare he cast aspersions on Maddie? After all she'd been through.

Heywood pressed a hand onto Nash's shoulder, pushing him back into his seat. He hadn't known he'd risen.

"Mrs. Madeline Quinn's brother-in-law is Earl of Shaftsbury."

"A peer who would rather throw a lawn party than assist us in our time of need. Wetherby, a mere viscount, has promised funds and billets for troops." Malbanks's gaze settled on Nash. The man knew the whole of it.

Rage growled from his gut. Malbanks lapped it up, nearly grinning. Nash forced his feelings down. He would not give the bastard any pleasure.

"Be sure to get Wetherby's money in cash," Nash said.

Clayton's voice startled them both. "I second that. This latest Lord Wetherby is a horror, from what I hear."

Deprived of entertainment from Nash, Malbanks flicked his attention to the older man. "He takes the major general to his hunting lodge today. I say he is a good friend."

Heywood used his gavel, for the first time. "Gentlemen, let us hold to the topic. We have accepted the petition. The meeting will occur. Now what?"

"Pull it that morning. Find a way."

"Fatal. You'd create the very riot you with to avoid," Nash said.

Clayton nodded. "Quinn's right. Let them have their say. If they get out of hand, we'll read the Riot Act and send them home."

"They will get out of hand, and our yeomanry will be ready." Malbanks was the first on his feet. "This meeting is over."

Heywood harrumphed, but could not call back men so eager to be gone. Clayton caught at Nash's sleeve as he passed. "A word, Quinn."

"You're interested in those silks, after all?"

He shook his head, his jowls following behind.

"You know this is all just for show."

"How is that?"

"Malbanks had Trefford write to the major general. They already control that horde of know-nothings in the guard."

"They wouldn't set that pack of drunkards on the people."

"They might well, if only to act the threat. You know how these things can get out of hand." Clayton pushed his spectacles up to rub at his eyes.

"The weavers are saying no one is to carry weapons. They would be sitting ducks." The thought sent a chill down Nash's spine. Maddie's sister would be there.

"It's the numbers they fear. Is there any way to split the rally?"

"There's only one Hunt. That's who they want to see."

"Let's hope they get to see him, then. But don't deceive yourself about who is in charge. If you want your view to prevail, it will take more than words."

"Any stronger words could get me arrested, as well as the workers."

"A fine line, true, but you're just the man to walk it." Clayton clapped Nash on the shoulder. "I understand you need merchandise. Malbanks's portion of the proposal."

"We've lost it. Only a week to go." It meant his near-bankruptcy, and his worst nightmare—falling back onto his family for support. Right now, though, Nash could only shrug. All the balls were in the air, and he had to keep juggling them.

"I believe I can make you good. It's finished cotton, you said?"

Nash stared at him. "If you're serious, you're a savior, man."

Clayton touched the side of his nose with an index finger. "One man's chaos is another's opportunity. I've had a windfall from the Americas. I believe the trade was twenty for five?"

"Twenty for four."

Clayton sucked in his cheeks and changed his stance. Nash matched him. Now they could negotiate. Then he remembered they were in a pub, filled with mercantile ears. Clayton looked away, seeming to realize the same. He leaned in. "Make it quick. Four and a half. Accept a bit of unwanted advice from an old man and we've a deal."

"Four and a quarter. What's the advice?"

"Next time, choose your allies with more care."

They shook hands, and Nash hurried out of the room and down the street. If this deal held, and Clayton had always kept his word, he had saved their hides. Nash would have to think about that later. A quick check on the warehouse, and he could be home with Maddie by four.

Fear had outstripped reason this summer. Masters and men should both be on the same side. And here they were, less than a week from slitting one another's throats.

As DEACON'S carriage crossed the river Irk, Maddie panicked. She couldn't be alone, not yet. In the forest of her exhaustion and despair, Nash had coaxed a sapling of hope. But it was far too fragile to live on its own. Not yet.

Kitty leaned out the window to call the direction to the driver. She never let go of Maddie's hand, a grip that had held through the hours-long ride.

"He's to let me out past Shude Hill, then go on to take you home."

Maddie couldn't lose her. She'd woken, dazed, wondering at how she'd come to be in the blue bedroom again and not Nash's chambers. Had it all been a dream, and it still that first morning in May? Then she saw Kitty rocking in a chair near the window, and the whole of the day before crushed her back into the mattress.

Wetherby. Nash said she was rid of him, and Deacon had repeated it later at the breakfast table. The thought lifted ten stone from her shoulders, but she couldn't shake the feeling that it would soon tumble her down again. If only he never woke up from the pummeling she'd given him. That would have led to more difficulties, of course, but solved so many others. And what was her death, by hanging, to compare with the endless number of girls saved from his depravity?

Kitty had told Deacon that Wetherby was a poor seducer. She thought he took Maddie simply because she was there and he could. His family had bought her, and she should pay him back.

"Didn't she just." Deacon had smiled, the grin tinged with iron. "He'll not do it to anyone else. I'll make sure of it."

The stuff in Maddie's head had shifted loose. She'd spent years convincing herself what had happened to her was normal, and any hurt she still felt was due to her own weaknesses. Everyone else was more logical, more reasonable about it, and she should just grow up. Seeing Kitty at Wetherby's mercy had pulled apart that band of shoddy excuses for good. His groping Kitty was wrong, and if that was wrong, how could what he had done to her be right? The band snapped, and her world tumbled apart.

Not a day later, it remained rather gingerly rigged, built on Nash's still-fresh ministrations of love, Deacon's protectiveness, and Kitty's acceptance. Perhaps as she prayed, she could use her own strength to cement these bricks into a whole.

The carriage, which had been traveling at a walk for a few

minutes, slowed to a crawl. The buildings here stood so close its wheels had less than two feet of space between them and a court-yard wall. She felt the outrider step off the back, springing them in their seats. Kitty scooted toward the door.

Maddie tugged her back. "Take me with you."

"Home? Don't be a duck egg."

She shrugged, trying to appear nonchalant and failing so badly that her eyes rimmed with tears. "I can't be alone."

"Nash said he would be home in a few hours."

"That's forever. I need to be with someone now. With family."

Kitty looked at her steadily, that Amazon gaze Maddie so wanted to learn to copy. What did her sister see? An overgrown baby in a lady's striped muslin?

"You needs be gone by three."

Nash would be back by three. "You're a saint."

"I'm cracked is what I am. Come along."

They stepped out, into haze and damp and the smell of rotten cabbage and something underneath, worse. Maddie picked up the hem of her skirt, but the ground was swept clean. The filth was in the air. She waved the coachman to leave; he paused to make sure she meant it.

"Clock Alley. For clock-lace, you know? Two dozen families along the sides, privies and ash pit at the back and our own tree smack in the middle." A girl stood at the pump beside the tree, drawing water. No one else was to be seen.

"Is everyone at work?"

Kitty shook her head. "Some's too hungry to come out and play. The men are at the worker's meeting. That's why it's safe for you to come in."

Maddie tried not to think on why her father would not want her in his home, and why she needed to see it anyway.

Perhaps he was ashamed. The houses were two- and three-storey affairs, nearly cottages but built in the narrow, connected way of the city.

"Ours is a through-house, best on the block. Here." Kitty waved proudly at a narrow three-storey, gray as soot, with one window per floor and just the door below. The designers had tried to make it look like the better stock of housing, but the builders had cheapened the materials. It seemed to sag to the right.

"You's what bought us this."

"I?"

"Da used the death money from your people to buy it. We are the only ones living here who own the lease to our home."

"Even Nash rents."

"Da said if he knew as it would get so tough, so much clemming, he would have bought another house, just to lease it to folks for free for a time. Instead he sent me for school."

"Progressive of him."

"Guilty, more like. He knew you had a made life, and I think he wanted to give me a chance at a merchant's trade. Something better than the mills."

"But you followed his footsteps instead."

"Started a spinner, so's my work feeds into his. I love that we can work together. We starve together when the work dries up, so's I work the mills, as well. Should have stayed in school another year, and really learned my letters."

"You can read?"

"Slow but sure. With figures, I'm flash as any cove, just like me Da. Wish we had more of them adding up and not as many to subtract." She unlatched the door and waved Maddie in.

The room was as big as Maddie's closet, and held three wooden chairs and the cooking fireplace. Straight stairs stood against a wall; a closet in back acted as the pantry. Unlike the cottage Jem Smith and his family inhabited, this one had a small window in the back wall, offering a shaft of morning light.

"You keep a neat home."

"It ain't no castle, but it'll do."

She moved deeper into the room as Kitty came in, shutting them in. A quarter-moon window cut into the door offered a sliver of light, but even at noon the room was dim.

"Why the shades?"

Kitty glanced at the window, blinded by cloth. "Can't have too much privacy. Come up and see the looms."

They sped by the first floor, which looked to hold two sleeping rooms. As they turned toward the top floor, sunlight edged the treads on the stairs.

This floor stretched the breadth of their cottage plus the one behind it. A higher ceiling and four large windows gave good light. Two looms, standard cotton-weaving jennies, took up the bulk of the space, and chairs and stools stood in the front and back of the room by each pair of windows. A narrow cot sat in the back corner.

"I spend most of my time in here, in good weather. Do my spinning at the window while Da works this loom and George works his, there. It's right nice here."

"You sleep up here?"

"He does. I sleep below, and our tenant takes t'other."

"But there's no heat on this floor."

"I don't see you doing much better, for all your husband has money." Kitty's look cut as sharp as her voice.

Maddie flushed and paled and flushed again. "I'm sorry," she said, her voice faltering as if she might collapse.

"No, you have the right of it. Sometimes Da's joints bother him, so he sleeps on the kitchen bench pulled out beside the fire."

"How can he work the shuttle if his joints ache?"

She shrugged. "You don't work, you don't eat."

Maddie didn't want to see her family like this. She had so much; they should have at least enough. "Would he ever take money? A stipend, perhaps, quarterly?"

"He's a proud man." Kitty fingered the strings on the loom.

"But you hold the purse strings?"

She grinned, and Maddie felt a surge of pleasure, as if she'd given the winning answer in a spelling contest. "And if a little extra came my way, say, because I was working longer at the rectory, well, who's to say it didn't?"

"The rectory?"

Kitty drew her finger down a string. "Where I went for schooling, myself. Sometimes I act the tutor for the smaller ones at the school. It's pennies, only, but having some bit coming in is better than none."

Maddie sat at his loom. "Show me a little."

"These are the straight threads, the warp." Kitty picked up an oversized bobbin. "I wind my spinning around bobbins like these. Goes in the shuttle, see, and Da passes it back and forth through the shed, picking over. The beater, here, packs the threads tight between."

"How long does it take?"

"To do a napkin, one round of "O God Our Help." Enough for a shirt, four or five evensongs. A tablecloth's measure takes the whole day."

Maddie took mental stock of all the linens, calicoes, and cottons in her home. It would have taken hand-weavers months if not years to make the things in her house alone. The amount it would take to fill the cabinets at Shaftsbury castle made her head spin.

"And the machines?"

"Oh, one of those can do a tablecloth in less than an hour." Maddie gasped, and Kitty set the shuttle down hard. "We do twice the work now for the same coin. Lucky for us, the machines keep breaking; they're broken more than not. But they'll find new ways to build them, and we'll be cut out for good."

"You could switch to weaving silk."

"Same method. Guaranteed a 'factory man is tinkering up a silk loom as we speak."

"That's not fair."

Kitty shrugged. "God be mysterious, all right."

The door opened downstairs. Kitty's gaze locked with Maddie's, her eyes wide. "He's early. Stay here. Maybe he'll go straight out again."

But before she could get to the stairs, they heard footfalls coming up.

Maddie scooted off the seat and to a stand just as her father came into view.

He was scowling to himself, and when he saw them, he froze, mouth wide open. He looked from one to the other, finally landing on Maddie, and took a deep breath.

"Wot are yo', an' weer dun yo' come fro'?"

Maddie weaved, in the wake of his roar, and even Kitty flinched. But her face grew just as hard as his.

"She's me sister, and she can visit wit' me if she wishes."

"Had yo' yesterday, dino she? Nae enough?"

His eyes were blue darker than Kitty's, but they looked smaller in his face, with its wide rounds of cheekbones and large nose. His face seemed to stretch over his head, unimpeded but by a wreath of graying hair. The beard made a bear of him. Maddie felt the hard edge of the seat behind her. She must have backed up without thinking of it.

"Dunna sech a fine picnic yesterday?"

Was he talking to her? She barely understood him. She didn't remember having such trouble before. Did he want an answer? Maddie struggled to answer. She couldn't think. Kitty took her hand, but even that calmed her only a little.

"Maddie's brother-in-law be a fine cove."

"The peer spake at ye?"

"Danced a jig wit' me. Handsome enough, for a scarecrow."

Her father reared back and laughed. "You didna say that to his face." He looked at Maddie again, sobering instantly. She thought she might faint.

"What's it they grow at Shaftsbury? Maize?"

"Yes." Maddie nearly slapped herself on the forehead. "No. Barley. It's barley."

He looked at Kitty. "Simple. It's the fall as done that."

Maddie wanted nothing more than to drop through the floorboards. She had dreamed of making a strong impression on her father, and now she had. He thought her a simpleton.

"She's just had a bear of a time of it. So's I said she could stay for tea."

"I'll not, then." He looked at her and then at his loom, as if he thought she might harm it in her idiocy. She took a step away from it.

At the head of the stair, he turned back. "Tell your husband Black Tulip, after seven, do he mean to parlay." He looked at Kitty. "Write it down, so he can read it."

As he stomped down the stair and out the door, Maddie sank onto the bench. "Oh dear lord."

Kitty pulled her up again and together they descended the stair. "Don't fash yourself. His accents go broad when he's het up. It's probably better that he thinks you're soft."

"Why?"

"Then he won't be so afeered of you, with your carriages and fine silks. Everybody loves the simple bodies."

Maddie couldn't imagine herself frightening that man. She would never impress him, at this rate, but at least he did not reject her or threaten her.

She could build on that.

THIRTY-TWO

The moment he heard the door click shut, Nash was on his feet, the newspaper falling to the floor. He barreled so hard into the hall that Maddie drew back, startled out of her tentative smile.

"Where the devil have you been? Mrs. Willis was worried sick." The words must have come out too sharp. Her mouth set in that familiar tight-lipped way, but her eyes took on a new, shrewd look. Like her sister's. "You've been with Kitty all this time?" At least she didn't flinch when he reached for the ribbons on her bonnet. He untied them and together they swept it off her head. Now she was home. As he hung it on its hook, she spoke.

"You weren't home, and Kitty said tea might help." She could slay him not only with her tears but also with her voice, raw and lost. He stared at the mirror over the sideboard, cursing the safety committee and its endless meetings, the warehouse with its relentless demands, that bastard Wetherby, and the entire house of blasted Lords. Not to mention the man in the reflection.

"I'm sorry for not coming home with you."

Her shrug looked the same, even reversed. "You had important business elsewhere."

"Nothing is more important than you." He took her hands. "We're not perfect, but we're all that we have."

Face carefully composed, she slipped away, into the sitting room. She picked up the *Observer* from the floor, shaking it out. "Manchester Public Meeting" stood out in large type at the top. "If the working men want the vote, and you and the other men of business want the vote, then why don't all of you attend the meeting?"

Why was she on about this? Why wouldn't she be, with the streets plastered with political placards? "Because each don't care for the other to have it. Can't say I disagree entirely. Suffrage should be a privilege, with requirements."

"Such as one's father was an earl?"

"Such as one knows how to write and to cipher, and has found such success in the world that he owns property."

"My father has all those attributes."

Perfect. "You went to see your father."

"He used the Wetherbys' money to buy his cottage, and Kitty's schooling. And the gravestone."

"He welcomed you with open arms, then?"

"We made a start." He couldn't hide the doubt on his face. "We did," she said, softer.

He sank onto the sofa, rubbing his face with his hand.

"Don't we have enough trouble without inviting more? This week, especially?"

He imagined the hash Malbanks would make of this—*consorting with the enemy, keep your wife on a leash*—he could see it already.

The paper hit the floor again, the pages slipping apart. Her rump hit the chair, across the room from him. He tried to call up some compassion, but after yesterday, and today, and this entire blasted summer, he was drained dry.

He dropped his hands to the cushions. She really was a handsome woman. Beautiful coloring, nice proportions, smooth in swift currents. Even her dress, a medium-weight green-striped gingham, brightened the room, a splash of color and line against the simplicity of the furniture. If only she didn't look so mutinous. "Could not you have waited until this is over?"

"I've waited my whole life."

She'd waited two months. "It's not worth arguing about."

"You mean your argument is so weak you can't win?"

"I mean, it's no use arguing with a woman. She'll never change her mind."

She crossed her arms, a mutinous set to her mouth. "That is patently untrue. I've changed my thinking on any number of things, if you can recall."

He turned his palms up, complete surrender. Maddie had been forced to reconsider herself again and again these past months. It was a miracle she wasn't abed with migraines every day.

"All it is, I worry about you."

"About your fellow committee men, rather."

"About all of it. You should have heard the talk this afternoon. They are the ones with minds like clay bricks. Once fired, set as stone."

"You could try the reformers. They meet at seven."

"At the Tulip?" He'd tried the tavern twice already, and come up empty. He was starting to think Bamford had played him for a fool.

"My father extended you a personal invitation."

"Don't be that way. I'm just afraid he'll hurt you."

"Yet you don't think we suit." Her voice betrayed her insecurities.

"What are you talking about? We suit in many ways."

"That's not what you said last week."

"When? Just before I fell asleep? I was already gone."

"No. It's what you truly believe. The sleeping don't lie."

"Better pun than proverb." He pushed himself to his feet and went to her. Untangling her arms, he pulled her up and back to the sofa.

"Listen, we are husband and wife. Nothing changes that. No two people suit exactly. We will just keep rubbing and scratching along our bumps and ridges until all is smooth between us."

"You promise?" He cursed Wetherby again for that small tremor in her voice, for the moisture in her eye.

"Again and again." Until he damned well got it right.

MILLER STREET WAS ODDLY quiet when Nash appeared just past seven at the Black Tulip. His entry killed conversation inside the tavern room entirely. The keep must have been told to watch for him, for he waved his hand up toward the stairs leading to a sort of balcony, open but for a railing. Nash took the stairs two at a time. Let them stick that in their craws, those men who grumble their betters grow fat and lazy off their work.

He scolded himself. No one was the better of anyone else. Though one couldn't always prove that by shouting.

Bamford sat at a round table with the young lad and a tall gentleman who must be Hunt. Maddie's father, a bit more red in his cheeks than Nash remembered from the standoff at the Exchange, sat to his left.

Hunt, farthest from the stair, rose and came to greet him, hand outstretched. Nash shook it. The others started to rise, but Nash nodded at each, and they settled back into their seats. The empty chair had its back to the stair, the weakest position.

"Thank you for having me. I know our last meeting pleased no one."

Hunt had returned to his chair, but didn't sit. Instead, he grabbed hold of its back and drew in a great breath. He spread his free arm wide, encompassing the whole of their floor and the taproom below.

"I have always been an enemy to private meetings—of reformers or magistrates alike. True reform does not require privacy." He pulled the chair out and plumped down, peacock proud in his doubled waistcoat and snow-white cravat.

Young George Swift, in the seat to Hunt's left, gulped audibly. Nash doubted the boy could even speak at the moment, as awestruck as he looked. Swift's back was to the railing; for Hunt he must represent the whole of the establishment's audience.

Bamford must have read Nash's thoughts in his expression. "Easy to see how he can draw a crowd," he said cheerily.

"Mr. Bamford, I admired your riposte to the magistrates' advert in the *Observer*. You make your points well."

"Liked this line, did you? We don't want your property; we have nobler aims in view."

Moore snorted. "Pigtail gentry, nae hear truth in it."

Nash didn't see the need to respond to the man's complaint. He nodded again to young Swift, who probably had no idea anyone was in the room besides Hunt.

Hunt, though, focused on Nash. "So, what must we do to ensure our meeting goes as planned?"

"You must swear it is not a meeting to overthrow the government."

At that, all four threw up their hands, even Swift, as if they were under arrest. Nash knew Bamford and Moore had already been arrested a time or two.

Hunt looked to be gearing up for more operatics, but Bamford found his voice first. "I swear by all's holy, we never wish to overthrow his majesty, or Parliament, or the Government, harsh as Sidmouth and his minions may be. What we want is to join in the government, not break it. We want our seat."

"So you say in the petition. The magistrates find it hard to believe."

Bamford shrugged. "They should read more Cobbett, and his Register. He has taught us that our ills be from misgovernment, and to save ourselves we need to reform such. There's been no rioting these past three years."

"Out with it, then. What do we do?" Moore had a temper to match those appled cheeks. Maddie must have inherited her mother's calm temperament, not this burly fire-head's.

"First, show yourselves these next few days as planning a simple meeting. No collecting pikes and cudgels. No marching." Reports of bands of men drilling in parade formations had even Heywood concerned. Their drillmasters were said to be former military.

"Idjits. What care how we step?" Moore spread his hands on the table.

"Think how it looks to a nervous merchant. You look to be drilling yourselves into a bloody army."

Moore held his hands out, palms up. "We carry naught."

"One doesn't need to carry arms to learn to march. The magistrates know contraband weapons are buried all about Lancashire."

"Nae true anymore."

"Isn't it." Nash shrugged, pasting unconcern on his face.

"Mr. Moore, if I might have the floor." Hunt stood and tugged his vest down, perhaps to draw attention to his fine figure.

Moore crossed his arms, leaning back.

"At past events, Mr. Quinn, the good men and women attending have seen themselves referred to in the papers as trash, sloppy, unable to dress or comport themselves properly. This has been used as an argument that their cause is unjust—if a man is slovenly, why ought we to give him the vote, you see."

Hunt's voice rose, surely loud enough for the drunkest man down below to comprehend. "But this time will be nothing of the sort. This time we will step together, singing the most patriotic of songs. This time, we will wear our Sunday best. This time, we will give no one the ammunition to shoot our cause down. We will have reform. Reform!"

"Reform!" George Swift echoed, and then cut himself off as he saw no one else had followed.

Hunt sat again, his eyes popping a bit. "We've done nothing wrong. We plan on doing nothing wrong."

Bamford pushed his tankard toward the taller man, who took it. "Good beer," Hunt said.

"Aye, for an ale." Bamford didn't seem at all cowed by the Southerner.

Nash tried again. "That may be, Mr. Hunt, but it's not the reality, it's the fancies in the committee-men's heads you need to battle."

Bamford turned back to Nash. "Will you help us? We know you hold sway among your people."

"How do you know that?"

"Because they did not reject the petition outright." He held up a hand, stopping Nash's retort. "It may well be legal in the eyes of the Parliament, but in Manchester town the law lies in the magistrate's hands. They're the sort to shoot first and ask questions later."

"That can't be true."

Moore laughed unpleasantly. "Missed the last time, you did. Ran away afore that."

Nash let that pass, but not without a struggle. What bug was up Moore's arse? "I'll argue your case to the committee, especially if it seems to be veering from proper legal form."

Hunt set down the tankard, now half-empty. "Tell them this: We will be completely unarmed."

Moore roared his disapproval. "Ye lost yer mind?" Even young Swift looked shocked.

Bamford stayed cool, but his eyebrows crept up toward his

hairline. "I cannot like that idea. I walk with my neighbors into a town both personally and politically against us, without any means to defend ourselves?" He looked to Nash. "And ain't it true that scores of men have been sworn special constables, and the yeomanry increased, and weapons liberally distributed to all of them?"

Nash had to nod yes. He wasn't sure he disagreed with the man from Middleton. Deacon was fortunate to have him in his district. Nash wished he had a few men the likes of this Bamford on his own committee.

Hunt held up a hand, Roman style, but at least he did not rise from his chair. "If we are in the right, as we are, are not these constables our sworn guardians?"

"More fool talk," Moore muttered, wiping the top of his bald head with a handkerchief.

Hunt ignored him. "If we were wrong, or they considered us wrong, would they not send us home by simply reading the Riot Act? Assuredly, while we respect the law, they will respect us. All will be well on our side."

Hunt's three comrades took a minute to digest this speech. Nash did not believe they would accept it. Hunt, a Londoner, didn't understand the hard-edged men and masters of Lancashire, who would not stand down from a fight until the other man saw stars.

At last, Bamford sighed. "We've forgotten the old times. Back before we became infested with spies and their dupes— distracting, misleading, betraying—no one spoke of physical force. They and their warlike ways have lost us many who might have been friendly to our cause."

"You side with him?" Moore stood up, hands on the table.

"How can they fight us if we will not fight?" Hunt's conviction gave Moore pause, but he shook his head.

"This be a mummer's play for the committee man. You think Quinn as addle-pated as his missus." Nash wasn't sure he'd heard correctly, but the faces of the others registered the same shock.

Moore stormed on. "A sweet piece, sure, but simple. Could you nae ha' done better?"

Nash had had quite enough of people attacking his wife. Here in a room full of idled workers angry at their masters was not the best time to express that opinion. *Cool down.* This was business, not family; it required reason, not passion.

"Mrs. Quinn does the books for the warehouse, and she straightened out the estate."

Moore's hand slapped the table. "Either the girl's simple, or a liar. Cannae trust her."

Bamford interrupted before Nash could speak. "Moore, what ails you? Kitty is a right good girl."

"Not Kitty. The other. His wife." Moore flicked his thumb toward Nash.

Hunt's jaw dropped; he snapped it shut. "The child you sold is this merchant's bride?"

"I didn't sell her."

Bamford snorted. "No, you traded her for money."

Nash jumped on this information. "Bamford? Did you know of the case? Maddie has a lot of questions about that time."

Bamford's wise eyes flicked quickly to Moore. "I know only what he told me. A story that has changed over the years, and even today sounds different to my ears."

"If you believe they won't knock us about, you're all as addled as his wife," Moore said.

Nash stood up and stepped toward Moore. "What do you know of my wife? You deserted her nineteen years ago, never wrote a word, never tried to make contact. If that's how you intend to lead your men and this meeting, the magistrates may as well cancel it. You'll be gone already."

Both men lurched toward each other. Bamford, between them, jumped to his feet and pushed each away with a hand, breaking their locked stare.

"Moore. Richard, this isn't to the purpose. We need Mr. Quinn's help, not another enemy." Bamford turned to Nash. "This isn't like him. I've known him these thirty years and more."

Nash bit down his retort, and nodded stiffly. Hunt appeared at his elbow.

"So, Quinn, you have what you need from us? Neat attire, neat manners, and nothing but neat speechifying. Nothing to argue with."

It took Nash a moment to unclench his jaw. "Aye."

"Then let me show you to the door."

"Please pass along my salutations to your fine wife," Bamford called behind him, turning to look a stern plea at his compatriot.

"As be mine," he heard Moore mutter.

Nash said nothing. The rage was too close.

He'd damned well be dead before he passed any message from that cretin of a father to his Maddie.

THE SATURDAY before Monday's meeting, Manchester was bathed in placards, plastered on every wall, post, or slow-moving dog. They promised readers the event would be an afternoon stroll, a picnic, a peaceable assembly, a rally for justice, a blow to tyranny, a call to arms, a danger to the economy, a deadly threat to Christendom. One could read a novel's worth of words merely walking the quarter mile from the Exchange to the warehouse, if one could stand the whipsawing. Judging by the sluggishness of foot traffic, it appeared many people were doing just that.

As Nash returned from the Exchange, damp from one of the town's two-minute rains, the carts carrying the day's final orders rolled past out of the warehouse yard. Jem Smith was just inside the wide door, counting over a much-diminished stock of tins of tea.

"Shipping out a bit late?"

Smith scratched his hip, shrugging. "Some as wanted Tuesday's stock, as well. Good sign, that."

"Why?"

"Were me, I wouldn't have ordered any. If a man thinks his house is about to be burned down, he doesn't order furniture."

Nash slapped him on the shoulder, grinning. "That's the best damned thing I've heard all week. As for the sops at the 'Change, they've turned tail. Closed till Tuesday."

"We'll be shut, then?"

"If the orders are out, why not? Let me check the books."

Jem had no trouble pivoting on his heel; the leg was nearly whole again. "If'n it doesn't, I'd like to be off meself."

"To see Hunt?"

"Just me, I'd go for an hour, but the missus is set upon it, and she'll be at it all day."

A boy ran up with a last-minute order for five tins of coffee. Nash watched as Jem tied the tins together so the child could carry them over his shoulder.

"And your boy?"

"Might as well take him. He can cheer the banner she made."

"I didn't know you to be such a reformist."

Jem's brows shot up, startled. "No sir. I work well enough with you. The wife, she has family in the mills. Women who must work to feed themselves and their bairns. Decent folk don't hire rough women." He shrugged as they reached the door to the office.

"You think I should hire women?" Nash had never considered it. What could they do at a warehouse? Jem tilted his head toward the door. Nash opened it, and saw his wife on the rolling step, pulling an old ledger from the shelf. Jem was right—he already did employ females.

After the Wetherby skirmish, he'd brought her here just so he could keep an eye on her. She'd been so restless and worried at things when she was alone. She'd been ready and standing by the door every day since, and as Jem preferred the back-shop work, Nash had let her have the run of the office again.

"Quicker at the books, she is," Jem said softly. "Could be she might draw more trade from the lady manufacturers."

"All one of them." At the sound of his voice, Maddie turned, a smile rising to her lips, lighting her face. An answering grin bloomed on his. Her eyes might still carry a haunted cast, but she'd slept through the night last night. He might plump her out yet.

She'd been a good investment, if not in terms of money or time. She didn't always give good return on love, either. But Nash had found surprising satisfaction in giving love, not expecting a return. That she did return it was pure profit.

"One today," Jem said. "Tomorrow's another tale."

THIRTY-THREE

Deacon's note said only that he had business in town and would call on Maddie in the afternoon to go for a ride. It said nothing about Kitty's accompanying them. When her sister arrived on the doorstep at two, breathless and excited, shortly after Maddie's own return from the warehouse, Maddie could not hide her surprise, or her delight.

Kitty's smile, though, wavered. "Do you mind I don't return your dress quite yet?"

"I said you could have it. The blue makes your eyes sparkle."

"It does." Kitty smiled, one of her rare rays of sunshine. By the time Deacon drove up to Stevenson Square, the sisters had dressed and re-dressed their hair, argued and made up, and taken tea. Maddie tried not to notice the first piece of bread Kitty buttered had disappeared into the hanging pockets along the folds of the dress. But she ran down to the kitchen to ask Mrs.

357

Willis to get another four-pound loaf to give Kitty when they returned.

Her sister was already in the open barouche, to the far side of Deacon. "I think we all might squeeze onto the facing seat," he said, reaching down to hand her up and into the coach. "No need for anyone to ride backwards. Save it for the picnic basket."

Kitty laughed. "You should have seen the faces along the alley when your fancy livery boy knocked at my door."

"You sent a messenger?"

"Same as for you." Deacon patted Maddie's hand, but saved the full wattage of his smile for her sister. Could something be going on there? Maddie chastised herself for over-imagining things already. More likely Kitty was an amusing oddity, a dancing bear, in Deacon's world, just as Deacon was in Kitty's.

"So how do my pretty radical relations this fine day? What do you call yourselves again?"

"Manchester Female Reform—not radical—Society. After we heard about the matrons at the Blackburn meeting, we had to show our colors. Now we're the biggest of the lot, more than a thousand members in just a month."

"A thousand rebellious misses? Isn't that a bit, shall we say, profligate?"

"None a bit. We don't seek glory for ourselves, but ask only for what's right by our men—and our wee'uns. It's the small folk need the food we can't afford to buy, cost of bread what it is and all of us on half-work."

"And the men?" Deacon's smile seemed patronizing to Maddie, but Kitty took to it like live bait.

"As for the men, they be needin' that certain stiffness—in

their spine, a'course—that only the support of a good woman can give."

Deacon laughed. Maddie wished she could do the same. Every little thing felt so life-and-death urgent to her lately. Nash's saying they wouldn't suit, the push-pull over Maddie's bathing, the dread day at the castle, the discovery of a sister and father still living. Everything changed and changed again so quickly in Manchester, she was breathless trying to keep up.

It seemed so easy for the others. Jealousy bit her in the belly. Kitty knew exactly who she was, and she wasn't afraid to try something new. Maddie had had to screw up all her calm and courage to walk into Kitty's world, and she hadn't performed nearly as well in it as Kitty had in Maddie's world. She wondered if Deacon noticed how Kitty's accent broadened when she was around him.

They pulled onto Long Millgate, heading north. Kitty slanted her eyes at Deacon. "Where do we go?"

"Lady's pleasure."

"Middleton, then. I hear the posies are a'bloomin'." Deacon directed the driver. Maddie noticed he hadn't checked with her first—or at all. As they crossed the river, though, he did search her face, and press her gloved hand. "Nash writes that you are recovered. I think he might overestimate from love."

"The sun will do me good, and the country air."

"My thoughts exactly." He winked, surprising a laugh out of her. He raised his voice. "Sister Maddie, what do you think of this new breed of female, the reformer?" Kitty leaned forward to look around him for her reaction.

"I'm of two minds. I must admit, it all feels a little... masculine. I've been reading those tracts of Cobbett's, though, and he reminds us of our queens and noblewomen who blessed the knights of old, with banners and tokens. Even proclamations."

"We be queens. Princesses of the worker class."

"But these are men, not warriors," Deacon said.

"They fight for what's right."

"Fighting assumes violence." Was Deacon playing devil's advocate?

"Not a bit. Peaceable protest, that's all we're about."

"Might I continue?" They both turned such guilty faces to Maddie she had to laugh. "Also, did not Mary Wollstonecraft argue thirty years ago—or was it forty?—that as women are equal to men, they should have the vote, too. So why don't our reformers ask for it all?"

Deacon leaned forward. "Don't look at me, I'm doing all I can for the women in my life. Look here, fresh rolls and jam, delivered by mine own hands." He pulled the basket to his knees.

"Aye, but who made it?"

"Believe you me, pretty Miss Kitty, you don't want my clumsy hands anywhere near the kitchen fires. Just ask Cook."

The rolling hills were drenched in posies, tiny bits of color adding up to a blanket of white and reds against the greens of the grasses. They passed many women, with and without children, walking out of the town.

"Trading day," Kitty said past a mouthful of bun. "They start at dawn, trade their finished pieces for new yarn at the merchants, and then return home by mid-afternoon. Nearly a day lost for working, but it's fine to be outside."

Maddie watched a woman turn and beckon her dawdling

son. "A lost day for them. Someone should arrange a cart to carry them, once a week."

"That's a day lost for the carter, then."

The horses slowed of their own accord as they drew up Cheatham Hill. Maddie thought she could see the pocket hamlet of Middleton, a half-mile or so away. Before she could look more closely, the action on the ridge captured her attention.

Hundreds of working-men stood in rows and columns in the field, seeming to march in place. A single man headed each of four squares with another two on the sides to keep the order. Deacon had the driver pull to the side of the road. Maddie lost count as she tried to track the lines across the meadow.

"Can you hear the drums beat?" Kitty clapped in time.

"Are they military men?" They looked too strong and healthy to be of the army, which had fallen on hard times after the war.

"Weavers and mill workers. By Monday's meeting, they'll be sharper than even the coves in the school parades."

The men already stepped tight in rhythm with one another, Maddie could see. Some carried sticks, but most swung arms empty-handed. "They do look well. They must have taken time away from their work, for practice."

"It's that important. The papers are always on about us being clumsy, dirty mobs. This time, we'll be in our Sunday best and stepping in time. Let the naysayers find fault with that."

"They look like they are preparing for an invasion." The bite in Deacon's voice surprised Maddie, but then he shrugged it off. "They should practice dancing in the line. That would truly impress the magistrates."

"You'd have us minuet for your pleasure?" Kitty shot him a glare.

"My pleasure? Darling, I want nothing from you. You might consider the consequences of your actions, though. How they sound—and look—to others."

"Such fatherly advice. You treat us like children."

"Do I now?" Deacon's lilting voice carried a harder edge. "Perhaps you shouldn't throw so many tantrums."

"If you think meeting lawful-like to discuss our grievances is throwing a tantrum, you're not worth talking to." She jumped out of the coach.

"Kitty, come back." Maddie stepped carefully off the side-runner and followed her.

"I'd rather walk than listen to another lecture."

Deacon clapped slowly. "A fine performance."

Kitty tossed her hair and kept moving, taking them away from the carriage and toward the marchers across ground throbbing in rhythmic sympathy with the drums. "Maddie, do you hear him? That's how they all are."

"Nash isn't like that."

"Took long enough to change his mind, and he's not full one of us now." They had reached the outer ring of spectators, women, children, and old folks sitting on blankets in the sun. Kitty paced back and forth behind them.

"They've set it up so we cannot win, Maddie, when all we want is the same voice they have."

Maddie could see her passion and her point, but Nash's view made sense to her, too. Must one be in the wrong for the other to be in the right?

"Can't you see how terrifying that might be to them? No one wishes to give up power, and how can you obtain some if not by taking power away from another?"

"We'd not take anything from them. Our voices would be additions." Kitty's body twisted with her logic, her arms swinging open as if to encompass the entire field. "Every man—every woman—should have a say in how the world is run. Oh, I don't know. Leaders should be leaders, aye, but they should at least be required to listen to their followers. Not treat them as mindless sheep."

She stopped directly in front of Maddie, striking her fist into her palm like a gavel. "Sister, you'll march with us?"

Maddie took a step back. Could Kitty be serious? Panic raced her heart. She looked at the marching men, at the children playing at marching, at the women laughing and gossiping. What was the right answer? She stalled, her mind careening.

"You wish me to join you?"

"Are you not voiceless, too? Wear white, step in time, and demand your due."

"I don't think Nash would approve."

"Your lord and master?"

"He doesn't own me."

"He took you in trade, for five thousand pounds, courtesy of that pretty lordling over yonder. Told me himself."

"That's not how it was." Did everyone think her marriage truly such a sham? They were wrong, weren't they?

Kitty waved a hand in her face, and wrenching her thoughts back to the present. "Maddie, it's just a meeting."

"If it's just a meeting, why should I bother?"

"Why stick your neck out, you mean." Kitty grabbed her arm, nearly hurting her. She pulled their foreheads to almost touch. "Reform for us is life or death. Our people starve in this land of plenty. If we don't gain reform, we'll resort to riot. We must eat."

She let Maddie go, and turned to look at the men as they pivoted in the drill. Maddie looked at the children. She so wanted to be a mother, but how could she bring a child into a world where he might well die hungry? Her own life had held no guarantees. If she could do something to make sure these children, already living, could eat, shouldn't she?

"Call it just a meeting. But it would mean the world to our Da."

Maddie's gaze snapped back to Kitty. "Why?"

"It would show you aren't ashamed of where you came from, wouldn't it? Prove you ain't ashamed of him."

"I'm not. Why would I need to prove it?"

Kitty took both her hands, gentler this time, swinging her arms in time with the tattoo of the drummers. "Join us, Maddie. It will be a grand day, the likes of which none in Manchester has seen. A day to remember, and tell your wee bairns about."

She dropped her hands and stepped back. "Show your mettle. Are you a mouse or a Moore?"

Maddie longed to reach for Kitty's hand again, swing circles like the littlest girls on the blankets. It might not be wise to join this march, but whom would it hurt? No one. Whom could it help? Her family. Herself.

"I'll do it."

"Excellent. We can march together. I'm to join with this clan, from Middleton. They lead in Orator Hunt himself."

The incessant drumming was making Maddie's head pound. She had to get away. "Let's return to Shaftsbury. I need to get back to town."

"I told you, I'm not riding anywhere with the likes of him. Although you may thank him from me for the ride out here."

"I thought you enjoyed flirting with him."

"It's flirting with the devil. He is nice enough in the moment, and then you find yourself covered in brimstone." She puckered her face, making Maddie laugh.

"You can walk this far?"

"Twice over. You saw the porter-women? I do that route, too, twice a week sometimes. Don't you worry about me."

Maddie gave her the small purse she'd made up, and left her to cheer the trooping weavers.

When she reached Deacon and the barouche, he was pacing and the horses were stamping, restless. "Call your sister, and we'll go." He reached out to hand her up.

"She stays here."

"Nonsense." He turned and scanned the rows of women.

"Don't follow her. She'll only spit at you."

"Then you'll have to hit me with a tankard, like poor Wetherby." He stepped up to the seat again, sobered. "Wetherby deserved everything he got, and more."

Amen, Maddie added silently. As the driver maneuvered the horses to face back to the town, she imagined the view from Deacon's eyes. "Do you really see these men as a new army?"

"Not in the martial sense, though they do look quite fierce. In the sense of how they wish to change our world, certainly."

"They just want a sliver of what we take for granted."

"They want more than that. Opening the vote to unlanded

men would put them in the immediate majority. If they voted *en masse* against our interests, they would win." Deacon shivered theatrically. Maddie didn't smile.

"They want the same things we do: Safety, security, family."

"The means they wish to secure them by—that marks the difference. They wish us to give our money to them. Simple as that."

"I don't believe it is that simple."

"Now you really do sound like Nash."

Maddie turned to face him almost straight on. "Did you pay for Nash to marry me?"

Deacon's mouth turned down. "I did and I didn't. Don't look at me like that. I did supply a dowry for you, but Nash would never have married solely for money. In the event, he played me for a fool: You are a treasure."

After a mile of silence, Maddie could hold it in no longer. "I'm going to march."

Deacon jerked back from her. "Driver, stop!" The carriage lurched to a start so violently she was nearly thrown. He caught her by the waist and settled her back on the bench as he spoke to the driver at the door.

"Check on the horses. One might have a stone in its shoe. Now." The man obediently stepped down and checked his horses.

"Saints have mercy," Deacon hissed at her. "Did Kitty put you up to it?"

"Women should have the vote, too."

"Don't even start. But answer me: Did you decide this of your own will?"

"Why?"

"Because this would be great political theater, my dear. How much ink would be given to a poor weaver's daughter marching for her vision of justice? None. How much would be given to the wife of the biggest goods trader in Manchester, the sister of the local earl no less, doing the same? Columns."

"That has nothing to do with it."

"Doesn't it? Kitty will tell her hero, that Orator fellow, who will trumpet it from the stage. He might even call you out of the crowd. How proud Nash will be."

"It's nothing like that." Maddie suddenly wanted to cry.

"You think a sister of reform wouldn't use you for her own purposes? Why ever not? She knows a good deal when she sees it."

"You're not being fair." Kitty was her sister, and would only want what was best for her and the family. Then again, she and Kitty could well have different pictures of what was good for the family. Was she being manipulated? No. This was her decision, and it was the right one. She should be represented in her government, and so should the workers be. The surge of doubt left an ache in Maddie's heart. "Stop. I'm sorry. Don't cry." Deacon's movements were all agitation. He waved his scented handkerchief at her, nearly choking her. It had his initials in five places. With so much stitching, it would scratch the nose of anyone who dared to use it. She had to laugh.

"Merciful heavens." Deacon leaned out the door of the carriage to call the coachman back. "Nothing? How odd. Let us resume." Soon they were rolling again for Manchester.

"Do what you must, Maddie. I'm with you, despite your

minx of a sister. I must give you a word of warning, though; I know how appearances can work against you. If you wish to preserve the peace at home, lay low. Don't lead a regiment, above all. If anything goes wrong, know that you can come to me, always. Above all, don't breathe a word of what you are doing to Nash."

THIRTY-FOUR

Nash forced himself admit it. He was jealous of his brother.

Deacon could take Maddie out to the country, give her a lark of an afternoon, just the thing her heart needed. Nash could only cage her in this sooty, seething town he could never seem to find time to escape. Just a few more days, and then perhaps he'd take her to Liverpool, or even to London. If the Netherlands deal went belly-up, though that seemed less likely by the day, they'd best have their fun while his funds allowed.

After she'd left the warehouse, the afternoon had ground so to a halt he'd checked to make sure the clocks were running. He'd stuck it out, though, rearranging boxes in a new order Jem suggested. There was no rush to the project, but he hated coming home to an empty house now.

He thrust open the door and saw her bonnet, hung neatly as always. He matched it with his hat, and lit up the stairs to Maddie's sitting room. She was already standing when he crossed into the room, a pattern magazine on the table beside her, with cuttings of fine white cotton. She set down the shears and came to embrace him. He drew in the scent of her—sun, meadow, and fragrant skin.

This was a proper homecoming.

He dropped into the seat across the small table from hers. "A dress?"

"Apron. Deacon says hello. He says you work too much. He says you should have come."

"Next time. Did he tell you tales out of school?"

"We talked mostly of the meeting, like everyone else. We saw the workers rehearsing for parade."

Nash sat up straight. Of all the bone-headed maneuvers. "You went to see the drilling?"

"It isn't drilling, or not for any martial purpose."

"But you went?"

"Deacon took us. It was just a ride in the country."

"A ride that took you directly to one of its most dangerous areas?"

Maddie rolled her eyes. "You do sound like a magistrate. There were no guns, no cudgels, no pikes. There were babies, and women, and children. Families, Nash."

Something was wrong. She picked up the scissors, but her hands shook and she set them back down. Nash's chest went cold. He didn't say anything. Best to wait her out.

All that churching must have trained her well. She neither moved nor spoke.

Nash rubbed his chin. In all the excitement, he'd forgotten to shave today. "How did Deacon decide to drive to Middleton? He usually prefers the dells."

Her hands twisted in her lap.

"Maddie?"

"Kitty decided."

Kitty. That one was getting too familiar for his tastes. No doubt she knew exactly what they would find on their little drive.

"Deacon listened to her?"

"They were flirting."

"My god."

"It wasn't real, and besides, it's over now. They argued, and she refused to go home with us."

"Smart lass."

"What do you know of it?" Maddie's attack took Nash by surprise, and immediately made him suspicious. He didn't rise to her bait.

She looked at him as if trying to read him. He held out his hands, an open book. "How did Kitty come riding with you?"

"He sent a messenger to her house, inviting her."

"Treating her like a lady, proper miss."

"She is so a proper miss, at least, as much as I am."

"You are my wife."

"Is that all I am to you?"

Here it came. "What do you mean?"

"I don't know. Sometimes I think women aren't allowed to have ideas of their own."

"Certainly they may."

"We may have the courage of our convictions, true, so long as we do not act on them."

What could she be on about? "What do you want, Maddie? You're a cipher."

She put her hands palms down on the table. "Why can't women have the vote?"

"Sweet mother of pearl, do we need to talk about that now? I have enough on my plate."

"Kitty speaks at the reform meetings, and votes, and the world has not come to an end. Men respect her because her words carry wisdom. Mine don't?"

"It's not the same, voting in the back room of a noisome bar and electing a member to Parliament."

"Can we not start somewhere?"

"Let's talk about this later. Everyone's nerves are set on edge tonight."

"You mean mine, of course. Men don't have nerves."

"We have plenty." She was still too fragile. He'd been wrong about her speedy recovery. Dark circles under her eyes, and the lines at the corners of her mouth, spoke volumes. She still startled at every sound, even some he couldn't hear.

The tension this weekend was affecting everyone; surely it was harming her. He had to get her away from here. He'd miss her in his bed, but knowing she was safe and on the mend at Shaftsbury would ease his mind, if not his loins.

"Maddie, listen. Tomorrow, I want you to go to Deacon's pile and stay there."

"Why?"

"I want you out of the city in case anything happens."

"You keep telling anyone who will listen that nothing is going to happen."

"I'm willing to consider I may be wrong. I won't risk you." She'd had enough pain in her life already. He thought he saw her face soften a moment, and then she crossed her arms, scowling.

"I see no reason to go to Shaftsbury. Do you order me to go?"

"Not an order, a request. It will be deadly dull here, in any case. Why not spend some time with Deacon's ledgers?"

Her face hardened, and Nash realized with a curse he had said the exact wrong thing.

"I do not need to be protected from the mob, as you put it, because I will be one of them."

Did she mean she would go to the meeting? She couldn't be serious.

She was. Pride and fear crossed and re-crossed her face. She seemed to be holding her breath waiting for his reaction. Nash held his breath, as well. Otherwise he would explode all over her. He counted slowly to ten. And ten again.

"Absolutely not."

"You forbid it?"

"I do."

"If I do march, despite your misgivings?"

"Misgivings? Frankly, Maddie, right now I fear more for the safety of your mob than any danger that might spring from it. Let them have their meeting. This is not your fight."

"It is. For all women. For my family."

"I am your family now."

She sat silent, eyes closed. He thought back to when they first met in May, her determination, the steady pressure of her moral strength.

He might lose this argument, he realized. His Maddie might have the soft manners of a Southerner, but she'd been born with a spine of pure Lancashire iron, strengthened by all she'd endured.

She'd fought for her place with Deacon, and lost graciously. She fought for a place at the warehouse, and wasn't she there again? Now she had found what looked to her a family; what made him think she would not fight to keep it?

She had to know she was his family now; he couldn't lose her. She filled his days, his life. She fit with him. Their edges might be rough, but he had faith they'd smooth out as they rubbed along. Faith, patience, and love.

"I love you, Madeline."

She blinked, and her gaze locked on his. Her mouth opened in that inviting way. It was the first time he had spoken those words to her. All the other times had been silent promises, said over dinner, or on the walk home, or over her sleeping form.

"Oh, Nash." Her gaze shuttered, locking him out. Her disappointment seared his bones.

"I want to keep you safe."

"You don't fight fair." She stood and headed for the door.

He scrambled in his mind for something to say, something that would hold her here. She could not go. He would not let her go. "Don't do it."

She reached the doorway and grasped the doorknob, then looked back at him. "Or what?"

He let out a gust of breath. His throat ached; even his eyes ached. "Or we are through."

THIRTY-FIVE

Maddie nearly fell down the stair, afraid Nash would chase and catch her and at the same time afraid that he would not. There was no sound of pursuit, no hand on her shoulder as she threw on her bonnet and pushed herself out the door. Before she knew it, she had crossed two streets, and her chest heaved, gasping for breath.

He told her he loved her. He told her to obey. He said he was forever family, and he would never leave her. He said that if she defied him, he would cut her loose.

Maddie hardly registered the greater numbers of people in the streets on a Saturday night. Once she saw where her feet were taking her, she could only wish to arrive faster. No one was in the graveyard where her mother lay. Maddie brushed a leaf off the marker. She sank to the ground and leaned against it, the edges of the letters and numbers that marked her mother's life cutting into her back.

Kitty wanted her to prove her love to her family by marching. Nash wanted her to prove her love to his family by not marching. What would her mother want?

Only to love her, by the heartful. Maddie sank her fingers into the ground, as if to find her, even as she knew what she wanted to find—a flesh-and-blood woman ready to embrace her —did not exist. Maddie's chest ached, disappointment and growing despair and a grief her heart could no longer contain. She turned toward the stone and traced the letters, one by one.

"She were so young. You be older now than she ever was."

Over top of the marker, she could see the head and shoulders of her father. He sat, his back against the other side of the marker. "It were a different time, then. Wives had babes soon as they could, not like now."

"You talk to her, too?"

"She gives good counsel."

Maddie blinked back tears. He was talking with her! She struggled with what to say next. She took too long; he was the first to speak again.

"My Kitty says you would march. Didn't sound right to me. Thought I'd ask my Mary."

Softly, she said, "Did you love her?"

"I did. I'll never look at another." He lapsed into silence.

It warmed her soul to think she had been conceived in love, a wanted child, a joy. If only she had that with Nash. His love was conditional, which really was no love at all.

She closed her eyes. She'd say goodbye tomorrow, and start looking for employment. She'd need to make her own way. Perhaps Mr. Heywood would make good on his offer of a book-keeper's position, but she knew better than to expect anyone to keep a promise.

He stirred, sighed. "That be the problem with thee. To look upon you is to see your Ma. Couldn't bear it when you were wee, and it's worse now you are grown. Strikes me a blow fierce every time I catch sight of you."

His words made no sense to her. "I look just like Kitty."

"My blue-eyed devil? None a bit of it. You have the angel in you, and it's the weakness in me that cannae stomach it. Can ye forgive me?"

Of course she could forgive him, but how would that change anything? Perhaps if she could please him, he might alter his opinion. Her mother was gone, but part of her lived on in Maddie. Couldn't he love that part? And perhaps that love might—someday, not tomorrow—it might extend to the whole of her. She had to try.

"Do you think you could stand it if I marched?"

"I believe so. She would have it so."

Maddie rose to her feet, her knees creaking in protest. The sky was purpled with oncoming night. She stepped back on the path, away from her father. She could see a leg stretched out, but no more.

"Then I'll see you at the meeting."

She would go to Middleton with Kitty. They could stay at Shaftsbury overnight; it was only a mile or two from the village. She would join the marchers.

Her mother would have it so.

AFTER SHE RETURNED HOME, Maddie and Nash sat to supper, and then sat together reading until time for bed.

Looking in the window, their evening looked much like many others. Inside, though, one could hear the difference. No one spoke.

At eleven, they readied themselves for bed, still like a theater piece without sound. Maddie used the washbasin first as Nash disrobed, then they switched places, a mockery of a minuet.

Without a word, they slid under the sheets from separate sides of the bed. Maddie wore her night rail; Nash, as usual, wore nothing.

For a long minute they lay side by side on their backs, not touching. Maddie wondered if she ever would touch him again.

Nash had made it clear that should she disobey, should she march, he was through with her. She would march. There was nothing more to say.

She closed her eyes. Only a few months ago the idea of leading a quiet life as a bookkeeper for a man like Mr. Heywood seemed the best of a ream of bad choices. Now it felt unbearable.

What the people were doing was right. She should help them. She must. It was her cause, too. She could work; she would not starve. Perhaps she could set up a small school, as Miss Marsden had done in Bath. Perhaps, in a decade or so, she would have buried her longings and her loss in good deeds and those beautiful moments of discovery that shone in children's faces.

That imagined joy was years away. Right now, she loved Nash's touch, his breath, his scent of new wood, coppery tea, and man. His rumbling tenor voice in the other room. The constant surprise at his grace though he was such a big man.

He was starting to understand her, too. To know her, as no

one else ever had. As no one else ever would. Or so she'd made herself believe. Her breath hitched.

His hand took her hip and rolled her to her side. Pulling her close, he wrapped himself around her. Their bodies quickened, unfettered by their minds' arguments against the connection.

He planted kisses behind her ear and along her neck and shoulder while his hand massaged the deep curve in her back. The gentle touch seemed to push her fears away.

"Stay, Maddie." The words croaked out of him, rusted from an evening's disuse. She spun to face him, his eyes wide in the darkness. "Please."

She took his mouth with such passion it pushed him onto his back. Without letting go for one second, she moved over him, hiking up her rail and fitting her bared hips into his.

He groaned and arched against her, his bulge pressing against her. His body wanted her, but she wanted it more. Without waiting for Nash to do it, she took the base of his cock and positioned it. Inch by inch, she slowly sank onto him, taking him fully inside, as far as she could. She savored every moment, every thrust and gasp and drop of sweat on her skin.

She memorized the lines of his body, the rhythms of his breathing and thrusting and calling out. The wonder that was Nash.

She would need to recall these things in the life to come. She knew they would not be repeated.

THIRTY-SIX

N ash had never been inside the office of the constable before, but the cold welcome he received Sunday afternoon matched the stories he'd heard about the place. Heywood looked surprised and a bit guilty; Malbanks positively hissed. Constable Nadin and Trefford, in full yeomanry blue, seemed to be rehearsing their truncheon faces.

"How did you find us?"

"Good afternoon to you, too, Malbanks. Star Inn's keep forwarded your direction." That was only partly true. The keep had merely said the meeting was elsewhere. Bamford had told him where it likely was.

The man had interrupted Nash's breakfast by pounding at the door. A grim Bamford told him of the events at White Moss that dawn. A man sent to spy on the drilling near Middleton was discovered and beaten, but not by reformers, by country boys who didn't even plan to march. They picked the wrong sot to toy with though—now they sat in New Bailey jail as James 'Gingerbread' Murray lay at home in his bed nursing his wounds.

Bamford wanted to go with Nash to the committee meeting he was sure would be called today, to explain again the peaceful intent of the true marchers. Nash had agreed, but at the Star, the weaver had faltered, saying he would not willingly submit himself to the vagaries of constables, especially this day. Even Nash's influence could not protect the likes of him in that lair, he'd said. Their hopes would have to ride on Nash.

He wasn't sure he was up to it. All he wanted to do was go back to bed and roll over his wife as she had rocked him over last night. There would be plenty of time for that after tomorrow.

Heywood stepped up to him. "Did you hear what they did to Murray? One of their militias set upon him, beat him nearly to death." His mentor had gone fully to the opposition. "I tell you, these hooligans must be stopped. Why, they could attack us as we sleep!"

"They could do that any day." Nash knew that was not the right track to take, but it did shut the man up. His face reddened until Nash thought the man might faint of apoplexy. Malbanks merely gave his sickly grin.

"You don't seem surprised. Perhaps because your family attended?"

"What are you on about?"

"Your lord brother was seen observing the buildup of the civilian army last week. At the side of your wife."

"They passed by, playing the tourist."

"When earls treat with weavers, what manner of world do we live in?" Malbanks's grin could poison the air.

Nash bit down hard, reminding himself to stay to the

purpose. "I did hear of White Moss, though I hadn't heard of this meeting."

"We sent a messenger to the warehouse," Malbanks said. "He must have missed you. Perhaps you were attending services."

"Gingerbread Murray makes a worse spy than he does a baker."

Heywood sat down heavily. "He wasn't a spy. Nothing like."

"He just happened to be taking a stroll, at eleven at night?"

Heywood glared at Nash. "It isn't against the law. He was attacked without provocation."

"Again, I heard they were provoked. He was indeed set upon, but not by the marchers. By some vagabond youths who don't even work for a living."

"If this is the sort of person coming into our town tomorrow, I say call the whole thing off," Malbanks said.

"I just said it wasn't this sort of person." Nash brushed the hair away from his forehead. He needed a haircut. "Nadin, was Murray a spy?"

"Can't say one way t'other." The bullish man wilted under Nash's glare. "I didna send him out."

"I sent him." Malbanks stomped his foot once as if starting a marching band. "He performed admirably. Now we know the true intent of these rabblers."

Malbanks minion Trefford's face was alight, an amateur spoiling for a fight, but the professional peace-keeper, Nadin, did not look as positive. His gaze flicked from Malbanks to Nash to Heywood. He was the one who led the constables.

If Nash could convince him, all might still be well. "This does look ill. And it may appear that all your fears are justified.

The truth of the matter is we have the promises—hard promises—of the organizers that tomorrow they will keep their people under control. And, the weavers' union head told me, these men accused will not be any part of it."

"That's certainly true," Malbanks said. "We've arrested them, haven't we, Nadin?"

Nash couldn't believe it. "For brawling?"

"For attempted murder. They've already been remanded to Highgate."

"Where they will just be released at session."

"Which is weeks from now. They are out of our hair until then." Malbanks wiped his hands clean in emphasis.

Heywood pinched the bridge of his nose. "If only we could jail them all for two weeks. Let everyone cool their heels."

Even Trefford looked surprised, but it was Nash who spoke. "Who would work the mills?"

Malbanks waved his hand. "You men of business. That's all you think about. We have anarchy on our hands."

"You yourself are such a man, Malbanks." Heywood's face mirrored Nash's confusion.

"No longer. Sold out to Clayton, for quite a nice sum. The fool doesn't know what he's in for." That explained Clayton's newly excess capacity. No wonder the man offered to help Nash. He needed the quick return on his investment.

Malbanks spat, hitting the spittoon in the corner. "The worst possible spirit pervades the country. This morning's incident is proof positive they intend an armed uprising."

"With sticks and pitchforks?" Nash rolled his eyes.

"They are steps away from open rebellion, and I won't have

them doing it in my jurisdiction." Malbanks was almost shouting. "Who's with me?"

The tavern-keep stepped up, eyes blazing. "I demand the town's own yeomanry have the honor of making the first charge."

"Saints alive," Heywood started out of his chair. "No one is charging at anyone tomorrow."

The yeoman hadn't expected attack from that quarter, but quickly found his footing. "We'll have our blades sharpened, just in case," he muttered.

Malbanks slapped him on the back. "Gentlemen, we have anarchy on our hands."

Nash nearly shouted with frustration. Even Nadin's flat face showed dismay. "Nothing like," Nash repeated. "The marchers plan to sing tunes and bring their families with them. Does that sound like an invitation to mob?"

"Damned dangerous to have women and children there," Malbanks said. "At the least, we should forbid that."

Trefford found his voice, if not his intellect. "Why could they not terrorize another town?"

"The terror is all in your head," Nash said.

"Tell that to the French king," Malbanks retorted.

"We are not France, thank the Lord. Though if we keep starving the peasantry, we may as well be."

Heywood cleared his throat, but waited to speak until the air had settled. "We proceed as planned. Watch and wait. They must act first."

Nadin nodded once, and under his hoary eye the yeoman nodded his resentful agreement. Malbanks shrugged. "Tell the yeomanry to stand ready. No true patriot is going to be injured by that mob."

Nadin squinted at Heywood. "If they don't carry weapons in, they won't find any on St. Peter's fields. We picked up all the likely stones yesterday."

"You sent constables to clear the field?"

"Yeomanry. Right eager, they are."

Nash shook his head. "This is a meeting, not a battle."

"This is war, man." Malbanks, despite his small frame, could roar. "One we must not lose."

THIRTY-SEVEN

The trunks were gone. Maddie had gone. Nash breathed a sigh of relief as he pushed the rowhouse's door shut. Malbanks could hang, the radicals could hang; they could hang one another. So long as Maddie was out in the country, safe.

The scent of her lingered in the entry, a trace of cinnamon from the soap he'd given her amid her own sweet fragrance. She had been wanton last night, so changed from the first time. Was it only a few months past? For a moment, he considered riding out to join her. No, he had to be here at dawn, to make sure those tarted-up shopkeepers kept their swords sheathed.

He sat on the lowest stair step, savoring the quiet. The front door was ship-tight, blocking the sounds of the city, even a city roiled as wild as this one. The smell of potatoes and stew set his stomach growling. Mrs. Willis was cooking only half-rations tonight. Back to his bachelor habits; what a relief those days were done.

Then he saw it, something in the basket reserved for the calling cards that never came. A letter, in Maddie's script. His stomach sank, appetite gone. He'd sent her away for her own good. Surely she could see that. If she had agreed with his reasoning, if she'd done what he asked, why leave a note behind?

His hand didn't obey his first command to reach out for it. He forced himself to snatch it up. He stalked through the sitting room, to the window overlooking their tiny garden. Better light here than at the great window in front, facing the street.

Leaning against the window frame as if it were a ship's mast in stormy seas, he battened down his baseless fears and unsealed the vellum. His eyes sought the signature first. Just *M*. No *Yours faithfully*, no *Until tomorrow*. No *Love*.

She hadn't gone peaceably into the country, after all.

These last months have been wondrous strange. I honor and thank you for your assistance, your bravery and strength, for all you have given me. I regret that they are not enough.

I see that for you, family is a heavy burden. For me, it is every-thing. Family begets a love that is unconditional. I love you, and I grieve that I cannot meet your conditions.

What is a wife to Manchester merchants, who glory in being the makers of their own fate? I wished to be a helpmeet, as Mrs. Heywood is, but I feel you would prefer a Mrs. Malbanks, a living ghost, or perhaps a true ghost. If so, feel free to declare me dead. I will use my earliest name in place of yours.

How could she not see that her family was here, was him? She'd understood last night. Or had she? He sagged into the wood, left hand gripping the sill as if it were the house pitching and not his world. He'd done it all for her, for their life together. How could she not see that?

The afternoon rain plodded down, tapping at the window, mocking him. The rains were short, but nothing stopped them.

Where would she go? Maddie would hate to live in one of those squalid cottages. The cottagers lived so close, no one had room to breathe. No running water, not even for the privy. She'd need to go to the baths twice a day.

He looked around their sitting room, which also served as their dining room, and receiving room, and music room, and reading room, and writing room. Mrs. Willis had taken his luncheon plate but had yet to return to fold the dining table away. The thing took up half the space in the room. He folded it himself, admiring the clever way it compacted nearly flat. Shipshape. He'd loved how everything had its place on board a ship, and its purpose, so different from the ramshackle castle. Here in his first home, he'd copied as many of the good ideas he'd learned onboard as he could.

And one bad one: Ladies weren't welcome onboard. Their skirts mussed the coils of line, their hoops made it impossible—scandalous—to negotiate the ladders. Worse, on ship, ladies had no purpose.

Nash had made Maddie feel unwelcome here. He'd moved the writing desk downstairs, but he hadn't built her decent closets. He'd set her up to consort with the wives of manufacturers but saddled her with a reception room that could not hold a table and three music stands at the same time. When she wanted to be useful, he'd tried her at the warehouse, where he had to admit she shone, and then snatched the opportunity away. Sure, he'd brought her back, but she knew it was at his whim, and he was starting to see that people—even females—wished to be masters of their own fates. Just as he did.

A life of one's choosing versus one at a capricious master's beck and call—who wouldn't choose the first? Especially when one considered herself mere goods.

I admire and respect you too much to wish you to continue to act the hypocrite. You took me on as unwanted trade to obtain capital from your brother. At least I can be grateful that you did not set me on a shelf in that high room in the warehouse.

I go to the castle, as you wished. But tomorrow I march, from Middleton. I release you from your burden. I wish you great success and fortune.

How could he defend against that? He couldn't deny it. Looking through her eyes, he saw no white knight but a greedy merchant scrabbling for spoils, never recognizing the treasure among the dross.

Hypocrites, weren't they all? Every event in Maddie's short life had proved to her she carried no value, while every person mouthed the empty platitudes: *You are special; I have plans for you; you are part of our family; I love you.*

He couldn't bear the pain he pictured in her heart. He couldn't bear the knowledge that instead of easing it, he had compounded it. He couldn't see how she hadn't simply sunk, with all that rancid freight about.

He couldn't just give her up, and he couldn't allow her to cut her own throat, either. She needed support, if only financial. At the least, he could arrange that. There was precious little he could do to soften the blows from society, though they might remain estranged, forever tied but by this loosest of threads, to give her a cover of respectability. That course of action also dangled the chance she would return. And he would damned well do her better then.

No, she would want a clean break. He would, in her place. He would never wish to be connected, even loosely, to someone he thought treated him as unwanted goods. He would just have to change her mind, with all he had: his words.

Nash pushed himself upright and marched to his writing desk. He would answer her letter with his own. If it caught the evening post, it would get to her by seven or eight. He would courier it if it took too long to compose. He pulled the table open, dropping the leaf onto its two spindled supports. He pulled out a sheet of the good vellum, prepared the ink, and trimmed the pen. He must right this ship. He stared the blank sheet for one minute, two, three. And then he wrote, scratching his heart across the page. And then he prayed.

THIRTY-EIGHT

Maddie could see that Deacon had the right of it; neither the coach much less the crested carriage would have made it to within a mile of Middleton this morning. The road, lanes, and paths were filled with folk heading in the same direction. Maddie and the driver barely made it to the edge of town in the field wagon, but were able to give a dozen of the older walkers a ride in the bed of the cart. The driver was supposed to wait on her return from the meeting to transport her back to the castle, but she told him he could leave as soon as the path cleared. She would not be returning to the castle.

Though the day was fine and fair, the air warm even at this early hour, she shivered and held herself close. So many people! There must be hundreds, even thousands, in Middleton alone. Women in simple white dresses and aprons and bonnets, just as she wore; men in their Sunday best. She'd never been alone among so many strangers, and none of her kind, or what she'd been brought up to think were her kind. She'd been so wrong.

As disconcerting as the scene was, her fears faded quickly. The people jostled her, sure, but only in their eagerness to get into the square to join their fellow marchers, who met them with smiles and hearty slaps on the back. They did not frown at her, a stranger, but did not jump to welcome her, either. At last, the hubbub resolved itself. Men were forming up into the sort of contingents she'd seen rehearsing on the hill. Older folk and younger lined the road, looking on, the smaller children running in and out of the columns, practicing for their own parade. The women were forming themselves up farther down the road. She pressed her hands down, smoothing her apron and settling the butterflies in her stomach, and hurried alongside the columns to join them. Though the roadway here was cobbled, it smelled of fresh-turned earth after rain.

After a half-hearted attempt to dissuade her, Deacon had agreed to store her things until she sorted out where she would be living next. He suggested it be the castle, and she remain Mrs. Quinn, if in name only, but Maddie retorted that as he himself had paid his brother to take her off his hands, he shouldn't expect her to believe he wanted her to live with him now. He protested that his feelings about her had changed. Well, so had her feelings about him—about all the Quinns.

It hurt to wrench herself away from the castle, from every-thing, in the dawn-dark of early morning. Maddie knew this track would take her, finally, to her true family, but this first step was not solid, more a footfall on a swaying bridge, with Kitty and her father on the far side.

A bugle blast at her shoulder made her jump. Mr.

Bamford stood at the musician's side, waiting for his tune to quiet the crowd. As all faces turned expectantly toward him, Maddie saw Kitty, only a few yards away. Her sister waved her over.

"Cut it a bit fine, didn't you? Should have stayed the night like I said. We sang and talked till dawn." She held a slip of green cloth.

"That's your banner?"

Kitty unrolled it. Gold lettering on silk, *Suffrage Universal* on one side, *Parliaments Annual* on the other. "Made it ourselves, didn't we? My words is in the speech, the prockle."

"Proclamation?"

"Our president, Mrs. Fildes, is to give it to Hunt on the hustings, and he'll read it out to the crowd. 'May our flag never be unfurled but in the cause of peace and reform. And may a female's curse pursue the coward who deserts the standard.' I suggested the curse bit."

"Will he really read it aloud?"

"He did at Blackburn, didn't he? And Mrs. Fildes is to stand up with him, and we might as well. To hold the banner."

Maddie's breath caught in her throat. Stand before all these people? Her gaze darted from head to head. Far too many to count. The bugle shocked her into attention again, and Bamford started to speak.

"We are here assembled to attend the most important meeting that has ever been held for Parliamentary Reform, and we will show the steadiness and seriousness befitting the occasion. In our Sunday best, in step with the music, we will cast shame on our opponents, on those who call us a mob, who call us a rabble, who say we don't deserve justice. They will see their error today. They will see in us a mirror of themselves, true patriots."

The crowd roared and stamped, their sounding a tattoo on the cobbles. Maddie wondered if what he said could come true. The committee men she'd met seemed far from recognizing working folk as human, much less mirrors of themselves.

Bamford waved his arm, and the crowed quickly quieted.

The gesture was familiar. Deacon had used the same pat-on-the-head motion last night during supper. "Nash is a fool to give you up," he'd said.

"He doesn't want me. He wants another biddable worker."

"I don't believe that for a second. Something is wrong, and as you're sitting here mope-faced, I lay the blame at his door. I truly thought he was getting better, you were serving as good influence, but obviously he's more truculent than even I could imagine. Cutting you loose is by far the stupidest thing he's ever done, and the sooner he realizes that and makes it up to you, the better."

The pain behind her ribs tightened. She was also to blame for their troubles, no matter how Deacon saw it. Their marriage was a casualty of Nash's ambition, Maddie's accident of birth, and Manchester itself.

Bamford raised his arms. "Stay in your forms; follow your leaders. There may be those among us who would take advantage of our numbers by causing a riot. Do not follow them. Our hatbands sport sprigs of laurel, emblem of purity and peace. Offer insult to no one; on this day, suffer insult if you must to keep the peace, but know this. The first man who picks up a stick or a rock, the first man who raises a shiv or a cudgel against his fellow Englishman, that man ruins all. For that man will have proved to the nobs that we are nothing more than the rabble they believe us to be. It may be I am arrested, or others. We will offer no resistance, and do not you offer resistance on my behalf. I prefer to appeal to the laws of my country rather than to force. Is that not the very reason we meet today?"

The crowd's cheering forced him to pause again. "Now, my country sisters and brothers, let us carry our banners, made with pride by our own hands. Let the band lead us. And let us bring our festive ways into the heart of this Puritanical town of strangers. A reformer's wake, with us the rushcarts. For Reform!"

Another roar of cheers swelled past Maddie and down the road. As it subsided, line leaders called for order, and the band struck up "God Save the King". She lined herself up just behind Kitty, who held one edge of the banner at the front of the first row. From the bonnet on her head to the high hem of her white skirt, Maddie matched the others. But her sturdy boots stood out. She hadn't thought to obtain clogs.

There must be one hundred women, a lake of white against the blues and browns of the men following. Their husbands, sons, lovers. Of those Maddie now had none, but today they were all her brothers.

The heaviness lifted from her lungs. She was part of something bigger than herself, something hopeful and good and true. With more spirit than she'd felt in months, she joined her voice to the others in praising "our gracious king."

AT THE NORTH edge of town, near the gate entering on Shude Hill, Nash and Trefford stood by their horses as they watched workers march past by the thousands.

Trefford's blue-and-white yeoman's uniform drew quite a few looks, but no one missed a step or a note of song. As he was alone on the hill with Nash, he must not be considered much of a threat, despite the nasty truncheon tied to his belt. His hands were busy with his flask at the moment.

Row after neat row of singing or smiling, Sunday-best men and wives filed past. Nash could see a few breaks in the column as it swept down Cheetham Hill Road, but he did not see a tail end as yet. Just as the drumbeat and fiddle sound of one group faded, that of the next could be heard.

The people held banners rather than pulling wakes carts, and they were clearly more sober than at wakes, but he felt the same sense of holiday as during those jubilant parades. Today's purpose might be serious, but their aspect, at least on this long march south to St. Peter's fields, was boisterous and gay.

He couldn't help grinning. "It's wakes, or an overgrown Sunday school scholars' parade, isn't it?"

Trefford did not share their enthusiasm.

Nash pressed him. "Look at their organization. Even their arms swing in step."

"These rebels are taking orders, all right, but from whom? Shades of the Jacobins." Trefford spit, hitting too close to his horse, which shied off. Nash's rented gelding didn't flick an ear.

"Nonsense. Take another look. Not one has a weapon. They've brought their children, for god's sake. Who would start a riot with their children on the field?"

"Men who carry banners like that." Trefford pointed to a

large black banner, white letters spelling *Equal Representation or Death*. Beneath the dire words was another, *Love*, and an image of two hands clasping over a heart.

Nash's eyebrows arched. "I do prefer the blue one: *Unity and Strength, Liberty and Brotherhood*."

"See that green one, *No Corn Laws, Annual Parliaments*. Precious little chance of that. Just look at those women." Trefford whistled.

A new regiment was following, at least four score women in the lead, their white bonnets tied at the same jaunty angle. But their banner, a beautiful green and red silk, carried a slogan oddly dour: *Let us DIE like men and not be SOLD as slaves*.

Trefford pursed his lips, and then quickly glanced at his horse. "Jezebels all, and dressed to match the French mob."

"Or the vestal virgins."

Trefford snorted. "If they wish to act like men, by god we'll treat them as men. Into the New Bailey with the lot of them."

"You can't jail a man without cause, nor a woman, either." They'd done it before, though. The thought chilled Nash to the marrow. What had Maddie gotten herself into? She should be at his side, watching, a silent witness or even a cheering one. Instead he'd let her fly into the fray.

No, he'd pushed her into it. He knew she wouldn't find herself at the hands of Trefford and his lot, but what other mischief could accost her?

His grip tightened on the lead, tugging the horse closer. Patting her calm helped restore his temper.

A man stood to the edge of the paraders. Nash recognized Bamford, even under that ancient hat, and beckoned to him. The weaver waved and hiked up the short hill, his bugler in tow.

Nash shook his hand, and turned to introduce Trefford, who quickly stepped aside to avoid the introduction. Nash spoke loudly, to rise over the din of the marchers and ensure Trefford heard every word.

"A right fine turnout, Mr. Bamford. I trust you still intend no harm?"

"None at all, Mr. Quinn. I would pledge my life for their entire peaceableness." He turned and swept his hand across the line. "Do they look like persons wishing to outrage the law? Are they not, clearly, heads of decent working households, and their kin?"

"Much like." Nash's gaze flicked to Trefford, obviously listening though pretending to see to his horse's bridle.

"Just so. If any wrong or violence take play, they will be committed by men of a different stamp than these."

"Glad to hear it."

"I did think we might be stopped at the toll-gates, but no trouble there. Does that mean the meeting won't be prevented?"

"The meeting is on."

"Then all will be well." He touched the sprig in his cap and led his man back to the tail end of a column. They led the band in "Cherry Ripe."

"So, Trefford, what will you report? I don't see a massed army surrounding the town, ready to invade."

The yeoman used a downed log to hoist himself onto his horse.

"Then you're blind. Are wives arm-in-arm with their husbands? Hand-in-hand with their children? No. They are regimented up just like the men, and in the front, like cannon fodder. This is no family meeting." He kicked his horse into a fast walk, then a trot.

Nash had to scramble onto his own horse and fly down the side track to catch up. Trefford's report best not be the only one the sitting magistrates heard.

MADDIE WAS glad to march behind the banner that read *Liberty and Fraternity. Brothers, sisters, and freedom.* It seemed positively English, and increasingly possible, as judged from the center of thousands of marchers stepping lively on a bright-blue summer morning. Even the weather, dry if a shade warm, favored them.

At the last resting stop, Mr. Bamford had spoken of their possibly being detained outside the city, but as they passed the gate, they saw only one of the yeomanry standing among the onlookers. No one was going to stop them. A three-part cheer rose from behind her, and then the singing started up again, "Cherry Ripe." But Maddie's voice jammed in her throat. Nash stood next to that official.

Did he see her? She stepped closer to the woman beside her, hanging in her faint shadow. Surely he was too far away to distinguish her from the others.

Why had he come? Of course. He was an official, too. A pig-tailed gentry, a know-nothing, a dangerous fool. She'd heard all three epithets, plus more she couldn't quite understand, hurled at the magistrates and their committee by the marchers. Were they wrong? Not if one based judgment on the actions of others. Yes, if one based judgment on empathy, or understanding.

For a moment, amid all these bodies and their melodic shouting, Maddie felt alone, singled out, even as she knew she was invisible. How was it that only she could see both sides of the argument, that only she could see how the antipathy between the people and their masters only hurt them both? She didn't want this special sight, if that was what it was. She wanted to be as straight and sure as Kitty, or as Mr. Malbanks, or anyone else, really. It was easy to stay in one's place when one knew what one's place was.

As they neared the town, more and more spectators lined the roads, as well as white-smocked weavers, spinners, and other workers forming into their own contingents. They were entering the narrower streets now, and their party split, one taking the high road. The second, with the women's contingent, dropped down the lane to Smedley Cottage, to lead Mr. Hunt's carriage to the fields.

"We need a fiddler or three," Kitty called out. Bamford waved the closest two, a woman and her daughter, to keep their time.

The sound of music and cheering seemed to come from every direction, though they could only see themselves in the narrow street. Finally they reached the cottage, where stood a carriage with no horses but young men to pull it. Hunt was handing a well-dressed working woman into the coach.

"That's Mrs. Mary Fildes, with young George Swift. They're going to speak to the whole crowd. Who says women can't do what the men can do?" Kitty gave a loud huzzah.

The sound turned Hunt's head. He waved them over to join them in the coach. Kitty clambered on eagerly, the banner with her, but Maddie shook her head. The carriage smacked of her old life. She needed to walk to get to her new one.

Then she spied her father, among the men pulling the coach. She pushed over to him.

"Hie on up to the coach with you."

She shook her head "Can I help you?"

"No, but take this." He pulled a tambourine out from under his shirt. It was warm from his body and scented of him. "Lead us. You'll need to make a lot of noise to get anyone's attention." He nodded at her.

She took the tambourine and gave it a shake. Joy filled her heart so fast she thought it might burst. This is where she belonged.

Despite the jostle and general hubbub, the chariot finally set off, Kitty sitting beside the driver, and Mrs. Fildes, who truly was as pretty as everyone said, beside the Orator. The young man sat post.

The convoy set off at a pace almost as slow as a funeral. It took an hour just to carry on down Deansgate. All Maddie could see, though, was her father, pulling with a dozen other men, smiling if he couldn't sing. He looked a different man when he smiled.

All was giddy excitement as they made the last turning and could see the fields beside St. Peter's church. And the more than sixty thousand faces looking for them.

Her father must have heard the stutter in her rhythm at the shock of the sight. Their gazes locked, and he grinned at her. She grinned right back. Even as the din threatened to burst her eardrums, she felt as if he were the only other person there.

THIRTY-NINE

"Hunt! Hunt! Huzzah!"

The roar of the gathered crowd carried the force of an ocean wave, pushing Maddie back on her heels. She turned to see Mr. Hunt standing in the carriage, a stern smile on his lips, his legs braced by his fellow passengers.

The bands took up the refrain to "See the Conquering Hero Come" as the women and carriage pushed into the crowd. Though the path from Mount Street to the speakers' platform was lined by special constables, the carriage could not easily make its way down the street to reach it. Maddie and the other women made no headway against the thickening tide of people. Each contingent on the field had clumped together around its banner, leaving barely the width of one person between. The Middleton contingent was forced to press ever closer together.

Her father, in the lead of the cart, called for the women to fall back. Maddie and the others gratefully stepped to the side to let the barouche pass. Even Mr. Hunt, sitting straight in the seat, and taller in his signature white top hat, looked a bit taken aback by the size of the crowd. Mrs. Fildes beside him waved a small flag. Kitty waved her larger one side to side, her arms pumping as if there were a great wind. Her grin rivaled the sun, bright and high at one o'clock.

Maddie fell in behind the carriage, its wheels kicking up dust even on ground as hard-packed at St. Peter's field in high summer. There would be no shelter from the sun—not the smallest cloud marred the blue of the sky. She began to wish she'd had more than a few sips of water at the last stop.

After they breached the first of the two single rows of constables, protecting a path from lower Mount Street to the speaker's platform, it was only a minute's work to reach it. Two flat wagons lashed together, a short stair between them, formed the platform, or what the country folk called hustings. The men pulled the barouche to the side, and Hunt jumped to the ground, then handed Mrs. Fildes and Kitty down. Other women took up places in the carriage for a bit of rest. One looked as if she might give birth at any moment.

Kitty was the first up the steps, joining some two dozen others already on the platform. She took a place on the far right, away from the constables, seating herself on a large drum. She held the banner out so all could see the image: Justice, an elegant woman dressed in pale blue, carrying scales in one hand and treading the serpent of corruption under her boot.

Maddie didn't recognize the handful of other women on the stand, nor the many men. Mr. Bamford was not there; he must have remained with their contingent. Kitty's head swiveled side to side, her smile dimming. Was she looking for her?

Maddie pushed through the crowd to reach her before the space in front of the hustings packed too tight with people. Those in the back were surging toward the front, pushing the women who circled the wagons even closer. For the first time, she felt uneasy. She was well and truly trapped here, even if it was blue sky overhead and not a prison ceiling.

When Kitty caught sight of her, at the edge of the wagon, she gestured frantically for Maddie to come up, patting the edge of the drum to offer her a perch. Her mouth moved, but the cacophony of voices around her stole the words away. Clapping and chanting skittered over their heads, with the chatter of thousands rumbling underneath.

Maddie started to slide past the last few women in her path, but a picture of Nash flashed through her mind. It was bad enough a committee man's wife attended a workers' meeting, but to stand on its stage? Could she truly break from him so completely?

Why not? In for a penny, in for a pound. She made it to the back of the "stage" and took the steps up. Kitty pulled her into a sideways hug on top of the drum. She grinned, twin to her sister's.

Where was their father? If he were on the platform, too, it would be perfect. But Hunt's head popped up from the stairwell; as he stepped onto the hustings, it rocked. Too many feet on it already. Their Da must have gone around the other way.

Hunt held up a hand. A pocket of quiet washed across the field. Then a roar the likes of which Maddie had never heard rumbled through the field, resolving itself into a single word: "Hunt! Hunt! Hunt!"

"So, a Sunday-school parade, after all."

Nash stepped into the first-floor parlor of a Mr. Buxton's house on Mount Street, his mouth gripping a smile. Trefford might have told him the magistrates had moved from the Inn to here, across the street from St. Peter's fields.

Most of the men didn't turn from where they stood, staring out the wide bowed windows at the swirl of bodies that filled the field, but Heywood, seated at a writing desk, looked at him and frowned. He was too late. The first words out of Malbanks's mouth proved it.

"Nothing like. Trefford reported in already. Death threats sewn lovingly into flags. And look at the women. All in white, impudent hags."

Nash joined them at the window. The first dozen rows rounding the stand were women, a sea of white faces, dresses and bonnets, as if the two dozen people on the hustings were the center of a daisy and the first rows of listeners its petals. "Mothers and daughters, all," Nash said.

Chief constable Nadin crossed his roast-beef arms in front of his porcine chest. "Not our mothers and daughters. Harlots all, drunk on the poison of reform."

"Need to be taught a lesson," agreed Malbanks.

A cold foreboding brushed Nash's forehead. Maddie was out there somewhere, marching and singing. She had deserted him in favor of the family that had once deserted her. The pain of it seemed lodged in his gut.

"What lesson?" At their silence, he pictured the worst. "You'd throw them all into jail?"

The church bells chimed over the top of the hour. Nash tried to follow the tune to quell his rising sense of panic. Then a wave of roaring noise crashed against the house, rattling the window frames.

He'd never heard a sound at such volume, far greater even than the steady rumble-roar of the largest manufactory. "Hunt! Hunt! Huzzah!"

Nash leaned out the window. Past the heads of Malbanks and Nadin leaning from the window beside him, he saw a barouche and the white top hat that was Hunt's. He had women in the carriage with them, waving more of those banners.

Nash was sorry to recognize "Hail the Conquering Hero Comes," on the trumpets and drums. The scene did remind him of the stories of Roman coliseums and gladiators primed for battle. Hunt planned to fight today with only words. How could he win?

They pulled their heads back in and turned to stare at one another, eyes wide. Even now, with all they had expected, the sheer force of a crowd this size shocked them.

Heywood approached the window. "Gentlemen?"

"A riot, just waiting for Hunt to set spark to tinder," Malbanks said.

"Nothing of the sort." Nash had to shout to be heard over the crowd.

Malbanks pointed at the banners. "*Liberty or Death. Equal Representation or Death*. There's no other interpretation."

Nahs tried to remember those he'd seen. "Labour is the Source of Wealth. Taxation without Representation is Unjust?"

"Enough." Heywood stepped up to the window and handed

a sheet of paper out to Nadin. "Constable, please arrest Mr. Hunt and his fellow organizers."

Nadin pulled his head from the window's opening. "I'll need more help, with this crowd."

Malbanks nearly skipped to the window. "My yeomanry will back you up."

Heywood walked heavily back to the writing table. "We'll call the cavalry first."

Nash stepped in front of the desk, startling Heywood into dropping the pen. "You never intended to let this happen." Heywood stared at him as if he were an insect, letting Malbanks talk for him.

"On the contrary. This is exactly what we intend. Show the people that these gatherings are a danger, to us and to them. Especially to them."

Nash couldn't let this go. Heywood had the ultimate power. He could still stop this.

He grabbed the man's wrist. "You are going to attack women and children?"

"We attack no one. We intend simply to arrest the men on the stands. We will read the Riot Act, and the people will disperse. This is too big for us, Quinn. We can't control a mob."

Malbanks stared out at his unsuspecting victims and smacked his lips. "Without the head of the snake to lead them, the tail will straggle back to their homes. Tails between their legs."

"Snakes don't have legs," Nash said softly.

"Details. An enemy that would not hesitate to commit murder. That is what we have saved our country from today."

Heywood wrenched his hand from Nash's grip. "Call in the message-riders, Quinn, on your way out."

Malbanks slapped the window's sill. "Perhaps you'd wish to accompany them. It's your bruiser of a wife riding post with Hunt. No doubt she'll join him on the hustings."

"You lie." Nash ran to the window. He could see only the back of her, tawny curls under the band of a classic bonnet.

"Loose hair, loose morals, my mam always said. You heard what she did to poor Wetherby."

Nash closed his eyes. It could not be true. "He deserved it."

"Careful, man, or I'll have you arrested as a Radical spy," Malbanks said. "As well as for slander."

On the hustings, Maddie found the sights and especially the sounds overwhelming, but Kitty seemed to bask in the roar. Her feet square to the corner of the platform, she stood tall, surveying the tens of thousands of people facing her. The tallest heads in the crowd seemed high enough only to kiss her clogs.

Another lady reformer stood parallel to Kitty on the right side of the hustings, waving one of Stockton's rather militant black flags. Kitty's gorgeous deep-green silk seemed more appropriate.

From her perch at the back of the platform, Maddie gave up trying to guess the numbers in the crowd. It filled the huge field, overflowing onto the streets at the rear, and people still pushed in. The women in the front rows were now squeezed so tight they looked like threads pressed out of pattern. Washerwomen, cotton batters, weavers, hand laborers, and hawkers of all sorts, all in white, all calling and clapping.

Hunt held up a second hand, and the chanting ceased. Maddie swayed; her ears had grown so accustomed to the chants and roars, their sudden absence threw her off balance. Now she could hear the regiments' flags snapping behind him on the hustings and before him on the ground.

"My friends, we are here peaceably assembled." The hush settled on the crowd, at least those who could hear his voice, ready to listen to a speech she expected would last a good hour or more.

Hunt projected his voice out, but somehow it also rolled back and around her. She'd always been in the midst of the crowd before. The odd ricochet made her feel singled out, as if she were helping Hunt speak.

Hunt's cadences seemed to draw the attention of even the double row of special constables. What had Kitty called them? Penny-pinching pawnbrokers, second-rate inn keeps who sold watered ale, and men of business who kept their boot on the throats of their workers, taxing their wages for imagined infractions while dressing their wives in French thread. How could they stand there so blithely among thousands who resented them?

As he spoke the word "countrymen," Hunt waved his arm, drawing her gaze toward the far end of the corridor of specials. A movement. Horses, with men upon them, tossed their heads, mincing in place.

That must be the yeomanry Nash talked about. High upon their saddles, making their way down the aisle of constables, they were going to arrest Hunt. Many had expected Hunt would be arrested by day's end, but his speech had only just started. What could he have said already that was seditious?

Most in the crowd strained to hear the vibrant sentences of the speaker, but the sound of murmuring grew as more and more people saw the horses.

"Steady, friends," Hunt called out. "Welcome them. Show them our new ways. If they want me, they will have me. No striking back."

The lead horseman raised an unsteady sword, as if in drunken greeting. The crowd closest to him raised their arms and their voices, calling and responding, as if they were at the loom, or the spinning-wheel, or church on Sunday. The chorus spread across the crowd, a wave of salutes sparkling like water over pebbles in a brook.

The horses looked nervous, side-stepping, coming too close to the tightly packed bodies. The lead horseman turned, perhaps to see if his men were following him, but that turned his horse's head as well. The horse lurched into the crowd, which spilled into the open aisle to get away from it.

"Stand fast!" Hunt's call was picked up by the leaders of the regiments across the field. "They ride among us, stand fast."

Other horses and their riders had lodged themselves in pockets along the route, people jamming their paths, unable to move. The horses snorted in panic. The lead man—did he grin? —lifted his sword and slashed it down. Blood spurted from the head of a defenseless woman.

Other riders had drawn and were cutting. But the bulk of the yeomanry was pounding toward the hustings, toward her, their swords out, their horses' eyes crazed.

Fear punched Maddie in the chest. She stepped back, against

the drum, and almost fell off the platform. A man in the platform's center was waving, standing halfway up the stairs. "Women this way!"

Maddie reached for Kitty, and they locked hands. Her sister's face was wild with anger, but the noise was such Maddy couldn't hear what she was shouting. As they were pushed down the stairs, Kitty's hand let go.

Maddie turned back, pulling herself out of the stream of ladies running for the carriage to go back for Kitty. The wagons were rocking, the ties binding them together pulling apart. The yeoman must be boarding from the front.

The short stair collapsed.

FORTY

"Good god, sir, don't you see they are attacking the yeomanry? Disperse the meeting!"

Heywood's voice was ragged as he stood at the top of the steps to Buxton's house, but his eyes were clear with rage. From the base of the steps, Nash watched him order Lt. Col. L'Estrange to send his trained cavalry troops into battle as if he were watching a play upon the stage. This couldn't be real.

Ethelston leaned out the balcony's window, speaking the words to the Riot Act in a voice that only the soldiers and committee men could hear. At least the Act allowed the crowd an hour to disperse. Nothing serious could happen till then.

They intended to arrest Hunt. To arrest Maddie. He played through his mind the steps he'd need to take to get her released from jail. He wasn't sure who the magistrate on duty was this week, but surely no one would want women held in that cesspit overnight. He'd pledge the warehouse as surety; they couldn't want more. But what if they charged her with gross sedition? There might be no bail at all.

The thought of her locked away from him tore at his chest. He pushed it out of mind, concentrating on the military arrayed against her. L'Estrange had mounted and was shouting orders. Nash grabbed the man's ankle, careful to avoid spooking his charger. The lieutenant was young but cool under fire, and he'd put up with the committee with no more than the occasional locked jaw and reminder that they were no longer at war.

"You'll not wait the hour?"

"I have my orders." He'd just ordered them to present. They were going in now.

Nash didn't let go. "But there are women and children here."

"I have my orders, sir." But he put a hand on Nash's shoulder. "I'm not a monster, man. We won't wage war on the people." But that was exactly what the yeomanry were doing, Nash saw as he trailed the horses to the edge of the street. Those part-time soldiers had not been in danger, yet had lashed out. He knew reinforcements, infantry and artillery, stood in the streets to his left and right. If this caught fire, no one would escape it.

Maddie, his Maddie, was in the thick of it.

Malbanks stood beside him and grimaced. "A right scheme, this was. Every district in Britain is in revolt. At least Manchester will be preserved. We will not be taken."

Nash couldn't help responding, though he knew nothing could reverse the man's mind. "You've made it so they cannot escape, even the innocent. The exits are blocked."

"Just as well. Quicker this way."

"May all the souls who die today wait for you at the pearly gates." St. Peter himself must surely be watching.

"They are traitors, Quinn. They will rest in hell."

Nash mounted his horse, trying to steady his mind so he wouldn't spook her. As he turned the mare's head toward lower Mosley Street, away from the field, he watched L'Estrange's Fifteenth Hussars lining themselves along the eastern end of the field. They would be the bottom pincer, with the yeomanry at the north the top, pressing the people into the fixed bayonets of the Eighty-eighth Infantry. A slaughter waiting to happen. Nash knew he couldn't stop it. He knew he should run. In battle, weapons don't discriminate.

He turned his horse back toward the crowd. Toward Maddie.

He followed the wake of the first line of cavalry. As they met the crowd, they slowed, and he shot through them toward the hustings, barely registering the bloody gashes and moans of constables and crowd alike. The field was screaming. He opened his mouth to match it, to keep the scream from lodging inside him.

Fewer than a dozen people still stood on the hustings, constables in blue pushing men in brown down. A flash of white at the front, skirts swinging. Her bonnet pushed back, her arms wielding the pole like a scythe, Maddie seemed to be floating in midair.

She must have tried to jump and caught herself on a piece of the wagon. She couldn't reach the ground. She couldn't get away.

A yeoman galloped past, slashing the pole apart damned

close to her hands. She wriggled and reached back, trying to free herself, as the man turned his horse to charge her again.

Nash gouged his horse's belly, pushing her to run. He had to get there first.

Her arms crossed in front of her, the short pole facing away, as she swung to nearly facing him. The front of her dress was dark red with blood. Someone had already gotten to her.

Bile rose to his throat, his nose. His horse snorted at the pain of his kicks. He would kill that yeoman.

As he rode past Trefford, arm raised for another blow, Nash stripped the sword from his hand. Not slowing down as he reached the platform, he swung the blade to just behind Maddie. His arm rang at the impact of the weapon on the nail, but the blade won out. She was free. He leaned to wrap his left arm around her shoulders, but she'd slid water-fast to the ground.

With a powerful underswing, he knocked the charging yeoman's sword away. As the man passed, the surprise on his face turned to pain as Nash punched him in the side hard enough to knock him off his beast.

Nash dropped down beside her. The screams, the shouts, the sickening crunch of bone and suck of wounded flesh that had assaulted him while astride fell to nothing. All he heard was her too-loud gasps, the gurgle of blood punctuating the end of each breath.

She lay in a ball, trying to protect her insides. From the front, he could see her shoulder blades between the pulses of her heart.

"Cross your arms tight, sweetheart. Hold yourself in."

He scooped her up, and pushed himself to stand. Her head lolled back, eyes closed, pain altering her features beyond recognition. He had to get her help. The hospital, or Lady Egerton's house. Heywood's, if he had to. Her hand scrabbled at his shirt, but had no strength to grasp it.

"That's him!"

He looked up at L'Estrange riding toward him. Then eye level, at the angry young yeoman he'd felled. The first punch, to his jaw, only made him stagger. The second, at his temple, stunned him enough that he let go of Maddie. She hit the ground without a whimper.

"Enough! He's under arrest. I'll take him myself. Yeoman, move on."

Nash dropped to his knees, trying to scoop her up again. As he touched her shoulder, her body gave way.

Her dress gaped open, exposing all she had lost. He slipped off his coat and draped it over her, shielding her innards from the sun.

He wiped the gore from her beautiful face. Her head fell back, lids opening, her unseeing eyes a pure reflection of the sky's perfect blue.

Kitty.

FASTER THAN THE day's faint breeze, panic swept across the field. The crowd that had been pressing so persistently toward the hustings now was fleeing it. Maddie quickly made her way to the front of the platform.

On the boards, the dark-clad special constables had their truncheons out, clubbing whomever stood in their path, their weapons rising and falling. One constable tugged Hunt by the coattails as if to throw him off the stand and onto the ground. Others were ripping the flags and breaking their poles, some by swinging them at the people on the stands. She saw the older lady fall. Chivalry be damned; they were not going to spare the women today.

A man jumped from the wagon, falling into the path of one of the part-time cavalry. Maddie quickly looked away, but she couldn't block out the sound of crunching bone and howling voice. It took her eyes panicked seconds to find Kitty in the melee. Her sister had backed up, pushing the giant drum between her and the club-wielding men. But two of them had longer reach, landing blows on her shoulders. One knocked her hand back into her face, blacking her eye.

The pain of each blow seemed to echo in Maddie's body. Her vision blurred.

"Jump, Kit! I'll catch ye." Her father's voice cut through the din. He was as far away as Maddie, but back and to the side, pushing against a tide of fleeing women. The truncheons would lay Kitty low before he got to her.

Maddie got to the front edge of the hustings first. "No! Jump here. Here!" She pounded on the bed of the wagon, as if her puny force could distract anyone from the grisly dance on stage.

Kitty must have heard her; they locked gazes. Another blow knocked Kitty's shoulder crooked, but she kicked the drum at him, pushing him back and giving her room to run straight off the front of the stage. Maddie stepped back to give her space to fall. She held out her arms and held in her breath, bracing for her sister's dead weight.

She didn't hear the horseman until the force of another

flailing body hit her from behind. She was thrust forward, past the corner of the stage, landing on her hands and hips a good yard from where Kitty should have landed. Maddie's face and hair were wet with blood. A young man, his shoulder cleaved from his body, lay across her.

She had to get back to Kitty. She rolled out from under him, not listening, not hearing his screams, and scrambled to her knees. Spitting dust and blood, she blinked hard to clear her vision, and then wished she hadn't.

In front of her were the deadly prancing steps of giant horse-shoes. Which meant above her was one of those killing swords. She froze, her fear so great it sharpened every sense while dulling her power of volition. "This is Waterloo for you!" His sword hand wobbled, a sign of poor practice, but it did not stop its arc directly at her.

It was only inches away when she regained control of her limbs. She pushed herself backwards, trying to get away, but the movement first raised her chest, pushing it toward the blade.

The force of the blow severed the plackets of her dress and pounded her heart into a solid bruise. But it also pushed her farther back and down, where he couldn't reach her to deal a second blow from way up on that high horse. She told her limbs to move, scramble away from those sharpened hooves, but they did not respond. She wasn't going to be able to help Kitty. She couldn't even help herself.

She closed her eyes, shutting the blood and din and smell and chaos out. In the safety of her mind, she said farewell to Kitty, to her friends from school, to her parents, one by one.

Then Nash's face flashed behind her eyelids. She couldn't say goodbye to him. He refused to listen, even in her own imagination. He would not let go, would not believe she was through. Get up, he said, and fight for your family. That's how you prove you deserve one.

She opened her eyes. She lay on her side beside the bloodied man, now merely groaning. The cavalryman had turned away from her, looking for more live meat. She moved her arm and pressed her palm against her chest. Dry. No blood.

Shocked into sense, she ran her fingers up and down. The blade had split one of the stays in her corset. The stays were bone, two inches wide and a quarter-inch thick, she knew from the corset maker's advert. Her skin might be scratched enough to scar, but nothing more.

If she could just catch her breath, she could get away from here. Windmill Street wasn't but twenty yards behind her. She struggled to sit up, and wiped at the blood on the side of her neck and face.

A thought floated by. She wasn't modestly attired at the moment, her dress gapping like that and blood all in her hair. She shouldn't really be seen in public. The idea somehow calmed her, and she took a sip of air.

"There ye be." Strong hands under her arms jerked her to her feet. Her father, a gash on his temple but still seeming to have all his senses. He must have helped Kitty, and then come back for her. "Can ye run or must I carry ye?"

She took a step and did not fall. He clasped her hand in his, both slippery, hers from blood, his simple sweat. They slipped under the wagons and then dashed onto the street. The yeomanry must have massed here, she could see their trampling, but all were on the field now.

Step by labored step, they slid past the carnage. Screams and a crunch of metal behind them turned her head. Between the horses, she saw a pile of arms and legs and torsos tumbling down one of the cellars of a rowhouse.

With each step, Maddie's dim hopes rose. She might live through this.

"Keep moving, lass. We're not safe yet."

But safety felt just a step ahead. Beside them stumbled women and men with cuts across their faces and hands and children whose faces were streaked only with terror.

"Just around the bend."

With a sigh of relief, they passed the crowd at Mount Street and could see the sign for lower Moseley and escape. But as they passed the final knot of men and horses, the flow of frightened people around them stopped.

Turning the corner, blocking their escape, came an army, bayonets fixed and aimed straight at them.

Maddie and the others froze in terror. Then they realized the soldiers were only creeping at them. They weren't going to mow them down, merely slowly crush them underfoot. They did not leave room enough for a body to pass. Regular troops, trained and cool under the heat of the sun, they would not stop.

Maddie recovered her wits before her father did. She tugged him to the side of the street. His feet trod slowly, as if his clogs were sticking to the cobblestones.

There—an eighteen inch alley between houses, not meant for any but the night-soil man. She dragged him to the entry and pushed him in ahead of her. He was a tight squeeze, and unwilling. The stench stalled her too, but holding her breath she pressed them on. They had no other option.

They popped out into a closed space less than the width of

Nash's bed and holding three privies, ancient but still in use. Maddie bent, hands on her thighs, to recover her breath. But her nose refused to take in the air her lungs were screaming for. She forced herself to inhale; the air scorched her nose and burned its way down to her already bruised lungs. Her body felt as if it were working at one-quarter capacity, her heart as leaden as that artillery's cannon.

The courtyard's filth hurt her eyes, but the picture of what had occurred on the field blotted it out. Impressions she had not had time to notice in their pell-mell escape now crowded her mind for attention. One woman screaming as another's forehead split open. A man, clutching his hand, hanging from a fold of skin, his attacker riding away with the pole he had been holding. Mounds of clothing writhing in the dust and dirt. A boy, unhurt, not running away but crouching beside his fallen mother, crying for help. So much blood.

"Go ahead, cry, sweeting." Her father laid his heavy hand on her shoulder. She felt him shudder. "Hunt and them had it wrong. City rules don't hold for Manchester men."

Maddie sobbed, as deep as her bruised chest could stand, her horror mixed with wonder. Her father had come to her. Her true father. She leaned into his embrace, the brightest of silver linings in this death-cloud of a day.

How could this have happened to her, to them? Her first meeting ever, and it ended in bloodshed. Nash would never forgive her now. Could she ever forgive him? A committee man, he must have agreed to call this attack. He, at least, knew better.

It was right for her to leave him. Her true supporter stood at her side now, or rather leaned against the brick wall. She'd waited all her life for someone to choose her, just her, and now someone had. She turned her tear-streaked face up to his.

He pulled the cap off his head and wiped at her teary face absently, looking down the alley. "Rum foul in here, but it's still commotion without."

"How long, do you think?"

"Gudgeons will make short work of us." Then he froze, head tilted, as if listening to a silent bird in his head.

Or repeating her upper-crust accents.

He spun her to face him, pushing her shoulders into the brick. She winced as he shoved her bonnet back.

"Look on me!"

She looked full at him, watching the darks of his eyes grow round. He dropped her shoulders and brought his hands to his face as if he didn't believe they were his own. A keening came from his throat, resolving into a hissing whisper.

"Where is my daughter?"

FORTY-ONE

"What ha' thee done with my Kitty?"

Her father slapped the sides of his head once, twice, three times before Maddie thought to take his hands in hers.

"I thought you knew." Hadn't he said she was nothing like Kitty? How could he pretend to be surprised? Yet in the cramped courtyard, fouled by generations of waste, here he stood, flabbergasted.

He wrenched his hands away, tipping her off balance across the opening to the alley. Before he could enter it, he had to stop and turn his hips sideways, which gave her time enough to take his hand again.

"Wait. You don't know if they're through."

He didn't even try to release her grip, just dragged her behind him as he side-stepped back to the street. Back into fresh air—and danger. They emerged onto the street, and saw a nearly deserted field. Her father stopped, gasping for breath, as if he

427

could not understand what he was seeing. Where tens of thousands of people had stood and cheered, now stood only remnants of their presence, the wounded and the dead.

The sun shone blindly on an array of caps and bonnets, shawls and coats, misshapen, bloody. Shoes and clogs their owners' feet had run directly out of in their flight. So many, as if a hurricane had whisked the people up, and everyone had dropped whatever they held in their hands. To their right, near the corner house, the cavalry had dismounted, seeing to their horses and cleaning their swords. Laughing and slapping one another on the back, they evidently thought their work well done.

Maddie almost couldn't bear to look at the larger bundles of clothing strewn across the field, each a being either in distress or recently released from it. She forced herself back onto the field: One of them could be Kitty. Now it was she who took the lead, pulling them toward the hustings. The two wagons remained, broken flag-staves rising from their beds. The banners were taken or destroyed, the people only taken, she prayed.

The densest number of casualties lay closest to the wagons. Maddie took some to be children, their bodies so small, and then she realized they had been crushed into the earth. At each mound, she looked for Kitty's auburn curls. She was too weak to look into their faces. A woman, a man, a woman, another woman. Others, Samaritans or fearful relations, also stepped from one to the next, seeking the living.

Kitty.

The curls spilled out from under a man's coat cut like Nash's. Maddie swallowed hard, her mouth suddenly too dry to call to her father, who was searching near the other wagon. He must have seen her stop, for he rushed to her side.

"Damn Tory fabric." He thrust the coat away from her, and then recoiled. Kitty's lively face held the red marks of a beating, marks that never would bruise. Even with her arms across her belly, parts spilled into the dirt in front of her. She hadn't been merely killed, she'd been gutted.

Maddie fell into blinding pain all over her body, mirroring Kitty's wounds. To regain herself, she looked away, up, anywhere, everywhere else. Set her eyes and ears adrift. Rows of houses, all their curtains pulled, blinds closed, doors shut tight. Horse's harnesses glittering in the sun. The steady tramp of soldiers' boots melting into a confusion of strides as they were called out of formation. The keening of a man mourning his wreck of a daughter. His tones melting into the moans and cries of other fathers. Her father.

Maddie sank to her knees. The discarded coat lay before her. She picked it up and wrapped herself in it, fastening its familiar buttons. So like Nash's, she let herself imagine it smelled of him, too. She tried to focus her senses on the memory of that scent, chamomile and musk, to mask the harsher smells of blood and despair. She looked down the field to the horses and their scarlet-plumed masters. Cavalry, against cloggers. The world had no sense of proportion, no measure. She hated the soldiers, and the world they represented. If she'd been a reluctant radical before, she was a full-blooded one now.

Her father's grief was attracting the attention of one of the soldiers, which could only mean ill. She dared put a hand on her father's shoulder, only slightly less dangerous than facing those dragoons. "She shouldn't be in the dirt, like this. Take her to hospital?"

He pushed her away, leaning over the body, a mother hen after the fox has raided the coop. He pulled Kitty toward him, and lurched to his feet, pressing her belly to his. "Out of the way." Step by staggering step, he carried Kitty across the field, toward the church. He hadn't gone three dozen steps before his knees folded and he sank to the ground, holding Kitty as Mary does her child in the Pietà sculpture. "I dinnae want your help," he insisted, his sobs making the words a dirge.

"Your home is more than a mile away. Let me find a wagon, at least." He nodded, perhaps; she left him there, his shoulders shaking under the pressure of his unshed tears. But not a wagon, nor a coach, nor a carriage was to be found. The hospital wagon transported only the living, and the morgue wagon would only take her there. The sun's steady glare mocked Maddie, stealing her energy. She weaved on her feet as she went from house to house, closed shop to closed shop. She started calling out, a town crier of death, pleading for final transport.

At last, a man appeared from the courtyard of a house she'd just passed, pushing a wheelbarrow. He dropped the handles, setting the barrow at the edge of the street, and retreated. At his locked door, she called out her thanks and her father's address.

The church bells rang half past two before she got back to the field with the barrow, and seven before they got Kitty home. Moore had insisted he push her every step of the way, and it took all Maddie's will just to keep up with even his slow pace. He'd covered Kitty with his own shirt, and wore only his vest. He'd been whipped sometime in the past.

Twice, they had to pull to the side and take shelter in an alley as riders passed by. They had to skirt Shude Hill and Market Street, where shouts and clacking stones and metal warned of conflict best avoided. By the time they reached the cottage in Clock Alley, Maddie felt beaten down to her soul.

❧

MADDIE FORCED herself to keep moving, collecting all the pans and buckets in the house to carry to the pump in the court-yard. A neighbor woman sent her boy to help carry them back to the cottage.

After draping his daughter onto the table, Moore collapsed onto the floor, his head hanging so low it nearly touched the swept earth. Maddie fetched the stool from beside the cold fire-place and set it beside him.

"It would help if you hold her hand while I make her ready."

He pushed himself up and onto the stool, his face a creased mask of sorrow. He gripped Kitty's good hand and sat silent witness as Maddie folded up the cuffs of her coat and started to cleanse the body. Had her three-year-old face looked so ravaged as she held her mother's hand while they prepared her for her eternal journey? Her adopted mother.

Dusk deepened into gloom as she worked, first to get the body clean, then to shape it back into her sister. Finally, she asked for a needle and thread. He fetched it for her, but just as she bit off a length of it, he shuddered and retreated back up the stair. She sighed in relief. Now she could light the candles; he hadn't wanted any light. She wanted this part done as quickly as possible.

Above her head, she heard a click-click-clack, click-click-clack. He must be at the loom, weaving. The rhythm soothed her. She hoped it soothed him.

Kitty and she were so alike. Long legs, fine fingers. They'd slashed at her breasts, but she was so small they'd only taken the tips. Maddie's breasts ached in angry sympathy. There was little she could do with the cuts to the hands but make the stitches as neat as possible. She could do nothing with the chest, but merely wrapped it with strips from her petticoat.

Finished, she kissed the closed lids of Kitty's eyes, then her forehead. The sister she never knew she'd always wanted.

She sat on the stool for just a minute before going up to look for Kitty's other dress. But the click-clack lulled her into a sleep so deep the new nightmares couldn't touch her.

MONEY HAD DONE what his weakened influence could not, and by evening Nash found himself in the best accommodations the New Bailey jail could offer. He could only pray that Maddie was as secure.

The turnkey had recognized him and gone against constable's orders to install him and some of the others in a largish room on the second floor with six cots and two slop-pails. He'd also given them pen and paper—or rather sold it to them at a usurious rate. Nash had gotten a letter out to Deacon; if only his brother could wield his power to conjure up Maddie.

He should have known it would be Kitty on the hustings. He should have known not to believe Malbanks's eyes. He should have known to trust Maddie's good judgment. All the things he should have known filled the space of the room, spilling out along the corridors. What he didn't know was acid eating him slowly from inside.

Where was she? Was she hurt or frightened? There were no woods to hide oneself in Manchester, but there were two rivers. She'd promised him not to consider it again, but he'd promised in return that he'd never leave her. Would she consider that contract broken? After seeing the carnage of this day, was she—were any of them—thinking rationally tonight?

She must be with her father. He knew Moore wasn't locked in here; the old reform hand had likely not risked standing on stage. A reporter from London was not so fortunate. Not known to the constables and not believed by the yeomanry, he sat across from Nash penning his own batch of correspondence. Dark curls and an amiable round face offset the sharpness of his gaze.

"It's a rare thing these days not to carry a stick, or even a cudgel when one walks the streets and byways. My impression is that the people purposely refrained from bringing any such implements of alarm. Is that your impression, as well?"

"The committee told them not to. They counted on the protection of the state."

"More fool them. You don't look the rabid radical."

"Nor you."

He sighed, all but draping the back of his hand across his forehead. "Bragge. *London Beacon*. So I say."

"*The Beacon's* Tory. Or barely Whig. Why report on a protest? Just bloviate against it."

"Like your Manchester rags? The biggest story in Britain, of course I'm here. Sadly, current circumstances will make it difficult for me to meet my deadline. I never thought this would happen on our soil. We're not the French, after all."

"What did you hear of the women?"

"Anyone in the coach or on the hustings arrested or maimed. Three here with us, confusing the guards on the floor below."

Had Maddie really been in the coach? He couldn't say for sure now. "Names?"

Bragge looked at the ceiling, thinking. "Two they're calling Mary Fildes, though neither looks like the lady I met this morning. The other appears very ill—and very pregnant." His account matched what the turnkey had told Nash. Maddie wasn't here.

He'd been an idiot to believe Malbanks. The man couldn't tell an enemy from a rock. It was Kitty in that coach, Kitty on the stands, Kitty dead in the dirt. Maddie might not even have been at the rally. But he knew her better than that. She followed her older sister like a lapdog, hoping for any scrap of love she or her blasted father threw her way. Why was their love so much more valuable than his?

It had certainly cost her more. A marriage, a secure life, and now a sister. Perhaps, heaven forbid, her own life. His mind skittered away from the thought.

Had she read his letter? Had it made a difference? Sitting in here, deprived of his freedom and his power, just as she so often must have felt, he saw how foolish he had been. Why had he forced her to choose between him and her family? It made so much sense politically, and even economically. But woman was a creature of emotion, as was man, if he would but admit it.

To meet others' expectations, he'd cut out his own heart.

When those others were tested, they failed him. Maddie was the true partner, the truthful friend.

He never wanted to see Heywood again. He was glad to be in jail tonight; otherwise he would hunt down Malbanks and flay him with his own sword or, better, with Trefford's, after he had done with that piece of offal first.

But as the night darkened to chill black, Nash forced himself to face a deeper truth. He was his worst enemy. Those men had followed their own rules, but he'd bent his, trying to stay in their good graces. He had broken his promise to always hold and honor his wife. He hadn't kept it for even four months.

She'd read the letter; he was sure of it. She'd probably burned it, just like Deacon, just as she should have. What mere words could convince her when she'd seen his true colors in his actions?

The red-orange of dawn promised to lift the chill of the cell's walls. It would do nothing to cauterize the gaping wound that was his heart.

FORTY-TWO

Morning did not bring renewal to the broken and battered families of Manchester, much less hope.

Maddie wasn't sure what woke her. She heard nothing unusual, only the shuffles and murmurs of people in the yard, and not much of that. The residents had barricaded themselves in, closing off the street to avoid clashes with both constables and mobs. No, it was the absence of sound that had woken her. The loom upstairs had stopped.

She started to stretch her arms, but shooting pain forced her back into a hunch. She unbuttoned the coat. The bruising now stretched across her chest, but her ribs did not hurt when she pressed on them. Nothing broken. She said a prayer of thanks to whoever had invented the corset. Little did they know it could act as armor in battle.

She heard Moore's heavy tread down the stair. Had he not slept at all?

He drew up to the table on which Kitty lay, his face dark, a piece of thick buff linen draped over his arm. He pulled it taut and stretched it over and under her body, from head to crushed foot.

His hands fell heavy to the table. His bruised eyes leached tears. She knew he would wish to be alone with her. She rose, and he startled, crystal eyes shining confusion and aching pain. He didn't seem to know her.

"She can wear the blue dress. Upstairs."

"No. Like this."

Maddie swallowed her own pain. "I'll fetch breakfast. Want I should call the rector?"

"She'll take my place, next to her Ma. Happen they can comfort t'other."

"But where will you rest?"

"As far away from here as God sees fit." He scanned the small but tidy cottage as if its very air poisoned him. "Sell this piece; use the coin to get out."

"And leave them here, alone?" Maddie's voice broke. Would he not even consider making a family with her?

"They're God's kin now. I have no family." His gaze snapped to hers. The pain of it, the hurt should have burned her to her black-bruised heart, but she was too tired to even whimper. Instead she shuffled to the back of the cottage.

She found dried oats for porridge, and used the rest of the water to get it to cooking. Fetching yet another pail of water from the pump, she spied a lady with chickens, and bought an egg to crack over the gruel.

Moore took the meal without comment, just as he'd taken her efforts at setting Kitty to rights.

He never would call her his daughter, not now. She would

never be welcome here. He would rather leave and desert them all than stay and admit he was wrong.

She almost dropped her spoon in her shock at the thought. If he took her back, he would have to admit he'd made a grievous mistake in letting her go, all those years ago. He'd sold her. Over the past nearly two decades, he'd built such a wall around his heart against her she could never scale it, and he, clearly, refused to tear it down.

He was lost to her. He always had been. Perhaps she could have made her way with Kitty, but never him.

She tipped the lid on her roiling cauldron of emotions, opening it just a crack. Deep disappointment spilled out. She'd thrown away the opportunity to build something lasting with Nash to grasp instead at the slicked rope of this family's love. Now she had neither. Maddie expected these thoughts would crush her, but she breathed easy for the first time in a day. At least now she knew. She'd tried and failed, but at least she'd tried.

She would see Kitty off, and then leave Manchester to its hard-driving ways. She'd already said farewell to life as a countess, as a town wife, and now as a daughter of reform. Surely something equally surprising was in store. She would survive it, a shard of her at least.

Her body's tension now released, sleep overtook Maddie so quickly she nearly fell into the cook fire. She stole up the stair to the bedroom and lost herself in the exhausted slumber of a motherless child.

THE TURNKEY UNLOCKED the door into the jail yard and Nash stepped out, again a free man. The air here was not yet free enough, but as he started to hurry his steps through the tunneled opening, he stopped short.

Deacon, resplendent, lounged in the shadow of the gate. Top to toe the earl, if the colors were a shade more muted than usual. He'd be bearing some of the king's crowns, Nash expected, as did the weasel-faced turnkey fawning over him.

His brother raised an eyebrow, asking if Nash would wish to be recognized here, among these men. Nash had no time to worry over what jailers and radicals thought of his relations. He did not fully embrace the man, but he did clasp both his hands.

"Where's Maddie?"

"I'm not the dunderhead who lost her, and yes, you are quite welcome for my having to rise before I've even slept to come and rescue you."

"Didn't need it. Magistrate released me immediately." The words tasted bitter.

The turnkey spat. Deacon gave him the Quinn stare until he shuffled a few more steps away. "Some might argue that justice is not always so accommodating," he said. "Or quick." The factotum Ethelston had presided, hurried in from his breakfast, it appeared. Thanks to the last of his good coin slipped to the chief jailer, Nash was the first prisoner he saw.

"My god, man, you are supposed to be standing in my place." Ethelston fingered the page before him. "I should be having a fine cup of coffee, not sitting while you stand before me."

"I hit a man who was killing a lady."

"So it says. Birley. He was plenty hale enough to meet up

with another scuffle along Shude Hill by evening. No harm done. Release him."

The jailer undid the metal cuffs, and Nash chafed the life back into his wrists and hands. "Is the town in riot?"

"Riot? We won, man. Or did you miss it in the scuffle? Malbanks has written Home Office such a report as will win us all medals. The papers sing our praises."

"Take care to release the man Bragge today, then. He writes for *The Beacon*."

"I'm sure they won't have missed him."

That portly cherub of a man himself stepped into the yard, blinking at the light just as Nash had done.

"No worse for wear, Mr. Bragge?"

"Like a ship at sea, Mr. Quinn. And I a landlubber." He tipped his cap to them. "Good voyage, shipmate."

"Good quarters."

Deacon watched him pass with interest. "Your constables imprisoned an unusual quality of men yesterday."

"That's the least of it. What do you hear?"

"Britannia is safe from the likes of you, reports the *Observer*. Its august editor seemed to expect mayhem from all counties, but could find none to report by deadline."

"What of my people?" Where the hell is Maddie?

"Your man, the gawky one, Jem? He came to the castle ahead of your letter, full of news of your adventure. Brave man."

"Was he hurt?"

"No. He took his family to the warehouse to ride out the storm. He also kept your chattel safe, of course."

Nash couldn't care less about the warehouse. "Everyone is safe."

"All accounted for, he says." Deacon's gaze slid behind Nash. The turnkey had sidled closer. "Let's take this conversation outside."

Nash matched his steps "Can't say the same for the Moores. Kitty is dead."

Deacon stopped still, directly under the heavy iron gate, mouth agape. Nash pushed him a step forward. Bad luck to stand in the path of a falling gate.

"Kitty? Impossible. She carried more life in that saucy body of hers than my entire family. Are you sure?"

"I watched it." The images replayed again in his memory. Blood and sweat and terror and she was fighting. Falling but not falling. Fighting for honor, fighting for life.

Nash's vision blurred. Sweat broke over his brow and he started to shake.

Deacon took his arm. "You thought she was Maddie."

The shaking heat spread through his face and neck. He choked the words out. "She was dead. And I—I—"

"Broke your heart."

"No. When I saw it wasn't Maddie, all I felt was relief." The joy had shot through him like heat lightning.

"Bad, little baby brother, cheering at another's grave. Don't we all dance when the reaper takes another?" Deacon patted his arm awkwardly. "Miss Kitty does deserve better, though." He thought a moment, mouth pursed. "I know. Here and now, in the shadow of this grim shelter, I pledge to continue her quixotic fight. Suffrage cannot hurt me. I'll take my seat in Lords and agitate from the inside. And when I have my great victory, I'll call the bill the Kitty Moore Act." He raised his arm, a petty, pretty Caesar.

Despite himself, Nash choked out a guffaw. "You do know Lords sits in London?"

"Right. Well, maybe I won't then." He winked. "The cause will carry without me."

Not bloody likely. The cause was dead, its leaders jailed or slaughtered. "Has her blasted father seen her?"

"That part of town is blocked off. Martial law. If she didn't get there immediately, she's not there now."

The turnkey was at their shoulder, even as they neared the carriage. "The 'Change is shut another day. Best for you gents to go straight on home, if you value your goods."

Nash turned on him, the frustration of a night in the clink and his fears for Maddie adding to the venom in his voice. "You think I care more for coin than mine own wife?" The man blinked and jumped back as if struck in the face by a lash.

"Don't assault another man, brother." Deacon's tone carried both warning and appeasement. "Remember where you are." He held out a sovereign; the man slipped past Nash to take it, and then fled. The coachman opened the carriage door, and Deacon stepped in.

"It's not as if he's far wrong, either. You do know where your goods are, after all."

Nash ignored his implication, pushing him to the side so they could both sit facing front. "What are they thinking, to close the 'Change? No one is fighting against trade. Are the mails shut as well?"

"Delayed, since the weekend. Here." Deacon pulled out Nash's letter to Maddie.

He took it, dumbfounded. He'd spent the day and the night wondering if she would listen to him, or if she would still choose her family over what they had together. It had never occurred to him that she wouldn't have the choice at all.

"Astray?"

"This one stopped first at Wetherby's."

"Why?"

"You have had a busy few days if you haven't heard this. His workers left him, but not before they burned the crops in the field. I believe they may have heard the story of how he mistreated his ward, and I hear there were others as well. The mail coach was called into service to fight the blaze, or at least to enjoy the spectacle. Arson, obviously. The fires started on the edges and burned inward. Nothing of mine or Egerton's was touched."

"He'll be ruined."

"I'd say. He's crazed at the moment. Works out well for us, though; Shaftsbury might acquire more land, at fire-sale prices, so to speak."

"Maddie would be glad." Even as he said it, he knew she would not; she would feel scant joy at such ruin. Perhaps she could feel no joy at all, anymore.

"No sobbing. You'll make me cry and muss my powder. Who's to say our Maddie is in any trouble? She's landed on her feet before. Come to the castle, and we'll drink to the Navy's failure to cure your rebellious ways."

"No. Take me home. I have to find her."

Deacon sighed theatrically. "So be it. I'll need to send for my things, of course. May as well collect another sturdy man or two, to help with the footwork."

"You're coming home with me?"

"What is family for, if not to butt into all your adventures?"

ON WHAT FELT like her hundredth trip to the water pump and back, Maddie surprised an old man about to rap on the Moores' door. He jumped back from her too nimbly, his hands in the air.

"Mrs. Quinn," he said with a sigh, resting a hand on his heart. "You gave me such a turn."

Under an old felt hat and long gray locks, his eyes seemed familiar.

"Your father knows me." He winked.

"He doesn't know me." Seeing the pitying look in those eyes, she wished she could wrench the words back. She led him into the cottage. Kitty's box lay against the near wall, her father crumpled on the stool beside it.

The stranger knelt beside the box, the hem of his long-waisted jacket wiping the floor. Pulling off the hat and hair—it was a wig—and pulling the kerchief about his face down, he became Mr. Bamford again.

"She was the spark to our flame."

At his friend's touch, a fresh wave of sobs overtook Kitty's father. Bamford rocked onto his heels and waited out the storm of grief.

Maddie tried to feel compassion for his loss. All she felt was weariness and anger. How could he turn away as if she did not feel pain, too? She settled by the fire to make some tea. He was still human, and despite her hurt and dismay at his betrayal, she must be charitable. She didn't have to like it, though, or him.

She could not stay here. Once martial law was lifted, she

would need to find a place to live. Another new life. She was not as strong as Kitty, though, and look what had happened to her.

Kitty was the one who believed most of all of them that showing their troubles would convince others to help. Instead, it convinced others she should be attacked. Maddie did not doubt that Kitty had fought back. She did not deserve to be attacked in the first place. What had happened to the English that gutting women was considered the moral course of action? Men were cowards. Tyrants, and then cowards.

As the tea steeped, Bamford led Moore to the table. After Maddie poured for them, he gestured for her to sit with them. She sat to Bamford's other side, across from Moore, so the man would have to look at her. She was so weary of his bull-headedness.

Bamford considered her a moment. "One thing ironical in all this. That banner of Kitty's, the green one? It ended up in Tate's window over on Oldham Street, not a stone's throw from the Quinns."

Maddie pictured the stores along Oldham. "The grocer's?"

"Aye. Yeoman gave it him, or so he said, and he hung it up, *'Manchester Female Reform Society'* still clear to see. Some of the women knew it for Kitty's, and, well, they didn't like to see that. They came around, and brung their children, and smashed every window in the place. Riot lasted till this morning, from what I heard."

He saw Maddie looking at the old-fashioned knotted buttons on his coat. "You can hear a lot when folks take you for nothing but an old, deaf codger. I passed people who should have known me—constables, even—and they didn't bat an eye."

"Did the yeoman attack?"

"Shots fired; one dead."

Moore lifted his cup, and then set it down, untouched. "Add Tate's to the boycott listing, then."

"At least it's not another ale-house. More than half of them are already off-limits."

"She lost the banner."

"She fought for it," Bamford said, "and we'll keep fighting, man. Her life will not have been in vain."

Moore frowned, staring at Maddie. She felt the force of his pain and anger like a saber to the throat. This time, instead of meekly accepting it as she had all this time she flashed it right back. He didn't own sorrow, or grief, or anger.

His gaze flicked away, to Bamford. "What is it like, outside?"

"Confusion, generally. Artillery on Market Street, though we could steal it or break it easily enough. Shops shut tight, warehouses padlocked. The foulest rumor on the streets and in the pubs is of thousands of pikemen on the march to Manchester, from Oldham and Middleton, of all places. I were both places this morning, and saw not one pike."

"They tell themselves their own horror stories." Maddie gave up on drinking her tea, as well, pressing her palms on the table. "The magistrates dreamt of mobs, and created one.."

Bamford patted her hand. "Well put, daughter of the movement. General opinion is the authorities are stunned and unsure how to proceed. Even the nobs are looking askance at those magistrates, saying they put everyone else in jeopardy. And the men of business are crab-pot boiling mad that the Exchange is closed another day."

"And the reformers?"

Bamford pulled his hand back and wiped his brow. "A man

shot dead on Deansgate, not even part of the meeting. Yeomanry and constables picking fights in Oldham, and all over creation. Yesterday, an innocent babe knocked out of his mam's arms by a yeoman in too much hurry to get to St. Peter's field."

"They've lost everything, too." Moore's gaze slipped past Maddie to the casket by the door.

Maddie slapped the table. "You have not lost everything. You do have me. You gave me life. How am I nothing now?" She sat back, as surprised as they at her outburst.

Moore looked down into his mug. "I had another girl. Emily died with her mother, rest her soul."

Maddie blinked, replaying his words over and again. "Emily was my name. Before they changed it. Can you not see?" It hurt her throat to push the words out. She had no more breath.

"Not mine. Another case of nobs killing decent folk. I say revenge is past due."

He was wrong. She might not be called Madeline Wetherby, or Maddie Quinn, or Emily Moore, but she was herself. She was not dead. His words—all their words—might harm her, but she would carry on.

Bamford jumped in. "Cool yourself, Richard. Your burdens are heavy, but do we that, anything close, and we lose the fine sentiment of the powerful folk. This is the first time in my memory the rads, the reformers, and the rich agree on something."

Failing to get purchase on her father, Maddie had turned on Bamford. "They slaughtered us, and you wish to make political hay?"

"No, dear, not I. I merely wish to pay my respects. Might I stay the night with you? The service is in the morning?"

Moore shrugged, his eyes returning to the casket. Rising heavily, his feet followed the track of his gaze.

Bamford rose as well. "I've more people to see, and then I'll pick up a little bite for our supper, shall I?"

Maddie's stomach growled, a surprise after more than a day of torpor. She roused herself as he adjusted his wig.

"Might I return to Middleton with you tomorrow? I'd feel better walking with a companion."

"Headed to the castle? A wise course, I'm afraid." His smile was sad. "How about if I see if the baths are open? You want to be clean and proper for saying your goodbyes."

Maddie looked down, suddenly seeing herself through his eyes. Uncombed hair, with who knew what in it. A man's coat over a torn skirt, both stiff with dried blood. She hadn't washed in more than a day, and never noticed.

Madeline Quinn would never have let herself go in this way.

FORTY-THREE

The next day, with martial law lifted, Nash and Deacon could not stop themselves from returning to St. Peter's field. Even two days after the event, rubbish and clothing lay strewn across the stamped flat ground. The wagons were gone, and the bodies, but the rust-red dirt remembered.

Deacon picked up a tiny clog, alone without its mate. "It looks like a toy battlefield."

"The screams were real enough, and the blood." Was any of it Maddie's? Deacon's man hadn't found her at the morgue or the infirmary, but Jem had heard something of her lookalike over in Clock Alley. He prayed she wasn't mortally injured. She might not have dared go to the infirmary; he'd heard the doctors there had turned their backs on a man who would not retract his reformist views, even as his arm hung nearly off his body. Other marchers rightly feared the loss of their livelihoods if it was known they took part in what the Tory papers now called a mob. The radical papers were calling it "Peterloo," coined from Waterloo. He hoped the word stuck.

Maddie must be well, because she had to read his letter. She couldn't go to her grave thinking so ill of him. He saw Trefford hurrying down Peter Street. "The meeting's on."

Deacon, face set as stern as their father's ever had been, tucked the tiny shoe into his pocket. "Good. We won't have to hunt them down to give them our medicine."

It wasn't so much a meeting as a wake. "They brought it on themselves," Malbanks shrilled out at the room in general and an exhausted-looking Nadin in particular. "The London papers blame us. How can they so misunderstand the matter?"

"Perhaps you shouldn't have jailed their correspondents." Nash's entrance, as usual lately, took them by surprise. Heywood, sitting on the far side of the room, looked to him with something like hope in his eyes. Nash slid his gaze past the man, not trusting his face to hide the disgust he felt at the old man's deeds. He set them in their places by introducing his brother as rudely as possible.

"Shaftsbury, these are the committee men Malbanks, and Trefford. You know Heywood and the constable, of course. Gentlemen, my brother, Lord Shaftsbury."

"A good friend of one of the blameless young women your cronies beat to death on Monday." Deacon looked down the straightedge of his nose at Malbanks, who quivered, though not with the fear Nash expected.

"Then she deserved it. The women were the worst of it. What will the world come to—women out running for Parliament and men and infants dying at home for want of a good meal?"

Showing how little he cared for the man or his blather, Deacon turned his back to Malbanks and marched to one of the tall windows that looked onto the field. The committee man then set his sights on Nash. "I hear your wife's funeral is today. A pity."

So he didn't know, or he was playing some double game Nash had no time for. He thought of all the pain this man had caused him, had caused families across the county. It took all his strength not to leap across the bare three feet that stood between them and dash that simpering face into the table.

Malbanks evidently mistook his restraint for sorrow. "We thought we'd leave you to your grieving. Such a pretty thing but, it's true, breeding will tell."

Nash's hand struck out, serpent fast, for the man's throat, the better to rip his tongue out, and smiled grimly at the flash of terror that replaced the usual smirk. He'd barely touched the man when the crash of a trestle to the tiles startled them both.

Heywood had kicked it over, though he remained seated. Nash looked hard at him, and was shocked at the change. Heywood looked to have aged twenty years in the past two days. *Good.*

Malbanks took advantage of the moment's respite to sidle away from Nash, but found his way blocked by an unsmiling Deacon. Instead, he reached for one of the papers strewn across the table.

"Look at this," Malbanks pleaded, picking one up. "Even *The Beacon* scolds us. *The Beacon*!"

"No country-wide rebellion, after all." Deacon could not sound more cutting.

"My spies told me wrong. How could I know?"

"You might have listened to the good men of Manchester."

"Which would those be? Merchant and worker, owner and weaver, who can tell anymore?"

"You might start with not arresting your own kind. Nash here spent the evening in the clink, thanks to the idiots you deputized into the yeomanry."

Malbanks cringed. "He did accost a man charged with keeping the peace."

Deacon pulled the clog from his pocket. "You accosted women and children, frightening them so that they deserted even their shoes."

Malbanks stood straighter. "Aye, I would have, but it were Heywood there signed the order."

Nash crouched beside Heywood's chair. His old mentor took his hand between his own. "I cannot believe I allowed this to happen. It breaks my heart even to touch on the idea of those women, those babes. Your Maddie."

"Not mine. It were her sister struck down. My Maddie lives."

"Could that be true?"

"I heard it from my foreman, who heard it from Bamford, who saw her with his own eyes yesterday. That's all I have, but I believe she may be well enough." For a woman whose husband had deserted her and whose sister had been killed by his band of brothers, he amended silently.

"Thank the Lord." Heywood sighed. His head seemed to quiver, as if he could no longer hold it quite still. "If only you were still on the committee, I would gladly hand over the reins. To give them to one such as that?" He glanced toward Malbanks. "I'd die first."

"Your service did precious little good."

"A Judas, my wife calls me. Malbanks has the right of it: I did sign the order." He shuddered, his eyes closing. "She's leaving for her sister's. Magistrates are paid nothing, and it's cost me so much. I'd go with her."

"It's the least you could do." But Nash frowned, remembering. "Her sister? She's not in Lancashire, is she?"

"Lower Canada."

"You'd leave the country?"

"I don't recognize this country. I didn't wish to cause it; I don't wish to remain part of it."

Nash, still holding Heywood's oddly frail hand, tried to reconcile the man in front of him with his mental image of his old mentor. All fathers were frail. All men. He'd thought he'd have a fight on his hands, but instead he felt driven to save this man, who did not deserve to be saved. Was mental anguish and self-enforced banishment penance enough?

He patted the hand. "Here's what we'll do. The Quinns served by tradition as magistrates for the county, but father instead gave the role to you. Now it's time for Lord Shaftsbury to take it back."

A shard of light returned to Heywood's eyes. "Would he buy out my business holdings as well?"

"No. But I will, along with Clayton. With the new Netherlands contract, and your portion of the profit from the trial contract, we will cover your holdings in town, at the least."

"Might work. You buy me out and Shaftsbury takes his due..." Heywood stroked his chin, looking past him, at the others around the table. Nash wasn't sure what the man saw.

Deacon and Malbanks already were claw to claw. Deacon waved a copy of *The Beacon* in the other man's face.

"So have you told the papers you apologize yet?"

"Balderdash. They got what they deserved. The question is, how can we get Fleet Street to see it our way?"

"There is one way." Deacon tapped the paper against his chin as if in thought.

"Yes?"

"We could write to another town, perhaps Plymouth or Bath."

"And ask for their support?"

"Yes. Ask them to go out and cut down a hundred of their citizens. That will make the dozens killed here look insignificant."

Malbanks had to sit down. Nadin guffawed. Deacon nodded towards him, acknowledging the praise.

Heywood rose, reaching for Nash for support. "Getting a taste for your new chief magistrate, Malbanks?"

Nash nodded confirmation to Deacon, whose scowl melted into the sweetest of smiles. "Now that I've met you, Mr. Malbanks, I'm twice as pleased to join your little party."

Malbanks shuddered. Nash thought he might truly be shocked. But the shrewd man of business quickly recovered. "It's no party. This is hard, difficult work."

Deacon pulled out the chair beside him. "Then we should begin immediately. Share the burden. Shall we start with reviewing the minutes of the past few meetings?"

"Minutes?"

"To be sure. We'll need to send them to the Home Office, at the very least. I'll help you organize them. I have an excellent hand. And, of course, I'll frank the letters myself, so we may be ever as detailed as can be."

Trefford stumbled into the conversation. "But we don't keep minutes." Malbanks's glare staked him to his chair.

Nash put his arm around Heywood, who leaned into it gratefully. "I'll take you home."

"Take the coach. It looks like we'll be here quite a while," Deacon added cheerfully. "Won't we now, gentlemen?"

MADDIE WISHED she'd never seen her mother's grave. Nor her living father, so strong in form and so weak in substance. He stood at the foot of the reopened gravesite, as still as an ancient oak, and just as expressive.

The reformers' public meeting hadn't merely stolen Kitty's life, it had spirited away her friends, as well. Only Mr. Bamford joined them for the prayer of farewell. Mrs. Fildes was recovering from her wounds; others sat trapped in jail or equally trapped at home, not daring to admit they took part in what now had been declared an illegal meeting.

If they did not come to the churchyard, many had shown their respect in other ways. As the cart carrying Kitty's coffin trundled through Long Millgate Street, the working people came to a sudden halt. Men doffed their caps, women held their children close. The blocks fell silent as they passed, a sign of respect to the woman and to her father, walking behind her.

When their eyes fell on Maddie, though, some in the street did a double-take. Others simply stared. After the first block of this, she pulled her bonnet closer to her face, tucking the forever stray curls deep into its cap. At least no one recognized the dress, the one Kitty had worn to the lawn party. There had been no other dress in the cottage.

Maddie scooped a handful of the fresh-turned ground that had rested so long. She held it a moment before casting her final farewell. The tang of the clay mixed with the honeysuckle of soap she'd used at the public baths this morning. The soil pricked her ungloved fingers, gritty and infertile.

She let it go, spraying across the center of the unadorned box. With it, she let go her dreams of making a family of the Moores. Her father's rejection knifed her, but it was her own expectations that had made the deepest cut. She had wanted him to come at her with open heart and open arms, and only because she wanted it so. That he did not—that he could not—should not have been such a surprise. As Nash said, if her father wanted to know her, he would have sought her out. Instead, he treated her as dead. Still, she couldn't bring herself to declare that it had been a complete mistake to seek him out. If she hadn't, she always would have wondered. At least now she knew, hard as it was to hear.

She knew a bit more about Manchester, as well. As poorly as some in high society might take her "fall," they took the search for basic rights for all even more ill. Would anyone speak out on behalf of the working-man now? The publishers of sympathetic journals and tracts would be closed down or thrown into jail again, just as a decade earlier. Fear overcame logic; terror trumped sense. There was no room for dreamers here, or Utopians.

As the digger crunched his shovel into the clay earth, she turned her back on that life. Her steps felt lighter, as if her expectations had been a weight around her hips, now released. She wasn't quite ready to face the future, but found some contentment in the moment, in the sudden change from chill to warm as she moved out of the shadow of the church.

Mr. Bamford caught up to her, taking her arm. "Can't say how sorry I am. He's a good man, but her death—your Ma's—took the stuffing right out of him. Kitty's glow gave him life, but now I see it were a trick of the light."

"We all of us have feet of clay." She leaned closer, comforting the comforter. He'd fetched his good clothes for the services, and looked the proper country gentleman. She pictured how it would be were he her father, but quickly let the impulse pass. Her imagination was what got her into these troubles in the first place.

The Shaftsbury coach and four stood to the side of the street before the cemetery gate. They'd passed it as they entered, a half-hour before. Empty, its presence was appropriate to an acquaintance of the peerage, but a mighty sign of respect for a weaver's daughter. But then an earl could afford the luxury of a public drubbing of the town's leaders.

As they passed by this time, though, the door sprang open. Bamford pulled her back a step, protecting her.

It was no highwayman, but Nash. Solid and real.

Had it been only three days since she'd seen him? He carried a new tension about his chocolate eyes, set deeper in their sockets than usual. And that bruise on his temple must ache. Had he slept at all?

Maddie's skin seemed to stretch toward him, trying to taste his smell through the thick summer air. Then shame overcame her, the heat of it burning away any faint scent. She'd rejected him, and here he was, the generous prince.

"My condolences. Wasn't sure of my welcome."

Bamford's grip on Maddie tightened. "You aren't welcome. No magistrate would be."

"Not a committee man anymore. They booted me out before the meeting." He looked steadily at Bamford, only rarely flicking a glance at her. She didn't dare look at him, or she'd dissolve into tears right here on the street. She was the biggest idiot in Manchester. In Christendom.

They stood awkward a long minute, Maddie alternately frozen in shame and melting in regret, Bamford the protective bantam rooster puffed up and breathing through his nose, Nash stiff in Navy stance as if awaiting orders. Then he snapped his hand to his vest pocket.

"I forgot. Here." He held out a letter, folded and franked.

"What is it?" Bamford reached for it, but Maddie was quicker. She snatched at it, but Nash held on, held her, a second before letting go. After releasing his grip, he seemed to have trouble controlling his stance, as if the ground were swelling like the sea. His hands chopped up and down, punctuating his words.

"For you. Mailed Sunday, to Deacon's, but it missed you. Honored it you'd read it, at your leisure, of course."

Were Bamford not tugging at her, she'd drop to the ground and rip it open right now. Instead, she pressed her lips together and nodded once, just as she'd learned in school. She allowed Bamford to lead her away from the man who still held her battered heart. She didn't deserve a second chance.

She shouldn't even hope for it.

Frustration boxing his ears, Nash stepped into the street to let Maddie and Bamford pass. A man didn't push, especially not at a wounded lady. She had his letter now, with everything he wanted to say in order, not tumbled and scattered like his thoughts and words were now.

What an idiot he'd sounded, honking his condolences at her, accosting her with his missive. Still, all he wanted to do was grab her, toss her in the coach and drive away for good.

He could so easily reach past the bantam man, wrap his hand around her elbow, and pull her to him. Then he could inhale her warm scent, now hidden behind the tracings of soot in the summer-heavy air. Then he could feel the throb of her pulse under the thin fabric of that familiar blue dress. Then he might taste the ruddy plumpness of her lower lip, which she worried at when she was upset. Who had made her so? He had.

Half an hour ago, he'd sat in the dark of the coach watching her pass into the cemetery, her back straight as royalty, and called himself content to see her hale and safe. More fool him.

He fisted his hands and thrust them into the pockets of his wedding jacket. Had she noticed? She glanced at him as she passed. Beneath the white on the pinches of her nose, and the gray-blue of the circles under her eyes, she seemed calm, like a mild sea under strong winds.

Something about her was magnetic. Even her shuttered gaze pulled him in. Even her backside, walking away from him. If she turned around, if she looked back, just a glance, he would breathe again. With every step, she tore at the line holding his heart to his body, taking it with her.

Fanciful rubbish, he chided himself, pressing a fist against his chest. Half a block, a block, another. She didn't turn around. And he just stood there.

He should return the coach to Deacon at the Inn. She might turn around. He should follow her, slowly, in the coach. The blood fled his clenched hands, whitening his knuckles. He needed to punch something. In a pocket of quiet on the street, he heard the crunch and tumble of the gravedigger hard at work.

Nash turned and entered the cemetery. Angled across its square of land, the solid gray of the church spoke of generations unbroken. The soot draped like icing down the stones changed it to a gingerbread chapel, for a patchwork marriage, basted together and easily rent.

Staring into the grave as the digger rhythmically filled it in, Maddie's father stood alone. Moore hadn't aged well. Bamford said he'd been a handsome lad, and the wife as beautiful as her daughters. Moore's hair had fled, his stubbled cheeks sagged unevenly, even his tall frame canted at the wrong angle. What could be called feisty in Kitty, in Moore was simple boorishness.

How could Maddie have chosen him? Nash ached to drop the man to the ground, kick him into the new-turned dirt. How dare the man steal his wife from him? He stepped closer, crooked his arm, and took a deep breath.

The tang of the clay earth stung his throat, and brought him back to his senses. The man was burying his child. Moore's shoulders bowed with the weight of it. His arms wrapped around his middle. His face, usually as guarded as Maddie's, today could not contain all his pain, flashing pale to red to patchy pale again.

His poor Maddie. She had known so much death, but at a

distance. Did she feel Kitty's wounds as her own? What if this were Deacon's grave? Nash choked on his breath, and coughed.

Moore looked at him, and then at the gravestone. "Come to see the fruits of thy labor?"

"I told them not to do it."

"Have to carve a new one, they say. Kitty so different than Richard."

Nash stepped away from the man. He slid his palms over the edge of the stone as he walked to its smooth backside. "Tell them to use the other side."

Moore's mouth turned down like a cupped hand. "Might be."

"I'm sorry." Nash slapped his fist against the top of the cool stone.

"If not this, summat else. She shone too bright. They had to snuff her out afore long."

"It's consolation, though, having her sister still?"

"Sister?" Moore frowned, his round, blue-green gaze clouded, and then cleared. "That's a rum 'un. Kitty like as wanted a sister, and happen I played along. It did make my girl happy." He shrugged, oversized shoulders in an undersized linen shirt.

The man was stone blind. Nash's hands tightened, vises gripping the top of the granite. "How can you say that? They're a matched set."

"Not a bit of it." Nash could read in the ease of the man's jaw, the still stare in his eyes. Moore believed it. No man so blind as one who will not see.

The stone's edge cut into Nash's palms. She'd given her heart to that? "I gave her up. For you."

"Never asked ye."

How could he not see her value? Persistence and spirit, and generosity—Lord knew—thrift, kindness. Radiant from her soul. Not lost, never wandering.

The screaming ache in his fingers startled some sense into Nash. He was tugging at the stone, did he think to lift it out of the clay and knock the blasted man's head straight? Besting her idiot father wouldn't ease Maddie's troubles; precious little had been solved at St. Peter's field on Monday. How manly would it be to knock a grieving man to the ground, no matter how much he might need it? Nash loosened his grip, shoving his hands into his pockets without inspecting for damage.

The digger tamped the top of the new mound with his shovel again, waiting for a coin. Nash tossed him a bit of silver. He caught it and smiled. His teeth were silver.

Moore stretched his shoulders, but they dropped to the same hunch. "Good work, grave digging. Might try it."

The man was a fool. He was no competition.

Nash blinked, slow, as if the air had turned to water. Maddie was free. Hope gut-punched him. He might yet reel her back in.

He'd already set the lure, the letter, but he'd thought that was just to get them back on speaking terms. He should have aimed higher. Since when did he haggle for the small prize? Certainly not in the Navy, and not in trade.

He might have it all, have her back, make a family. Gain his heart back.

Would she ever allow him back into hers? After everything he'd said, and everything he'd not said. His bull-headedness about family, when really that was all he wanted, too.

Everyone—especially him—had tried to fit her into a cage of

their own design. And in her goodness she tried to fit, every time. She wasn't a countess, nor a radical, nor a viscount's whore. She was Maddie, and wasn't that enough? Plenty enough for him. But how could he convince her? More than words, he needed to act. Now.

He walked beside Moore on the path toward the street, and the rest of their lives. "Headed home alone?"

"How I like it."

"Where did the woman go?"

"Sam took her. North?"

There was nothing for her in the North. Nash was sure he had taken her west, to Shaftsbury Castle.

Perfect.

FORTY-FOUR

Late-afternoon light shimmered amber against the walls of the last coaching inn before Middleton. In the quiet shade of the lawn outside, Maddie tried to smile as Mr. Bamford trod carefully toward her carrying two mugs of brew.

"Warm ale and ginger. Best thing in the world after a wet day."

Sharp and sweet, it tickled her nose and eased a fraction of the tightness in her chest. "I'm sorry. I've cried nearly the whole way."

"Least you're a leaker and not a wailer. We'd have needed more beer to keep you in voice." He tapped her mug with his, and then downed half his stout. "Still mean to go straight on to the castle? Won't get there afore dark."

She nodded, swishing another mouthful of the brew in her mouth before swallowing, like a child. If it grew too late she might take the forest path and sleep in the stable, truly reverting to her childhood. "You're too kind to stop and drink with me when your home is just over the hill."

"Nay, I'm already home. Hear the shuttles singing in the looms in the cottages there? Settles my heart, as the drink settles my belly."

Maddie felt far from settled. Her feet throbbed, her face stung, her insides ached. A good night's rest would set her body right, but it would also revive the snarling harpies of her fears. She found she preferred this weary numbness.

"I've ruined everything." She sighed. "My father—"

He slapped the bench. "Your Da's got nothing for you, lass. It breaks his heart just to look at you. Get ye gone, and live a right life. What says your man?"

"He won't have me back, either." Nash had given her the power to choose, and she had chosen against him. How could she have been so blind?

"Your man? The moon-eyed one at the churchyard?"

She frowned into her beer. He couldn't have the right of it. Nash had almond-shaped eyes.

Bamford leaned back, watching her over his tankard. "Would you take him back, after all this?"

"He told me to wait, just until after the meeting. Why didn't I?"

"Is that it?" He set the tankard on the bench beside him and patted her knee. "Here, let me tell you my little Minna's trial on Monday."

"Was she hurt?" At the thought that she was keeping him from tending to his injured wife, Maddie's tears dried instantly.

"Nay, be easy. But we were separated in the fracas, as you might imagine. She ran to a house nearby, where they took her in until the worst was past. Then she made her way up to Shude Hill and home."

He tapped on the edge of the tankard. "But that's not the story. The first Middleton man she met, she asked after me. Can you believe, he said I was dead! Well, you can imagine her state. She's a sentimental thing."

"She loves you."

"So she does. Here, then, she's wandering out the town, a river of tears much as you, and she meets another Middleton bloke, and he says no, I'm not dead, but in the infirmary. Just as she's deciding to return and look for my broken body, she hears I'm in prison. Then that I'm already on the road home."

"What did she do?"

"She decided she couldn't help me that day were I dead, or in jail, or even in hospital. She's not much of a nurse. She could give comfort to our little girl. So she turned her feet for home. When she saw me on the road at Harperhey, not fifteen minutes later, she cried again, but this time with joy."

"You're so lucky."

He tipped his head back to drain his mug, and stood. "I hear your man took a like journey that day. A rough swell. Could have jostled his thinking a bit, you never know."

Something clicked in Maddie's mind, puzzle pieces locking into place. That coat, the one that she'd pretended smelled of Nash, with buttons like his. It was his coat. Nash had seen Kitty die.

What if he'd thought it was her? Had he come to rescue her, or to cut her down? No, he'd been booted out before then, he'd said. Why?

Had he truly chosen her over his own good standing? She

wanted to believe it. But hadn't wanting to believe the best of others gotten her into such trouble in the first place? She frowned into the tankard, resting between her hands on her lap. What could she trust, a man's words, his actions—or her own heart?

A touch on her shoulder knocked her out of spiraling reverie. "I bid you good day, ma'am, and godspeed." Bamford winked. "Something in your pocket?"

Maddie's hand went to the spot. Nash's letter. Hope fluttered, and then went still. What good could a letter do? Hadn't muddled correspondence gotten them all into this fix? She put no stock in letters anymore.

She pushed the vellum deeper into her pocket. It tilted, the corner pricking her palm, as the contents shifted under it. His buttons. She'd cut them off the ruined coat, thinking to give them to Moore to sell, and forgotten them. They belonged to Nash; mislaid, like the letter.

She pulled it out. Marred by creases, dirt, and pocket lint, the seal on the back broke only when she cracked it. Half a page of Nash's vertical hand. She'd once thought of it as skeletons dancing.

I did not tell you directly about the money. I did not stop Shaftsbury from burning the letters. I did not tell you that you are my other and better self. For all this, I am well and truly sorry.

You think it best to leave me, and I will let you go, but know this: You are my world. How could I ever stop thinking of you, worrying about you, loving you?

Now that I see how important family is to you, I find I must try to reconcile with my own. My father wasn't the monster I painted him as a child, but it's too late to mend that rent now. I have much to regret, but some things I might set right. I have earned back Shaftsbury's dowry, and I will settle the full amount on you. You shall always have the means to live a simple life, come what may.

She had to stop reading to take this in. She was secure? Even as a merchant's wife she hadn't been completely free of that knot of fear that it all might fall to ruin. As the idea settled in, the knot unraveled, kink by kink. In its place she sensed a sort of peace.

With such funds, she might even start a school for girls without families. Plans started spinning about her mind. Perhaps she could work with one of the churches, and use a room. The need was so great right here. Why not stay?

It was just like Nash, to focus on the financials of the arrangement. Romantic, even, for him. She turned back to the letter.

Whatever you wish, I'll agree to. All I wish is your happiness. And if it made you happy to reconsider your decision to leave, I would welcome it. For you, Madeline, my door is open, and always will be. I hope to see you pass through it one day.

I dream of it.

She had no room to breathe. The love she held in her heart for him spilled out, filling her limbs, filling her mind with a ginger-scented joy. She wanted to run all the way back to his house, to their house, and tell him. Touch him and taste him and lay with him.

Then the knot drew tight again. She'd lost that privilege on Monday afternoon. Hadn't this letter been written before the reformers' meeting? She had marched; everyone would know it.

She must be as poison to the minds of Nash's customers and friends. What must the Heywoods think?

Still, he had loved her once—really loved her—and only days ago. Was his love a tender bud, crushed under the clogs of militancy, or a sturdy shoot, bent but springing back whole? He'd run through a melee to find her in St. Peter's fields. There must be a chance.

The sultry air and quiet space seemed to show everything so clearly. She could not make her father love her. She could not recover the love lost with the deaths of her mother and the Wetherbys, and now Kitty. Nash could not replace that. Might she could accept what he could give her, a love that might grow, that might multiply?

She'd thought him bull-headed and rigid, but she'd put just as many conditions on her affections, hadn't she?

He said he dreamed of her.

She tapped the vellum against her lip. Might a letter do some good? She would write him a mirror of his words. Make him feel as beautiful—as beloved—as his vision of her did her. Tell him she dreamed of him, too. Every night.

She had to get to Deacon's. He would frank another letter, even for hand delivery tonight, if she could get it done by quarter of eight. Maddie drained the last of the ale, catching a piece of ginger between her teeth. Handing the mug back to the serving girl, she set off as fast as her worn feet and sorely tried heart would take her.

FORTY-FIVE

From a quarter-mile away, Nash could see the purpose in her stride. As he drew closer, he could see the set in her shoulders.

His Maddie.

He knew when she heard the wagon; she stepped out of the track and turned around. Dusty and rumpled, color in her cheeks, a spray of curls wildly escaping from the back of her bonnet. Only in the carriage of her spine and the purse of her full lips did she appear the young miss he'd met along this path just last spring. Now he knew better.

"Lost your carriage, ma'am?"

She tilted her head, a hand shading her eyes from the steep-angled sun. He must have said the same thing to her then; was she remembering? Or was she simply trying to determine how to best set him in his place? If so, she was succeeding. With every silent second that ticked by, his stomach clenched tighter, his throat grew more parched.

She really had turned her back on him. He'd been a fool to think mere words on paper could argue his case. Actions spoke a thousand times louder, actions that convicted him.

She shrugged delicately. There were new freckles across her nose. "I seem always to be in need of your rescue."

In two seconds, he had set the reins, leapt out of the cart, and taken her hand. "If only that were so." He breathed her in, sun and honey and ginger. Her hand warmed his. Her breaths were slow, with that pause between that scared him so when she was sleeping. All he wanted to say crowded his throat. He couldn't push the words out. Any words. She looked at him with those too-round, too-wise eyes, but her mouth did not judge.

She let him lead her to the wagon and up to sitting on its bench. He hoisted himself up beside her. She slid a hand's length away. He took her hand, no gloves today. She looked hard into his eyes as if she could reach his soul through them. He let her look her fill.

She blinked, her gaze flicking away to the bed of the wagon. "Empty?"

He cleared his throat. "Thought I'd pick up a wardrobe, maybe two. Could always use extra storage. That is, until we remove to somewhere larger."

He winced. We. Too fast.

She turned, pulling her hand free and dropping it into her lap. He hied the team and the wagon jerked into motion.

"Your settlement is generous."

Settlement? She must mean Deacon's money. Business again. Why did everyone think him a merchant first? Because that's what he pretended to be. To admit how he felt about things—about her—would be to invite heartbreak. Not to admit it, he had discovered, would guarantee it. He swallowed hard.

"All I need is you. The rest is merely commerce." He glanced at her, and back to the horses. Steady on gait. Was her lower lip trembling? He chanced another look. Now she was frowning. No, worrying her lip. She was thinking. Could be a good sign.

Her gaze caught his, and they both looked away, startled and sheepish. Her hands clasped and unclasped. A sigh rumbled her lungs. She held his letter, crushed in the palm of her far hand. He fought to keep his wrists easy, the horses in rhythm. Let her think it out. Let her drink him in. Let her let herself change her mind.

Let her say yes.

As the wagon turned into the long drive up to the castle, its weight shifting on its axles, she slid closer to him. Before she could resettle herself, he put his hand around her, resting it on the seat. A small push, and their hips met. She held herself stiff, but she didn't move away.

The rocking of the wagon settled her deeper into him with each step. He took shallow breaths, so she wouldn't wake to their growing intimacy.

With her beside him, even by feint, the castle did not loom as foreboding as usual. He wished he could give it to her. A wardrobe or two was poor consolation. But she might think of it as interest on the future.

"We won the Netherlands contract. It might treble my profit next year, and keep two hundred men working—and women—through the winter."

She sighed and said nothing. He could have punched

himself. Commerce, again. As he scrambled for something artistic to say, she cleared her throat. He leaned closer.

"You saw Kitty?"

Her thoughts were not of him at all. Of course not. She'd just buried her sister, and left her ramshackle father. "Too late. I could do nothing for her but close her eyes. I'm sorry."

"You left your coat." She jostled her skirts, digging in a pocket. Her shoulder pushed into his chest, and then away. She held rounded buttons in her hand. "It was ruined, but I saved these."

"You knew they were mine?"

"Only today. I thank you." She tried to hand them to him, but he pushed her hand away with his forearm.

"I did it for you. I thought it was you." The vision raced back to the front of his mind, the strength of it clenching his hands. The horses stuttered a step before he righted the reins. "I couldn't help it, Maddie, the joy I felt when I saw it wasn't you. I'll go to hell for it, sure." He shook the vision from his thoughts. Maddie watched him, that oddly direct stare. She must hate him now. He scrambled for words. "Losing your sister, and so soon after you'd met her, I don't know, it must be—"

She put a hand on his knee, startling him into silence. She lifted it off. He watched it fall to her own knee. The horses slowed. She sighed deeper into him. "I'm so tired of running away."

The harness jangled, and he pulled the team off the track. With the wheels stopped, he could hear an orchestra of cicadas in the shade of the wood.

"Folk commit grave errors every day, Maddie. Somehow, they go on. Could we?" He cupped her hands in his.

She held her breath so long. So many expressions, her face clouded, cleared, clouded again. He feared the worst. His chest began to cave in, his ears to swell the quiet evening into a dull roar. Then her face cleared, settling on a look of unguarded hope.

"I could be a better wife."

He exhaled, relief streaming from his veins.

"You couldn't." She stiffened, and tried to pull her hands free. "You're already perfect."

She snorted. He'd never before thought it such a welcoming sign.

"I could be a better husband. What say you to that?"

"I see what you mean." Her lips wobbled into a smile. He started to lift his hand to run it down the soft rounding of her cheek, but she turned to look over her shoulder. The roaring he'd heard was real—Deacon's carriage and four, returning from town. The driver slowed his team as the coach drew near. Deacon rolled down the window and leaned out.

"Am I late to the party?"

"Might we stay to dinner? And perhaps borrow a wardrobe or two?"

"Have at it. Take some curtains, too, we have plenty enough. Hurry on in, though. Wrestling with Malbanks has given me a prodigious appetite."

He unlatched the door and smiled past Nash at Maddie. "Wish to ride in comfort the rest of the way?"

Nash's hands clamped down on hers. He should let go, help

her into the carriage next to the lord she was supposed to marry. The one with that lady-killer smile.

But she didn't tug away. She just sat there, still with that crooked smile on her too wide, too beautiful face.

"Thank you kindly, but I'm well enough here."

"Sure?"

She dropped her gaze to his, smile wobbling again. "I can stay?"

"Do you want to?"

"Forever."

"Let's do."

He heard the door latch, and the coach move on. Still, that crooked smile turned to him. Only him.

He grinned. She wasn't going anywhere without him.

Author's Note

The Peterloo Massacre, as it became known, shocked people across England, according to accounts at the time. While the government quickly praised the actions of the magistrates' committee, public sentiment was not so sanguine. People from around the country donated funds to help the injured, and bought commemorative items—plates, jugs, handkerchiefs, medals—that carried what became the iconic image of Peterloo: cavalrymen with swords drawn slashing at bare-armed civilians.

Some formerly anti-reform newspapers turned toward reform, including the influential Times of London, whose reporter was among those arrested on the speaker's stand that day. But political reform did not come until 1832, more than a decade later. The immediate effect of the summer of protests was more government crackdown, including the Six Acts, which allowed houses to be searched without a warrant and declared that "every meeting for radical reform is an overt act of treasonable conspiracy."

Orator Hunt and Sam Bamford, along with eight others, were charged with sedition for their parts in the meeting on 16 August; both were found guilty and went to jail, Hunt for four years, Bamford for one.

In this story, I have taken liberties with some of the history, particularly with the members of the magistrates' committee. I did not base my likenesses of Nash Quinn or any of the others on the people who did serve on that panel, partly because no one on the committee actually lived in Manchester. I also took major artistic license with the bathing rooms in Manchester; while they did sit on the grounds of the Manchester Hospital, in style they were more Spartan than Roman.

The injuries the marchers and yeomanry sustained at Peterloo are taken from eyewitness accounts.

KEEP IN TOUCH!

If you'd like to know when my next book is available, you can sign up for my new release email list at nickypenttila.com

ALSO BY NICKY PENTTILA

About the Author

Nicky Penttila writes about women who push back and the men sharp enough to keep up. Her novels have been featured by USA Today and the Historical Fiction Society. She also writes science fiction and fantasy—but ink and upheaval came first.
Find more at nickypenttila.com.

www.ingramcontent.com/pod-product-compliance
Lightning Source LLC
Chambersburg PA
CBHW020824030726
47496CB00001B/84